Rosilee A. Bartlett
RR 3 Box 345
Grafton, WV 26354

E THE
FOLK.

"It's high time Sawtooth was put on the map. Our town will finally gain the respectability it deserves. And if civilization means losing a few saloons"—he slanted a glance at Miss Wade—"or gambling halls, so be it. I'll be glad to see them go."

Scattered applause greeted his short speech.

Gabby strode up the aisle toward him, her heels clicking on the floor like an army drummer's cadence. Although the top of her head didn't even reach his shoulder, she glared up at him and jabbed a forefinger into his chest.

"Just because you live an utterly boring life doesn't mean the other residents don't like to have a drink or engage in a friendly game of poker." Her eyes narrowed to topaz slits. "You, Mr. Ashburn, need to learn there is more to life than tallying your profits."

A few men clapped in support, while some of the women gasped at her audacity.

Ty's face burned. His first mayor, he decided, would be outspoken woman gagged. "If me, Miss Wade, I'd see you stagecoach out of town!"

MAUREEN McKADE
RITA Finalist for WINTER
for Best First Book

Other **AVON ROMANCES**

THE BELOVED ONE *by Danelle Harmon*
THE DARKEST KNIGHT *by Gayle Callen*
THE FORBIDDEN LORD *by Sabrina Jeffries*
KISSING A STRANGER *by Margaret Evans Porter*
THE MACKENZIES: PETER *by Ana Leigh*
THE MEN OF PRIDE COUNTY: THE REBEL
by Rosalyn West
ONCE A MISTRESS *by Debra Mullins*

Coming Soon

MY LORD STRANGER *by Eve Byron*
A SCOUNDREL'S KISS *by Margaret Moore*

And Don't Miss These
ROMANTIC TREASURES
from Avon Books

BECAUSE OF YOU *by Cathy Maxwell*
ON BENDED KNEE *by Tanya Anne Crosby*
UPON A WICKED TIME *by Karen Ranney*

Avon Books are available at special quantity discounts for bulk purchases for sales promotions, premiums, fund raising or educational use. Special books, or book excerpts, can also be created to fit specific needs.

For details write or telephone the office of the Director of Special Markets, Avon Books, Inc., Dept. FP, 1350 Avenue of the Americas, New York, New York 10019, 1-800-238-0658.

Maureen McKade

Untamed Heart

AVON BOOKS ◆ NEW YORK

This is a work of fiction. Names, characters, places, and incidents either are the product of the author's imagination or are used fictitiously. Any resemblance to actual events, locales, organizations, or persons, living or dead, is entirely coincidental and beyond the intent of either the author or the publisher.

AVON BOOKS, INC.
1350 Avenue of the Americas
New York, New York 10019

Copyright © 1999 by Maureen Webster
Inside cover author photo by Bezy Photography
Published by arrangement with the author
Visit our website at **http://www.AvonBooks.com**
Library of Congress Catalog Card Number: 98-93538
ISBN: 0-380-80284-8

All rights reserved, which includes the right to reproduce this book or portions thereof in any form whatsoever except as provided by the U.S. Copyright Law. For information address Avon Books, Inc.

First Avon Books Printing: February 1999

AVON TRADEMARK REG. U.S. PAT. OFF. AND IN OTHER COUNTRIES, MARCA REGISTRADA, HECHO EN U.S.A.

Printed in the U.S.A.

WCD   10   9   8   7   6   5   4   3   2   1

If you purchased this book without a cover, you should be aware that this book is stolen property. It was reported as ''unsold and destroyed'' to the publisher, and neither the author nor the publisher has received any payment for this ''stripped book.''

*For the M7 Posse, who reminded me
of the power of faith and perseverance.
Let 'em ride!*

Chapter 1

Wyoming, 1887

"I object!"

As the defiant voice echoed through the hall, Tyler Ashburn swiveled in his pew at the front of the Sawtooth Baptist Church and searched for the lone dissenter at the town meeting. He spotted the firebrand standing by the church doors, but almost didn't recognize her with her long hair hidden beneath a faded purple bonnet sporting drooping feathers and two equally bedraggled stuffed sparrows. What on earth was *she* doing here, pretending to be a respectable member of the community?

A jerk on his coat sleeve demanded his attention and he turned to the woman sitting on his left.

"It's that *woman*," Eleanor Gatewood whispered hoarsely, holding a kid-gloved palm in front of her mouth. "That's Miss Gabby Wade. She owns the—"

"I know who she is," he interrupted.

"How do *you* know her, Tyler?" Eleanor demanded, her indignant shock replaced by suspicion.

"I haul her merchandise in from Rawlins."

"Merchandise? You mean her"—Eleanor low-

1

ered her voice even further—"spirits?"

"That and other supplies," Ty replied.

"You actually conduct *business* with *her*?"

He stifled his growing annoyance, reminding himself that Eleanor had been sheltered all her life from the likes of Miss Gabby Wade. Patting the back of his fiancée's dainty hand, he reassured her, "It's strictly business, Eleanor."

Her plump lips settled into a childish pout, and she smoothed an imaginary wrinkle from her fashionable claret silk cape. "Who does she think she is, attending a meeting of decent folks—and wearing such an abominable hat?"

Eleanor had a point: it *was* the ugliest hat he'd ever laid eyes on. Ty looked at his fiancée's delicate features. She'd had a privileged childhood and been pampered like a china doll. As her future husband, Ty had the responsibility to shield her from the seamier side of life, and from the forces that would seek to corrupt her ladylike sensibilities. Miss Wade represented both. Giving Eleanor's slender fingers a reassuring squeeze, he turned back to listen to the Wyoming territorial politician at the front of the packed room.

"Miss Wade," Tom Bailey said patiently, "this is not a court of law. You cannot object. You can, however, make a motion for the floor to recognize you."

Her indignant expression faltered, and she brushed at the dowdy bonnet with a nervous hand. "Well, I think most of you recognize me, but for those of you who don't, my name is Miss Gabby Wade and I'm a *legitimate* business owner here in Sawtooth."

Muffled coughs and snorts, along with a few out-right guffaws, met her statement.

Sparks rekindled in her eyes, and small fists pressed into the skirt folds at her hips. The look in her eyes reminded Ty of a thundercloud readying to unleash its fury, and he braced for the storm.

"It's my right as a citizen to object if my rights are being violated. And what you're proposing, sir, violates my right to earn a living," Miss Wade said in a clear, strong voice that belied her petite stature.

Outraged mutterings and rustlings erupted in the wake of her clipped words.

Bailey sighed in exasperation. "I would think incorporating Sawtooth into a real town would be good for your saloon."

"Gambling hall," she corrected curtly. "And if Sawtooth elects a mayor and a town council is appointed, they will impose taxes on my place of business. And that, Mr. Bailey, will raise the price of that fancy French cognac you like so well."

She tipped her bonneted head to one side, the shabby feathers dipping to her shoulder. The gesture seemed oddly youthful and almost innocent for a woman in her profession.

"And," she continued, "I would be willing to bet it will also force you to hand over a percentage of your poker winnings to the town's coffers. *That* is the price of incorporating."

Bailey tugged at his stiff white collar as his apple-red cheeks deepened to scarlet. "That, of course, is true, Miss Wade. But you will also be getting a bridge that will cut twenty miles off the trip to Rawlins. People will come and settle in Sawtooth, giving you more business. I would think that would more than compensate for the taxes that have to be paid—if, as you say, taxes are imposed by the town government." He paused. "I can assure you, though, that without incorporation, the territory will build the bridge someplace else."

Miss Wade folded her arms below her abundant bosom and tapped her boot-clad foot. "I've seen gambling halls disappear overnight because of mandates other town councils have put into effect. Mandates such as restrictions on the amount of liquor we can serve and earlier closing times."

Ty wasn't much for talking in front of an audience, but the madam's defense of saloons aroused his ire. If it were up to him, Miss Gabby Wade and her "business" would be shut down for good. He uncoiled his lanky frame and stood to face the crowd, clenching his hands behind his back. He deliberately allowed his gaze to settle on fellow businessmen and customers of his freighting company. "I say it's high time Sawtooth was put on the map. Our town will finally gain the respectability it deserves. And if civilization means losing a few saloons"—he slanted a glance at the pugnacious woman—"or gambling halls, so be it. I, for one, will not be sorry to see them go."

Scattered applause greeted his short speech.

Miss Wade strode up the aisle toward him, her heels clicking on the wood floor like an army drummer's cadence. Although the top of her head didn't even reach his shoulder, she glared up at him, jabbed a forefinger into his chest, and fired the first volley. "Just because you live an utterly boring life doesn't mean the other residents don't like to have a drink or engage in a friendly game of poker." She paused, her eyes narrowing to topaz slits. "You, Mr. Ashburn, need to learn there is more to life than tallying your profits."

A few men clapped in support, while some of the women gasped at Miss Wade's audacity.

Ty's face burned under her scathing assault. If a man had dared criticize him in public, he would have had a taste of Ty's knuckles. "This town can do without you taking men's hard-earned money—money that should've been used to buy food for their families," he said through clenched teeth. "If it were up to me, Miss Wade, I would ensure that every single saloon and gambling hall in Sawtooth was boarded up—and I'd see you on the next stage out of town."

The women applauded enthusiastically.

"Then it's a good thing it's not up to you!"

Her upturned face blazed with rosy-cheeked defiance. He met the challenge in her eyes and opened his mouth to respond. Then the clean scent of soap and rose water wafted around him, a gentle assault of unexpected innocence, and he was unable to remember what he'd meant to say.

"Mr. Bailey, may I be recognized?"

Ty glanced over at his future father-in-law. With thick, leonine white hair and dressed in an elegant black pinstriped suit, Vernon Gatewood appeared every inch the successful businessman.

Bailey sighed in relief, then said deferentially, "Yes, Mr. Gatewood?"

"I realize this isn't a platform for political purposes, but I wish to say something that I believe would be relevant to the cause of gaining incorporation." Gatewood gripped his lapels and stepped up to the lectern. "I am in complete agreement with Tyler, and feel it's high time our community moves past the lawless frontier to rightly take its place in the civilized world. And to help do that, as a representative of the Republican Party, I nominate Tyler Ashburn for mayor."

If Gatewood had announced the Second Coming had arrived, Ty doubted he would have been more shocked. Vaguely aware of the explosion of comments that followed, he looked down to find Miss Wade's lips pressed firmly together in a disapproving frown.

Eleanor jumped to her feet, elbowing Miss Wade aside and wrapping her arms around him. "Oh, Tyler, that would be wonderful! Just imagine, me as the mayor's wife."

"Yes, imagine," Miss Wade said, her words oozing sarcasm.

Ty glared at her, then extricated himself from his fiancée's overly enthusiastic embrace. Moving to Gatewood's side at the front of the room, he said in a low voice to the older man, "I have a freight business to run. I don't have time to be mayor."

"Nonsense, Tyler," Gatewood said under his breath. "You have people working for you who can take care of the schedules and books. You have a fine head on your shoulders and that's what Sawtooth needs to bring us into a new era."

"But—"

"But nothing. Think of all the good you could do. It would be within your power to rid the town of licentious dens like Miss Gabby's Gambling Emporium. You can make Sawtooth a place where folks can come and raise their children without being surrounded by the moral depravity of people like her." Gatewood turned away from Ty and raised his hands to quiet the noisy crowd. "Everybody, may I have your attention? Who will second

Tyler Ashburn's candidacy for mayor?"

"I second," the Reverend Tusk said sonorously, as if proclaiming an amen.

"All in favor?" Gatewood called.

The ayes nearly raised the house of worship's roof.

"Those opposed?"

"Me!" Miss Wade's single voice rang out.

As his first official act as mayor, Ty decided he would have the outspoken Miss Wade gagged.

Gatewood threw an arm around Ty's shoulders. "Looks like you're going to be Sawtooth's first mayor."

"Not so fast," Bailey broke in reluctantly. "Mr. Ashburn must be voted into office through the proper procedures."

Gatewood scowled. "And what are the 'proper procedures'?"

Bailey appeared uncomfortable. "Well, you have to hold an official election, and there has to be a grace period of at least one month for any other interested candidate to enter the mayoral race."

"There isn't anybody in town who doesn't respect Mr. Ashburn. I sincerely doubt anyone will challenge him."

"I wouldn't be so sure of that, Mr. Gatewood," Miss Wade called out, then fixed her blistering gaze on Ty. "This isn't over, Mr. Ashburn."

Spinning around, the unstoppable Miss Gabby flounced down the center aisle and out of the church.

Ty's gaze followed her dramatic exit, and a shiver of warning chased down his spine. He shrugged it aside. How much trouble could one pint-sized woman be, anyway?

*   *   *

Gabby burst into her gambling hall and nodded to a few of the regular customers at the poker and faro tables. Absently, she noted that a couple of lamps needed oil, and the chandelier, lowered and cleaned only a few days ago, already had cobwebs stretched across its prisms. Despite more pressing problems, she'd be sure those items were taken care of after closing. The Emporium was a reflection of herself, and Gabby wanted to cast both in the best light possible.

Rose James, one of her barmaids as well as her best friend, joined her at the polished mahogany bar. "How'd it go?" Her excited smile faded to a grimace. "I hope it wasn't as bad as you look."

"Worse," Gabby replied dourly. She removed her mother's bonnet and laid it on the bar reverently, soothing the sparrows' ruffled feathers. Pulling the pins from her blond hair, Gabby allowed the long tresses to spill down her back. Rid of the respectable trappings, she heaved a sigh.

Rose pointed at the hat. "Didn't that help?"

Gabby shook her head. "Trying to pass myself off as one of them was like a fox trying to get in the coop dressed like a chicken."

"Maybe you should've bought a new hat, one a little more fashionable?" Rose suggested hesitantly.

"There is nothing wrong with this bonnet," Gabby said defensively. Her thoughts returned to the meeting. "Everybody wants Sawtooth on the map, and the territory won't build the bridge unless the town's incorporated, which means a mayor has to be elected. Vernon Gatewood nominated Tyler Ashburn to run for office."

Rose's kohl-shadowed eyes widened. "Tyler

Ashburn of the A-B Freight Company?"

"The same."

Rose gave Gabby a wicked grin. "I would give a month's wages to spend a night with that man."

Gabby stared openmouthed at her. "Tyler Ashburn? He's a sour-faced grouch who wouldn't know how to have fun if his life depended on it. All he cares about is his money and getting in good with Vernon Gatewood." She scowled. "Even going so far as to become engaged to Gatewood's spoiled brat."

"Who cares about that?" Rose said with a negligent wave of her hand. "It's just his body I want."

Gabby recalled the breadth of his shoulders and his firm chest beneath her prodding finger, and a hot wave shimmered through her. Rose had a point: Tyler Ashburn's fine physique could turn any girl's head. But she wasn't an impressionable young girl. She'd grown up around men and learned about their crude behavior with women early on.

Gabby didn't care what a man and a consenting woman did behind closed doors, but she wasn't about to encourage it by allowing her upstairs rooms to be used for such debasing activities. And although Rose and the other barmaids wore brightly colored knee-length dresses typical of saloon girls, they only sold drinks—not their bodies.

"Now, Rose," Gabby began, "I thought you put your past behind you."

"I have—I wouldn't charge him." Rose winked. "I'd *pay* him. Besides, just because I don't do it for money anymore doesn't mean I don't enjoy a romp with a good-lookin' man."

Imagining Tyler Ashburn in her own bed

brought an unexpected rush of heat to Gabby's cheeks, and she took a deep breath, casting aside the unwanted images. Once a man took his pleasure with a woman, he figured he owned her. And Gabby wasn't about to let any man boss her around—not even one whose rugged good looks could coax a spinster out of her proper petticoats.

"Men are more trouble than they're worth," Gabby said. "You mark my words. If Mr. Ashburn becomes mayor, we may as well pack our bags."

She leaned against the bar and gazed about her gambling hall. After she'd bought the place, she'd put in countless hours transforming the common saloon into a bright, airy room with tasteful oil paintings adorning the walls and rich velvet maroon curtains draped from floor to ceiling at the entrance.

She'd put her heart, soul, and sweat into Miss Gabby's Gambling Emporium, and nobody was going to chase her out of her home. She'd spent fifteen of her twenty-three years moving from one place to another, sometimes forced to leave by irate townsfolk, sometimes because her uncle had decided to find a greener pasture to hawk his wares.

"We have to come up with a way to stop Ashburn from becoming the mayor," Gabby stated.

"I have a double-barrel derringer in my room upstairs," Rose offered helpfully.

"That's good, Rose," Gabby said dryly. "You can use your charms to lure him up to your room, then shoot him. I can see the newspapers now." She lifted her arm, pointing to an imaginary headline. " 'One of Sawtooth's Upstanding Citizens Killed While Cavorting in Bed with Soiled Dove.' Great idea."

"I promise he'll go a happy man." Rose waggled her eyebrows suggestively.

"Unfortunately, Tyler Ashburn is so upstanding he'd make Abraham Lincoln look like a scoundrel."

"Nobody's that perfect," Rose scoffed.

"Then we'll have to find something in his background to use against him—tarnish his squeaky-clean image so that people will think twice before voting for him." She rubbed her palms together. "But somebody has to run against him. Somebody sympathetic to our cause."

"Why don't *you* run against him?"

Gabby wrinkled her nose. "That's worse than the derringer idea."

"No, listen to me." Rose began to pace excitedly. "It just might work. This is the one territory in the country where women can vote and hold office. Declare yourself a candidate, and beat Ashburn at his own game."

"Come on, Rose, I wouldn't have a chance against him. You should've seen the folks at the meeting when I stood up to him. I thought they were going to have an old-fashioned witch burning."

"I'll bet it was mainly the women who were ready to strike the match. Most of the men in this town have been in here a few times, and I haven't heard any complaints. If you can get them behind you, you *could* win."

"But I don't know anything about being a mayor," Gabby objected. "I'd only make a fool of myself."

"No, you wouldn't. You own your own business, Gabby, and that makes you smarter than most.

And you're friendly and don't hold to airs like those snooty folks who live on the other side of town. Besides, you're the most honest person I know, and you've never done anything you're ashamed of, right?"

Gabby nibbled on her thumbnail. "What about Soapy? What if folks find out about him and what he did? I might lose before I even got started."

"That was a long time ago. And even if somebody remembers, I doubt they'd blame you. You were only a girl at the time."

Gabby's Uncle Soapy, an itinerant gambler and huckster, had taken on the responsibility of raising his seven-year-old orphaned niece. She'd followed him from one town to another, learning the tricks of his trade, from playing the shill in one of his con games to recognizing a marked deck of cards. She had been an apt student, but had put it all behind her when she bought Miss Gabby's Gambling Emporium.

She fished for another excuse. "Even if I did agree to run, which I won't, I can't just yell it from the rooftops. I'm sure there's some kind of official rules we have to follow."

Rose frowned. She glanced at the bartender and brightened. "Let's ask William. He studied at some fancy school back East. He should know."

She grabbed Gabby's wrist and dragged her down to the other end of the twelve-foot gleaming expanse of mahogany.

"We got a question for you, William," Rose said without preamble.

"Hey, Rose, ain't you gonna say hello?"

She turned to the customer who'd spoken and smiled saucily. Placing a hand on his shoulder and leaning against his side, she said, "Been a while, Pete. You been keeping out of trouble?"

Pete wrapped a burly arm around Rose's waist. "Yeah, and it ain't been any fun at all. I signed on with the crew that's aimin' to build that bridge for the new road they're surveyin'."

Gabby stepped closer to them. "I thought they were going to wait and see if Sawtooth became an official town."

Pete shrugged meaty shoulders and turned to look at her. "I don't know nothin' about that, Miss Gabby. All I know is the pay's good and the work's better'n sitting in a saddle fourteen hours a day like I was doin' at the Rocking H spread."

Gabby tapped her lower lip with her fingertip. "So Mr. Bailey assumed we'd vote to incorporate. I wouldn't put it past Ashburn and Gatewood to give him a bit of an incentive to get the territory started on the road right away. William, what do you know about electing someone to run for office?"

The young bookish bartender appeared startled by the question. "Well, I know that the person has to be affiliated with a political party, and you have to hold a meeting of that party to nominate and endorse a candidate. I've got a copy of *Roberts Rules of Order*. It tells how to hold an organized, legal meeting."

"Could you get the book, William? We can't waste a minute planning our offense."

William shrugged. "Sure, but who's going to watch the bar?"

"Rose can. She likes to play bartender."

"Who am I to deny Rose her fun?" he commented dryly. After removing his apron, he hurried out of the Emporium.

Rose slipped out of Pete's friendly hold and sashayed behind the bar. Flipping a towel over her shoulder, she moved down to wait on another customer.

Gabby rubbed her chin with her forefinger. Men like Ty Ashburn thought they owned the world simply because they wore a cloak of respectability. But no more. Gabby wasn't going to be railroaded out of town; she was going to take a stand. And if she had to run for mayor, she would—for the sake of herself, her friends, her employees, and her beliefs!

Her excitement grew. She needed a political affiliation and a group of people to attend her meeting. Who could she get who would support her? Most of the people at the town meeting wouldn't openly attend a meeting she organized—but what about those who hadn't attended?

"Rose, run over to the other establishments and tell the owners we need to have an emergency meeting tomorrow morning. We're going to give Tyler Ashburn and Vernon Gatewood a little competition."

Rose squealed in delight. "You're going to run against him!"

Gabby held up her hand. "Only as a last resort. But we definitely need to nominate *someone* who's on our side."

"Do you really think they'll come?"

"Their places are in as much danger as mine of getting closed up. They'll come." Then she grinned. "But just to make sure we get enough people to form a party, tell them the drinks are free during the meeting."

Rose cast Gabby a skeptical look, but refrained from commenting. "I'll go as soon as William gets back."

Gabby shook her head. "No. I want you to go right away."

With a sigh of surrender and a longing look usually reserved for a lover, Rose left her post behind the bar and disappeared around the curtained entrance.

Pete set his empty glass down. "I hate to mention this, Miss Gabby, but I'd sure like another drink."

Gabby grinned as she stepped around behind the bar and donned William's apron. "Another whiskey coming right up."

Chapter 2

Ty leaned forward in his chair and braced his elbows on the cluttered desk in his office at the A-B Freight Company. "Look, Vernon, I appreciate your confidence in me, but I did a lot of thinking last night and I've decided I don't want to become Sawtooth's first mayor. The fact is, I've never wanted to run for any political office."

Gatewood clasped his hands and formed a steeple with his fingers. "Didn't you mean what you said about cleaning up this town?"

Ty scowled. "Sure I did, but somebody else could do the job better than me. Like you, for instance."

The distinguished-looking man chuckled. "I thought about it, but I've got six businesses to look after, plus I've got holdings in most of the town's other places of commerce."

"Then how about Sam Ramey? Or Bill Danvers? Either one of them would make a good mayor."

Gatewood shook his head. "Neither one of them has your reputation for honesty and fair dealing." He paused, and a sly smile slid across his features. "And neither one of them is engaged to my only daughter."

Resentment surged through Ty, and he tamped down the emotion. He owed Vernon Gatewood a great deal for taking him under his wing when he'd first arrived in Sawtooth. Keeping his voice calm, he said, "I may be marrying Eleanor, but that doesn't give you the right to arrange my life."

Gatewood waved a placating hand. "Settle down, Tyler. You know you're like a son to me, and I only want what's best for you. You possess a great deal of promise in the political arena, and I know for a fact Eleanor would be more than pleased to be Sawtooth's first lady."

Ty didn't doubt that: Eleanor was already planning the dinner parties they'd host for visiting dignitaries, even though Sawtooth had few visitors, much less important ones. His head began to pound and he rubbed the back of his neck. "I'm sorry, Vernon, but I really don't want to be the damned mayor. I want to give my full attention to the business."

"You want to become the largest freight company in the territory, don't you?"

Ty lifted his head sharply. "You know I do. We've talked about it, and you said you'd back me. Are you reconsidering?"

"Of course I plan on financing you, but there are certain conditions we need to be aware of." Gatewood eyed Ty with a narrowed gaze, and a frisson of unease skittered down Ty's spine.

"This is business, pure and simple," Gatewood began. "We need that bridge and the only way we'll get it is to incorporate the town. Without that bridge, I may have trouble justifying the money you need to expand. If you refuse the candidacy for mayor, we can't be sure we'll get what we need."

"So you'll only finance me if the bridge is built?"

"It's too risky without it, son," Gatewood said, his calculating gaze at odds with the apology in his voice. "I didn't get where I am today by making foolhardy business decisions. I thought you didn't like to take unnecessary risks, either—or was I wrong about that?"

The cutting question grated on Ty's nerves, and angry heat rose in his face. "I saved every penny I made, built the A-B from the ground up, and never overextended myself. I'm *not* a gambler, and I *won't* take any chances where the A-B is concerned."

Gatewood sat back in his chair, looking as pleased as a cat that had cornered a mouse. "That's good to hear, because there's also the little matter of Miss Gabby and her associates. Besides that bridge, we need to make Sawtooth a place where families will want to settle. By imposing sanctions on the saloons and gambling halls, we should be able to run them out of town legally. And with your moral code and the fortitude to stand behind it, you, Tyler, are the perfect man to do so."

Ty had worked hard to build a respectable life in Sawtooth, and with Vernon Gatewood backing the A-B's expansion, he could finally cut the strings to his past—a past he'd tried to forget for twenty-two years. Still, he didn't like being manipulated. "So the loan is contingent on my running for mayor?"

Gatewood shook his head. "No." His affable expression disappeared, replaced by a banker's implacability. "It's contingent on your *becoming* mayor."

Ty seethed with helplessness, an emotion he'd spent years purging from his life. Very few people had the ability to rattle him, but Vernon Gatewood was one of those people. "I don't appreciate you putting me between a rock and a hard place."

Gatewood's quicksilver smile returned. "Now, Tyler, there's no reason to feel that way. You'll have no trouble getting elected. Then all you have to do is put together a town charter that will encourage the less savory elements to depart from our fair town. After that, you can give the company your undivided attention. In fact, I'll help oversee the town's affairs so that they don't distract you from the A-B."

Gatewood made it sound so simple, Ty thought— but then that was one of his strengths. That and knowing where others were vulnerable. The A-B was doing well. He was ready to double the number of wagons he had and set up a second office in Rawlins. Gatewood's support would seal his plans. How could he blame him for wanting to see Sawtooth turned into a decent town, when Ty wanted the same thing?

With a muttered oath, he nodded. "All right, Vernon, I'll do it. But only for one term. After that, someone else can have it."

"Fair enough, son." Gatewood stood. "I heard that Miss Wade is having a meeting at her place this morning."

"What kind of meeting?"

"She's planning on getting one of the other saloon owners to run against you." Gatewood laughed. "Imagine someone like Big Louie on the ballot."

Ty pictured the burly bartender, his perpetually

soiled apron stretched over a belly the size of a flour barrel. "She doesn't really think they'd have a chance, does she?" he asked in disbelief.

"You saw her last night at the meeting. She's not about to go down without a fight."

Ty recalled the stubborn glint in her eyes, and he felt a reluctant respect for her standing up for her unpopular view in an opposition-filled room. "I've dealt with her when we drew up the contract to transport her liquor and I never figured her to be a troublemaker."

"By virtue of her profession, she's a trouble-maker," Gatewood said flatly. "She shamelessly flouts civilized society's rules, and I'm afraid she's going to be even more of a nuisance with this election. If she gets too far out of hand, we'll just have to nip the problem in the bud."

"What do you mean?"

"Nothing illegal, of course. Perhaps you could find a loophole in her contract that you could exploit, and legally break the contract," Gatewood suggested, a scheming glint in his dark eyes.

Ty clenched his jaw. "I won't break a contract—with anyone. I do that once, and my word isn't worth anything."

"Then we'll find another way, if it becomes necessary."

"She's only one woman. There can't be much she can do."

"I hope you're right, Tyler. I'm going over to see what she has to say. Care to join me?"

Ty glanced at the pile of papers on his desk, but curiosity urged him to accompany Gatewood. And in spite of his objection to her livelihood, Ty was tempted to see the fiery Miss Wade in action again.

He stood. "I guess it'd be better to be forewarned about who I'm going to be up against."

Together, Ty and Gatewood strolled down the boardwalk. Ty glanced up at the Green Mountains to the west, which reflected the glow of the late September sun. Leaves were already beginning to turn color in the early autumn, littering the hillsides with splashes of yellow. With the added burden of an election, Ty hoped he'd get the extra trips to Rawlins completed before the first snow, or Sawtooth would suffer without a winter cache of supplies.

As they approached the Emporium, Ty noticed a handwritten announcement about the meeting tacked to a knotty post outside the saloon. The neat, curvy penmanship was obviously a woman's, and Ty suspected Miss Gabby Wade had been busy organizing the opposition since last night.

Side by side, Ty and Gatewood pressed through the batwing doors and walked between garish tasseled curtains to enter the main room. The low hum of conversation met Ty's ears. He was surprised to note the place was neater than he'd imagined. He'd expected a dark, smoke-filled room with tobacco-stained floors and rickety tables covered with dirty beer mugs. Instead, glass gleamed under the chandelier's bright lights and the wood bar shone from repeated polishing. Fresh sawdust covered the floor and the spittoons had recently been emptied. The shelves behind the bar were well-stocked with brown bottles bearing labels he recognized from past shipping invoices.

Spying an empty table near the back of the high-ceilinged room, he led Gatewood toward it. Ty settled in a chair and continued his perusal of Miss

Wade's domain. A long staircase led to the upper floor. How many men had trod those steps with Miss Wade? he wondered. Unbidden images of the feisty woman sitting on a brass bed wearing nothing but her unbound wheat-colored hair made him shift uncomfortably.

Thankfully, the unwelcome mental picture faded as a brunette clad in a short violet dress and black stockings came to a halt beside their table. "Why, Mr. Ashburn, this is the first time I've seen you in here."

"I only came to hear what Miss Wade has to say," he said tersely.

"Well, any reason's a good reason for you to stop in. By the way, my name's Rose. I just want to tell you I've seen you around town, and I do so admire your imposing"—her gaze swept down to his lap and back up—"manliness."

Ty stared at the saloon gal, wondering if he'd heard her correctly. "Have we ever met?"

Rose pressed her hip against his shoulder. "We just did, honey."

Ty shifted his position to escape her blatant invitation, but she followed like a flea on a dog.

"Could I get you a drink? Or anything else you might . . . desire?" Rose asked without a whit of modesty.

"I'd like a cup of coffee, miss," Gatewood interrupted. "And I believe Tyler will have the same."

Rose kept her gaze fixed on Ty, giving him the uncomfortable impression she'd undressed and hog-tied him with her eyes. "Are you sure?"

"Yes, we're sure," Ty snapped.

She shrugged. "Suit yourself. But if I was you,

I'd have a drink. They're free until the end of the meeting."

Rose sauntered away, swaying her hips like a front porch swing in a northern gale.

"She's about as subtle as a twister," Ty commented in disgust. After he was elected mayor, women like her wouldn't be bothering anyone.

"There she is," Gatewood announced.

Ty glanced up to see Miss Wade descend the stairs gracefully. He'd expected to see her in red satin; instead, she wore a sky-blue dress with a modest neckline trimmed with white lace. Her long blond ringlets covered her back and spilled over her shoulders to caress her full breasts, reminding him too much of his earlier image.

"Look at her, parading around like some kind of bawdy queen," Gatewood commented venomously.

Ty looked at Vernon and was surprised to see him watching Gabby Wade with an expression that bordered on loathing. He couldn't remember Gatewood ever expressing such animosity for a person. Frowning, Ty wondered if Miss Wade had personally insulted the older man.

"Actually, she doesn't look like I thought she would," Ty said.

"What do you mean?"

"I figured she'd be dressed in something less ladylike."

"You can dress a whore in a pure white gown, but she's still a whore underneath it. Nothing can change that type of woman." Gatewood spit out the last words as if he had dirt in his mouth.

Ty studied the older man, wondering at his vehemence.

"May I have your attention?" Miss Wade called out as she reached the bar, her voice rising above the din. Slowly the noise subsided. "Thank you. I think most of you know why I asked you all to come here this morning."

"For the free drinks," a man's slurred voice called out.

Miss Wade smiled slightly. "I didn't think you drank, Owen."

"I didn't till I come here."

Laughter tumbled around the room.

She waited until everyone quieted and began again. "As most of you know, the territorial authorities are proposing to build a bridge across the river, which will cut close to twenty miles off the trip to Rawlins."

"That's good news, ain't it?"

Ty recognized the speaker as Big Louie, clad in his familiar stained apron.

"Yes and no. If built, the bridge will bring more business to Sawtooth, but there is a price to be paid." She took a deep breath. "Sawtooth would have to become an incorporated township, with a town government established before the final construction plans can go into effect. And that's where the problem lies."

The room's silence was broken by a booming belch.

" 'Scuse me. Just slipped out," the man apologized.

Miss Wade acknowledged his apology with a teacher's scolding expression, though Ty noticed the twinkle in her eyes. "Let's try to keep this meeting as civilized as possible, shall we?"

The guilty party's ears reddened with embarrassment as he nodded. Ty drew the side of his hand along his mouth to curb a smile that tugged at the corners of his lips.

"So what's the problem with having a town government?" Big Louie demanded, bringing the subject back on track.

"Mr. Tyler Ashburn has been nominated as a candidate for mayor," she replied, her stare pinpointing Ty.

Heads swiveled to follow her gaze, and curious looks landed on him. Ty was surprised she'd known he was there. He scanned the room, meeting the eyes of those men he knew, and storing the names in his memory for future reference.

"And he has stated that when he is elected, he will do everything in his power to rid Sawtooth of saloons and gambling halls," Miss Wade concluded.

Unrestrained muttering broke out, and Ty parried the now-hostile looks with a hard stare of his own.

"We can't let him shut down the saloons!" one voice rose above the rest.

Miss Wade held up her arms for silence. "He has the right to stand up for what he believes in." She paused dramatically. "But so do we! To protect our interests, I'm asking for one person to volunteer to run against Mr. Ashburn."

For a moment Ty could have heard a feather drop, then all hell broke loose.

"Run against Ashburn?"

"Nobody could—"

"One of us?"

"You got to be crazy, Miss Gabby."

"Who knows anything about—"

"Quiet down," she shouted above the remarks. "Please, everyone, quiet!"

Slowly, the voices subsided.

Louie stood and shifted his considerable weight from one foot to the other. "We don't know nothin' about politickin', Miss Gabby. Most of us just pour drinks and try to keep the fights from getting out of hand. Besides, who would vote for one of us?"

Gatewood rose. "He's right, Miss Wade. The good folks of Sawtooth want to do away with places such as this—gambling hells where men get drunk and lose their hard-earned money in crooked poker games."

"I run a straight house, Mr. Gatewood," Miss Wade defended hotly. "And nobody here twists those men's arms. If they want a drink, I sell it to them. And if they want to gamble, I offer them a poker table. They know the risks."

Dark memories and a fierce bitterness filled Ty, and he came to his feet. "Then maybe it's our duty to take away temptation so men don't lose everything they own at one of your tables."

"You're not God, Mr. Ashburn, and it's not your right to decide what's best for everyone." She glared pointedly at Ty, who bristled. "People have the right to make their own choices."

"Even if that choice means their children will go hungry?" Ty's stomach clenched in remembered pain; his own childhood was a testament to such selfish choices.

"I never let a man bet everything he owns on the turn of a card," Gabby said. "It's bad for business."

Gatewood took hold of Ty's arm. "Let it go, Tyler," he said in a low voice. "You'll have numerous chances to air your views before the official election."

Fuming inwardly, Ty reluctantly lowered himself back into his chair.

Gabby had no idea Tyler Ashburn and Vernon Gatewood would be attending the meeting until she'd noticed the two men as she'd come downstairs. She'd been fighting to regain control of herself ever since. She took a deep breath to still her agitated nerves, and raised her voice. "Now that we know without equivocation where Mr. Ashburn stands, it's imperative that we nominate our own candidate so *our* voice can be heard."

"How 'bout you, Miss Gabby?" Louie asked.

"I don't know anything about running for office, or what would be expected of me if I became mayor."

"You probably know more'n anybody else in this room," another saloon owner said.

A chorus of agreements arose from the gathering.

Against her will, her gaze strayed to Tyler Ashburn, who studied her with unfathomable, icy blue eyes. He was probably laughing at her behind that cool mask.

If nobody else would challenge Ashburn, she'd be driven out of town by his inflexible and impossible moral standards. But she liked Sawtooth, and she liked waking up in her own room every morning.

Rose sidled over to her. "I told you, Gabby. You have to run against him."

The twinkle in her friend's eye steadied Gabby's resolve and she gave in to the inevitable. "All right," she called out. "I will accept the candidacy, but we have to do this right or I could be disqualified from the ballot."

She turned to William, who handed her the copy of *Roberts Rules of Order* that she'd spent most of the night trying to understand. Mentally crossing her fingers, she silently cursed Robert and all his stupid rules and hoped she did things right with know-it-all Ashburn sitting in judgment.

"According to these rules of order for an official meeting, we have to have someone make a motion, then we need somebody else to second it."

Blank gazes met her statement.

"A motion?" Louie asked in confusion. "What the heck's that?"

"Someone has to make a move to nominate the candidate," she explained.

Their vacant looks told her she was getting nowhere.

Gabby surreptitiously glanced at Ashburn and found him leaning back in his chair, his arms folded across his broad chest, and laughter glinting in his eyes. She restrained the urge to throw the book at his smug face.

"I move to nominate Miss Gabby Wade as candidate for mayor of Sawtooth," William spoke up.

Gabby sent her bartender a grateful look. "Who will second the motion?"

Louie shrugged. "I will."

"You have to say, 'I second the motion.' "

"Why?"

She held up the bible of meeting proceedings. "Because *this* says so."

Louie shrugged. "Okay. I second whatever you said."

Gabby's racing heart settled down; she might actually make it through the meeting. "Everyone in favor, say aye."

A few scattered ayes responded, and Gabby glanced at her bartender, who nodded.

"Anyone opposed?" she asked, and held her breath.

"Nay," Ty and Gatewood chorused.

Ignoring the minority opposition, Gabby said, "Motion carried."

Ashburn raised his hand. Though Gabby wanted to pretend she didn't see him, the book said she couldn't, and she was determined to do everything by the book. "Mr. Ashburn."

"Point of order, Miss Wade."

Gabby blinked. Point of order. She'd read about that somewhere, hadn't she? As she leafed through the pages, several of the men moved to the bar to get refills. Soon, other men followed, and Gabby found herself jostled aside in the mass movement for more free liquor.

There it was. She skimmed the section. All he wanted to do was point out something she'd forgotten.

"What is your point of order, Mr. Ashburn?" she hollered above the uproar.

He stood and hooked his thumbs in his belt, distracting Gabby as her gaze slid down denim jeans stretched across hard thighs. An unfamiliar tingle started in her belly and moved outward. In her few business dealings with Ashburn, she'd never noticed the snug fit of his trousers. Of course, he was usually seated behind his desk then.

"It seems to me you can't have a candidate without a party affiliation," he said, bringing Gabby out of her reverie.

"Ah, well, that was my next order of business, Mr. Ashburn." Hadn't William told her that last night? How could she have forgotten? "Everybody, we have one more item to vote on."

It took her ten minutes to get the men settled back in their chairs. Wiping a bead of perspiration from her brow, she continued the meeting. "For me to run for mayor, I have to be affiliated with a political party."

"You mean like a Democrat?" Louie asked.

Gabby nodded with excitement. This wouldn't be so hard after all. "That's right. Since Mr. Ashburn is running as a Republican, I could very well run as a Democrat."

"I ain't going to vote for any stinkin' Democrat, even if it's you, Miss Gabby," Slim Talman, the owner of Slim's Place, shouted, a drunken slur to his words.

Gabby groaned.

"I told you you shouldn't have lured them here with free booze," Rose said in an aside.

Gabby ignored her. "Then what party would you support, Mr. Talman?"

"How about the Working Party?"

"They're a bunch of socialists, and I won't vote for anyone who runs under their shingle," another man called out.

Gabby's optimism died amid the cacophony of name calling. Out of the corner of her eye she noticed Ashburn and Gatewood leaving, and for a moment she was tempted to join their retreat. Then she saw Ashburn's shoulders shaking, and she steeled her backbone.

He might be laughing at her now, but she'd have the last laugh on election day.

Chapter 3

Ty added the last column of figures and scrupulously wrote the total beneath the numbers. He laid aside the fountain pen Eleanor had given him for his thirty-third birthday a few months ago. It was the only present out of many she'd given him that he'd been able to actually use. He hoped that once they were married she'd become more practical, as well as curb her habit of extravagant spending.

Rubbing his eyes, he had to admit the pampered only child of Vernon Gatewood was more interested in the latest New York fashions than the routine of everyday living. But she'd also attended the best schools and had learned how to manage a household, as well as organize parties and dances. Besides her social skills, she was gifted with a tall, slender figure and luxurious auburn hair. There was no doubt she'd be the perfect wife.

So why did he have a vague sense of restlessness when he thought about his upcoming wedding?

The sound of traces jangling and hooves on hard-packed ground distracted his troubled thoughts. He rose and strode out of his office to the boardwalk. Shading his eyes against the afternoon sun,

he watched one of his freight wagons roll into
town. He checked his pocketwatch. Right on time,
he thought proudly.

The driver pulled his team to a halt in front of
the office and wrapped the leather reins around the
hand brake. The horses snorted, their sides heaving
from the last few upward-sloping miles.

Ty walked over to the lead horses and stroked
their damp necks. "Any problems, Joe?"

Joe Hedley, a man about Ty's age, removed his
hat, leaving carrot-red curls plastered against his
sweat-dampened forehead. He drew his arm across
his brow. "Nope." He hopped down from the
wagon seat and winced, rubbing his backside. With
ginger steps, he joined Ty and growled, "Next time
we're a man short, you're taking the run."

Ty smiled wryly. "I wish I'd gone this time."

"Why's that?"

"There was a town meeting a couple nights ago.
Vernon nominated me to run for mayor."

"You, a mayor?" Joe hooted. "You didn't go
along with it, did you?"

Stung, Ty demanded, "What's wrong with me
being mayor?"

"Nothing, other than you got the tact of a charging bull." Although Joe was six inches shorter than
him, he'd never backed down to Ty, which was one
of the reasons they'd become friends.

"You've got a point. I told Vernon I wasn't interested, but he didn't give me a helluva lot of
choice."

"He said he wouldn't give you the loan if you
didn't run, right?"

Ty shouldn't have been startled by Joe's percep-
tive guess. They had started out as teamsters to-

gether years ago, and Joe knew how much a successful business meant to him.

"What was I supposed to do?" he demanded.

The shorter man shrugged "Got me. I guess if I was in your place, I would've done the same. But I'm glad I ain't. I wouldn't want your headaches for all the Arbuckles in the country."

"Sometimes I feel that way myself." Ty clapped him on the back. "Why don't you go get something to eat? I'll take the wagon over to the general store and get it unloaded."

"Thanks, Ty. I think I'll head on down to Miss Gabby's place for a beer or two first."

"Don't!"

Joe paused, and gazed at Ty like he didn't know one end of a horse from the other. "What?"

"Don't go over there."

"Why not?"

Just then, Miss Wade herself rounded the corner, halting Ty's explanation. She wore a high-collared forest-green dress, but she'd forsaken the dilapidated bonnet and her thick, wavy hair shimmered down her back and over her shoulders like a golden waterfall. Ty could almost feel the silky strands caressing his skin, and his pulse quickened.

"Good morning, Mr. Ashburn." She turned to Joe and her expression warmed. "I see you made it back in one piece, Joe."

"Sure did, Miss Gabby. I was just telling Ty I was going to head over to your place to wash down the dust," Joe said, slanting Ty a challenging gaze.

"I'm surprised he didn't forbid you from darkening the Emporium's door."

"Actually—" Joe began.

"I was just about to," Ty broke in irritably. It

irked him that his best friend and his opponent were on such good terms, and he hadn't even realized they knew each other.

"What's going on?" Joe demanded impatiently.

Miss Wade displayed one of the sheets of paper in her hands: *Miss Gabby Wade for Mayor, The Working Men and Women Party's Candidate.*

"She's running against you, Ty?" Joe guffawed and slapped his hat against his thigh, pluming dust from his trousers. "This is going to be one hell of an interesting election."

"Do I have your support, Joe?" she asked.

Joe's laughter stopped in midchuckle. "Well, uh, Miss Gabby, you know me and Ty go way back."

She smiled sweetly. "What would Rose think if she knew you were supporting him and not me?"

"Aw, Miss Gabby, that's not fair! You wouldn't want me to have to choose between my best friend and my best girl."

"Everything's fair in love or war," she replied with a twinkle in her eye. "Now if you'll excuse me, I have to speak to Mr. Ashburn about the ground rules for this election."

She turned to Ty, and Joe sent him a helpless shrug.

"Go on," Ty said. He held up a warning finger. "But you might remember who pays you."

With a grunt of disgust, Joe strode away.

"That wasn't very nice. Joe's been coming to the Emporium ever since I opened," Miss Wade said.

"Maybe it's time he stopped." Ty glanced around and noticed that several people were watching them with open curiosity. He gestured toward his door. "Why don't we step inside before we draw any more attention?"

Gabby nodded regally and entered the tiny office. She lowered herself to a seat in front of his paper-littered desk and crossed one leg over the other. Ty caught a glimpse of a well-turned ankle and quickly brought his gaze back to her fair features.

Taking sanctuary in his own chair behind the desk, he folded his arms across his chest. "All right. What is it we need to discuss?"

"I believe we need to establish some ground rules as to how this election will be run," she began.

"That shouldn't be up to us, should it?"

She fidgeted in her chair. "I assume a committee has to be put together to come up with a few guidelines."

"I suppose."

"So, ah, how do you think that should be done?"

Ty shrugged. "Someone will have to appoint committee members."

"Like who?" she asked tentatively.

She seemed unable to look him in the eye. "You have no idea how to run for office, either, do you?" he asked.

Her ramrod posture slumped, and laughter spilled out of her, startling Ty with the musical tone. Unexpected warmth flared within him.

"I haven't even voted before." She raised her hands helplessly. "I've never lived in a place where women could vote until I moved here."

He picked up his fountain pen and toyed with it, hiding his discomfort at her candor and the affinity it invited. "Well, I've voted once or twice, but that's a whole lot different than being on the ballot."

"So what do we do besides put up notices like these?" she asked, holding up her sheaf of handbills.

"I guess we should stage a debate where folks can ask us questions and we can lay out our platforms."

"What's a platform?"

"It's where you stand on issues."

"Like you wanting to shut down the saloons and gambling halls, and me wanting to keep them open?"

"That's one, but there's other things we'll be asked about, like taxes."

"I won't have any," she stated flatly.

"Then who'll pay the sheriff?"

"We don't have a sheriff."

"Not now, but after we're incorporated, we'll need one to uphold the town's laws," Ty explained.

"Why don't we just pass a hat around? If folks want the laws upheld, they can throw some money in. If they don't, they won't," she suggested.

Ty didn't know whether to laugh or rail at her naïveté. "A sheriff isn't like a preacher, Miss Wade," he began, straining to keep the impatience from his tone. "He has to be ensured a certain income."

"Why? You and I aren't ensured an income. It depends on how much business we do."

"So we should pay him per arrest?"

His sarcasm slipped right past her, and excitement animated her face. "Good idea! We can give him so much for each murderer he catches, so much for each robber, and so on. We could have a whole chart drawn up for each offense, and then we'd have the criminal pay the sheriff instead of the fine citizens of Sawtooth."

"That's ridiculous!"

"I don't think so. In fact, it's such a good idea, it's going to be one of my platforms," she said, looking quite satisfied with herself.

A runaway stagecoach would be easier to stop than Gabby Wade once she got rolling. "Suit yourself, but you'd better be prepared to defend it." If she wanted to make a fool of herself, he shouldn't care. It would only make him look better—not that he needed the added advantage.

"About this committee. We need to come up with a few people who'll be impartial," he said.

"How about Joe?"

"He doesn't know anything about election rules."

"He knows as much as you and I do about being mayor," she said, raising a dark blond eyebrow as if daring him to dispute her.

"Aren't you afraid he won't be objective?"

"No. We've already put him in the middle. He may as well stay there."

Much as Ty hated to admit it, she had a point. For the next fifteen minutes, they chose and discarded names until they came up with five people—Joe, Vernon Gatewood, Big Louie, Tom Bailey, and Reverend Tusk—to make up the committee.

"Can I ask you a question, Miss Wade?" Ty asked suddenly.

"Go ahead. I've got nothing to hide."

"Why are you putting up such a fight? I would think it'd be easier to pack up and leave than go through this whole bother of an election."

"Why are *you* doing it?"

"Because my business and home are here."

She tipped her head to the side, a sunny curl spilling across her smooth brow. "Those are my reasons, too, Mr. Ashburn, even though you're of the mind that my business isn't as important as yours, and that it shouldn't be allowed to continue."

"You may not understand this, Miss Wade, but I'm doing it for your own good," Ty said in a tone that even he realized was condescending. "Maybe if you left here, you could change your name and find a man who didn't know about your past, then raise a passel of children. Women weren't meant to run a business, especially a gambling hall."

Her shocked expression revealed disbelief mingled with amazement. "You're scared I might win, aren't you?"

Ty couldn't have been more surprised if an Indian war party had just swooped down on the town. "Are you crazy? You don't have a snowball's chance in hell."

"I've been told that before, Mr. Ashburn, and I haven't melted yet." She stared at him defiantly. "I'll make you a little wager. If you win, I'll pack up and leave town immediately, giving you a clear path to push out the rest of the saloons." Gabby's eyes narrowed challengingly, but not before Ty noticed the mischief lurking in their depths. "And if I win, you have to dance a jig in the middle of the street."

Ty's mouth dropped open. She belonged in an asylum. There was no other explanation for her insane wager.

"Well?" she prompted.

He snapped his mouth shut and rallied his jolted senses. "Why should I make a wager like that when you'll be driven out of town anyhow?"

She leaned forward in her chair, her face aglow. "Wagers make life more interesting, Mr. Ashburn. If everything in life was predictable, people would die of boredom. Come on—take a chance. What have you got to lose?"

Her dancing eyes and flushed cheeks captivated Ty, bringing a rush of heat to his blood. Startled, he looked away, to a fly caught in a sun-spangled spider web in the window. For a moment he understood how that fly felt, trapped in the silken strands.

"No." The single word came out harsher than he'd intended.

Instead of being cowed by his tone, she shrugged. "Suit yourself. But even though you won't take me up on my bet, I'll wager that by the end of this election, you'll have learned there is more to life than numbers in ledgers."

He aimed his pen at her. "And you, Miss Wade, will learn that life is not all fun and games."

Her smile grew, and for a moment Ty could only stare at the sunshine and laughter reflected in her amber eyes.

"We shall see who learns what, Mr. Ashburn." She stood, and he automatically got to his feet. "When would you like to get the committee together?"

He checked the calendar on his desk. "How about seven o'clock tomorrow evening here in my office?"

She glanced around and wrinkled her nose. "It's

kind of small. How about in the back room of the Emporium?"

"How would that look to folks if I agreed to that?"

Gabby shrugged. "Who cares? You have to stop thinking about how it looks to other people. You'll only make yourself miserable trying to please everyone. Of course"—she paused, giving him an assessing look—"you might actually like being miserable."

Ty scowled. Maybe she didn't care what other people thought, but he did. Still, she had a point; his place *was* too cramped. "What about the church?"

She shook her head. "The quilting bee meets there every Tuesday night."

"How would you know?"

"I tried to join."

Although she'd spoken matter-of-factly, Ty detected a note of bitterness in her tone. Why had she even attempted to join? Had she expected Sawtooth's proper matrons to accept her into their midst with open arms? If so, she was even more naive than he'd first believed.

He tried to think of another place to have the meeting, but came up blank. Resigned, Ty nodded. "As long as you don't supply free drinks again."

"That's fine by me. It was an expensive lesson," she admitted with a chagrined look. "Is a pot of coffee acceptable?"

He didn't want to accept anything from her, but he couldn't see anything wrong with coffee. "All right."

"Seven o'clock in my back room, then."

Ty nodded and moved to open the door. He accidentally wrapped his fingers around Gabby's small hand, which had already settled on the doorknob. Awareness shot through him, startling him with its potency, and his thumb lightly swept across her smooth knuckles. She glanced up at him in surprise and he could see bronze flecks in her eyes and a few golden brown freckles scattered across her nose and cheeks.

"Thank you," she said quietly.

Her voice brought back his reason, and he stepped back, almost tripping in his haste. "You're welcome."

Outside, she walked directly to the wooden post in front of his office and tacked up one of her posters. Sending him a sweet smile, she continued down the boardwalk. With a muttered oath, Ty strode over and tore down the paper, crushing it in his palm.

Gabby glanced around her back room. How fitting that the first meeting of the election committee would gather here: a room reserved for high-stakes gambling, where Gabby was about to ante up for the biggest gamble of her life.

A pot of freshly made coffee sat on the sideboard along with platters bearing pickles, cheese, crackers, and tiny sandwiches.

Rose entered carrying a tray laden with small frosted cakes. "Here's a little something I made for the party."

Gabby studied the confections appreciatively yet warily. In the year they'd lived together, Rose and Gabby had taken turns cooking their meals, and Rose had never shown any inclination to bake, or even any sign that she knew how.

"Go ahead, try one," Rose urged.

With trepidation, Gabby tasted one of the small desserts. The delicate sweetness melted in her mouth. "Ummm. Where did you learn how to bake like this?"

"Good, aren't they?" Rose said with a cocky smile. "My folks owned a bakery. When I turned six, they made me work with them. For twelve, fourteen hours a day, I'd sit in that kitchen cutting out cookies or frosting cakes or whatever they wanted me to do. I felt like a prisoner and came to hate everything about baking." She shrugged, but the nonchalant gesture didn't fool Gabby. "Guess I didn't forget everything I learned."

Rose didn't often talk about her childhood or what had led her to become a prostitute, and Gabby had never asked. Knowing her friend despised sympathetic platitudes, she kept her voice light. "And you just happened to remember how to make these the evening both Joe and Mr. Ashburn will be here?"

"Yeah, kind of amazing, isn't it?" Rose replied impishly.

Gabby gave her shoulders a fond squeeze. "Why don't you put them down beside the rest of the food?"

Rose set the tray down and eyed the miniature feast. "With all this food and coffee, you'll probably need someone to help keep cups filled and serve the food. Don't you think so?"

"I knew there was more to those cakes than met the eye: they're a bribe to let you stay in here during the meeting."

Rose assumed a mask of innocence. "You *could*

use a friend in that nest of vipers, and I'm available."

"All right. Let William know you'll be giving me a hand, and have Liz and Mary cover your tables until the meeting's over."

A triumphant grin lit Rose's face, and she hurried out. A few minutes later she returned and helped Gabby put the finishing touches on the room.

"You know, Vernon Gatewood isn't going to be impartial, and I'll be surprised if the reverend even shows up," Rose commented. "Why did you agree to let them be on the committee?"

Gabby adjusted the fanned napkins on the green-velvet-covered poker table. "It would look strange if the town's leading citizen wasn't included, and despite Reverend Tusk's stand against gambling, he'll feel he has a moral obligation to keep the election a fair one."

"I don't want to see you hurt, Gabby, and those men are going to do everything in their power to see you're disqualified," Rose said seriously.

"They might try, but Ty Ashburn won't let them get away with it."

"If you haven't noticed, Ashburn is just like them."

"I thought you liked Mr. Ashburn."

Rose rolled her eyes in exasperation. "I didn't say I liked him. I said I liked his *body*. Those are two completely separate things. And quit changing the subject."

"Look, Rose, I know men just as well as you—"

"Oh, no, you don't," she interrupted. "For six years, I got to know men a whole lot better than I wanted to, and I know for a fact you haven't—"

"It's his eyes!"

Rose's mouth dropped open. "His eyes are colder than a dead man's—"

Gabby held up her hand. "Stop! I get the picture."

"I was going to say nose," she finished with a smirk.

Gabby bit back her chuckle, then turned to Rose. "I see honesty in his eyes. Even though I know he doesn't approve of me, he's never tried to cheat me."

"But you've never run against him before, either."

"That's true, but I trust my instincts, and I'm betting he'll keep the election a fair one."

"I hope so, for your sake," Rose said.

"Me, too," Gabby said prayerfully. "Me, too."

Chapter 4

~~~~⌒✺⌒~~~~

He'd managed to steer clear of establishments like Miss Gabby's Gambling Emporium for most of his adult life, but now, for the second time in three days, Ty found himself in a saloon. Or gambling hall, as Miss Wade liked to call it, although the difference between the two escaped him. They both served liquor and promoted gambling to line their owners' pockets, with no more concern for the poor bastard who lost everything than for a starving stray cur.

Ignoring the sudden silence his presence produced, Ty strode to the Emporium's bar. "Where's the back room?"

The bartender motioned to a door off to the left. "Right through there, Mr. Ashburn."

"Is anyone else here yet?"

"You're the last one to arrive."

He was both relieved and oddly disappointed that he wouldn't have to endure Miss Wade's company alone. He opened the door and stepped into the smoke-hazed room.

"About time you got here, Ty," Joe called out.

Ty noticed the tart-tongued saloon gal named Rose was also in attendance, and seemed to be attending Joe. "I doubt you even noticed I was missing," he said dryly.

Joe's wounded expression almost brought a smile to Ty's lips.

"Mr. Ashburn, I'm glad to see you finally made it."

Miss Wade stepped forward with a warm, welcoming expression that startled him. If their roles had been reversed, he wouldn't have been so amiable.

"Sorry I'm late. I had a few things to do at the office," he apologized. "Have you started yet?"

"We couldn't very well start without you," Gatewood said, and pulled a fat cigar from between his lips. "Have a seat, Tyler, so we can get this tedious business over with and go home."

Ty moved to the chair at Gatewood's right, and Rose brought him a cup of coffee. "Thank you," he said.

"Would you like something to eat?" she asked politely.

"I thought Miss Wade was only supplying coffee."

"Gabby made a little something to keep everyone awake for the meeting."

Ty's stomach growled, reminding him he hadn't eaten any supper, and lunch had been a long time ago.

Rose smiled and patted his shoulder. "I'll fill a plate for you."

Gatewood took command of the meeting. "Everyone sit down so we can get started."

Miss Wade sat on Gatewood's left; seated on her other side was Joe, then Big Louie, whom Ty almost didn't recognize without his bartender's apron. In its stead was a brand-new black suit, and Ty felt a grudging regard for Louie's attempt at respectability. Beside Ty sat Tom Bailey, then the Reverend Tusk to Tom's right.

Rose set a plate overflowing with small sandwiches, cheese, and tiny cakes next to his elbow. Surprised by the "little something" Miss Wade had made, Ty said, "Thank you."

"You're more than welcome." Rose moved to a shadowed corner to lean against the wall.

"The first and only order of business is to determine the basic rules for the mayoral election," Gatewood began.

"Like what?" Louie asked, planting his elbows on the table and forcing Joe closer to Miss Wade.

"Like no hitting below the belt," Joe quipped.

Miss Wade grinned widely. "And don't forget no gouging or biting."

"I hope you'll be able to restrain yourself, Miss Wade," Ty said wryly. "I think what Vernon means is that we need to establish the qualifications for a mayoral candidate, as well as who can actually vote in the election."

"Very good points, Mr. Ashburn," Tom Bailey said. He removed his spectacles and rubbed the lenses across his shirtfront. "Let me offer a few suggestions. Usually there's a minimum amount of time a person has to live in the town before he or she can run for political office or vote."

"What kind of time are we looking at?" Gabby asked.

"It could be a year, could be ninety days. It's up to your committee."

"I move that candidates must have lived in Sawtooth for at least one year," Gatewood said without hesitation.

Joe held up his hands. "Hold it, now, Mr. Gatewood. You know darn well that would disqualify Miss Gabby."

"Your point?" Gatewood prompted.

Joe's face turned as red as his hair, and Ty recognized his friend's rising temper.

"We can't have an election with only one candidate," Joe stated impatiently. "I know you're all for Ty getting to be mayor, but this is going to be a clean election."

Miss Wade laid her hand on Joe's arm and turned to Gatewood. "I have a better idea. Maybe we should have some type of physical test, where only people who can run a mile with a one-hundred-pound sack of flour over their shoulder qualify? Or maybe only those who can handle a team of eight wild horses pulling a freight wagon through the middle of town? Personally, I find both of those more creative than the one-year stipulation, and they would still disqualify me."

Ty pictured Miss Wade trying to balance a sack of flour bigger than herself, and an unexpected chuckle rose in his throat. He choked back his humor. "Much as I hate to admit it, Joe's right, Vernon. It would look like we were deliberately keeping her off the ballot if we go with a one-year resident time."

"Thank you, Mr. Ashburn. I appreciate your support," Miss Wade said with a pleased expression.

Ty shook his head. "You didn't let me finish. If we do that, people will think we're afraid of her competition, which is nowhere near the truth."

She smiled ruefully. "For a moment there, I

thought you were overcome with a case of open-mindedness."

He ignored her. "I make a motion that mayoral candidates and voters must have lived in Sawtooth for at least ninety days and be at least twenty-one years of age."

"I second what you said," Louie spoke up.

"Is there anybody here who's writing all this down?" Bailey asked curiously.

"I can do it," Rose volunteered.

Gatewood leveled her a quelling look. "I wouldn't have thought a woman with your background would know how to read or write."

"And I would've thought a man of your breeding would have some manners," Rose retorted. "Obviously we were both wrong."

Big Louie's guffaw roared in the enclosed room, but Joe pushed back his chair and stood, steam nearly roiling from his ears.

"Gatewood, you got no cause insulting Rose like that," Joe said. "And if you say anything else against her, I'm going to take you outside and teach you some manners, old man or not."

Ty rose and leaned across the table to lay a hand on Joe's shoulder. "Calm down. Vernon didn't mean anything by it, did you?"

Gatewood smiled, although it didn't reach his eyes. "I was merely under a mistaken assumption." He tipped his head to Rose. "No offense meant, ma'am."

"No offense taken, Mr. Gatewood," she replied, her tone as blatantly insincere as Gatewood's.

Ty kept his grip fastened on his friend until Joe's muscles relaxed and he again lowered himself into his chair. Ty sat down, but watched him closely.

Joe's hair-trigger temper and Rose's obvious occupation made for a powder keg ready to explode at the slightest provocation.

"There's another item which needs to be addressed," Miss Wade said. "The subject of name-calling."

Ty switched his attention to her. "I can keep a civil tongue. Can you?"

"Referring to me as a saloon madam isn't keeping a civil tongue."

"That's what you are!" Ty retorted. "It's like people calling me a teamster or freighter. I'm not insulted by that."

"But the connotation for those isn't bad," she argued. "By using madam for me, you're insinuating that I'm less respectable. I'm a businessperson, just like yourself."

Ty snorted, then leaned forward and laid his forearms on the table. "All right. What *do* I call you?"

"Either Miss Gabby or just plain old Gabby."

His gaze swept across her delicate features, her intelligent eyes, and her voluptuous figure. There was nothing old or plain about Gabby Wade, as evidenced by his body's traitorous reaction to her abundant charms. "All right, *Miss* Gabby. I'll restrain myself in referring to your line of business."

"Thank you, Mr. Ashburn."

"Could we get back to the business at hand?" Gatewood asked.

"I don't think we've strayed from it," Miss Gabby replied. She turned to Rose. "There's paper and pencil in the office."

Rose left, and an awkward silence filled the tense room. Miss Gabby took a deep breath, and Ty unwillingly noticed how her breasts rose and fell beneath her amber dress—a dress the same unusual hue as her eyes. He drew a hand across his damp brow and decided his second official act as mayor would be to enact a law that forbade Miss Gabby from breathing.

Rose returned a couple minutes later, sat across the table from Gatewood, and licked the lead of her pencil. After scribbling a few words, she lifted her head. "I've got Mr. Ashburn's motion that mayoral candidates and voters must be residents of Sawtooth no less than ninety days and be at least twenty-one years of age. I also have Louie's second. I believe you need a vote now."

Surprised by her recall, Ty glanced at Gabby, who arched an eyebrow at him. Irritated by her smug expression, he looked at Gatewood.

"All in favor of Tyler's motion, say aye," Gatewood said without enthusiasm.

Ty, Miss Gabby, Joe, Bailey, and Louie affirmed.

Gatewood and the reverend nayed the motion.

"Motion passed," Gatewood said reluctantly. "The next item discussed should be the definition of a resident of Sawtooth for voting purposes."

"What do you mean?" Miss Gabby asked with a quizzical frown.

"Should the voters be only those who live within the town's limits, or should it be expanded to those who live on the nearby ranches," Gatewood explained in a condescending tone.

"Anyone who does their business here in town should be allowed to vote," Gabby said.

"That means everyone from Rawlins who does business with me or Vernon or anybody else would be able to vote," Ty stated.

"That isn't what I meant. I'm talking about the ranchers and their hired men who come to Sawtooth every week—they should be allowed to vote."

"She's got a point there," Louie said. "Maybe if we say anybody who lives within twenty miles in any direction can vote."

"I would go along with that," Joe stated.

Gatewood scowled. "Those men frequent saloons and thus are not residents of good standing."

"And who are you to say that?" Miss Gabby demanded. "Besides spending their money in saloons, they also buy goods at *your* mercantile and open accounts at *your* bank. And don't forget they patronize *your* leather shop and drugstore, too. If they aren't allowed to vote, I'm going to make sure they know why."

Ty studied Miss Gabby, impressed by her pluck. "I make a motion that folks who live up to twenty miles from Sawtooth can vote, and that they need not be landowners," he said.

Gatewood pinned him with a baleful gaze that Ty refused to acknowledge.

"I second," Joe said.

"All in favor?" Louie called out, jumping into the spirit of the meeting.

Ayes echoed around the table.

"Opposed?"

Gatewood glowered, but remained silent.

After more discussion, they agreed on October 28 for the election—less than a week before Ty's wedding to Eleanor. She'd be ecstatic at the idea of marrying Sawtooth's mayor, Ty thought wryly.

Dates for debates between the two candidates were established, and by the time the meeting ended, it was nearly half past ten. Joe, Bailey, and Louie stopped to thank Gabby, but Ty, Gatewood, and the reverend headed for the door immediately.

"Mr. Ashburn, could I speak to you a moment?" Gabby called out.

Impatiently, he waited by the door until everybody else had gone. "What is it, Miss Gabby?"

She heard the censure in his voice and controlled her inclination to answer in kind. "I only wanted to thank you for not allowing Mr. Gatewood to run roughshod over the proceedings. I know how much it took for you to stand up to him."

He frowned, further darkening his somber countenance. "You don't know anything."

Taken aback by his gruff reply, she said stiffly, "Maybe not, but I felt I should thank you. And I wanted to tell you I'm looking forward to running against you."

"Why?"

"Because you've got something most people don't have: integrity. And although you think I don't even know the meaning of the word, I do. I've known a lot of men, and only a few of them had even a trace of your principles."

"You may *think* you know what integrity means, but if you really understood the meaning of the word, you wouldn't own a place like this," he said, his voice as sharp as a butcher's knife.

Taken aback by his vehemence, she searched his steely eyes. "Why do you hate me? What have I ever done to you?"

"I don't hate you, Miss Gabby," he said tightly. "I don't approve of what you do for a living. And I intend to do something about it when I become mayor."

"*If* you become mayor."

"No 'if' about it. You don't have a chance and I think deep down you know it, too." He turned to the door. "Now, if you'll excuse me, I've got work to do."

She laid her palm on his forearm, feeling corded muscle through his suit's fabric. Her fingers tingled with the warmth emanating from his arm, and she suddenly felt as if someone had laced her corset too tightly. "You're going back to your office?" she asked with a breathy voice.

He jerked his arm away from her. "That's where I usually do my work."

Gabby twined her fingers together behind her back and tried to ignore her disappointment at his abrupt withdrawal. "It just proves my point that you work too hard and don't take any time to enjoy life."

He stared past her for a moment, and Gabby caught a momentary unveiling of his curtained eyes and saw a sliver of soul-deep pain. Then the chilly aloofness was back, and he met her gaze. "There's a lot of things a helluva lot worse than working hard. Good night, Miss Gabby."

Ashburn moved out of the back room, and Gabby watched as he passed through the crowded gambling hall. A few people greeted him, and he managed to nod politely.

"Ashburn, I wanna talk to you!" a drunken voice called out.

Gabby recognized the unruly cowboy as one of the ranchhands from the Rocking H spread north of town. Tensing with sudden foreboding, she moved quickly toward the young man.

Ashburn stopped and approached the man. "What do you want?"

The cowboy hitched up his gunbelt, swayed for a moment, then laid a hand on the butt of his revolver. "I heared you're goin' to run Miss Gabby out of town."

Gabby stopped about five feet from the two men, her fingernails digging into her palms. She gave the boy a smile and forced her voice to remain friendly. "Come on, cowboy, let's you and me go have a drink at the bar."

"Not now, Miss Gabby," the man slurred. "I gotta take care of this fella for you first."

"Stay out of this, Gabby," Ashburn ordered, holding up his hand. He returned his attention to the drunk. "Look, mister, I don't want any trouble."

"I can't be lettin' you run Miss Gabby out of town. Wouldn't be right." He lifted the gun out of his holster and aimed it at Ty.

The barrel wavered, but Gabby knew he couldn't miss at such close range. The hall had gone silent as everybody waited to see what would happen. William had come out from behind the bar, a shotgun held steady in his hands. He might unintentionally cause the cowboy to do something foolish and she shook her head at him. William lowered the shotgun, reluctance in his face.

Gabby boldly stepped between the drunken young man and Ashburn. "You don't want to do this. Mr. Ashburn isn't going to make me go anywhere. In fact, we get along just fine, don't we, Ty?"

He hesitated.

She turned her head and glared at him. "Tell him we're friends."

Ty shook his head. "You're right, cowboy. I *am* going to clean up this town and get rid of Miss Gabby and others like her."

Damn reckless men and their stupid pride! Nobody had ever been killed in her Emporium, and she'd be damned if she let Ashburn spoil her unblemished record. "He's wrong, cowboy, so there's no reason for you to be doing this." She slowly reached for the pistol.

The cowboy staggered back out of range. "I'm doin' this for you, Miss Gabby," he said, his bleary gaze on her.

Ty exploded into motion, shoving Gabby out of danger. He grabbed the cowboy's hand, wresting the gun from his grasp, then drew back his right hand and slugged the young man in the jaw.

Gabby hurried to Ty's side and planted her hands on her hips. "What were you doing? I would've had his gun in another minute!"

Ty rubbed his skinned knuckles. "He could've shot you!"

"He wasn't going to hurt me," she hurled back.

"He was so drunk he didn't know what he was doing. You give boys like him too much to drink and violence erupts. That's one of the reasons I plan on shutting down places like this."

Ty handed her the cowboy's revolver, and the weight of the weapon filled her palm.

"And another thing," he continued. "When I'm mayor, men won't be allowed to carry weapons within the town's limits. I'm going to turn Sawtooth into a safe place where decent families can live without worrying about getting shot by a stray bullet from a liquored-up cowboy."

"This was your own fault! You shouldn't have provoked him."

Ty took a menacing step toward her, and Gabby forced herself to hold her ground. She stared up into his silver-blue eyes and an involuntary shiver shimmied down her spine. His jaw, carved in granite, radiated an anger so intense Gabby could almost touch it.

"Without *you*, this wouldn't have happened, because the Emporium wouldn't have been here and he wouldn't have gotten drunk," he said, his voice dangerously low. "If I were you, I'd have them check their guns at the door when they come in. Next time you may not be so lucky."

Righteous indignation overcame Gabby's prudence. "If you weren't so hell-bent on being everybody's lord and master, this wouldn't have happened. Why don't *you* mind your own business and let people live their own lives?"

Ty shook his head, and he balled his hands into fists at his sides. "The time is coming when you're going to be put on the stagecoach out of Sawtooth and these doors will be locked for good. Why don't you spare everyone a lot of trouble and leave now?"

"It seems to me it's you who's causing the trouble," she said recklessly.

His jaw muscle clenched as he looked around at the crowd gathered about them. "Everyone, go on home to your families. Don't be spending good money on liquor and cards when your wife and children need food and clothing."

Muttering erupted among the men, and they directed their unfriendly gazes toward Ashburn. Most of them sat back down, ignoring Ty's order, but a couple men shuffled out.

"How dare you!" Gabby sputtered. "You have no right—"

"I have every right! This is only the beginning, Miss Wade. By the time the election is over and I'm mayor, you're going to be more than ready to leave town."

He spun around and strode out, his broad shoulders disappearing behind the velvet curtains.

A couple Rocking H cowhands stepped forward to help their partner up, and Gabby handed one the gun.

"Make sure he doesn't get it back until he's completely sober," she warned. "And when he wakes up, tell him that if he ever tries a stunt like that again, he won't be allowed to set foot in here."

"Don't worry, Miss Gabby—though I don't blame him for what he done. It ain't right for Ashburn to be tryin' to throw you out of your own place," the grizzled cowboy said.

Gabby forced a smile. "Thanks, but I can handle Tyler Ashburn by myself."

The two men said good night and dragged their unconscious friend out.

Pale-faced, Rose hurried over to Gabby and put an arm around her shoulders. "Are you all right? That cowboy was so drunk, I was afraid he was going to shoot you!"

"I wasn't in any danger, and if Ashburn had played along with me, I could've gotten the gun without his foolish heroics."

"I wonder why he didn't do that?"

Gabby thought for a moment, picturing the fierce

pride in Ty's face. "Probably for the same reason that I respect him: he's always honest, no matter the consequences."

"Doesn't seem to me that that's always such a good thing. The only thing *I* know is that my heart has finally stopped clacking like a train. In all the times you've dealt with drunks, I've never been scared for you—until now." She paused a moment. "Maybe getting out of this business isn't such a bad idea."

"Don't tell me Ashburn's getting to you, too."

Rose shook her head. "No, it's not that. But maybe owning a restaurant would be safer. I'd even do the baking if you wanted."

"And you'd be miserable. Forget it, Rose. We have a good life here." She studied her best friend a moment. "You can leave if you want, though. You know I would never hold it against you."

"This is the best life I've ever had, thanks to you. And I have no intention of deserting you." She tossed her long hair over her shoulder, her flippancy returning. "Besides, you still might need my derringer."

Rose strutted away, and Gabby wondered if her friend had a point. Maybe that *was* the only way to convince Tyler Ashburn he didn't have the right to be every person's conscience.

Chapter 5

Ty rolled his shirtsleeves up to his elbows and squinted at the clear blue sky as he and Joe walked toward town. "It's going to be a warm one," he commented.

Joe nodded and wiped his brow with his forearm. "We'll need a lot more days like this to make all the runs before winter sets in."

"I know. With this election and all, I'm relying on you to keep the wagons on schedule."

"You could back out, y'know."

"There's too much at stake." Ty thought of Miss Gabby and the war she'd declared on him. "Besides, I don't want my opponent thinking that I'm afraid of her."

Joe snorted. "Maybe you should be."

Children's laughter grew louder as they approached the outskirts of Sawtooth, where the Home for Orphaned Children was situated. Ty smiled at the carefree sound and wasn't surprised to see kids on the two swings he'd hung from a massive oak tree's limbs the previous spring. Only Mrs. Edwards, the orphanage manager, knew he had done it.

"Hey, mister, give me a push," a small boy hollered from one of the swings.

Ty glanced at Joe, who sent him a crooked grin.

"Go ahead, Ty," he suggested. "I'll get over to the office and start working. I should be able to get something done before that meeting." At Ty's blank expression, he continued. "The one about the debating platform."

Ty grimaced at the reminder. "I'd better go with you. I've got a lot of work—"

"You need to relax a little, and a few minutes won't hurt. Besides, I know where those swings came from."

"How'd you know?"

"Anybody with two eyes can see you got a soft spot for those kids. See you later." Joe gave him a friendly shove and continued on into town.

Ty smiled and shook his head, then strode across the yard. He stood behind the boy who was swinging and gave him a push.

"Me, too!" a young girl with whitish blond hair yelled from the other swing.

Ty accommodated the child, enjoying her shrieks of excitement as she rose higher and higher, her stubby legs pumping to keep her momentum going. "Hang on tight so you don't fall off," he called out.

"I will," she assured him.

A handful of other children chattered and giggled as they gathered fallen leaves into a huge pile. The warm breeze tickled Ty's nose with autumn's fragrances, and the orphans' joy in such simple pleasures filled him with bittersweet melancholy. His own childhood had been lost when he wasn't much older than these youngsters, and he was determined that they wouldn't be forced to grow up as quickly as he'd had to.

Mrs. Edwards stuck her head out of the home's back door and called out, "It's time to get to school!"

A collective groan arose from the children, and Ty couldn't blame them—he wasn't exactly thrilled to go to his small office, either.

"Come on, children. No lollygagging, now," the jolly-looking woman said with practiced patience. "Good morning, Mr. Ashburn."

"Morning, Mrs. Edwards," he greeted.

"What brings you here so early?"

"I was just passing by on my way to the office. How's everything going?"

"As good as can be expected," Mrs. Edwards replied. "Could use some more room, though."

"I know," Ty said. "But it's not a good time financially."

"It never is." Mrs. Edwards didn't sound angry, only resigned. "I'd best get back to my chores. Have a nice day, now." She hurried back into the house.

"Watch me," the girl on the swing hollered, drawing Ty's attention.

She launched herself from her seat and flew through the air to land in the gigantic pile of leaves. Ty's heart leaped into his throat as he ran over to the girl, expecting a broken bone or two. She popped out of the leaves with a huge grin on her face, and, relieved, Ty shook his head at her antics. She held up her hands and Ty took hold of them, lifting her out of the pile and setting her on the ground.

* * *

Gabby heard the orphans playing in the back-yard, and her steps lightened as she skipped around the corner of the home. Spotting Tyler Ashburn amid the gaggle of children, she halted in her tracks. What in the world was stuffy Ashburn doing here?

She backed up quickly before someone spotted her, and peeked around the house to watch the fascinating scene unfold. Ty hunkered down beside a young girl Gabby recognized as April, who had leaves stuck to her hair and jacket. She said something to Ashburn and his face lit with a smile, shocking Gabby even further.

So he *could* do something other than glower.

He began to pick the dried leaves from April's hair and clothing and Gabby stared, enchanted by this surprisingly gentle side of Ashburn. His long, tanned fingers removed the ribbon at the end of the girl's disheveled braid, and with endearing awkwardness he rebraided her long blond hair.

Gabby's stomach curled with a yearning to have him caress her with such tenderness. She imagined his work-roughened hands skimming across her hair, then over her bare skin, and her body heated with the too-vivid fantasy.

For a moment she was tempted to jump into the leaf pile herself; then she decided a tub of cold water might be better.

"Get a hold of yourself, Gabrielle Lucille Wade," she muttered. "A lot of men like kids."

But few of them went out of their way for hapless orphans.

And even fewer were as dangerously handsome as Tyler Ashburn.

He stood and placed his hand on April's head,

his smile making Gabby's knees feel like apple butter.

April wrapped her short little arms around his waist for a quick hug, then dashed away.

Gabby watched as Ty tipped his hat back off his forehead and gazed after the children. A few of them turned to wave at Ty and he waved back, fondness in his expression. Then he, too, went on his way toward town.

Leaning against the house, Gabby pressed her hand to her heart, which tripped along at a merry pace. If she hadn't seen it with her own eyes, she wouldn't have believed it! Gabby couldn't recall when a man had so completely astonished her.

Or gave her an inkling of what Rose meant about the fun of a good romp in bed. Gabby's cheeks burned, but this time it wasn't from embarrassment.

"The structure should be built close to the house of God," Reverend Tusk stated vehemently as he stood on the boardwalk in the center of town. "It must be in God's sight so He can sanction the debates."

Ty folded his arms over his wool shirt, restraining his impatience by sheer force of will. It was bad enough to have an election committee meeting during a workday, but the decision on where to build the debating platform shouldn't have taken more than a few minutes. Reverend Tusk's proselytizing had already taken the better part of an hour.

"I didn't realize God was confined to only places of worship. I always thought He was everywhere," Miss Gabby said, one eyebrow pitched upward.

Reverend Tusk appeared tongue-tied by her

claim, and although Ty agreed with her, he resisted the urge to say it aloud.

"I suppose you think the debating stage should be constructed at your end of town," Gatewood retorted sarcastically.

"Why not?" Louie demanded, again wearing his beer- and food-splattered apron. "We got just as many rights as you."

"Louie's got a good point," Joe jumped in.

Ty sighed in exasperation, and frustration knotted his jaw muscle. If someone didn't take charge, they'd never come to an agreement.

"What do you think, Mr. Ashburn?" Miss Gabby suddenly asked, looking up at him with an intense gaze.

He glanced at her wind-pinkened cheeks, then switched his attention to Sawtooth's main street. At the respectable end of town, people scurried down the boardwalks, weaving in and out of the stone and brick buildings as they went about their business. At the end where the saloons and other disreputable places were situated, there was less activity. When darkness fell, the opposite would be true—the saloons would become busy and the upright citizens would be in their homes.

"I think we're wasting time," Ty said impatiently.

"Do you have an opinion or not?" Gatewood asked.

"I think we should build it in the center of town, halfway between the church and Miss Gabby's Emporium."

Gabby smiled and nodded. "I agree with Mr. Ashburn. It's the perfect solution."

The proposal was voted on, and it didn't surprise

Ty when Gatewood and the reverend were the only two who opposed it. Gatewood sent Ty a venomous look, which he ignored. The older man may have gotten him to run using extortion, but Ty hadn't forfeited the right to think for himself.

"Can we get back to work?" Ty asked curtly.

"After we decide who'll build the grandstand," Gatewood replied, his tone leaving no doubt he wasn't pleased with his candidate.

"When I talked to Bill Danvers last night at the Emporium, he said he'd donate the lumber from his mill," Gabby said.

The older man glanced sharply at her. "He didn't say anything to me about it."

"Maybe you didn't ask him nicely," she needled with a cloying smile.

Gatewood narrowed his eyes, but didn't comment. "We still need men to build it." He turned to Ty. "You have enough men on your payroll that they could do it."

"Why not some of your own employees?" Miss Gabby demanded. "You have just as many men working for you as Mr. Ashburn. And I know for a fact Mr. Ashburn's employees are all busy with the extra runs to Rawlins."

"Miss Gabby's right," Joe chimed in. "We're already being stretched pretty thin with winter just around the corner."

"You complaining, Joe?" Ty asked, his voice pitched low.

The shorter man shook his carrot-topped head. "You know it's the truth, Ty. Hell, you're working harder than anyone else."

"I'll get a few of my men to do it," Ty stated

flatly. He didn't want anyone accusing him of shirking his responsibilities.

"I think I can get a couple men to lend a hand, too," Miss Gabby offered.

"Don't bother. I don't need your help."

She drew back as if slapped by his curt refusal.

Unaccountably disturbed by her reaction, Ty almost apologized. Then he thought about the drunken cowboy who'd nearly shot him last night at her place. The incident had taken Ty back to his boyhood, to the night he'd found his father dead in the barn, a victim of his own weakness. He'd left Ty, his mother, and his younger brother Stephen alone, with no place to live and nothing to eat.

Ty clamped his lips together and turned away from Gabby. "Vernon, could you talk to Danvers? Let him know we need that lumber delivered tomorrow if we're going to have the platform up by Saturday evening."

The white-haired man nodded stiffly. "I'll tell him. Is there anything *else* you want me to do?"

Startled by Gatewood's cutting tone, Gabby glanced at Ty. Other than a narrowing of his steely eyes, she didn't notice any sign of defiance. If she'd been him, she would have told Gatewood where to get off the train, future father-in-law or not.

"No, I think that's it for now," Ty replied. "I suppose after the grandstand is finished, we'll need another meeting to approve it."

His echoing sarcasm made Gabby want to cheer.

"I don't think that'll be necessary," Gatewood said stiffly. "I'm sure each of us will be observing as it's constructed."

"Only those of us who have nothing better to do," Gabby retorted. "I'm sure it'll be fine. Mr.

Ashburn has my complete confidence—at least when it comes to building grandstands."

"If we're done, I'm going back to work," Ty announced, stony-faced.

The others nodded in assent, and everyone moved to disperse.

"I'd like a word with you, Mr. Ashburn," Gabby said.

His shoulders stiffened beneath his red plaid shirt, and he turned. "What is it now?" His voice was cold enough to give Gabby a case of pneumonia.

"About last night," she began hesitantly.

"What about it?" he asked, his tone thawing not a single degree.

She recalled his patience and gentleness with the children that morning. What had happened to that man? "When that drunken cowhand threatened to shoot you, I was only angry because I was scared."

He frowned. "He was after me—he wouldn't have shot you."

Gabby shook her head and wrapped her arms around her waist. "I wasn't worried about me. I was worried about you."

"I can take care of myself," he said gruffly. "Besides, if he'd shot me, you might've actually had a chance to win the election."

"Of all the . . ." She glared at him. "You're right, I shouldn't have worried about you—you're too stubborn to die. I bet you'd even argue with St. Peter at the gates to heaven—assuming you made it there, that is."

"And you'd probably sweet-talk the devil to get out of *your* rightful place," he said dryly, his lips quirking unexpectedly.

Gabby's temper cooled as quickly as it had boiled, and she laughed. "I wouldn't need to. I'd challenge him to a game of blackjack, winner take all."

Abruptly, Ty's face darkened. "Good day, Miss Gabby." He pivoted on his heel and strode away.

Gabby wondered what had caused his mercurial change of mood. Had it been her reference to gambling? Was Ty Ashburn's disapproval of gambling so great that he couldn't see past it to the humor in the joke?

Of course it was, she realized belatedly. He felt strongly enough about it that he would go to any extreme to see her gone from Sawtooth. A week ago, she wouldn't have had a second thought about Mr. Ashburn's opinion of her. Now she feared she was beginning to care a little too much.

Ty laid aside the last shipping invoice from the previous month and rubbed his eyes with his thumb and forefinger. Most customers paid their bills upon delivery of the goods, but a few hadn't yet made their payments and Ty made a list of those names. He would have to speak to them the next day. That was the worst aspect of owning his own company; he never knew when he'd run into a situation that brought echoes from his past. A few weeks ago, he'd talked to an overdue customer who'd lost most of his money gambling and couldn't afford to pay his bill.

Ty squeezed his eyes shut, trying to block out the image that had been burned into his mind. After so many years he should have been able to forget, but some memories were too powerful to release their victim.

And Ty hated his father for leaving him with that final bloody memory.

Pulling out his pocketwatch, he glanced at the time: nearly seven o'clock. He was supposed to have dinner with Eleanor and her father at seven.

He cursed aloud, his expletive unnaturally loud in the silent confines of his lantern-lit office. He could either show up on time in his work clothes or change into a suit and be late. After a moment of indecision, he chose the former.

He turned down the kerosene lamp, left his office, and headed toward the most pretentious house in Sawtooth. Although he knew little about architecture, Ty recognized the Victorian style so popular in the bigger cities like Denver and Cheyenne. The sharply pitched roof seemed a waste of inside space, but he liked the porch that stretched across the entire front of the building. It seemed a perfect place to sit in the evenings and watch the sun set. Of course, neither Vernon nor his daughter would have done something so common. A tower on each side of the house added to its impressive appearance, although Ty thought they were impractical.

He mounted the porch steps two at a time and paused in front of the double doors. Spying his reflection in the glazed windows, he finger-combed his wind-ruffled hair. For a moment he wondered if he should have taken the time to change, then discarded the thought. Once he and Eleanor were married, she'd have to get accustomed to seeing him in his work clothes.

He pounded on the door and waited a full minute before Bentley, the Gatewoods' ever-proper butler, opened the door.

Bentley's discriminating gaze swept across Ty, his thin nose wrinkling as if something distasteful were in the air. "Good evening, Mr. Ashburn."

Ty felt as if he'd been tried and sentenced. "Evening, Bentley. Miss Gatewood is expecting me."

"Of course, Mr. Ashburn." He stepped aside and allowed Ty to enter the vestibule between the outer doors and the inner panel. "Wait here. I shall announce your arrival."

"I don't think that's necessary." He'd already violated one rule involving proper dress for a dinner engagement; he didn't have much to lose by breaking another. "Is she in the parlor?"

"Yes, but it's highly improper—" Bentley began.

Too tired to humor Bentley's exaggerated sense of propriety, Ty strode past him. "She's going to be my wife in less than a month. I think that allows me a few privileges."

Ty imagined Bentley's disapproving scowl burning a hole between his shoulder blades, and he suddenly wondered how Miss Gabby would have handled the stuffy butler. The possible scenarios were endless. He chuckled, then coughed to cover the unexpected reaction.

His heels echoed on the brightly polished parquet floor as he walked past the elaborately carved winding staircase to the parlor. He slid open the pocket door and entered.

Eleanor, sitting on the sofa with a magazine in her lap, glanced up. Her face lit with a pleased expression that quickly faded.

"Tyler, what in the world are you wearing?" she asked incredulously.

"Clothes," he replied. Realizing he sounded like a petulant child, he added contritely, "I'm sorry,

Eleanor, but I came straight from the office. I thought you'd prefer me on time and in my work clothes rather than late because I changed into a jacket."

She laid aside the *Harper's Bazaar* and rose from the couch with an innate grace that Ty usually admired. Tonight, it irritated him. He blamed his ill-temper on his exhaustion and tried to banish the feeling.

Eleanor's welcoming smile appeared forced. "Of course; you're right."

She glided over to him and took his hands in hers, then turned her face so he could kiss her smooth cheek. Her skin was like marble beneath his lips, and when he pulled away, he felt like he'd just kissed an elderly aunt.

"You work too hard," Eleanor commented.

Ty recalled Miss Gabby saying the same words to him, and her concern seemed more genuine than his fiancée's.

"If I'm going to support a family, I'll have to *keep* working hard," he said.

Eleanor blushed. "Really, Tyler, it isn't seemly to be talking of children yet."

"Why not?"

"It's just not done." She leaned close and whispered, "To be speaking of marital duties before we're married is highly improper."

With a father like the sanctimonious Vernon, Eleanor was probably terrified at the thought of sleeping with her future husband. But Ty certainly wouldn't have to worry about her virginity—unlike his opponent, whose colorful lifestyle had doubtless given her plenty of experience in the boudoir.

Vernon Gatewood entered the parlor and surprise shown on his lined face. "Tyler, I didn't hear Bentley announce your arrival."

"He didn't," Ty said.

Gatewood frowned with displeasure. "He's usually very conscientious about carrying out his duties. It looks like I'll have to have a talk with him."

"It wasn't his fault. I told him not to bother."

The older man eyed Ty's clothing as if noticing it for the first time. "Becoming a bit remiss on good manners, aren't you?"

"He's been working all day, Father," Eleanor spoke up, surprising Ty.

"Already defending your betrothed." Gatewood smiled fondly at his only child, then looked at Ty. "See what a loyal wife she'll be?"

As long as I do as she wants, Ty thought, then shook aside the unfair assessment. Eleanor's defense had sounded sincere. He put an arm around her shoulders. "I'm a lucky man, all right."

"I suppose your oversight can be excused this one time. Let's go have dinner, shall we?" With a magnanimous wave of his hand, Vernon ushered Ty and Eleanor out before him.

Eleanor put her hand through the crook of Ty's arm, and he escorted her into the cavernous dining room. He led her to the far end of the long rosewood table where three settings had been laid out. After seating Eleanor at Vernon's right, Ty moved around to the chair across from her.

Ty remembered the unease he'd felt the first time he'd had dinner with the Gatewoods. He'd been in Sawtooth only a few months, working the hours of three men to get his business going, when Vernon had invited him to his house. Ty's awe had faded in the intervening years, but his out-of-place feeling hadn't. The home he'd lived in as a boy would have fit in the dining room, and the food the Gatewoods discarded in one meal would have fed Ty and his family for a week.

Vernon rang a small dinner bell and Bentley brought out a tray with three tureens of soup. Despite Ty's rumbling belly, he waited until Gatewood raised a spoonful of broth to his mouth.

"I was a bit disappointed in you today," Vernon said after tasting the first course.

Ty paused, his spoon held in midair. "Because I didn't blindly agree with you?"

"Because we're supposed to be working together," the older man corrected acerbically.

"We are." Ty swallowed the thin broth and drew a napkin across his lips. "We agree on the platforms. *That's* the important thing, not where the grandstand should be built."

"We should create a solid front even on the smaller issues. Siding with your opponent, even on such a minor detail, makes it appear you're softening your stand against her."

Ty aimed his forefinger at the older man. "Make no mistake, Vernon. I am dead set against Miss Gabby and her kind, and I will follow through with removing the saloon owners once I'm elected." He paused to let his statement sink in. "But I won't allow you to make decisions for me."

"Must you talk about *her* at the table?" Eleanor asked, her lips drawn into a thin line.

Gatewood patted the back of his daughter's hand. "I'm sorry, dear, but Tyler and I have to discuss some business despite the unpleasantries associated with it."

She lowered her gaze to the next course Bentley set in front of them. "All right, if you must. But once Tyler is elected mayor, no business conversations will be allowed at the table. According to Miss Phillipot at the Academy for Young Ladies, it is rude to speak of such things during meals."

"I'm sure Miss Phillipot would know," Ty said under his breath.

"What was that, Tyler?"

"I said, could you please pass the pepper?"

Eleanor handed him the pepper mill, looking unconvinced.

"Perhaps you have a point, Tyler," Vernon gave in grudgingly. "As long as you aren't swayed on larger issues by that woman, there shouldn't be a problem."

"Believe me, that won't happen."

"Good. Now, are you ready for the first debate?"

"What's there to be ready for? People will ask questions, and I'll answer them."

"You have to have some type of agenda when you step up there on Saturday evening."

Ty fiddled with the stem of his wine glass. "I know where I stand on the issues. What else is there to know?"

Gatewood lifted his napkin from his lap and plopped it on the table. "All right. Let's suppose I'm someone from the audience and I ask you this question: isn't it true that you of all people will benefit the most from the new bridge?"

"Everyone's going to benefit from lower freight costs," Ty refuted.

"But *you* stand to gain the most. As the mayor of Sawtooth, won't this be a conflict of interest?" Gatewood pressed.

"Dammit, Vernon, you were the one who wanted me to run."

"You shouldn't swear at the table, Tyler," Eleanor rebuked.

Ty took a deep breath. What did they want from him? "I'm sorry, Eleanor." He turned to Gatewood. "Look, I told you I wasn't a politician."

"You can be anything you want to be," Gatewood stated firmly. "You just need to be prepared for questions such as that, and you can't fly off the handle because it gets a little rough."

Ty studied the older man a long moment, noting the sly glint in his eyes. "So, how would you answer it?"

"I would be completely honest. I would say, 'Yes, I will benefit greatly by the bridge,' and then I'd appeal to their pocketbooks. Tell them how much money *they'll* save, from the freight customers all the way down to the lowliest hired hand. Everyone wants to save money."

"What about the tax issue? Miss Gabby said she won't have any taxes. She said that a sheriff shouldn't be paid by taxes, but on something like commission. For every arrest that he makes, he'll get a certain amount of money depending on the crime committed."

"That's ridiculous. It only goes to prove she's incompetent to hold political office. It also demonstrates her innate stupidity." Vernon smiled a gloating smile. "This is going to be even easier than I had thought."

There was no humor in Ty's harsh laugh. "Miss Gabby is anything but stupid. Naive, maybe, but definitely not stupid."

"And how do you draw that conclusion?"

"I've dealt with her, and I can guarantee she's sharper than most men," Ty replied.

Gatewood planted his elbows on the table and leaned forward. "Then that's another reason you need to be prepared when you face her."

Ty couldn't argue the logic. But now he'd have to take even more time away from his job to prepare for the debate. And time was the one thing he had too little of.

Chapter 6

◯◯◯◯

Ty stepped out of the restaurant where he'd just eaten a late lunch. The sun cast long shadows of the false-fronted buildings onto the dusty ground, creating cool eddies of air amid the warmer currents. He strode through town, heading back to his cabin to check on his horses and freight wagons. As he rounded the livery at the edge of town, he stumbled to a halt.

Kneeling on the ground in a circle were three boys and a woman. Long blond hair draped across her back and her petite figure gave away her identity immediately: Miss Gabby. His appreciative gaze settled on her nicely rounded derriere, which was aimed in his direction.

What in the world was she doing—teaching them how to play poker?

He walked silently over to the huddled group, but his shadow fell across their game and all four of them looked up at once. The boys appeared startled, but Miss Gabby merely shaded her eyes with her hand and grinned up at him.

"Hello, Mr. Ashburn," she greeted in such a friendly voice that Ty almost smiled in return. "It turned out to be a beautiful day, didn't it?" she

78

commented cheerfully, as if she hadn't a care in the world. "Makes a person want to take the afternoon off and just enjoy the last of the nice weather before winter."

"I guess," he responded neutrally. "What're you doing?"

"Playing marbles," one of the boys replied. "Miss Gabby's pretty good for a girl."

Ty's gaze flickered across her hourglass figure. He would hardly call her a girl.

"You boys better run on home now," Gabby suggested.

They gathered up their marbles into bags and hurried off as they called their farewells.

Gabby scooped her own marbles into a black bag and tightened the drawstring. Ty helped her to her feet, and once she was standing, Ty found himself staring down into her dust-streaked face. Her bow-shaped lips were parted slightly, as if beckoning him closer. He struggled against the urge to press his own lips upon hers, to feel their softness.

"Would you like to see my favorite one?"

Gabby's voice brought him back to reality and he released her, taking a step back.

"Your favorite one?" he asked huskily.

From the reticule she picked out a large brown marble with tan veins winding through it. "This is my favorite cat's-eye and it's the best one for playing Knock Out. I won it ten years ago when a bully challenged me." She winked conspiratorially. "He didn't know he was dealing with the Queen of Marbles."

Ty grinned crookedly. "I guess I'm lucky the election doesn't hinge on a marble game."

Gabby laughed, a clear, sweet sound. Her sunny

yellow dress had a film of dust covering the lower half of her skirt and the forearms of her sleeves, but she didn't seem at all concerned about it. "That's right, you are," she said. "Thank you for hurrying the negotiations along with the debating stage yesterday. I was getting tired of all the bickering."

"Don't thank me. I was getting ready to walk away from the whole mess."

"But you didn't, and the election committee agreed to do the fair thing." She gazed at him, all signs of lightheartedness gone. "You shouldn't have taken on the responsibility of building it, though. You should've had Mr. Gatewood get some men to do it."

Ty shrugged, not wanting to get into that argument again. "Was there anything else?"

"Nothing I can think of," she replied, then gave him another of her generous smiles. "Have a wonderful day, Mr. Ashburn."

Ty touched the brim of his hat. "You, too, Miss Gabby."

With twinkling eyes, she continued down the boardwalk, her steps light and lively, and her backside swinging enough to make her departure interesting. Ty glanced up at the clear sky and the bright sun, tempted to take her advice and enjoy the fall day. Then he reminded himself of all the work he had to do and thrust the temptation aside.

When you shirked your responsibilities, other people got hurt. He wasn't about to be guided by his impulses—and he would do everything in his power to see that others didn't, either.

* * *

Gabby wandered over to the door of the Emporium and gazed out into the dusk. Her keen eyes picked out two men moving about the uncompleted grandstand. She recognized Ty Ashburn and her heart quickened at the sight of his broad-shouldered, slim-hipped silhouette. She couldn't deny he was one good-looking man. Too bad he could make a dead fish seem warm and cuddly.

Gnawing on her thumbnail, she contemplated going out to speak with him. He should have taken her up on her offer and let her get a couple of other men to help him. Over the past few days, she'd watched Ashburn and Joe construct the platform with little or no help. Oftentimes it was Ashburn himself pounding nails into the two-by-fours after Gabby knew he'd already done a day's work.

Rose came around the tasseled curtains to stand beside her. "How come I knew I'd find you here?"

Heat rose in Gabby's cheeks. "Because you know everything that goes on, whether it's your business or not."

Rose snorted. "Ever since Ashburn started building that thing, you've taken a mighty powerful interest in the main street."

Gabby couldn't meet her friend's twinkling eyes. "I've got to get up on 'that thing' tomorrow night and debate him. Why wouldn't I be interested?"

Rose peeked past Gabby to the activity down the street. "I have a feeling it's not that grandstand you're so interested in, but what's wearing them tight Levi's."

"Tyler Ashburn is an engaged man and he thinks I'm a cousin to the devil. Besides, he's no different than any other man—though I have to admit he does fill those Levi's out pretty well." Gabby couldn't help but grin.

Rose stepped back to assess her friend. "If I didn't know better, I'd say you're looking at him a whole different way than you've looked at any other man."

Rose was right, but Gabby couldn't determine why Tyler Ashburn affected her this way. No man had ever made her wonder about the flex of his muscles beneath the cover of clothing. Or the softness of the ebony curls that peeped out of his open collar.

She shook her head to clear the tantalizing thoughts from her mind. Men held little regard for women, except when they were trying to sweet-talk them into bed—and she suspected deep down Ty wasn't much different from the others. And no man was going to take away her good sense with a few honeyed words—not even one with a body that ought to be outlawed during daylight hours.

"Don't be silly, Rose," Gabby said. "Just because I respect him doesn't mean I have feelings for him. Besides, he's the most stubborn and aggravating man I've ever met." She spun around, intent on escaping Rose's speculations. "I'm going back to work."

"Suit yourself, but Ashburn's still out there and now he's by himself," Rose called after her.

Gabby paused. "I thought Joe was helping him."

"Nope. Joe's headed up the street, probably going back to his place." Rose's gaze didn't waver from Gabby. "Well?"

Gabby sighed in resignation and walked back to the door. She watched Ty move about the grandstand with an economy of movement that belied his tall stature, then she frowned in irritation. Why couldn't she simply ignore him?

Because try as she might, she couldn't banish the memory of his heartwarming smile that could melt butter off a knife.

"He's going to kill himself working as hard as he does. I'll bet that when it gets too dark for him to work on the platform, he goes back to his office and does a few more hours of work there," Gabby said, more to herself than to her friend.

Rose nodded. "That's what he did last night. I saw the lantern glowing in his office window when I went past."

"What were you doing over there?"

"I went to see Joe."

"What in the world would you be doing so late?"

One look at Rose's impish expression answered Gabby's question.

Rose took hold of Gabby's hand, reading her thoughts. "Don't worry, I'm not falling into old habits."

Gabby squeezed her fingers slightly. "That's good. After what that man did to you before I found you in that alley . . ."

Rose's face hardened, making her look older than her twenty-one years. "No man will ever do that to me again."

"But . . . I mean . . . well, I thought that included not doing other things, too." Gabby knew her cheeks were as red as Rose's dress.

The younger woman, so much older in experience, smiled gently. "I'll tell you something I learned the hard way. When a man needs a woman, it's lust pure and simple. When a woman wants a man, it's indecent. But when they want and need each other, it's love. Someday you'll learn the difference between what that man did to me and what Joe and me got together." A mischievous glint lit her eyes. "Now, why don't you go give hardheaded Ashburn hell for working so hard?"

After a moment of indecision, Gabby pushed open the door and walked down the street. Her heart thudded against her ribs. Ashburn was her political opponent; nothing more, nothing less. Why should she care if he worked too hard? It was only because she never could abide a person working himself to an early grave.

Crossing the street, Gabby stepped over the horse droppings scattered up and down the main thoroughfare, glad the usual summer stench had disappeared with the colder weather. When she arrived at the open lot near the center of town, she stopped to eye the well-built platform. Her wayward gaze preferred to rest on the well-built man, instead.

"Good evening, Mr. Ashburn," she called out as he brought the hammer down.

"Son of a b—" he cussed, and thrust his thumb into his mouth. He glared at Gabby. "Do you make a habit of sneaking up on folks?"

"No, just you." She stepped next to the platform where Ashburn was kneeling and tried to see the extent of the damage. Hard calluses covered his fingertips and the heel of his palm. She took his wide, strong hand in hers and studied the reddening thumb.

"Did you break it?" she asked in a husky voice.

He shook his head. "No thanks to you."

Gabby brushed her forefinger across his knuckles, feeling each ridge and vein, and the light dusting of hair. She pictured his fingers awkwardly braiding April's hair, and her heart beat a little faster.

"You mind if I have my hand back?" he asked.

Brought back to reality by his dry-as-tinder tone, Gabby released him with an embarrassed nod.

Ty gingerly pulled a nail from the breast pocket of his plaid wool shirt and pounded it through two pieces of lumber. "What do you want, Miss Gabby?"

She dragged her gaze away from his fascinating hands. "I came to see how you were doing on the grandstand."

Ashburn kept his attention on his task. "Don't worry, it'll be ready by tomorrow night."

"I'm not worried," she replied, irritated by his churlish response. "I know if you say you'll have it done, you will."

He turned and studied her, his ebony hair tousled across his furrowed brow. Did the etched lines ever disappear from his forehead, or had he been born with them?

"When did you get such faith in me?" he asked.

His sarcasm stung, but Gabby plowed ahead. "I've lived here long enough to learn a lot of things about a lot of people. And as shocking as this may sound, I've always admired you, Mr. Ashburn."

He appeared startled, but said gruffly, "If you're trying to soften me on my stand against saloons and gambling halls, it's not going to work."

Gabby propped her hands on her hips and snorted. "I wouldn't even try. Besides, even if you did by any miracle have a change of heart, your pride wouldn't let you admit it."

"You seem to *think* you know an awful lot about me," Ashburn said with narrowed eyes. "But you don't." With a dismissive turn, he went back to his work.

Ashburn hammered nail after nail with a steady, powerful rhythm. Gabby's gaze followed the flexing of his shoulders beneath his shirt. His biceps, which pressed against the coarse material, threatened to split the seams. Her palms moistened, and she licked her suddenly dry lips.

A slight breeze brought gooseflesh to Gabby's arms, and she hugged her waist against the chill.

"Go on back to your place. There's no reason for you to stand out here and catch cold," Ty said.

Surprised he'd noticed, Gabby studied his bold profile in the fast-fading light. He had a long, sloping forehead, a trait her uncle had said reflected intelligence. In this case, Gabby had to agree with him. The firm outline of Ty's aquiline nose led down to generous lips. It was a shame they were so often thinned in irritation. His strong, clean-shaven chin revealed a stubborn determination that Gabby found both admirable and aggravating.

"I'll stay here as long as you do," Gabby proclaimed. "What's good enough for one candidate is good enough for the other."

"Suit yourself," Ty said through tightly drawn lips.

"I always do."

He flashed her a glance, too quick for Gabby to see his expression, but she suspected he was thinking the worst of her again. And once again, his scorn disturbed her.

"I thought you said you'd have a few of your men build this," Gabby commented.

"I couldn't spare any."

"Joe's been helping you."

"He offered to do it on his own time." He jumped down from the three-foot-high platform, his mule-ear boots creating small plumes of dust. He stared down at her, his direct gaze piercing her. "How did you know he was helping?"

"I happened to glance out here earlier and saw him." She hoped he didn't see through her slight fib. "I thought I should know if you built a trap-door on my side of the platform."

His silvery eyes softened slightly, and Gabby thought she'd be rewarded with one of his devastating smiles. His lips remained set in a grim line, though, and disappointment flitted through her.

"I'm not that low down," Ty said. "Besides, like I told you, I don't need any advantage to win this election."

"You're awfully sure of yourself, Mr. Ashburn."

He shrugged. "Shouldn't I be? Most people want Sawtooth to have a good reputation. They don't want it to be known for drunken brawls or gambling hells."

"Why can't Sawtooth have its reputation *and* its social establishments? Why is everything black and white to you?"

"Why is everything a game to you?" he shot back.

"I take this election very seriously. If I didn't feel so strongly about my home, I wouldn't be running against you."

Ty leaned over to pick up his tools and tossed them in a wooden box with a crude handle. Gabby's eyes were drawn to his well-formed backside, temptingly outlined by his worn Levi's. Her imagination shucked his jeans, and her insides turned to warm syrup. Why couldn't he wear baggy trousers and suspenders like other men?

"Still, you treat it like a game of blackjack: if I win, you leave; if the house wins, I have to have fun according to your rules." He straightened and looked at her. "For you, life will always be a game of chance."

"And for you, life will always be a drudge without the thrill of risk or the joy of overcoming a challenge."

He lifted the toolbox in his steady hand. "My business is all the challenge I want. And risk is for fools and drunks. I'm neither." He nodded curtly. "Good night, Miss Gabby."

She stared at his back as he strode into the darkening night. Did he truly believe she was a fool? Or had he been referring to someone else?

Gabby turned and hurried back toward the Emporium, her thoughts churning. Her teeth chattered from the cool wind that smelled of fallen leaves and damp soil. She loved this time of the year, knowing she had a comfortable home with a warm fireplace. A place where she could watch winter tiptoe in with the first light snowfall, or rage with a blizzard so intense it would rattle the windows.

But if Ty Ashburn won the election, she would no longer have her sanctuary, and winter would again be an enemy to withstand rather than an opportunity to drink hot chocolate and cuddle up beside the fire.

Straightening her spine, she vowed she wouldn't go down without a fight. Men like Ashburn thought they could order people about like they were property. Gabby would show him that here in Sawtooth folks didn't need his high-handed ways—they could make their own decisions.

Ty glanced at his reflection in the crooked mirror on the wall of his small cabin and impatiently tugged at his lopsided tie. For the hundredth time that week, he wondered why he'd allowed Gatewood to pressure him into accepting the mayoral nomination.

The past week had been fraught with frenzied activity. He'd put in extra hours at the freight company, scheduling almost twice as many runs as normal to Rawlins in preparation for a long snowbound winter. With Gatewood's assistance, Ty had also managed to put together a few general issues to expound on at the debate this evening. Erecting the grandstand had been another headache.

Miss Gabby's appearance at the platform had unsettled him more than he cared to admit. While he'd worked, he'd felt her gaze upon him and wondered why she studied him so intently. He'd sent her a few sidelong glances himself, noticing her windblown hair and straight, proud posture, as well as her abundant curves that continued to slip into his thoughts at the most inopportune moments.

Why had she come? What had she hoped to gain? If she thought she'd trap him in her web like she'd undoubtedly done to other men, she'd been disappointed. She could tempt him all she wanted, but he wasn't about to fall for her deceptively innocent face or modest dress.

With a few impatient motions, Ty reknotted the tie and buttoned his vest. He shrugged into his jacket and glanced in the mirror one last time.

Scowling, he realized he'd forgotten his weekly barber stop. He settled a black, broad-brimmed hat on his head, hoping no one would notice that his hair touched his collar. Then, leaving his three-room cabin, he walked to the corral where his horse was hitched.

Joe stepped out of the shadows, leading his own saddled horse. "Want some company?"

Ty wasn't surprised to see his friend. "Been waiting long?"

"Long enough to see you fussin' with your tie. You never could get them right." Joe reached out and made a new bow of Ty's string tie. "There."

"Thanks," Ty said. He took a deep breath, letting it out in a gust of white vapor. "How the hell did I get myself into this, Joe?"

"You didn't stand up to old man Gatewood," Joe replied with characteristic bluntness.

Ty remained silent, knowing Joe was right, but also knowing he couldn't have done anything different. Gatewood's ultimatum had taken away any choice he may have had.

"If you're elected, you can't let him run rough-shod over you," Joe said quietly.

"*If* I'm elected—thanks a lot, friend," Ty said dryly.

"I don't think you'd be a bad mayor; I just think you're too damned worried about things that don't concern you."

"Like the saloons?"

Joe nodded. "I know you aren't one to go to them, but there's a lot of men, myself included, that like a place to go in the evenings and have a drink. Most of the men there don't have a woman or a home to go to at night, and Miss Gabby's gives them a friendly place to go. Not everyone drinks until they're pie-eyed or gambles all their money away."

"If I save only one man from losing everything, it'll be worth it."

"But what about people like Miss Gabby? You're going to destroy her life by shutting down her livelihood."

Ty grasped the saddle horn and mounted his horse. "I'm sure Miss Gabby can take care of herself." He tightened his hold on the reins. "You coming or not?"

With a scowl, Joe thrust his boot toe in the stirrup and hauled himself into the saddle. "I just want to know one thing, Ty. How did you get to be such an expert on Miss Gabby, when you don't even know her?" He nudged the horse's flanks, sending the animal into a smooth trot.

Ty stared after him for a long moment, wondering how Joe could be so blind to Miss Gabby's true nature.

Clamping his teeth together, Ty followed Joe. When he reached the town, he fell into the throng of people walking and riding in wagons, intent on attending the social event of the month. He responded to greetings as he rode ahead to get settled on the platform before the debate began. And, he hoped, before Miss Gabby arrived.

Joe's horse was already tied to a nearby hitching rail, and Ty dismounted beside it, securing his bay mare next to Joe's. Glancing around, he spotted Vernon and Eleanor seated in the front row of the benches that had been set up that afternoon. For a moment, he wondered if he could avoid speaking to the Gatewoods until after the debate. Realizing it would be rude if he didn't, Ty reluctantly walked over to them.

"Evening," he greeted.

Eleanor laid a hand on his arm and gave him an unnaturally bright smile. "Tyler, you look wonderfully handsome," she gushed. "So distinguished, just like a mayor."

He patted the back of her gloved hand, wishing she wouldn't be so obvious in her desire to be the mayor's wife. "Thank you, Eleanor. You look very nice yourself."

Although Eleanor's dress and cape were impeccably fashionable, Ty thought the drab browns and rusts washed out her milky complexion. She should be wearing brighter colors to give her some vibrancy. The image of Gabby wearing her bright blue dress drifted into his mind.

Surprised by the vagrant thought, Ty concentrated on his fiancée's words.

"Once we're married and settled in our house, I can entertain visiting governors and, who knows, maybe even the president." Eleanor sighed. "It'll be perfect, Tyler. The dining room is large enough to hold thirty people. Can you imagine the dinners we can host?"

Ty frowned. "What do you mean?"

"We're fortunate that Father will allow us to live with him when you become mayor. We'll easily have accommodations for all the important people who'll stay with us."

"I never said anything about us living with your father after we're married," Ty said in a low, tightly controlled voice.

Eleanor's lips curved into a pout. "You don't expect me to live in that horrible cabin, do you?"

"Yes, I do. After my business grows, I'll be able to afford to build us a bigger house."

"Really, Tyler, you're letting your pride get in the way of practicality," Vernon spoke up. "There's no reason you and Eleanor can't live with me. God knows the house is large enough for five families."

Ty's fingers curved into fists as he tried to control his fury. "That isn't the issue. I'm not going to live off my wife's father."

Eleanor's eyes filled with moisture. "Oh, Tyler, how can you be so cruel as to expect me to live in such a tiny, terrible place?"

The sight of her tears softened Ty, and he sat down beside her, taking her hands in his. "Maybe we should wait until I can afford to build you a bigger home. We could put off the wedding for a year."

"No," Eleanor replied vehemently. "After all the preparations, what would people think if we called it off? I want to get married as we've planned, Tyler. I *won't* become the laughingstock of Sawtooth."

Ty forced himself to hold back his exasperated sigh. "You're being melodramatic, Eleanor. We'll talk about this more later."

"There's nothing to talk about, Tyler. If you wish to marry me, you must do so in three weeks," Eleanor stated, all signs of her tears gone like rain in the desert. "And we shall live with Father until you have our house built."

The finality in her tone startled Ty. He'd never known Eleanor to take such a firm stand. Maybe she was so certain Ty wanted to marry her that she thought she could order him around. And he did want to marry her, he reminded himself. Not only would it ensure his standing in the community and in Vernon Gatewood's eyes, but marriage to Eleanor would be another step up to gaining respectability.

"She's right, Tyler," Vernon said. "There's no reason you can't live in the comfort she's accustomed to until you build a more suitable home; one that will rival my own."

Ty didn't want a mansion. He wanted a home: a comfortable place to go to at the end of a long day where he could sit by the fire and read the paper. A place where he could watch his children grow and enjoy a sunset from his porch in the evenings. He didn't want a cold mausoleum like Gatewood owned.

But this wasn't the time or place to discuss such plans. Right now he had to concentrate on the debate.

He looked around the gaslit area and tried to find his opponent. Close to a hundred people were gathered about, talking and gesturing and laughing like this whole spectacle was nothing but a theater show. He couldn't blame them. To see the town's most notorious saloon owner and a respected businessman face off could be considered a farce.

Except that both he and Miss Gabby were dead serious about the issues. They each believed they were right, and, if nothing else, Ty held a grudging admiration for her for standing up for her beliefs, no matter how wrong they were.

The gradual cessation of voices brought Ty to his feet to search for the cause. A moment later, he spotted Miss Gabby with Rose beside her approaching the grandstand. People stepped back to allow her through and she cast them a friendly smile.

Both women were dressed in conservative capes, although Rose's coat had scarlet trim that stood out against the midnight-black material. Joe came forward and Rose smiled, then he led her to a nearby seat he'd saved for her.

Ty inwardly cursed Joe's public display of affection for a whore. Everyone knew he and Ty were good friends, and Joe's relationship with Rose could damage Ty's chance at becoming mayor.

Eleanor's snickering caused Ty to glance at her questioningly.

"She's wearing that silly hat again. Poor thing probably doesn't even know how dreadful it is," Eleanor said, her lips curled in disdain.

Ty looked back at Miss Gabby, his eyes drawn immediately to the puce bonnet, with its drooping feathers and bedraggled stuffed birds eating faded berries. Eleanor was right; the hat was dreadful.

He stared at the homely thing, almost hypnotized by the bobbing of the deformed sparrows that wiggled as Miss Gabby walked toward him.

She came to a halt in front of him. "Good evening, Mr. Ashburn."

With a mental shake Ty drew his gaze away from the ridiculous hat, only to find himself staring at Gabby's dark conservative cape, which couldn't disguise the full curves beneath it. Ty's gaze nearly tripped in its haste to return to her face. "I was wondering if you had changed your mind."

"Sorry to disappoint you," she said, although her tone suggested she was anything but contrite. She turned to Vernon and Eleanor. "Hello, Mr.

Gatewood, Miss Gatewood. A beautiful evening for a debate, isn't it?"

Eleanor turned away, ignoring Miss Gabby completely, and Vernon narrowed his eyes. Ty was startled by the cold contempt in the older man's rigid expression.

"It would've been better for you and all involved if you had changed your mind," Vernon said menacingly.

Rather than cower, Miss Gabby took a step closer to the older man. "Is that a threat, Mr. Gatewood?"

He smiled a bone-cold smile. "I don't make threats, Miss Wade. Only promises."

Chapter 7

Gabby had never liked Vernon Gatewood, and his intimidation made her dislike the sanctimonious donkey even more. With a lift of her chin, she spun around and climbed the stairs to the platform. Heavy footsteps followed and the clean scent of shaving soap told Gabby that Ty Ashburn was close behind her.

"I hope you're not as full of yourself as your puppetmaster is," Gabby stated, keeping her voice pitched low.

Ty's jaw muscles clenched. "I'm not his puppet."

"We'll see about that."

After Gabby and Ty had taken their seats, Tom Bailey joined them. He straightened his vest across his generous girth and faced the crowd. "May I have your attention, please?"

The audience quieted and the clusters of people settled onto the benches ringing the platform.

"Tonight, a historic event is about to take place," Bailey began. "Tonight you will witness a debate between the *first* two mayoral candidates in the history of Sawtooth."

He paused and the audience applauded politely. "For those of you who don't already know them, I would like to introduce your two candidates." Bailey stepped back and held out his hand toward Ashburn. "The first is Tyler Ashburn, owner of the A-B Freight Company."

Ashburn sent the crowd a curt nod.

The Gatewoods clapped enthusiastically and others joined in.

Bailey motioned to Gabby. "The opposing candidate is Miss Gabby Wade, owner of Miss Gabby's Gambling Emporium."

Rowdy hoots and hollers ensued, the boisterous sound easily surpassing the conservative applause Ashburn had garnered.

Gabby stood and smiled, then threw a kiss toward the rambunctious ranchhands, which increased their enthusiastic shouts. Out of the corner of her eye she noticed Ty's condemning scowl, which brought laughter bubbling up like a spring. She winked at him as she returned to her seat, and was pleased to see a ruddy blush begin on his neck and move upward. Resuming an air of decorum, she folded her hands demurely in her lap.

Bailey waited until the crowd quieted once more, then continued. "The rules are simple. Anyone may ask either candidate, or both candidates, a question after they have been recognized by me. Then Mr. Ashburn and Miss Gabby will have a chance to answer the question. Is that understood?"

A wave of nods passed through the onlookers.

Gabby fidgeted in her seat. Now that the moment was upon her, anxiety swept through her. Would she be able to answer the questions without sounding like an idiot?

A few hands rose in the air, and Bailey pointed

to one. "Mr. Long, what is your question?"

Gabby recognized the owner of the leather shop.

"We been getting along just fine without a mayor and all the hogwash that goes with town politics. How will all this hoopla with the election and incorporating into a real town help us?" Long demanded.

"Mr. Ashburn, why don't you go first?" Bailey suggested.

Ty nodded and stood. "As most of you know, the territory plans to build a bridge in one of two places across the river. The location preferred by the representatives is the one nearer us and will cut some twenty miles off the trip into Rawlins. We'll be able to ship goods cheaper, which will lower your costs. The bridge will also bring more people to settle in Sawtooth, giving our town more importance to the territory. If we don't become a real town, complete with a mayor, we don't get the bridge. It's as simple as that."

He sat back down.

"Miss Gabby, would you like to add anything?" Bailey asked.

Gabby took a deep breath to quell her nerves. "Everything Mr. Ashburn said is correct." Her voice rang through the night air. "However, he left a couple facts out. Because he is the only shipping company in town, *he* will gain the most by this bridge. More people means more supplies to be shipped, and more profit for him. Also, I have no doubt he will lower the costs for his clients, but not as much as he could. He is, after all, a businessman first. This bridge represents a chance to increase his profit margin."

Ty jumped to his feet. "I will *not* increase my

profits at the expense of others," he refuted. "I want to do what's right for the town and those who live here, unlike *you*, who'll bleed a man dry at your poker tables without batting an eye."

Righteous anger leaped into Gabby's veins, but she forced herself to remain calm. "I provide a place for people to come, have a drink, relax, and visit with friends. If a man chooses to gamble, that's his choice. It seems to me you're only trying to draw everyone's attention away from the real issue—that of your own financial advancement at Sawtooth's expense."

"Now, just hold on one blamed minute—" Ty glared down at her.

"You mean you aren't planning on expanding your freight business?" she asked, batting her lashes innocently.

Ty sputtered in protest, and Gabby fought to stifle her laughter—she'd never seen a man's face turn the color of a ripe tomato.

"That has nothing to do with this election!"

"I think that's up to the people to decide." She raised her voice. "If the town's incorporated, we'll get that bridge, along with a new road, which will be used by Tyler Ashburn to increase his business. And that road will be maintained by taxes levied against each and every one of you."

Her uncle had always said the best way to rile folks was to threaten their wallets. If the mass muttering was any indication, Gabby had struck gold.

Ty raised his hands to quiet the crowd. "Nobody likes taxes, but they are a necessary evil. Think of all the good that can be done—the new road will be taken care of, making it easier for everyone to travel; a fire department can be maintained; our streets and boardwalks will be cleaned every day. Everybody will benefit."

"Taxes is just a legal way of stealin'," a cowboy shouted from the back. "Why do I care if there's a little horse shit in the street? Ain't nothin' to get all worked up about."

Men snickered and a few women gasped at the man's plain speech.

"What about the road? Don't you want to be able to get to Rawlins in less time?" Ty asked.

"Why would I wanna go there? Miss Gabby's got everythin' I need at her place," the man replied.

Most of the ranchhands waved their hats over their heads and whistled their agreement.

"Why, thank you. You boys are just too sweet," Gabby said with a smile that could have charmed the spots off a bobcat.

Ty wasn't going to be misled by her flirtatious appeal. He had a responsibility to Sawtooth's citizens, and Miss Gabby's dimpled cheeks and coquettish eyes weren't going to make him forget that. "Not everyone in this town feels that Miss Wade's Emporium is the key to happiness," he said dryly. "If I'm elected mayor, I will do everything in my power to make Sawtooth a safe and decent place to live."

One of the cowboys, a whipcord-thin man with a drooping mustache, called out, "Hey, Ashburn, what's this I hear about you wantin' to close down the saloons—it ain't true, is it?"

Ty stiffened his spine and nodded. "Yes, it is. When a man goes to a saloon after work instead of going home, he runs the risk of losing hard-earned money at the gaming tables. Entire savings can be lost, leaving the man's family poverty-stricken and without hope. And even if a person doesn't lose everything, there is still the loss of money that could've been better spent on food and clothing for his wife and children."

Gabby wondered how a man who didn't frequent saloons knew so much about them. The intensity of his voice made it clear the issue was important to him. Why?

"And it's not just the gambling," he continued. "When a man drinks too much, he is also more inclined to violence. Do you want one of your children killed by a stray bullet from a drunken cowboy?"

Gabby reluctantly found herself agreeing with him. Although she tried to keep close tabs on her guests, some of the other establishment owners didn't care how drunk a customer got. That kind of disregard led to dangerous recklessness. Maybe forbidding guns within the town's limit wasn't such a bad idea.

"I believe Sawtooth will be a better town, a safer town, without the likes of Miss Gabby and her colleagues," he continued, bringing Gabby back to the present. "We must make this a place where folks will want to settle and raise families. A place where folks can walk the streets without fear of being accosted by a drunk. A place where our womenfolk are spared the indignity of having to cross the street when they see one of the less virtuous ladies coming toward them."

Although Ty kept his gaze aimed at the crowd, Gabby felt his condemnation. He thought she was one of *those* ladies. Because she preferred freedom and independence to the strictures of being married to some overbearing lout, he assumed she was also free with her favors. For being such a fair businessman, Ty Ashburn had nothing but preconceptions as far as she was concerned.

"Miss Wade, would you like to make a rebuttal?" Bailey asked.

She'd like to give Ty Ashburn a kick in the butt, but Gabby restrained herself with herculean fortitude. "I don't like to see a man lose all his money at a poker table, either. That's why I make it a standard policy not to allow a man to make those kind of bets. I've also instructed my employees to stop serving a customer if he appears drunk—and I've further told my employees to remove the man's weapon so what Mr. Ashburn spoke of will not happen."

"What about the other night when one of your fine customers almost shot me?" Ty demanded.

Gabby refused to be cowed. "That was your own fault, Mr. Ashburn. That boy was only acting under a misguided notion of chivalry, and *you* were the one who goaded him."

Ty laughed a harsh, bitter laugh. "You can't be naive enough to believe that. I didn't force the liquor down that boy's throat. And I sure didn't put that gun in his hand."

"Neither did I, Mr. Ashburn!" Gabby faced the audience and straightened her shoulders. "As adults, we all have free will," she declared in a carrying voice. "My gambling emporium is not a trap for unsuspecting men to lose their hard-earned money. I simply operate an establishment and give men a choice: to come in, have a drink, play a few hands of poker, or not.

"I believe that we should be allowed to make our own decisions, not have them forced upon us as

Tyler Ashburn wants to do." Gabby paused, and she could have heard a falling star in the silence. "If he becomes mayor, *he* will make the decision to shut down the saloons. What will be next? What else will he outlaw? Eating fried chicken on Sunday? Smoking in public? Wearing your hat in the town limits?"

"Ain't nobody touchin' my hat," a cowboy shouted from the spectators.

The ranchhands nodded and muttered in agreement.

"When you make your choice on election day, choose the candidate who believes in *your* freedom," Gabby concluded.

More whistles and loud clapping met her statement, and a heady sense of victory filled her. She risked a glance at Ashburn and saw a fierce scowl directed her way. Gabby flashed him a sweet smile, which only deepened his frown. After tonight, Ashburn would have to take her seriously: he'd have to face the fact that his victory wasn't nearly as secure as he'd believed it to be.

Bailey called for the next question.

Mr. Gatewood raised his hand and spoke. "What would you do about a sheriff, Miss Wade?"

Gabby clasped her hands behind her back and rested them against the base of her spine. Mr. Gatewood had given her an opening to expound on one of her favorite issues. "I believe that we should have a lawman who works on commission. Instead of paying him a regular salary, we would pay him for every criminal he apprehends."

"And where would that money come from, Miss Wade?" Gatewood asked, raising his voice above the murmurings.

"From the fines that are paid by the lawbreakers. That way the honest citizens of Sawtooth won't have to dig into their own pockets—the criminals would be the only ones who would contribute to the sheriff's income."

"And who will collect those fines?"

"The sheriff, of course," Gabby replied.

Gatewood stood and hooked his thumbs in his vest pockets. Turning to the audience like an executioner ready to drop the guillotine, he said, "And who will ensure the sheriff will be honest enough to collect these fines instead of pocketing them?"

"Why, the mayor, I suppose," Gabby said, suddenly uneasy about his motive in raising the question.

Gatewood turned to face her, his expression altogether too congenial, except for the hard glint in his eyes. "So you're telling me that if you are elected, we have to trust you, a woman who owns a gambling emporium, to make sure the sheriff is honest." He barked a mocking laugh. "That would be like having a wolf guard the sheep."

Furious indignation caught Gabby by surprise and she stepped to the edge of the stage, her toes hovering above open air. She stared down at Gatewood, the platform giving her the advantage of towering above him. "I run an honest house." She gazed out across the faces lit by gaslight. "And if there's anyone out there who can prove otherwise, step forward now."

Nobody moved, not even Gatewood, who peered at her like a snake eyeing its prey. She stared into his eyes and saw the cold promise of her destruction. Gooseflesh arose on her arms. Gabby had never been afraid of a man before, but she'd never run into someone as ruthless as Gatewood. She knew he would do anything to see her lose the election.

Ty couldn't believe Gatewood had baited Miss Gabby so openly. He joined her and leaned toward Gatewood, who stood close to the platform. "I think you owe Miss Gabby an apology, Vernon," he said, keeping his tone low enough that nobody else in the audience could hear.

"I don't owe her anything," Gatewood fired back. "You and I both know what kind of woman she is."

"And what kind of woman is that?" Gabby demanded.

Gatewood leaned even closer. "You're a woman who has no shame in running a house of chance or in leading God-fearing men astray by your easy virtue."

Gabby threw back her head and laughed so hard Ty thought she'd become hysterical. He glanced uneasily at the audience, who appeared puzzled by the scene. People began to squirm on the benches and talk among themselves.

Gabby gathered her composure and wiped at her tearing eyes. "Mr. Gatewood, you may own most of the so-called legitimate businesses in town, but you don't know anything about me, so kindly keep your ignorance to yourself."

Gatewood's face blazed. "Who do you think you are, telling me what I can and cannot say, you—you Jezebel!"

Gabby leaned closer to Gatewood, and her foot slipped. Without thinking, Ty grabbed her around the waist to stop her fall. As he hauled her back onto the platform, one of her moth-eaten sparrows pecked him in the eye. He plopped Gabby down a few feet behind him and raised a hand to his watering eye, growling a hair-curling epithet against inane hats and stupid birds.

"Are you all right?"

Through hazy vision, he noticed the offending headpiece lay askew on Miss Gabby's thick waves.

"Just fine," he replied tightly. "Everything is just fine."

"Mr. Gatewood, please take your seat," Bailey finally spoke up. "And Miss Wade, Mr. Ashburn, could you please return to your positions?"

Gatewood shot a poisonous glare at Ty, who seethed with anger. Ty had thought Miss Gabby's associates would be the first to resort to name-calling; instead it had been his main supporter, a man supposedly above such things.

Disgusted with Gatewood and with himself, Ty returned to his chair. Miss Gabby had already taken her seat, her hat once again centered on her head and her backbone as straight as a pitchfork handle. He couldn't blame her for being upset; if he'd been the one who'd been insulted, he would have felt the same way.

His gaze moved down from her anger-flushed cheeks, and he recalled how her soft breasts had felt against his forearm when he'd rescued her from falling. The memory brought a sudden rush of heat to his groin. He curled his fingers into his palms and placed his fists on his thighs.

Out of the corner of his eye, he noticed her adjust her ridiculous hat for the umpteenth time. How could he be physically attracted to a woman whose damn moth-eaten bird had almost blinded him?

"That concludes the first debate between Miss

Gabby Wade and Mr. Tyler Ashburn," Bailey announced. "The next debate will be in two weeks, so have your questions ready for the candidates."

The crowd rose and began to disperse, although a few people remained, clustered together and gesturing as they spoke.

Gabby stood and approached Ty. "Thank you for participating in this debate, Mr. Ashburn," she stated, and held out her hand.

After a moment of hesitation, he gripped her small hand in his palm. He was surprised by the strength in her petite fingers.

"Thank you, Miss Gabby," he said stiffly. "And I want you to know I think Gatewood was rude to say what he said to you in front of everyone."

Her eyes, usually so easy to read, held little expression. "So you think it would've been all right if he'd said those things in private?"

He shook his head. "I didn't say that."

"But you were thinking it."

Ty tried to stare down her direct gaze, but found himself looking away first. "Since when are you a mind reader?"

"When you allow yourself to be read so easily. May I have my hand back?"

He released her quickly, as if her hand had turned into a branding iron. Abruptly reminded of how she'd done the same thing to him the night he'd been working on the grandstand, he felt himself flush.

Joe and Rose crowded up on the stage beside them.

"You did great, honey," Rose gushed, hugging her friend. "See, I told you there was nothing to worry about."

"Thanks, Rose, but I was shivering like a leaf in the wind," Gabby said with a smile.

Self-assured Gabby had been nervous about the debate? It didn't seem possible. Ty had assumed she was used to being the center of attention.

"What was going on between you two and Mr. Gatewood? We saw Gabby almost fall off the stage, but we couldn't hear a thing," Joe asked Ty.

"Mr. Gatewood called me a thief," Gabby replied before Ty could open his mouth.

"Why, that—" Joe began, his freckled face reddening.

"Hold on," Ty said, flattening his palm against Joe's chest. "That wasn't exactly what he said."

"No, but the sentiment was the same." Then Gabby shrugged. "But it really doesn't matter what he thinks. He doesn't want to know the truth. He believes everyone should see things his way, no matter if it's right or wrong."

Ty was startled to realize he was beginning to think the same of Vernon, but he kept his suspicions to himself and started toward the steps.

Joe caught his arm and spoke close to his ear. "As much as you don't like to hear this, I'm going say it anyhow. Miss Gabby made some good points, and she's got a lot of people on her side. This isn't going be a cakewalk for you."

Ty had already come to that conclusion himself. "You're right. I didn't want to hear it."

He pulled out of Joe's grasp and thundered down the steps, only to be captured by Eleanor. He stifled the urge to escape his fiancée's clinging embrace, then realized he was blaming the wrong person. It was Miss Gabby's disturbing presence that made him want to run for safety.

"You're coming over to the house, aren't you?" Eleanor's tone didn't give him a choice. "Father's already gone ahead, so I need someone to walk me home. Besides, Father said he would like to speak to you."

Ty wasn't surprised. Even though nobody besides Bailey and Miss Gabby had heard their disagreement, Ty knew Vernon wasn't going to let it pass.

He rubbed his forehead, hoping to ease the sharp throb in his temple. "I'll walk you home, but I can't stay long. It's late and I have to be at work early tomorrow."

"But tomorrow's Sunday. Aren't you going to church?"

"I'm going to get a few hours in at the office before service."

"Work is the most important thing to you, isn't it? If you had to choose between your business and me, I would lose," Eleanor said petulantly.

Ty sighed. He didn't need one of Eleanor's little tantrums tonight. "You know that's not true. It's only that I have to build up the business to give you the things you deserve."

The words left a bitter taste in his mouth. Why couldn't Eleanor see beyond her own little world?

He heard footsteps behind him and turned to see Miss Gabby, Rose, and Joe descending the stage.

"Where are you headed?" he asked Joe gruffly.

"It's not any of your business where I spend my off time," Joe replied tightly.

Gabby laid a hand on Joe's arm. "He's your friend. He's not asking out of meanness."

Surprised by Gabby's defense of him, Ty nodded. "She's right, Joe. But if you don't want to tell

me, that's fine. What you do on your own time is
your own business."

"We're going over to the Emporium," Joe admitted after a few moments.

For a second, Ty was tempted to join them. It
didn't matter that he'd made a promise to avoid
saloons; all he could think of was escaping the
Gatewoods. Then Eleanor tugged on his arm. This
woman was to be his wife. Vernon Gatewood
would be his father-in-law. This sudden sense of
being trapped was foolish and would pass; it *had*
to pass.

Ty offered Joe his hand. "I'll be seeing you in the
morning, then," he said.

"I reckon," Joe responded, accepting the peace
offering.

"Mr. Ashburn," Gabby said.

He glanced at her questioningly.

"Thank you," she continued.

"For what?"

"For stopping my fall. If not for you, I would've
fallen right on Mr. Gatewood." She pressed her
forefinger against her chin, as if imagining the consequences. "Actually, that might not have been
such a bad idea."

Eleanor snorted, the sound reminding Ty of a
piglet's snuffling, and he almost laughed. "You're
welcome," he managed to say with a straight face.

He looked at Gabby one more time and saw understanding in her eyes. It filled him with an unexpected sense of camaraderie. Then, as she
glanced at Eleanor and back at him, her expression
changed to one of sympathy.

Irrational anger swept through him. There was
no reason for her to pity him. As a child, he'd seen

that pitying look all too often, and he'd sworn no one would look at him that way again. He had everything he wanted, or would soon. She had *no* business feeling sorry for him.

He tucked Eleanor's arm in the crook of his own and patted her hand possessively. "Come on, Eleanor, let's not keep your father waiting."

He guided her away from the grandstand and toward the big house at the edge of town.

Chapter 8

Gabby watched the couple stroll away, and her stomach knotted. It was only natural that he'd escort her home. Just as it was only natural the two of them would marry—the most eligible bachelor in town and the only daughter of Sawtooth's leading citizen.

Rose shook her head. "I just can't figure out what little Miss Priss has that Ashburn wants so bad. I doubt if she's even let him kiss her."

"She has a rich pa who can give Ty what he wants," Joe said.

"But he has his own business. What does Gatewood have that he'd need?" Rose pressed.

Joe glanced around, then said in a lowered voice, "Gatewood basically blackmailed Ty into running for mayor."

"Come on, Joe," Gabby scoffed. "Ashburn can't wait to win so he can start cleaning up *his* town."

"That's probably the *only* thing he's looking forward to," Joe replied. "Gatewood didn't give him a choice."

"Everyone has a choice."

Joe shook his head. "Ty didn't think so. Unless

113

Ty's elected mayor, Gatewood won't finance the A-B's expansion."

"Why?" Gabby asked in disbelief. "What does Gatewood get if Ty wins?"

"Power," Rose replied, nodding in understanding. "Back East, it's done all the time. A lot of the politicians back home won because of the backing of some rich person. But once the politician got his position, he found he owed too much to the person who put him there, so he danced to whatever tune the piper played."

"That doesn't make sense. Gatewood could've run himself and won. Why use Ty—Mr. Ashburn?"

"Gatewood hasn't gotten where he's at without making some enemies," Joe said with a somber grimace.

Gabby counted herself as one of Gatewood's enemies. He'd made her a private proposal soon after she arrived in Sawtooth: become his mistress, and he would ensure her business thrived. She'd dealt with men like him since she'd started to fill out as a woman, and had spurned his "deal" as well as him, gaining Gatewood's enmity.

"Ty, though, is as straight as they come," Joe went on. "Everyone likes and respects him, except you."

Gabby shook her head. "I respect him. I just don't agree with him."

"You still going to respect him when he sends you packing?" Rose asked.

Gabby grinned wryly. "Probably not. Brrrr." She stamped her feet. "Let's get over to the Emporium and warm up."

Joe offered each woman a crooked arm and they

hurried down the boardwalk, three abreast. Gabby looked into the darkness, searching for Ty and his uppity fiancée. They were probably already in Gatewood's castle, with Ty and Gatewood sitting around the fire, sipping brandy like two old friends. Despite what Joe had said about blackmail, Gabby found it hard to believe Ty felt cornered in any way. She couldn't see Ty backing down to anyone. If Ashburn chose to bend under Gatewood's threat, that was his choice.

Gabby scurried inside the gambling hall, followed by Rose and Joe.

Suddenly someone stood and began to clap. Her other customers turned to gaze at her and they, too, rose and began to applaud and hoot their approval.

"Good job, Miss Gabby," one man called out.

"You showed Ashburn!"

"No one's gonna close you down."

"You done good!"

Surprised by the hearty support, Gabby glanced at Rose and Joe, who were grinning at her like two kids who had just found a penny.

Gabby's face warmed with embarrassment and delight and she waved at her supporters. "Thank you! Thank you very much. I'll try not to let you all down!"

She quickly retreated to her office, and the cheering in the main hall gradually ceased. She hadn't expected such a rousing reception. With the gratification also came the heavy weight of responsibility. The men out there were depending on her to win the election and keep the saloons open. She wanted the same—for herself, for them, for those who depended on her for their jobs and livelihood.

As she removed her coat, Rose and Joe joined her.

"That was some welcome, wasn't it?" Rose commented, her dark eyes dancing.

"You have a lot more supporters than Gatewood or Ty gave you credit for," Joe added.

"But is it enough?" Gabby asked, not convinced she would be able to give Ty Ashburn enough competition.

She unknotted the bonnet ribbon below her chin and removed the only possession she had left of her mother's. Reverently, she set the headpiece in a sturdy hatbox that smelled of camphor and placed the lid on it.

She walked over to the fire that had been kept fueled in the hearth. Holding out her palms to the welcome heat, Gabby stared into the dancing flames, knowing the crimson and orange tongues invited both comfort and danger.

Just like Tyler Ashburn.

"Move over and share some of that fire," Rose teased.

Gabby smiled absently and stepped away from the heat to allow Rose and Joe in front of it.

"You did a good job putting Ty in his place tonight," Joe commented.

"I thought you were his friend," Gabby accused.

"I am, but I also know him too well. He's a good man, but he's got too much mule-headed pride," Joe said. "I know he was figuring on beating you without any problem. After this debate, he has to rethink everything."

Gabby moved over to the chair behind her desk and sat down. She picked up a pencil and tapped the end on the desk's polished surface. A piece of wisdom from her uncle came back to her: *in order to defeat an enemy, one has to know him.*

"How long have you known Mr. Ashburn?" she asked Joe.

He shrugged and rubbed his hands together. "About ten, twelve years now. He and I started together as teamsters in Rawlins."

"Is that where his family's from?"

"I don't think so," Joe said hesitantly. "I'm not sure where he's from, only that his folks are dead, and that he's got a younger brother he hasn't seen in years."

Gabby considered the new information. "What's his younger brother do?"

Joe shrugged. "I don't know. Ty never talks about him."

Gabby didn't know why she was wasting her time trying to figure out Tyler Ashburn. She should be devising a scheme to beat him in the election. Still, she couldn't help but be intrigued by the infuriating man.

"I need to come up with a strategy," Gabby stated.

"What do you mean?" Joe asked.

"Somehow, I need to get more votes. I have to put a bigger dent in Ashburn's support."

Rose snorted. "If the women in this town couldn't vote, you'd have no trouble winning."

Gabby laughed. "If women couldn't vote, I wouldn't be able to run for office."

"Rose is right, though," Joe said. "It's the women you have to get on your side."

Gabby dragged the pencil across her lower lip as she thought. In all the marriages she'd seen, the men controlled their wives. So why couldn't the men merely tell their women how to vote? It seemed to Gabby that they governed every other part of their wives' lives. But what if some of the women needed a little incentive? She remembered a story her uncle had told her when she was a girl, and jumped to her feet. "I've got it! Lysistrata, the Greek play my uncle told me about."

"How did Soapy know about Greek stuff?" Rose demanded.

"He went to college back East years ago, before he turned to . . ." She glanced at Joe. "Before he became a peddler. He was the smartest man I ever knew."

"So what about this Lysistrata thing?" Joe asked. "How can that help you get votes?"

"A long long time ago, there was this war that went on for years and years. The women wanted the men to call a truce, but they refused to give an inch," Gabby began. "So the women decided to force their husbands and boyfriends to stop the war—by withholding their affections."

Rose laughed aloud. "I'll bet it worked in less'n a week, too."

Joe's face reddened, and he coughed to cover his embarrassment. "That's an interesting story and all, Miss Gabby, but how's that going to help you get the *female* votes? For women, it's their wifely duty to give their man, ah, affection, but for men, it's . . . well, it's . . ." He floundered and waved at Rose. "Geezus, you tell her, Rose."

"You're doing fine, Joe," she said, winking at Gabby.

Gabby grinned, taking wicked pleasure in his discomfort. "I understand that, Joe. What I'm saying is, husbands order their wives around, so all they should have to do is tell their wives how to vote. If for some reason that doesn't work, though, we need a contingency plan. Instead of withholding their affections, the men can withhold their money until their wives agree to vote for me."

"That just might work," Joe said. "Women are always wanting money."

Rose propped her hands on her hips. "Is that so?"

He moved behind Rose and put his arms around her waist, hugging her close. "I wasn't talking about you, darling."

Rose remained stiff in his embrace. "So you think a little sweet-talking will get you out of this one?"

He nuzzled her neck. "C'mon, sweetheart. You know I didn't mean you."

Rose closed her eyes and leaned back against him. "Well, maybe I'll forgive you this one time."

The exchange tugged at Gabby's heart, making her sad in a way she didn't understand. She was truly happy Rose had found a man who cared for her in spite of her background. And Gabby liked Joe.

So where did this uncharacteristic melancholy come from? She'd never missed the company of a man, never having known a man worth missing. Her wayward thoughts brought Ty Ashburn into focus. She recalled the low timbre of his voice during the debate, and his confidence that radiated from his powerful stance. Even though she didn't agree with most of his opinions, she admired him for his unshakable convictions.

What did a man like him see in a woman as vain and selfish as Eleanor Gatewood?

"Gabby, did you hear me?"

Rose's voice startled Gabby back to reality. "I'm sorry. I must've been woolgathering. What did you say?"

"I asked you how you were going to get your plan started," Rose repeated patiently.

"We need to have a meeting here one evening this next week. Tonight everyone got to hear exactly what Mr. Ashburn is going to do once he's elected, and I'd be willing to bet a lot of men didn't know about his plans to shut down the saloons."

"So you figure the men will come to the Emporium for a drink and listen to what you have to say?" Joe asked.

"That's right." Rubbing her palms together, she moved toward the door. "And I think we should start spreading the word tonight." She walked into the bustling Emporium, adrenaline coursing through her. If Ty Ashburn had thought she was going to roll over, he was sadly mistaken.

He'd underestimated Miss Gabby Wade, and that would be his downfall in the end.

Vernon Gatewood bade his daughter good night and watched her climb the stairs. He'd always been grateful she resembled him more than his late wife, with dark eyes and the same auburn hair he used to have. Eleanor had also proven herself more loyal. Vernon had only had to tell her his plans involving her and Tyler Ashburn, and she'd agreed that a liaison between them would be beneficial for all involved.

It was too bad her mother hadn't felt the same devotion. She had wanted a divorce, saying she'd fallen in love with another man—a kind and gentle man who also loved her. She'd turned Vernon into a cuckold, and if he'd granted her the divorce, everyone would have known. Instead, he'd done the only thing he could to someone who betrayed him—he'd had her killed. Although he had it appear an accident, too many people suspected what had really happened. So with his young daughter, who was on the verge of becoming a lovely woman, he'd moved to this backwoods town.

A knock sounded on the front door. Since Bentley was already retired for the night, Vernon answered the summons. He swung open the door, not surprised to see Tom Bailey on the porch.

"Come in, Tom, I was expecting you," Vernon greeted. He waved the man inside.

Bailey, clutching his derby hat in his hands, entered.

"Let's go into my office where we can talk," Vernon said.

Once inside the large study, Vernon shut the door and motioned for Bailey to sit down. Vernon lowered himself to his leather chair behind the massive desk.

"The debate didn't go quite as we'd hoped," Vernon began.

Bailey loosened his string tie, then unbuttoned the top button of his starched collar shirt. "There was nothing I could've done. Miss Gabby made some good points. Besides, I don't exactly like the idea of closing down the saloons myself."

"A temporary condition until I turn the former Emporium into a social hall. Then you'll have your liquor, cards, and something Miss Gabby Wade doesn't have—working girls."

"I don't know how you're going to get that past Ashburn. He's hell-bent against anything having to do with gambling," Bailey said doubtfully.

"Leave him to me," Vernon assured. "Tyler Ashburn will give me all the power I need once he's elected. All he cares about is his freight company. He thinks too small, not like you and me, Tom." Vernon gave Bailey a conspiratorial wink. "I'll make sure he appoints me the chairman of the town board."

"And if he doesn't?"

"He will." *One way or another.* "Has the survey team finished its initial work for the bridge and road?"

Bailey nodded and smiled. "Once I gave them your little 'incentive,' they had no problem getting it done. They're only waiting for the newly incorporated town of Sawtooth to draw up a charter, complete with city taxes, to guarantee that the road will be maintained."

Impatience made Vernon lean forward. "Tell the idiots to get started. If they can finish a portion of it before winter sets in, it'll put us that much ahead next spring."

"But what if Miss Gabby wins?"

Vernon slammed a fist on the desktop, and the thump echoed dully through the room. "She won't! The bitch is not going to ruin my plans."

The territorial representative paled. "What'll you do?"

"I'll do what I have to," Vernon stated. "Send a wire tomorrow morning and get those men started on the bridge."

"What if they need some more 'incentive'?" Bailey asked gingerly.

"Tell them they'll get all the 'incentive' they need once they finish." Vernon eyed Bailey, knowing he couldn't trust a politician with too many facts—it tended to confuse them. "I would assume you are being discreet about all this?"

Bailey nodded. "Of course. Nobody will be able to trace anything back to you."

"Good."

Bailey laced his trembling fingers together and rested them on his belly. He seemed to be gathering his thoughts and courage. "The same can't be said about my part in all of this," he began timidly, then spoke with more force. "I mean, I'm taking the risks if things don't work out or if someone learns what we're doing."

Vernon knew exactly where Bailey was going with his strained discourse, and he stifled his rising annoyance. "How much more do you want?" he asked, cutting to the quick.

"Five hundred dollars," Bailey said without hesitation.

Inwardly, Vernon seethed. He'd already lined the politician's pockets with a thousand dollars. For now, he needed Bailey. Later, after his usefulness came to an end, Vernon would take care of him like he took care of all his problems.

"All right," Vernon said. "I'll have the five hundred dollars for you Monday afternoon. Why don't you come over to the bank then?"

Bailey's chubby face split with a satisfied smile. "I'll see you Monday, Mr. Gatewood." He stood, then paused. "Oh, I spoke with William Lowe the other day. I think he could be of assistance to you."

Vernon tried to place the name and finally remembered where he'd heard it. "The bartender at the Emporium?"

"That's right."

"I thought he was loyal to his master," Vernon commented sarcastically.

"He's more loyal to himself. Good night."

Vernon escorted Bailey out. Locking the door behind him, Vernon returned to his study, where he did his best thinking. He sat down in the comfortable chair that had molded to his body's contours. His gaze wandered. Shelves filled with books lined three walls and a brick fireplace dominated the fourth. Although Vernon had never read a book in his life, he liked others to think he was a scholar as well as a shrewd businessman.

Appearances were everything. Vernon believed he could convince anyone of anything if he had the right mask to wear and the costume to go with it. And so far, it had worked. In the six years he and Eleanor had lived in Sawtooth, he'd worked his way up to leading businessman and concerned citizen.

He chuckled. Even Tyler Ashburn, who thought he was such a good judge of character, hadn't seen anything other than what he wanted to see.

After Ashburn was elected mayor, Vernon would have to decide what to do with him. As long as he didn't get suspicious, Vernon would let him live. If he started asking questions, then Vernon would have to arrange an "accident" for him, too. Even if he was Eleanor's husband and his son-in-law.

But what if Gabby Wade won?

Vernon settled his elbows on the armrests and steepled his fingers. The memory of her rejection of him brought hot rage simmering in his veins. The whore had laughed at him! Nobody laughed at Vernon Gatewood, especially someone like her.

He tamped down the burning anger. If the support seemed to shift in her direction, he'd make her another offer. If she refused him again, he wouldn't be so lenient. His adulterous wife had learned what happened to those who defied him. Miss Gabby Wade would get the same lesson if she refused to cooperate again.

He would get his way in the end—he always did.

Eleanor glanced at the list in her hands. "We have to stop at Mrs. Williams's dress shop next."

Ty swallowed a sigh. "Whatever you want."

"The wedding is less than a month away. Making sure everything gets done isn't any more pleasurable for me than it is for you, Tyler," his fiancée said sharply.

He doubted that. He thought of the stack of paperwork on his desk and the broken wagon wheel that needed fixing and the two horses that needed reshoeing and—

"Did you hear what I said?" Eleanor asked.

This time Ty didn't hide his impatience. "I heard, but I have other things on my mind that need doing, too."

"They can wait." She led him into the dress shop.

"Hello, Miss Gatewood," Mrs. Williams greeted stiffly.

"How is my dress coming?" Eleanor asked without preamble.

"I'm glad you stopped by. I need you to put it on so we can do a fitting." The birdlike woman motioned to the back. "Jane is back there. She can help you."

"Wait here. I'll be done shortly," Eleanor said to Ty, then sailed past Mrs. Williams.

Stunned by Eleanor's snobbishness, Ty sent the dressmaker an apologetic smile. "She has a lot on her mind with the wedding and all."

"I understand," she said in a tone that implied the opposite, then asked in a kinder voice, "How are you doing, Mr. Ashburn?"

"Busy," he replied.

"I suppose you are. That Miss Gabby is sure giving you some competition, isn't she?"

"Not really. I think most people in Sawtooth want places like hers gone."

"I wouldn't be so sure of that. My Earl stops by the Emporium now and again with some of his friends."

"Doesn't that bother you?" Ty asked curiously.

Mrs. Williams chuckled as she smoothed a dress on a hanger. "Not at all. It gets him out from underfoot so I can get some work done. Besides, he's smart enough to only have a drink or two and never lose more than a dollar gambling."

"You're lucky. Most men aren't like that."

"I don't know any that aren't, except for maybe a few of those wild cowboys that come in on Saturday nights."

Children's laughter drew Ty's attention to the window and he looked out to see a group of boys and girls rolling hoops down the street. Startled, he recognized Gabby Wade amid the crowd.

"Looks like Miss Gabby's at it again," Mrs. Williams said as she stood next to Ty.

"Does she do this often?"

"Heavens, yes. At least a couple times a week she'll be out playing like she's a kid again." Mrs.

Williams's voice grew wistful. "I sometimes wish I had the courage to be more like her."

Ty puzzled over her words as he looked back at Gabby and the youngsters. He stepped out of the shop and onto the boardwalk. Leaning his shoulder against a post, he watched them approach.

Gabby glanced up, then looked again when she spotted him. Steering her hoop in his direction, she joined him, panting and smiling with excitement. Her hoop bumped into Ty's leg. "Sorry," she said sheepishly as he rubbed his thigh. "Looks like you caught me again, Mr. Ashburn. Would you like to join us?"

Ty's gaze fell to her breasts, which moved up and down with each deep breath. His blood pounded through his veins and settled in his groin. Forcing his perusal back to her flushed face, he tried to regain control of his thundering heart. "I don't think so."

"C'mon, mister. It's fun," the young girl he'd plucked the leaves from spoke up.

"I'm sure it is, but I have important things to do."

Gabby leaned close to the girl and whispered in a voice loud enough that Ty could hear. "He's afraid he won't be as good as you."

"I'll teach him," she piped up, her huge violet eyes on Ty.

He smiled. "That's mighty generous of you, but I'm too busy right now."

"Buying a new dress?" Gabby teased.

"My fiancée's getting her wedding dress fitted," he replied, unable to stifle his annoyance.

"Then you have time to play," Gabby said, and grabbed his hand, tugging him onto the street. She gave him her stick and hoop. "Go ahead."

"I'll show you," the girl volunteered.

Too aware of Gabby close by his side, he watched the orphan get her hoop rolling with deceptive ease.

"April just learned a couple weeks ago. She's doing pretty good, isn't she?" Gabby asked proudly.

"She must've had a good teacher."

Gabby raised her face to him, and her eyes twinkled. "Thank you."

"With the election coming up, I'd think you'd have better things to do with your time."

"What could be more important than giving children love and attention?" she asked softly.

He blinked, startled by her heartfelt sincerity. Damp tendrils of hair framed her face, and her cheeks were red from playing with the children. When she drew her tongue along her lush lips, Ty's stomach curled with desire, and he barely registered footsteps on the boardwalk behind him.

"What in the world are you doing, Tyler?" Eleanor called out.

"Nothing," he replied, and gave Gabby back her hoop and stick. "Like I said, I'm too busy for games."

April rejoined them. "Aren't you going to try?"

Ty laid his palm on the girl's soft crown. "Maybe some other time. I have to go now." He dared to look at Gabby one more time. "Good day, Miss Gabby." He touched the brim of his hat, then extended his arm to Eleanor.

Her mouth formed a pout, and Eleanor hesitated before slipping her hand through the crook of Ty's arm. He led her away, all the while aware of Gabby's eyes on him.

"What was that all about?" Eleanor asked in a low voice.

"The little girl was showing me how to roll a hoop," Ty answered.

"She didn't look like a 'little girl.' "

"I didn't mean Miss Gabby," Ty said irritably. "Those kids were from the orphanage."

Eleanor shuddered. "Contributing some money to the home is commendable, but associating with those ragamuffins is something else entirely."

Angry dismay formed a ball in Ty's stomach. "Just because they don't have parents doesn't mean they should be treated like pariahs."

"Really, Tyler, you're exaggerating. Those children have food, clothing, and a roof over their heads. What else do they need?"

"Love and attention," he replied unhesitantly, then abruptly realized he'd repeated Gabby's words.

"I'm not a heartless woman, Tyler. You know that."

Did he? The more he saw of Eleanor, the more he wondered if he'd made a mistake in asking her to marry him. What would she say if she found out he'd been worse off than those so-called ragamuffins?

Chapter 9

Ty locked his office door behind him and glanced down the shadow-draped street. Most of the town appeared deserted, except for an unusually large crowd at Miss Gabby's Emporium. The hitching posts around the gambling hall were crammed with saddled horses and buckboard wagons.

He'd seen handbills advertising a meeting for those who supported her. It appeared her supporters weren't nearly as limited as he'd assumed.

He stood motionless, staring at the activity at the other end of town, deciding whether he should learn what his unorthodox opponent had up her deceptively modest sleeve. She'd done better at the debate than he'd expected, answering the questions cleverly and placing him on the defensive more than once.

He knew Gatewood had been surprised by her astuteness. The man's single-minded determination to make him mayor bothered Ty more than he cared to admit. To Ty, this mayoral election was nothing more than a business proposition, and it was he who had the most to lose, not Gatewood.

As much as Gabby's political platform annoyed him, she also stirred his blood and played havoc with his self-control, something no other woman had ever done. Not even his own fiancée.

Lately, Ty had felt even more doubts about his forthcoming nuptials. After Eleanor's callous remarks about the orphans, the thought of spending the rest of his life with her brought a cold emptiness to his chest.

Her insistence that they live with her father after their marriage didn't set well with him, either. He had no intention of staying under Vernon Gatewood's roof, and it was time he made that crystal clear to his future wife.

Absently, Ty rubbed his eye, which had remained red and swollen for a couple of hours after his misadventure with Gabby's hat. For a woman who dressed so fastidiously, Gabby had no taste when it came to bonnets.

Deciding to appease his curiosity about the meeting, Ty strode down the street. As he approached the Emporium, the sound of voices grew louder and more strident. With a trace of amusement, he wondered what Gabby had gotten herself into now.

Slipping in silently, Ty stood in the shadows at the back of the overflowing gambling hall. Gabby stood on the bar so she could be seen by everyone. Dressed in a forest-green skirt and matching jacket over a white blouse, she resembled a schoolteacher more than the queen of a vice-ridden domain. Only her flowing honey-gold hair belied the prim and proper image and reminded him of the woman he'd seen playing with the children.

"Why is it impossible?" she demanded, her voice filled with frustration. "Don't you men have any guts?"

Puzzled, Ty listened to the comments the gathered men flung back at Gabby.

"Sure we do, Miss Gabby, but you don't know my Emma," said one man, shaking his head. "She goes plumb loco if she don't get what she wants."

"Yeah, my Cara's the same way," Louie said. "And she ain't one to let anyone tell her what she can and can't do—even me," he added miserably.

Ty hadn't known the bartender was married, and to hear him admit he had little control over his wife surprised him even more.

"But that's the only way," Gabby responded. "How else will you get your women to do as you say? You have to stop giving them what they want the most."

Ty blinked and wondered what in the hell he'd walked into. What was Gabby talking about?

More grumbling erupted and Gabby whistled shrilly, startling everyone into silence.

"It's up to you!" she shouted. "If you want all the saloons in this town to be shut down, you go right on home to your wives like obedient little boys. But if you want to have a place to come to at the end of a long, tiring workday to have a drink and talk with friends, then you'd best do like I said. Without the women's votes, I will lose and Tyler Ashburn will win. And I guarantee you—he *will* follow through on his campaign promise and close down the saloons."

She leaned over, and Joe and her bespectacled bartender swung her down from the bartop. She disappeared into the ocean of men, and Ty glanced at the person beside him. Although Ty didn't know him, he pulled his hat brim low to hide his features in case the stranger might recognize him. He tapped the man on the shoulder.

"What was that all about?" Ty asked.

The young cowhand shrugged. "Miss Gabby wants all the men to get their women to vote for her."

"How does she figure the men can do that?"

"Somethin' about not lettin' them have any money to buy new clothes or gewgaws."

Comprehension struck Ty between the eyes. She was even more clever than he'd suspected. "So Miss Gabby figures if the men don't give their wives any money until they come around to their way of thinking, she'll get the votes she needs to win?"

"Yep. But iffen I was married, I'd just tell my wife how she's gonna vote. No need to go through all this foolishness," the young cowboy said, then spat a wad of tobacco into a nearby spittoon.

A few weeks ago Ty would have agreed with him, but his latest experience with Eleanor had opened his eyes. He suspected the young man would learn soon enough that women had minds of their own, too.

"Someday after you're married you're going to think back on this night and laugh," Ty said.

The cowhand pressed back his hat and scratched his forehead. He stared at Ty for a few moments, then walked away, shaking his head.

"Did you learn anything tonight?"

He whirled around to find Gabby directly behind him, her hands propped on her hips and her eyes sparkling.

Ty doffed his hat. "Quite a bit."

"Like what?"

"Like the fact you're playing with fire, Miss Gabby."

"You think so?"

"I *know* so. If these men do as you say, you're going to start a civil war here in Sawtooth."

"Don't be melodramatic, Mr. Ashburn. You're only upset because you didn't think of it."

He scowled. "*I* don't have to stoop that low. Besides, it's not going to work."

"When they can't buy a new dress or hat, those wives won't be able to come around to our side fast enough. You wait and see, Mr. Know-it-all."

Ty hooked a thumb in his belt and asked, "Have you ever been married, Miss Gabby?"

Her composure slipped. "No. Never. Why?"

"I thought so. If you had, you would know your tactic is only going to make enemies of those same constituents you want to come over to your side."

"How can you be so sure? You've never been married, either."

"No, but I'm engaged." His declaration left a brackish taste in his mouth. "And that's closer than you are."

Gabby studied him with her catlike eyes. Suddenly she smiled brightly, like the sun after a summer thunderstorm, and Ty found himself wanting to bask in her warmth.

"I'll have you know I have no intention of getting married," she said. "Once a man puts a ring on a woman's finger, he thinks he owns her, lock, stock, and barrel. No man is ever going to boss me around."

Ty snorted. "I pity the man who tries."

Her eyes glittered mischievously. "So do I, Mr. Ashburn. So do I."

He watched the sway of her hips as she returned to the bar and found himself comparing Gabby to Eleanor, and not liking his assessment.

Joe approached him. "What're you doing here, Ty?" he asked.

Ty dragged his attention away from Gabby and focused on Joe. "I was going to ask you the same thing."

"I came to see my girl and hear what Miss Gabby had to say," he replied, his chin raised in challenge.

"Are you courting Rose?"

"You got something against her?"

Ty recognized the threat in Joe's tone, but he wasn't going to let that deter him. He had a responsibility to talk him out of his foolish notion.

"Not personally," Ty began. "But she works in a saloon, Joe. She's not the kind of woman a man wants to marry."

"You mean she's not the kind of woman *you* want to marry."

"And you shouldn't, either," Ty added without hesitation. "What kind of life would you have, wondering when one of Rose's old customers will come calling, or if she'll go back to her old habits?"

"In other words, once a whore, always a whore?" Joe asked in a brittle tone.

Ty tipped his head slightly. "You said it, I didn't."

Joe stared at him a moment. Then his gaze went to Rose, who was picking up empty beer mugs, and his belligerent expression eased slightly. "The only problem with that is she wasn't always that way. And she isn't anymore, neither."

"At least that's what she tells you." Ty sighed. "Look, Joe, we've been friends a long time. I think that gives me the right to tell you when you're making a big mistake."

The shorter man moved toe-to-toe with Ty. "And if you want us to keep on being friends," Joe began, his temper rising, "you'd best not be insulting Rose."

He turned away, and Ty grabbed his arm, spinning him around. "Don't do this, Joe."

"Let me go."

"Not until you agree to leave with me now."

"Let me go!" Joe repeated with more force.

"No."

Ty's mind registered Joe's fist a moment before the blow struck the side of his face. He stumbled back, slamming into the wall behind him. Trembling with the effort, he curbed his reaction to hit Joe back.

Using the wall's support, Ty straightened and skimmed his fingers across his injured cheek. He glanced down and found blood on his fingertips.

He and Joe had never fought before. Not until this damn election.

Not until Gabby and Rose had placed a wedge between him and his oldest friend.

Gabby approached them, her eyes wide. "What happened?"

"None of your business," he growled, and pushed away from the wall. He fixed Joe with a glare and asked bitterly, "Feel better?"

Joe scrubbed his palms on his thighs. "You were asking for it."

"Is this the way you plan on handling every man who knew Rose before?" Ty asked, struggling to keep his voice calm. "If so, you're going to have some mighty sore fists."

He looked around for his hat and saw that Gabby held it between her hands. He reached for it; then, not even bothering to thank her, he started toward the door.

"Let me wash that cut for you," Gabby called out.

He paused and leveled a glare at her. "You've done more than enough."

Holding his hand to his swelling cheek, he left the Emporium.

The betrayal she'd seen in Ty Ashburn's eyes caused Gabby's heart to tighten in anguish. She watched the proud man disappear around the curtain and sighed. Turning back to Joe, she found Rose had joined him.

"What were you and Mr. Ashburn arguing about?" Gabby asked.

Joe looked down and stubbed his boot toe into the layer of fresh sawdust. "He insulted Rose."

"He wasn't the first, and he won't be the last," Rose said. "Don't you think I'm used to it?"

"Anybody says anything against you and they'll answer to me." Joe didn't seem to hear anything she said. "Besides, Ty's my friend. He had no right calling you a—calling you names." His face reddened.

Gabby noticed a shadow of pain cross Rose's face. Though she'd denied it, such comments clearly hurt her.

"He thinks he's helping you, and in my book that makes him your friend," Rose said to Joe. "You shouldn't have hit him."

"Maybe." Joe didn't sound convinced.

Gabby sighed. "Even though he's as misguided

and stubborn as a goat, and has more than enough pride for ten men, I think he's a decent person underneath it all. Of course, he's awfully arrogant, too, and thinks he's always right, but that's just the way he is. Mr. Ashburn—"

She broke off abruptly as Rose laughed. "Sounds like he got under your skin."

"Yeah, like a chigger's itch, but twice as irritating," Gabby retorted.

"Ain't that the truth," Joe muttered.

At Rose's knowing smile, Gabby scowled. Rose couldn't actually believe Gabby was *attracted* to Tyler Ashburn. When it came to her, Ty had the understanding of a grizzly bear and the sensitivity of a wounded mountain lion. Still, it bothered Gabby that she'd inadvertently created a rift between the two men.

"I'm going to go talk to him right now," Gabby announced. "Someone has to get him to see past the end of his nose."

"And that someone is you?" Rose asked slyly.

Gabby's face flushed, but without questioning her motives further, she hurried after Ty. Pausing outside her establishment, she looked both ways and spotted his familiar figure striding across the street, headed toward his cabin at the edge of town.

Lifting her skirt hem a few inches, she ran after him. The cool night air smelled exceptionally fresh after the stale tobacco and beer odors in the Emporium. She chased him into the woods, and darkness enveloped them both. Out of the sight and hearing of anyone who might still be awake, Gabby dared to holler after him.

"Mr. Ashburn, wait!"

She could barely see him, and nearly collided

with his broad chest. He caught hold of her arms to steady her.

"What the hell are you doing following me?" he demanded.

What in the world *was* she doing? She panted for a few moments, buying herself some time to come up with a plausible excuse. "I—I wanted to make sure you were all right."

"He used his fist, not a gun."

His intentional inference cut deep, and she pulled out of his grasp. Taking a step back from his imposing and unexpectedly frightening form, Gabby stared up at him in silence. Her gaze settled on his firm lips, and she wondered how his kisses would make her feel. She doubted she'd be repulsed, like she'd been by those few men who'd pawed her and kissed her with disgusting wet lips.

Shaking aside the thought, she said, "I just wanted to tell you not to worry about Joe and Rose. All she does is serve drinks now. She's not what you think she is."

"And I'm supposed to believe *you*?" Ty laughed harshly. "You and Rose are two of a kind."

She raised her head. "If you mean we're both women alone in the world, then I agree with you." She studied his rugged features, which seemed so haggard in the scant light. "I care for Rose, just like you care about Joe. Neither of us wants to see our friends hurt."

"What do you know about it?" Ty demanded. "I'm sure you have 'special' friends scattered in all the towns you've traveled through." His voice oozed sarcasm.

"Why is it you always believe the worst about me?" She took a deep breath. "In any case, don't take it out on Rose. She's paid her dues—more than you'll ever know. Let her have this happiness with Joe."

He stepped toward her, removing the space she'd created between them, and glared down at her, his expression intimidating. "I won't let my best friend be made a laughingstock by Rose, or whatever her name is. She's using him and he's too blind to see her for what she is—a whore."

Gabby wanted to lash out at him, but she saw concern and fear mingled with his anger. He cared deeply. Perhaps too deeply.

She wanted to touch him and soothe away the furrows in his brow, but knew her actions would be misconstrued. Little did he know she didn't know the first thing about seduction.

"Her real name is Isabella," Gabby said quietly.

Startled, Ty asked, "What?"

"You wanted to know Rose's real name." Gabby's gaze moved over his shoulder, to the rustling treetops. "It means 'consecrated to God.' When she had to start selling her body to keep from starving, she changed her name to Rose. She told me it was sacrilegious to keep Isabella."

She brought her attention back to Ty, who appeared unmoved by her disclosure. "Don't tell her I told you. She doesn't like anyone's pity."

"Or maybe so she won't tell me the truth?" Ty retorted. "That you and she just wanted to make money the easiest way you could?"

Gabby gripped her skirt folds firmly, restraining the impulse to slap his self-righteous face. "You think that, because I own a gambling hall and Rose serves drinks, we're not as good as everybody else in this town. Maybe you should pull your head out of your business long enough to take a good look around. Even people close to you are hiding secrets—" She stopped, realizing she'd said more than she'd meant to.

"What do you mean?" Ty demanded. "Who's hiding secrets?"

Gabby shook her head. "That isn't for me to say, Mr. Ashburn." She met his demanding gaze. "I'm sorry for whatever happened in your past that's made you the way you are. But I only have the truth, and if that's not enough, then I guess we'll always be enemies. And that's only going to hurt our friends."

"Why the hell did you and Rose have to settle in Sawtooth?" he asked plaintively. "Because of you two, Joe's life's going to be ruined."

Desolation settled on her shoulders. How could she possibly broach the wall of bitterness he'd erected around himself?

"If being loved and needed and cared for will ruin his life, then so be it," she said softly.

She reached up and carefully touched his cheek. He flinched slightly, and she brought her hand away, staring at the blood on her fingers. "Is it worth it to lose a friend because of pride? Life is too short and too precious to live without people you love and care for. I hope you come to understand that before it's too late, Mr. Ashburn."

Gabby looked up at him for a moment longer, then turned to walk back the way she'd come. Ty caught her arm and pulled her toward him. She regained her balance before her body collided with his, and glanced up at him. Her heart missed a beat at the fire that burned in his eyes, but she couldn't move if her life had depended on it.

"Why did you follow me?" he demanded.

"I was worried about you," she replied.

"Why?"

She sensed his bewilderment and a little-boy's vulnerability. "You seemed so alone . . . and I wanted to help."

"Why do you care?"

Gabby could feel the heat radiating from his body, and it seemed to melt her own resolve. "I don't know," she replied honestly. "Maybe it's because I saw you with the orphans the other morning." She laid her trembling hand against his jaw. "You were so different, like you weren't afraid to be yourself with them."

His warm, uneven breath caressed her cheek, and the fever in his eyes both frightened and fascinated her. Ty wrapped his arm around her waist, bringing her flush against his hard body. Her breasts were crushed to his chest, and her nipples hardened at the contact. He tipped his head, bringing his lips savagely down upon hers. The fierce kiss stole her breath, but she returned it with a reckless passion she hadn't even known existed within her. Her insides fluttered uncontrollably, and she locked her hands behind his neck. Hot fire burned within her, and when his hand brushed the side of her breast, she thought she'd burst into flames. Gabby groaned deep in her throat, and suddenly Ty drew away, leaving her gasping for air.

Ty breathed heavily as he battled to regain control of his emotions. His hands slid away from her and fell to his sides, where he clenched them into fists.

"That was a mistake," he stated hoarsely.

The cool air brought harsh reality with it, and

Gabby bowed her head. Ty was an engaged man, and she'd behaved unconscionably. She raised her gaze to his face, but it skittered down to the third button on his shirt. If she looked into his eyes, she wasn't sure she could resist the attraction that vibrated between them.

"You're right. It was," she replied, glad her voice didn't tremble. "I'd better get back."

Ty's hungry gaze followed her slight figure along the path until the darkness swallowed her, leaving him restless and edgy. He didn't try to rationalize his actions—all logical thought seemed to flee in the presence of Miss Gabby. The only thing he could do was make sure he didn't repeat what had just occurred. In the light of day, everything would be back to normal and the insanity of this evening would be forgotten.

He breathed deeply of the night air to erase Gabby's womanly scent that filled his senses. His body burned with unfulfilled desire, and he tried to picture Eleanor, but sparkling topaz eyes and silky blond hair continued to taunt him.

I only have the truth. . . . What if Gabby hadn't lied about anything? She didn't have to tell him Rose's real name or why she'd changed it. And Gabby certainly hadn't acted like any sporting girl he'd ever seen.

What had she meant about even those close to him having secrets? Who had she been referring to—Vernon Gatewood? Or Eleanor? The idea that either one of them hid some horrible secret was almost laughable. He had never known two people so upright and respectable.

Ty squared his shoulders. He couldn't let himself weaken again. If he allowed one speck of doubt,

Gabby would succeed in undermining all he'd striven for since he was eleven years old. And nobody could ever make him forget the anger and humiliation of that night so long ago.

Especially not a gambling hall owner, who could steal a child's father, as well as his dreams.

Chapter 10

⟨⟨○○⟩⟩

Gabby set aside the rag she'd been polishing the bar with and smiled at the four children who gathered about her.

"Have you finished your chores?" she asked.

"Yes, ma'am. We got the floor swept and the tables wiped and we even dusted that handrail that goes upstairs," Tommy, a feisty eleven-year-old, replied.

Gabby gazed at the towheaded boy she often played marbles with. "I don't think the seat of your trousers was meant to be used as a dusting cloth, Tommy."

Tommy's face blushed scarlet and the other children, a younger boy and two girls, giggled at his embarrassment.

Gabby took pity on the red-cheeked boy and allowed her laughter to tumble out. "I'm just teasing you, Tommy. In fact, I'll tell you a secret: I used to slide down banisters all the time."

"Really?" His blue eyes widened.

"I don't believe you," Sara challenged. She was a skinny girl with long brown hair braided into one thick plait, and far too young, Gabby thought sadly, to be such a cynic.

"And why not?" Gabby asked.

"Because," Sara began judiciously, "ladies don't do things like that, and you're a lady, Miss Gabby."

"Ladies can do whatever they want," Gabby said firmly. She stood. "Come on, I'll show you."

She took Sara's frail hand and led her and the rest of the children up the curved staircase. At the top she turned to the gathered orphans, who eyed the banister with glee. "Each one of us will take a turn. I'll go first."

Holding her skirts down in a futile attempt at propriety, Gabby swung a leg over the railing. "Here I go."

She pushed off and laughed in abandoned delight as she slid backward down the polished wood banister. At the bottom, she slipped off and landed gracefully on her feet. Brushing her hair back from her face, she looked up the stairs.

"Tommy, you go next and show them how it's done," she called.

With a jaunty grin, the boy quickly mounted the banister and slid down. Gabby caught him as he reached the bottom, his eyes sparkling with joy. Harold, the other boy, came next, then April, who'd been given that name because, as an infant, she'd been left on the orphanage steps during that month. Finally, only twelve-year-old Sara remained at the top.

"Okay, Sara, your turn," Gabby said.

"Are you sure it's all right for me to do this?" Sara asked, her face twisted in indecision.

"If I can do it, you can!"

Sara took a deep breath and awkwardly hitched a leg over the railing. For a long moment, she remained motionless.

"C'mon, scaredy cat," Harold shouted.

"That wasn't very nice," Gabby rebuked gently. "Sara needs your encouragement, not to be called names."

The tips of Harold's ears reddened, and he called up, "It's okay, Sara. It's fun, really!"

With a visible sigh, Sara pushed away and slid down, gathering speed as she went. At the bottom, she jumped off and Gabby caught her shoulders to steady her.

"That was fun!" Sara's cheeks blossomed with a healthy flush and her hazel eyes sparkled. "Can I do it again?"

"Let's all do it again," Gabby exclaimed. "Last one up the stairs is a rotten egg!"

In the midst of the giggling children, Gabby raced up the steps. She hung back to allow April, the youngest, to beat her.

Magnifying her huffing and puffing lest April figure out what she'd done, Gabby pressed her hand to her chest. "Goodness, you're all too fast for me. Looks like I'll have to go last this time."

Ty knocked on the Emporium doors, holding a new contract for Gabby, since her old one ran out at the end of the week. He didn't know if she'd want to continue having her liquor freighted in until the very end, but his sense of fair play compelled him to give her the option.

He pounded on the door again and shifted impatiently. No footsteps sounded from within, and he pressed his ear against the door. Children's shrill laughter rang from inside, and Ty frowned. What were children doing in a place like this?

He tried the knob and found the door unlocked.

With a wary glance around to see if anyone noticed, he swung the door open and stepped inside, then closed the door softly behind him. Walking on the balls of his feet, he went around the gaudy entrance curtain and froze.

The girl he'd pushed on the swing was sliding down the banister, and three other children waited for her at the bottom. Miss Gabby stood at the top of the stairs, clapping as she cheered on the child. Two of the older children caught the girl as she came to the end of her slide.

Then Gabby hoisted a leg over the rail and her skirt hem hiked up to midcalf, revealing a flurry of surprisingly demure eyelet petticoats. Ty's gaze latched on to her curved white-stockinged leg, then her round bottom, enticingly outlined on the wooden banister. His heart thundered in his chest like a runaway freight team and he couldn't seem to catch his breath.

"Here I come!" she shouted, startling Ty.

The children jumped up and down, shouting their excitement. Within moments, Gabby landed feet first on the floor and the boys and girls gathered around her.

Somehow Ty remembered to breathe, and he eased back into the folds of the curtain. Glancing down at the crumpled contract in his clenched hand, he forced himself to uncurl his fingers.

He looked over at Gabby and was struck anew by her angelic features, even as he mocked himself for the comparison. Her cheeks glowed and her eyes danced with pleasure. Giggling and behaving like a young girl, she appeared as innocent as the four orphans circling her. The scene should have seemed absurd, considering her profession.

Gabby and the children from the home raced up the stairs, and Ty watched them with a hungry, needy gaze. He tried to remember the last time he'd indulged in such carefree fun. Certainly not since his father had killed himself, leaving Ty to support his family at an age when *he* should have been sliding down banisters. For a moment, he longed to be as free and lighthearted as Gabby and the children.

At the top of the stairs, first the girls, then the boys slid down backward amid high-spirited laughter.

He'd never had time to mourn his lost childhood years—instead he'd worked two jobs to keep his family from starving. He'd been able to give them a roof over their heads and put food on the table. Granted, it was often only a handful of potatoes or a loaf of bread, but he'd done it without anyone's help. Vowing never to be that poor again, Ty had forsworn frivolity and had worked hard to get where he was at today. The cloak of respectability could never be removed, or he would become like his father, who'd been weak and unable to resist temptation—temptations Miss Gabby and her Emporium represented. A temptation he'd already succumbed to once.

As Gabby climbed aboard for another trip down the railing, Ty gathered what remained of his splintered self-control. He'd indulged in foolish sentimentality long enough. Miss Gabby was corrupting innocent children, and he had a duty to protect them. He stepped out of his hiding place and approached the banister. Their attention on Gabby, the youngsters didn't notice Ty standing behind them.

She began her downward slide and turned her head to glance down at the boys and girls. Then she spotted Ty. Her speed increased and she careened down the remaining distance. When the banister ended, Gabby's momentum sent her flying backward, straight into Ty's chest, and knocking him flat on his back.

"Ooomph," Ty grunted.

Gabby's skirts bunched around her knees as she straddled his torso, and at the sight of her shapely calves, Ty felt the blood rush to his groin. White-hot heat pulsed through him, obliterating everything but the thought of Gabby wrapping those smooth legs around him . . . her eyes lit with passion, and his name on her red lips as her body rose to meet his.

"Oh-oh," she murmured, and turned to look at him. "Are you all right, Mr. Ashburn?"

Ty tried to regain some control of his unbridled lust. He thought of an icy cold stream, then the numbers in his ledger, and his passion waned. But when he looked at her curvaceous backside perched on his chest, his erection throbbed with renewed enthusiasm.

He glared up at the reason for his lapse of control. "No, I am *not* all right! Would you get the he—heck off me?"

Gabby scrambled to her feet, tugging her skirts back in place. She leaned over, offering Ty a hand, which he ignored, fearful of his response to any more physical contact with her. He didn't want a repeat of what had occurred three nights ago, especially with an audience of impressionable children.

He climbed to his feet and glowered down at

Gabby. It was easier to be angry with her than to admit to himself how disturbing and irresistible her appeal was. Then he looked at the quiet, wide-eyed children. Damn—he hadn't meant to frighten them.

Gabby gathered the youngsters together and herded them toward the table where her abandoned ledger lay. Ty followed.

"Thank you all for your help," she said to the children, ignoring him.

She reached into her skirt pocket and withdrew four gold coins, placing one in each orphan's outstretched hand.

"Come by in a couple days and I'll have some more chores for you to help me with," she said.

"Can we play again?" April piped up.

"You bet we can, sweetheart." Gabby leaned over and brushed the young girl's bangs out of her eyes, drawing a gap-toothed grin from the child.

"I like to play with you, Miss Gabby," she said, then turned to Ty. "And you can come over and swing whenever you want."

Ty couldn't help but soften at the girl's sincere offer.

"You all better head on back to the home before Mrs. Edwards sends out a posse to look for you," Gabby said.

Tommy, Harold, and April skipped out of the Emporium, but Sara remained behind. Gabby could tell something was bothering the girl.

"What is it, Sara?" Gabby asked softly.

Sara's eyes slid to Ty, and back to Gabby. "Are you going to be in trouble?" she asked in a low voice. "Mr. Ashburn looks mad."

Gabby glanced over at Ty, who shifted his

weight from one foot to the other to make his impatience known.

"That's just the way he is, honey. I'll tell you a secret." Gabby leaned close to Sara's ear and cupped her hand over her mouth. "He doesn't know it yet, but I'm going to teach him how to laugh and have fun."

"I don't know, Miss Gabby," Sara said tentatively. "He doesn't look like he wants to learn."

"Sometimes bad things happen to people that make them sad, but deep down, they still want to laugh and smile. I think Mr. Ashburn is that way."

Sara was silent for a moment, then nodded sagely. "Kind of like after my mother died."

Gabby wrapped an arm around the girl's slight shoulders and gave her a hug. "That's right. And remember, if you ever feel sad, you can come talk to me. Okay?"

"All right. I'd better go." She turned and moved toward the door. "Bye, Miss Gabby. And thank you."

"You're welcome, Sara."

Gabby watched her walk away. For a moment she was reminded of another girl who had been orphaned. But that girl had had an uncle named Soapy. Sara had no one.

Her mind caught in the past, she almost forgot about her unexpected visitor. Almost.

Gabby turned to face Ty, crossing her arms, and tried not to remember the feel of his hard body beneath hers. She reminded herself of what she'd told Sara regarding him, and kept her voice cordial. "What brings you into the lion's den at this time of day?"

"What were those children doing in here?" Ty demanded, ignoring her question.

Somewhere, someplace deep down, Ty Ashburn wants to be a normal human being, one who laughs and enjoys life.

She smiled determinedly. "They do a few jobs around here to earn some money."

"Like what?"

He really wants to be happy like everyone else.

Her smile wavered a moment, and she took a deep, wary breath before answering. "Like sweeping and dusting."

"Don't you have people who work for you who do that?"

She gave up and threw her hands in the air. "That's it!" Taking a step closer to him, she tilted her head back to give him the full force of her glare. "Those children barely have enough clothing and food to keep them comfortable. There's certainly nothing extra for a toy or a stick of candy. By letting them do some chores around here, I give them a chance to earn money for things like that."

"But this a saloon!" Ty thundered. "Children don't belong in a place like this."

"This is *not* a saloon, it is a gambling emporium," Gabby corrected, enunciating carefully.

"I don't care what you call it, innocent children should not be around the likes of you."

Gabby's mouth dropped open. "And what does that mean—that instead they should spend time with proper folks like your precious Eleanor and her pompous father?"

Ty blinked and his gaze flitted away. "They'd be a better influence than you."

"Then tell Miss Prissy Gatewood to get her nose out of the clouds and do it!"

"Miss Pr—Gatewood is none of your concern," Ty stated. "I don't want you corrupting those children anymore. Is that understood?"

Gabby planted her hands on her hips. "I like those children and they like me, and neither you nor anybody else is going to tell me I can't see them."

If steam could rise from a person's ears, Gabby suspected Ty would be boiling. It was high time someone showed Mr. Tyler Ashburn that he didn't rule the world.

"All right, if that's the way you feel about it, I'll go speak to Mrs. Edwards and tell her what you've been up to. She'll make sure that the kids aren't allowed to come here anymore," Ty said.

Gabby grabbed his arm, and in spite of her fury, the feel of his skin triggered an avalanche of sensations he'd fanned to life when he'd kissed her. "Don't do that!"

He narrowed his eyes. "I don't think I've ever heard you beg before."

Anger straightened her backbone. "I am *not* begging. I am asking you not to speak to Mrs. Edwards."

He studied her a moment, his unflinching mask giving no clues as to his thoughts. "*Someone* has to look out for those children."

Gritting her teeth, she said scathingly, "Now's a fine time to think of them. Where were you when the home first opened? Did you help then?"

Ty wasn't about to tell her that he'd talked the town leaders into buying the house and having it fixed up. He had contributed the largest sum of

money, and continued to give a monthly stipend
to help pay for food and clothing.

"If you'll step aside, I won't have to move you,"
he stated through gritted teeth.

Gabby looked like she wanted to give him a
good, hearty shove, but after a moment she moved
out of his path.

"Thank you," he said mockingly.

"You're not welcome," she responded peevishly.

Ty strode out of the Emporium and down to the
Home for Orphaned Children at the other end of
town. Once he told Mrs. Edwards where some of
the children were spending their time, she'd put a
stop to it. She wouldn't want the orphans cor-
rupted, either.

The neat-looking house had been whitewashed
over the summer and the shutters painted bright
blue. For a poorhouse, it was in surprisingly good
condition.

His knock was answered almost immediately by
the matronly woman.

"Hello, Mr. Ashburn," she greeted heartily. "If I
had known you were coming, I would've had the
children clean their rooms."

Ty smiled thinly. "That's all right, Mrs. Edwards.
I just wanted to talk to you about a matter concerning the children's welfare."

"Of course. Come on in." She opened the door
further and he stepped across the threshold.

Familiar mouthwatering smells of baking bread
and frying chicken filled the warm rooms. Whenever he came to visit, he could always count on
Mrs. Edwards to be baking or cooking, usually
both. He'd been lucky to find her to oversee the
home and the twelve children who lived there.

"Why don't we go into the parlor? We won't be bothered there," she suggested.

"That's fine."

Ty followed her down a neat hallway into a room filled with a variety of furniture, including a sagging sofa covered with a bright afghan and a comfortable, well-worn rocking chair. A fire burned in the fireplace, giving the parlor a welcoming atmosphere.

"Won't you sit down?" Mrs. Edwards motioned to a cushioned chair with crocheted doilies on the armrests.

He stepped over to it, but waited until she seated herself before lowering himself into the comfortable chair.

Mrs. Edwards perched on the edge of her seat. "Now, what's so urgent that it couldn't wait until your next visit?"

"It's come to my attention that some of the orphaned children are spending time at Miss Gabby's."

"So?"

Her puzzled reaction wasn't what he'd expected, confusing him. "Doesn't that bother you?"

"Should it?"

Ty leaned forward, placing his elbows on his thighs. Maybe she didn't know Miss Gabby's profession and so couldn't understand the significance. "She owns a gambling hall. It seems to me that isn't a proper place for youngsters to be spending their time."

"Were they there while it was open to customers?"

Ty shook his head. "No, but I don't—"

"Then I don't see a problem," Mrs. Edwards said

dismissively. "Is that all you wanted to discuss?"

"Isn't it enough?" Ty asked, not bothering to hide his frustration.

Mrs. Edwards studied him a long moment, and Ty consciously kept himself from squirming beneath her penetrating gaze.

"How do you think Miss Gabby is harming the children?"

Was the woman daft? Ty wondered. "She owns a gambling hall. For a child to associate with her in any way is harmful enough."

Suddenly she chuckled. "I may be busy here at the home, but I do know that you and Miss Gabby are running for mayor."

Ty frowned with mounting irritation. "That has nothing to do with this."

"Oh, I think it does. I've heard that if you become mayor, you plan to run Miss Gabby and the other saloon owners out of town."

"Having impressionable children to care for, you should support my stand."

She shook her head, her gray sausage curls dancing across her creased brow. "To be perfectly honest, I haven't decided who I'm going to vote for."

Ty leaned back in his chair and stared at the older woman. How could she even consider voting for Miss Gabby? "Why?" he managed to ask.

"You don't know Gabby Wade half as well as you think you do, Mr. Ashburn. Did she tell you why the children go to her place?"

Ty nodded. "She pays them for doing some chores."

"That's right. I know you've been generous with your contributions to the home, but do you have any idea what it's like for the children not to have a coin or two of their own?"

Ty froze and remained silent. He remembered only too well the nights he'd gone to bed with an empty stomach; the times he'd watched other children play with a new toy. And how many times had he endured taunts about his patched and threadbare clothing, washed so many times no one could tell what color it had been?

"She gives them a sense of worth," Mrs. Edwards went on. "With the coins she pays them, they can buy something for themselves, just like you and me did when we got a penny or two from our folks."

Ty didn't bother to correct her assumption. "But that money comes from—"

"It comes from the townsfolk, whether they know it or not," Mrs. Edwards said sharply. "What Miss Gabby's customers lose at the tables brings a little happiness to the children. I'll let you in on a little secret: you and Miss Gabby fairly run the orphanage by your donations. Funny thing is, neither one of you wants anybody to know about your generosity." She shook her head. "I just don't understand either one of you. Now do you see why I'm having a hard time deciding who to vote for?"

The heavy weight of truth settled on Ty's chest.

The parlor door burst open and April bounced in. "I got a—" She spotted Ty and broke off. "Hi! Are you still mad at Miss Gabby for falling on you?"

"What in the world are you talking about, April?" Mrs. Edwards asked.

"When Miss Gabby was teaching us how to slide down the banister, she fell on top of him. He looked madder'n that rooster when you locked him out of the chicken coop." She giggled.

Mrs. Edwards laughed and slapped her thigh, and the knowing twinkle in her eyes disconcerted Ty. However, the girl's infectious mirth brought a reluctant smile to his lips. "I'm not mad anymore, April. I was just worried about you and the others."

"Miss Gabby wouldn't hurt us. She's our bestest friend," April said solemnly.

Ty glanced at Mrs. Edwards, who had managed to compose herself. "I just found that out." He stood, and she rose also.

"Thanks for your time, Mrs. Edwards."

"You will keep our conversation confidential, won't you?" she asked.

"Don't worry. I won't tell a soul." He leaned closer to her. "And I hope you'll do the same."

She smiled. "I will, and thank you, Mr. Ashburn. I hope you understand why I will not forbid the children to stay away from her."

It was obvious he hadn't quite figured out Miss Gabby after all, and the knowledge was maddening. "Yes, I see your point." He glanced at the girl, who stared up at him with huge violet eyes. "Good-bye April."

"Bye."

Mrs. Edwards led him to the front door, and Ty paused.

"If some of the older children would like to make some extra money, send them down to my place where I keep the horses and wagons. I'm sure I can find some chores for them."

She patted his arm. "Bless you, Mr. Ashburn."

Uncomfortable with her gratitude, he slipped out

without another word. The sun's rays splashed across him, warming his shoulders as he walked back into town.

Gabby's generosity crept into his heart and threatened his vow to maintain his distance from her. It seemed everything was conspiring against him, and he was going to have a heck of a time holding on to his antagonism toward her.

But he had no choice if he was to rid himself of his past for good.

Chapter 11

$\sim\!\!\infty\!\!\sim$

A few days later, Ty showed up at Miss
Gabby's with the unsigned contract in his
hand once more. He'd forgotten about it after his
confrontation over the orphans. Though he had
considered not informing her of the lapsed contract
and letting her learn about it when her usual ship-
ment of liquor wasn't delivered next week, his conscience had a differing opinion—especially after
his visit with Mrs. Edwards.

With a sense of familiarity, he knocked on the
door. This time it was answered immediately by
the subject of his thoughts.

She blocked the entrance with her petite form,
her arms folded across her chest. "The children
aren't here today," she said, her dainty chin thrust
out challengingly.

Ty admired her plucky spirit and nearly smiled.
"That's too bad," he said, intentionally throwing
her off guard.

She eyed him warily. "I thought you were determined to have them banned from my 'den of
iniquity.'"

"I changed my mind. Can I come in?"

She studied him for a long moment, then took a

step away from the door and waved magnani-
mously. "Welcome to my parlor."

Understanding her not-so-subtle allusion, he
grimaced and entered. His arm accidentally
brushed against her breasts, sparking a wildfire
that raced through his veins. He silently cursed,
and concentrated on the reason for his visit.

After she closed the door behind him, she led
him to a table where she'd been doing her account-
ing. As he sat down, he tried to read some of the
column headings, but she slammed it shut before
he could make out any names.

"What do you want?" Gabby asked flatly.

Ty studied her pugnacious expression, then
glanced around, pretending to search for something. "What happened to the fun-loving Miss
Gabby who used to own this place?"

Puzzled surprise flickered in her eyes. "She
doesn't like to deal with men who have too much
pigheaded pride for their own good."

He chuckled at her frank reply. He did enjoy her
sharp wit and her defiance of social convention. Or
maybe, in spite of their differences, he liked being
around her.

"That's probably for the best," he teased. "Every
time I'm around that other Miss Gabby, I either
have a gun pointed my way, get hit in the eye by
one of her hat's stuffed birds, get punched by my
best friend, or knocked down and sat on." *Or end
up kissing you.*

A crimson flush crossed her smooth cheeks, and
he felt strangely elated that he'd made her blush.

"When did the bird get you?" she asked, fighting
the smile that tempted her lips.

"When I saved you from taking a dive off the grandstand into Gatewood's arms."

She surrendered to her laughter. "I'm sorry. I didn't realize my hat was such a dangerous weapon."

Ty smiled at the return of her usual lightheartedness. Then he remembered the contract in his hand, and for a moment he wished life's circumstances hadn't put so many obstacles between them.

"No harm done." He laid the contract on the table in front of her. "I—"

"I know what it is," Gabby interrupted, her expression sobering. "My old contract expires in two days. This is a new one, right?"

He nodded, again surprised by her business acumen. "With the election hanging over us, I wasn't sure—" He broke off, uncomfortable with his role in her uncertain future.

"You weren't sure I would want to sign a new contract with you?" Gabby finished.

"That's right."

"To be perfectly honest, I don't know what to make of you." She held up the piece of paper. "You could've just let it lapse and not said anything to me."

Ty met her even gaze. "I couldn't do that to anybody."

"Not even me?" she asked, giving him a sarcastic look.

"Especially not you," Ty replied without pause. "I may not approve of what you do here, but you've always been fair and honest in your business dealings with me. I owed you the same consideration."

"Thank you for that." She read through the business agreement, then glanced up at him, bewildered. "This is a month-to-month contract."

"That's right. We don't know who's going to win the upcoming election. If I win, I'm going to shut down the saloons, yours included." He kept his voice intentionally unapologetic. "However, there is a slight possibility you'll win. In that case, we can renegotiate a longer-term contract."

Gabby shook her head and smiled without humor. "You're getting good at the politician talk— I'm not sure if I've been insulted or not."

Ty threaded his fingers together and rested his hands on the table. This was more difficult than he had anticipated. "I may have been a little hard on you since this election began, Miss Gabby, but there's no changing the fact that you own a gambling hall. And because of that, we're going to be on opposite sides of the fence. This contract is strictly business."

"A *little* hard on me?"

His backbone stiffened. "We *are* adversaries."

Gabby kept her dubious gaze on him a moment longer, then glanced down at the contract. "It's a fair compromise." She raised amber eyes to him. "You once told me you don't like signing contracts for less than three months. I appreciate your making an exception." She picked up her pen, signed the form, then dated it. Handing it back to him, she said, "I've always admired your integrity, Mr. Ashburn, and I'm sorry we have to be enemies."

Surprised that she'd been thinking along the same lines as himself, he studied his blunt fingertips for a moment to regain his composure. "I spoke to Mrs. Edwards about you the other day."

"I wish you hadn't."

Ty observed the pink that painted her cheeks, and he found himself reassessing her again. How had a woman in her profession retained the ability to blush? "She told me about your contributions to the home."

Gabby shrugged nonchalantly. "So what? I'll bet nearly everyone in town has given them something."

Ty had a sound reason for not wanting people to know about his contributions, but it made no sense to him why Gabby would be so secretive about her charity. Especially when she shamelessly flaunted her ownership of a gambling hall. "Mrs. Edwards said you give money for food and clothing for the kids."

She remained silent, her attention seemingly riveted to her forefinger, which idly traced the ledger's embossed lettering.

Ty leaned forward. "Why?"

She peered at him from beneath long, thick lashes. "Why what?"

Her innocent question didn't fool him. "You know what I'm asking. Why do you care about those orphans so much?"

"It's none of your business."

Her sharp reply jolted Ty.

"Do they remind you of you?" he asked quietly.

Gabby pushed back her chair and walked to the bar. Leaning her back against the solid wood and propping her elbows on the polished surface, she fixed him with a penetrating glare. "Like I said, it's none of your business, Mr. Ashburn. Now would you kindly leave?"

Suddenly a porcupine seemed less prickly than Gabby.

He shrugged and pushed himself upright. "If that's what you want."

Gabby said nothing, but her unwavering stare spoke volumes.

With the newly signed contract in hand, Ty moved toward the door. At the curtain, he paused a moment. "I don't know why you're hiding your charity to the orphanage. I would think it would help you gain support in the election."

Gabby shook her head. "I wouldn't use those children for my own personal gain. I know what you think of me, but for the orphans' sake, please keep quiet about my contributions."

"Don't worry. I don't plan on telling anyone."

"Thank you."

A shriek from outside startled Ty, and he hurried out, with Gabby close on his heels. On the boardwalk across the street, a woman nearly the size of a Concord coach held a broom over her head. Big Louie was cowering beneath the woman's wrath, trying in vain to shield his head with his hands.

"Come on, sugarplum, you know I'm doin' this for your own good," Louie pleaded with the woman.

"Don't you sugarplum me, Louis. You ain't going to make me change my mind. Iffen Mr. Ashburn wins, you'll have to find a new job!" The stout woman raised the broom even higher.

"But barkeepin' is the only thing I know," Louie whined.

"Then you'll learn somethin' new. I'm sick and tired of you comin' home smellin' like cheap whiskey and cigar smoke. Now, I'm wantin' some new cloth to make me a dress, so give me some money."

Ty glanced at Gabby; her eyes were wide and her mouth agape. Now she would learn the cost of her so-called election strategy—and it didn't look like the lesson would come cheap.

Louie drew his arms out of their protective position and straightened his backbone. "Not until you promise me you'll vote for Miss Gabby!"

His stout wife brought the broom's bristles down on Louie's shoulders with a dull whack. "I done told you no, and I mean it!"

"So do you still think your idea to get the women's votes is a good one?" Ty asked dryly.

Gabby's shock vanished, and she glowered at him. Then she bustled across the street, holding her clenched fists stiffly at her sides. With an exasperated sigh, Ty followed her.

Since Louie wasn't even trying to disarm his wife, Gabby decided she'd have to step in and take care of Cara Adams herself.

"Mrs. Adams, please stop this!" Gabby cried as she attempted to grab hold of the broom handle.

"You stay out of this, Miss Gabby," Louie's wife hollered. "Iffen you ask me, you done enough," she continued, her second and third chins quivering like a turkey's wattle.

With deceptive agility, Mrs. Adams kept the broom out of Gabby's reach.

A crowd gathered, and a few of the men laughed and poked each other in the ribs. Most of the women cheered for Cara Adams.

"Please, Mrs. Adams, this isn't going to solve anything," Gabby stated.

Mrs. Adams's eyes gleamed with renewed fervor. "Maybe it'll show my husband he can't order me around like I'm some simpleton. I got my own mind when it comes to this election and if he thinks he can make me vote his way, he's got another thing comin'."

"You tell him," one of the ladies in the crowd called out.

"You keep your mouth shut, Erma," the woman's husband scolded.

"I will not! You cannot tell me what to do, Winston. I don't care if you hold on to your money. I won't be treated like a slave." Erma's pointed chin thrust forward like a bulldog's.

Other women chorused their support, and the men bellowed in opposition.

Gabby's head began to pound. This wasn't going as she'd envisioned, and if she didn't think of something soon, the whole street would erupt into a free-for-all between the sexes.

"You put that broom down and go on home, Cara," Louie ordered, futilely trying to regain some control over his wife.

"I won't leave until you give me some money," the woman argued.

She raised her broom once more and brought it down with a vigorous swing, not caring that Gabby stood between her and her husband.

The straw bristles raked across Gabby's cheek, bringing involuntary tears to her eyes.

Ty grabbed the handle and jerked it from Mrs. Adams's tight grasp.

"All right, that's enough," he shouted, his forceful voice rising above the din. Mrs. Adams tried to snatch the broom back, but Ty easily sidestepped her. "I said, that's enough!"

The arguing quieted and everyone's attention fell on Ty.

"Let's break this up, and everybody go on their way," he called out. "You shouldn't be bringing your personal business to the streets of Sawtooth. You folks need to take care of your private squabbles in your own homes, not out here where everyone can see and hear."

Grumbling greeted his words.

With a palm pressed to her stinging cheek, Gabby looked at the hostile expressions of the surrounding crowd. Ty had been right. All she was going to do with her bright idea was make enemies of the women and earn the men's anger for having made such a foolish suggestion. She had truly believed her improvised tactic would work. She knew better now.

"Can I have your attention, please?" Gabby shouted.

The crowd paused to look at her, the women's faces sullen, the men's angry.

She swallowed. "I seem to have made a mistake." Gabby could feel Ty's gaze upon her, but she refused to look at his smug, I-told-you-so expression. "I thought that if the men withheld money from their wives, you women would come around to our side. But I judged the women unfairly. I thought your votes could be bought, and I apologize for my foolish supposition. As of right now, I'm calling a truce to this battle. Everyone deserves the right to vote on their own, and I had no right trying to sway the votes my way in such an underhanded manner."

Every pair of eyes remained fixed on her. Some were sympathetic, but most, including the men's, were antagonistic. Gabby swallowed back tears of frustration and helplessness. Due to her bungling, Ty's chance of winning the election had increased dramatically. And that meant she was one step closer to losing her home.

She squared her shoulders and raised her chin so no one would see her despair—just as she'd done numerous times when she and her uncle had been banished from a town. "I'm sorry," she said simply, and turned away.

Deafening silence followed her across the street to the Emporium. Inside, she went behind the bar and pumped some water into a basin, then saturated a cloth with the cool water. She held the damp material against her burning cheek.

Closing her eyes, she tried to block out the humiliation of her moral defeat. She had been so certain the strategy would work. The married men Gabby had known bragged about their dominance over their cowed spouses and had cheated on them without remorse. Yet the women of Sawtooth had rebelled. Maybe marriages weren't as one-sided as Gabby had believed.

"Are you all right?"

With a start, she opened her eyes to find Ty standing beside her, looking at her with something akin to concern. His closeness sent a bevy of butterflies flapping crazily in her stomach.

"Fine," she answered. "Did you come over to gloat?"

He pushed his hat back off his forehead with his forefinger and a recalcitrant curl spilled across his brow, giving him a younger, more carefree appearance.

"I came over to make sure you were all right."

Already filled with self-reproach, Gabby felt lower than a caterpillar's belly. "I'm sorry. It's just that this election means so much to me."

"And it doesn't to me?"

"At least you'll still have your home and business if you lose." Uncharacteristic bitterness crept into Gabby's voice.

Ty's expression darkened. "Maybe."

She recalled what Joe had said about Ty not feeling like he had a choice under Gatewood's pressure to run for mayor. "If you really didn't want to run for mayor, why didn't you just tell Gatewood that?" she asked.

"Nobody tells Vernon no," Ty said wryly.

"I have," Gabby said firmly. "And he's not the man everybody in this town thinks he is."

"You *would* say that," Ty defended. "He wants the saloons gone, too."

Gabby had to tread carefully. She didn't know if Ty actually believed Gatewood was a saint, or if he was only protecting himself. Or was Ty aware of Gatewood's true colors, yet remaining his partner despite that? "I wonder if it's for the same reasons you do," she said softly.

Ty drew the damp cloth from her cheek, and his fingers brushed her skin. A tingle of awareness shot through Gabby, and her heart jumped into her throat. Her gaze latched on to his lips, and she was both excited and fearful that he might kiss her again.

"Louie's wife got you better than she got him," he commented.

"Maybe I deserved it more than Louie did. After all, it was my stupid idea," she said wryly.

"We've all made a bad decision or two. There's

no reason to beat yourself up over it. You learn from it and move on."

He cupped her cheek in his callused palm, surprising Gabby with his gentleness. There was no hint of the savage hunger she'd seen the night he'd kissed her, but this tenderness was a more powerful aphrodisiac. The warmth of his skin and the scent of him—wool and horses and his own unique masculinity—sent her senses whirling. His thumb swept across her cheekbone, tightening the coil of delicious tension in her stomach.

"It's all red," Ty said.

Gabby thought she heard a slight tremble in his voice, but one look at his cool expression dispelled her fanciful notion. It was probably her own uneven breathing that made her imagine he'd felt something, too.

"I think maybe next time you should stay out of the middle of marital spats," he added.

Gabby concentrated on his words instead of the dizzying effect of his gentle caress. Her breathing grew ragged, as if she'd dashed up a mountain and stood at the edge of its precipice.

"I won't try that again," Gabby said, hoping her voice didn't come out as husky as she thought it did.

"I hope not. I'd hate to have to save you from Big Louie's wife again." Humor twinkled in his eyes.

He was devastatingly handsome, with a mischievous sparkle in his blue eyes. Shaking, she lifted her hand to his, intending to remove it from her cheek. Instead, her fingers curled around his work-roughened hand and refused to budge.

For a long moment they remained motionless,

and Gabby's heart pounded against her breast. If their first kiss had been a mistake, she knew with certainty the second would be even more wrong. But God forgive her, she didn't care.

Ty drew his hand away from her cheek and out of her grasp.

"I have to get back to my office," he said.

Gabby shook herself. "Of course."

She watched as Ty turned and strode out of the Emporium for the second time that day. But this time, he nearly took her heart with him.

His blood roaring in his ears, Ty tried to escape the spell Gabby had woven over him. Back on the street, he paused to let the crisp autumn air cool his overheated blood.

What had come over him? When he'd cupped her face, he'd had an overpowering urge to kiss her gently, to taste her once more. He wanted to bury his fingers in her long blond hair and see passion light her eyes with gold fire. Never before had he experienced such a powerful reaction to a woman. What was it about Gabby that made him forget he was an engaged man? Forget that she was a gambling hall owner? Forget that they were enemies?

Guilt filled him. He'd been unfaithful to Eleanor once; his resolve couldn't weaken again. She was the woman he was going to marry, not voluptuous Gabby with eyes the color of sunlit honey. Yet compared to Gabby's vibrancy and spirit, Eleanor seemed a pale shadow.

Maybe it would be better if he called the wedding off until he was more certain she was the woman he wanted to spend the rest of his life with. Eleanor *was* a pillar of respectability, the type of woman Ty had mapped his life around marrying. Was he willing to give up Eleanor because of his confusion over Gabby? Yet it wouldn't be fair to marry Eleanor if he was so fickle that a woman like Gabby could stir his lust. After he won the election and Gabby left town, maybe then he could give Eleanor the attention she deserved.

The following Sunday was the annual Harvest Picnic. He'd buy Eleanor's picnic basket at the church auction like he always did, then he would take her to a quiet, secluded spot to explain why he wanted to postpone the wedding. He would tell her that he would have too much to do, being the new mayor as well as ensuring that the A-B's expansion went smoothly.

As if a cumbersome weight had been lifted from his shoulders, he strode down the street, his steps lighter than they'd been for some time.

Chapter 12

Gabby glanced up from the green-felt-covered table where she was dealing cards and saw Rose return to the Emporium. The dark-haired woman caught her eye and sent her a tiny nod.

Gabby turned to the four poker players surrounding her. "If you'll excuse me a moment, I have to speak to Rose about an urgent matter."

The men nodded in acknowledgment and she hurried over to her friend. "Well, did you find out what kind of basket Eleanor Gatewood is going to have?" Gabby asked in an excited whisper.

Rose opened a brown sack and lifted out a large picnic basket overly decorated with fussy pink and white ribbons. "It looks exactly like this."

Gabby wrinkled her nose at the nauseatingly cute creation, then glanced up in alarm. "You shouldn't have brought it here. What if she misses it?"

Rose giggled. "Don't worry. This isn't hers; it's yours. I talked to the Gatewoods' cook myself. She was so proud of the basket, you would've thought it was hers instead of Eleanor's. She showed it to me, so I know for certain it looks just like this thing." Rose's tone suggested she shared Gabby's distaste for the frilly basket.

Relieved, Gabby rubbed her palms together. "Good. Now all I need to do is fill it up and I'll be ready to attend my first Harvest Picnic tomorrow."

Rose slipped the basket back into the bag. "I don't understand what you have in mind, Gabby. I thought you were going to come up with another plan to get more votes."

"This *is* my plan."

"I hope it works better than your last one," Rose said dourly.

"How was I to know that the women wouldn't listen to their men?" Gabby asked defensively.

"If you paid more attention to what goes on between a man and a woman, you would've known." Rose paused and smiled slyly. "I heard Ty Ashburn rescued you from Louie's wife and her broom."

Gabby didn't want to remember Ty's assistance, or his concern when he'd come to the Emporium to check on her. Dealing with Ty's somber aloofness was easy compared to the confusing mix of emotions his touch evoked.

"My plan is to put Eleanor's basket behind some others, and place mine in the front so Ashburn will think he's bidding on hers."

"Then what are you going to do?" Rose asked.

"Once Ty buys mine, he and I will spend the afternoon together in some secluded picnic spot; then I just let the town biddies do my work for me."

"You really think that's going to put a dent in his shiny armor?"

"I don't know," Gabby said ruefully as guilt

twinged her conscience. "But if it doesn't, maybe I can change his mind about closing us down. Besides, after what happened a couple days ago, I had to come up with something."

Rose nodded. "That Women's Temperance League is a real public nuisance."

The sign-carrying ladies had paraded around town most of the day, calling down the wrath of God upon anyone who dared to enter an establishment that served the "devil's brew," including the Emporium. "If Ty hadn't joined them, I probably wouldn't be doing this," Gabby said, her dander rising. "But when he started stumping in front of *my* place with all those women surrounding him, I had to come up with some way to lure votes away from him."

"I guess we'll find out if your plan will work," Rose said dubiously.

"You're going with me, aren't you?"

Rose's mouth gaped. "Me? Go to a church picnic? Are you out of your mind?"

"No, I'm perfectly serious. Tell Joe which basket is yours, and he'll buy it. Then you can spend the afternoon with him. Didn't you say you wanted to become more respectable?"

Rose leaned closer to Gabby. "I didn't mean around here. Everybody knows me."

Gabby stared at her friend. "Are you afraid to try?"

"I'm not afraid of anything," Rose retorted, and shuffled her feet. "I just don't want to embarrass Joe."

"At the debate last week, Joe was by your side the whole time and he didn't seem shy about it."

"That was different. You're talking about a church picnic, for God's sake!"

Gabby chuckled. "That's right, the picnic is for God's sake. Come with me, Rose. We'll show the fine folks of Sawtooth just how respectable we can be."

"I don't know—"

"You're coming with me, and that's that," Gabby exclaimed. She glanced over at the poker players she'd abandoned. "I have to get back to work. After we close tonight, we'll get your basket decorated, then fill both of them with food. Maybe you could even bake some goodies."

"All right, but don't say I didn't warn you."

Gabby gave her friend's arm a quick squeeze. "Don't forget to tell Joe."

She laughed at Rose's reluctant expression, then hurried back to the gaming table. She imagined Ty's look when he realized he'd bought her picnic basket and not Miss Gatewood's, but instead of elation, Gabby felt trepidation. His respectability was important to him, and it was that very respectability she was planning to attack. She'd come to like Ty Ashburn in spite of his opinionated judgments, and she had no desire to hurt him.

Gabby had wracked her brain to come up with an alternative to gain votes, but with the election looming closer, she didn't have much choice. If she wanted to save her home and business, she had to try anything, no matter how desperate. She hoped, in time, Ty would be able to understand, if not forgive her.

Sunday dawned clear and cool, but the sun promised to warm the air as the day progressed, making it a perfect day for a fall picnic.

"Are you ready yet?" Gabby hollered up the stairs.

"I'm coming," Rose shouted down.

Gabby glanced up as her friend descended the stairs. Rose wore a wool wine-colored short jacket with a braided vest beneath it. The ankle-length matching skirt had a bustle, giving her slim figure a more fashionable shape. Her black hair had been pulled back into a loose chignon, and a velvet bonnet the same color as her outfit was perched atop her head.

"You look beautiful. And very respectable," Gabby complimented sincerely. She smiled impishly. "Joe's going to fall all over himself when he sees you."

Rose stopped at the bottom of the stairs next to Gabby, her expression doubtful. "Do you really think so?"

Gabby patted her friend's hand. "I *know* so."

Rose took a deep breath and looked at Gabby, her sauciness returning. "You look pretty good yourself, Miss Gabby. If I didn't know better, I'd say you were trying to impress a man."

Gabby smoothed her straight skirt, then tugged the taffeta-lined jacket down over her small waist. With her natural hourglass shape, she didn't need a bustle to fill out her figure. Although her old bonnet didn't match her sapphire-blue suit, she'd worn it anyway. Wearing the hat always made her feel as if her mother was beside her, and today she needed the moral support more than ever.

"Nobody's going to notice me with you there."

"I'll bet Ty Ashburn notices you," Rose said with a laugh. "Fact is, I think he notices you more than an engaged man should notice another woman."

Did Rose know? How could she? Gabby had told no one. Instead, she'd relived Ty's kiss at night as she lay in her bed, and imagined their bodies pressed tightly together, but this time there was no clothing between them. She would remain awake long into the early hours of morning as her body craved relief for the restlessness the images brought her.

"Do you think I'm doing the right thing?" Gabby asked anxiously.

"Having second thoughts?"

Gabby nodded miserably. "I don't want to hurt him, only defeat him in the election."

"Don't you worry about Mr. Ashburn. I have a feeling he can take care of himself."

"I suppose so, but I wish I didn't feel so darned guilty doing this."

"All's fair in love and war, and this election definitely qualifies as a war." Rose hooked her arm through Gabby's. "Shall we make our debut in Sawtooth's highbrow society?"

"Do you think they're ready for us?"

"They'll never be ready for us, honey," Rose drawled.

Laughing, Gabby and Rose picked up their picnic baskets and sashayed out of the Emporium. Since most of the businesses were closed, the street was deserted, except for the far end of town where the whitewashed church stood.

Gabby and Rose climbed the steps into the steepled building and found a crowd of people had already gathered. Conversations stumbled to a halt, but Gabby refused to be intimidated by the stares they attracted. Rose tightened her hold on Gabby's arm, her face unusually pale.

"You're just as good as they are," Gabby whispered to Rose. "Their narrow-mindedness is their problem, not yours."

Folks began to speak again in hushed voices.

"Let's put our baskets with the others," Gabby said. "You're going to have to switch mine and Eleanor's while I keep everybody's attention on me."

Rose nodded, and they walked to the front of the church where Alma Tusk, the reverend's wife, stood like a sentinel guarding the picnic baskets. Although she appeared stern, Gabby knew she was a generous soul. It was that gentle giving that had joined the two very different women in their crusade to help the orphans.

"Good morning, Mrs. Tusk," Gabby greeted.

The plain woman regarded her a moment, then smiled nervously in return. "Good morning, Miss Wade. Who's your friend?"

"Mrs. Tusk, this is Miss Rose James," Gabby introduced.

"It's nice to meet you, Miss James. I see you brought picnic baskets."

"That's right. Rose, could you put our baskets on the table while I speak with Mrs. Tusk?" Gabby asked.

"Sure," Rose replied. She took Gabby's basket and moved around the table.

Gabby drew Alma Tusk's attention, and, she hoped, the curious onlookers' gazes, too. "I wanted to talk to you about the orphanage. With the addition of three more orphans this past summer, the home is getting too crowded."

"I know. But there aren't any funds to buy a new house for the poor dears," Alma said sympathetically.

"Maybe we could expand the home, add a few more rooms."

"If we could just get some of these so-called Christians to loosen their purse strings..." Alma sighed. "Maybe I can convince the reverend to bring it up at next week's service."

Although Gabby was accustomed to Alma's formal name for her husband, it still brought a flash of amusement. "Even if he does talk about it, I wonder how many folks will make a contribution. It seems they like to close their eyes and figure if they can't see the orphans, they don't exist. I just can't understand why people feel that way."

"They don't like to be reminded of their own mortality," Alma said. "And they don't like to part with their money. Mrs. Edwards said you gave even a larger contribution than usual this month."

"I'm not sure how much longer I'll be in Sawtooth." Gabby shrugged with a nonchalance she didn't feel.

"I know. Reverend Tusk has informed me I will vote for Mr. Ashburn."

"Will you?"

Mrs. Tusk shook her head. "No. He may think he can order me about, but what he doesn't know won't hurt him."

Gabby smiled sheepishly.

The reverend's wife glanced about anxiously. "Why did you come here?"

"If I only have a short time left in Sawtooth, I wanted to leave a good impression," Gabby fibbed, crossing her fingers behind her back. "And I thought it might help my chance at winning the election."

"It could also harm your chances."

"I don't have much to lose."

"Mrs. Tusk, come here," the reverend called out. She flashed Gabby an apologetic look and scurried to follow her husband's bidding.

Rose sidled over to Gabby. "Maybe you shouldn't have spoken to her in front of everyone like that. You could get her in trouble."

"Mrs. Tusk can take care of herself," Gabby reassured her. "She's had to, with a husband like the reverend. Did you get the baskets switched?"

Rose nodded and grinned victoriously. "Eleanor Gatewood's basket is now hidden behind a bunch of others and yours is sitting right in front where hers was."

"Good," Gabby said, trying to inject some enthusiasm into her voice. "Now we just have to hope Ty Ashburn shows up."

As if waiting for his cue, Ty entered the church, with Joe behind him. Gabby's admiring gaze swept across the black suit and white shirt that emphasized the breadth of Ty's shoulders. A fluttery sensation started in her chest and spread to her stomach. She forced herself to look at Joe, to ignore the overpowering magnetism of Ty Ashburn.

Joe immediately spied Rose and his eyes widened in pleasure. Without glancing at anyone else, he approached Rose and took her hands in his.

"I almost didn't recognize you," he said, his voice low and intimate. "You look downright beautiful."

"You mean I usually don't?" Rose asked, a teasing smile tempering her words.

Feeling like an eavesdropper, Gabby took a few steps away from the couple. She glanced around the room, trying not to look at Ty, but her eyes refused to follow her bidding. Like a morning glory seeking the sun, Gabby met Ty's hooded gaze. Smoldering heat curled between them, and for a moment Gabby wished he would come to her as freely as Joe had gone to Rose.

Eleanor's appearance at Ty's side doused Gabby's ardor like a bucket of ice. She swallowed back unexpected jealousy as Eleanor leaned close to him and Ty kissed her cheek. For the first time in her life, she wanted a man, but that man was destined to marry another woman.

She moved back to stand beside Rose and Joe.

"Hello, Joe," Gabby greeted him, forcing cheer into her voice. "So what do you think of Rose's new clothes?"

Joe ran a hand through his curly red hair. "They look mighty fine." He smiled at Gabby and said gallantly, "And you're looking mighty good yourself, Miss Gabby."

"Thank you, though we both know I can't hold a candle next to Rose." She glanced down at their twined hands, then back at Joe. "Do you know which basket is Rose's?"

He nodded. "I just hope I brought enough to get the bid."

"Don't worry. I doubt any other man will want it," Rose said.

Gabby glanced up to see Ty and Miss Gatewood walk to the front table. Eleanor picked up the basket she thought was hers, and Ty nodded.

Gabby glanced at Rose, who sent her a wink. It wouldn't be long before their deception was found out. Second thoughts deluged her. It wasn't too late to put Eleanor's basket back in its original place. She wasn't even sure her scheme would work—the plan could easily backfire, leaving her with less support than she had.

She moved toward the front of the church, intent on putting a stop to her ill-conceived plan, but the Reverend Tusk beat her to the table and began the auction. Gabby's time had run out. She had no choice but to follow through and hope for the best.

Rose's basket was the fourth one to come up, and three men besides Joe jumped into a bidding war. Joe ended up getting it at the amazingly high bid of six dollars and forty-three cents.

He walked up to pay Alma Tusk and grabbed Rose's basket. Then he wrapped an arm around Rose's waist and steered her out of the church.

Sitting alone, Gabby tried not to fidget in her seat. Out of the corner of her eye, she caught Ty studying her curiously. She could imagine his wrath when he discovered the switch, not to mention the anger of Eleanor Gatewood and her hypocritical father.

Two more baskets were auctioned off, then the reverend reached for her pink-and-white-ribboned one. Gabby's heart tripped into her throat and her stomach quivered. She rested her hands in her lap, her fingers clenched.

"Can I get the first bid for this beautiful basket?" Reverend Tusk began.

"One dollar," Ty called out.

Eleanor's lips thinned, and Gabby knew she was angry that Ty had started the bid so low.

"Two dollars," Vernon Gatewood countered.

Gabby stiffened. What if old man Gatewood got

her basket? She didn't care what the rules were; he'd eat alone.

"Three dollars," Ty said.

"Five dollars," Gatewood upped the bid.

"Five dollars and twenty five cents."

"Six dollars."

Although Ty appeared outwardly calm, Gabby noticed the white lines about his mouth.

"Seven dollars," Ty stated. "And that's my final bid."

Gatewood flashed his daughter a victorious smile.

"Going once, going twice." The reverend paused. "Sold for seven dollars to Tyler Ashburn."

Ty stood and walked up to claim his basket. Gabby consciously calmed herself as he strode past her to collect the woman who he thought owned the basket.

She'd come this far; she had to take it to the end. She stood.

"I think that's my basket," she stated, proud that her voice didn't falter.

Ty halted in his tracks, his expression a mixture of shock and disbelief.

"That is *my* picnic basket," Eleanor said sharply.

"Are you sure?" Gabby asked with a frown. "I decorated mine with pink and white bows just like that."

The folks remaining in the church watched the exchange in a silence so loud Gabby thought her eardrums would burst.

"There's one way to know for certain," Reverend Tusk said. "What's inside, Mr. Ashburn?"

Ty remained motionless, his gaze tripping between Gabby and his fiancée. Slowly, he opened one side of the picnic basket.

Eleanor's eyes widened. "I didn't put wine in mine." She glared at Gabby. "You did this on purpose. You knew Tyler would bid on my basket, and you wanted to make a fool of me."

Gabby shook her head and replied honestly, "That wasn't my intention."

Vernon Gatewood approached Gabby, and the hatred in his eyes chilled her. She held her ground, refusing to give in to the instinct to run and escape.

"My daughter will not be made a fool by you or anyone else, Miss Wade." Gatewood said her name like it was poison. "What did you do with her basket?"

"Is this it, Mr. Gatewood?" Alma Tusk asked, holding up a basket identical to the one Ty had in his hands. "It was behind some others."

Eleanor pointed to Gabby's basket. "I thought that was mine," she whined. "Can't Tyler get mine in exchange?"

"I'm sorry, Miss Gatewood, but rules are rules," Alma said, shaking her head in sympathy. "Mr. Ashburn bought Miss Wade's basket, and they'll have to share it."

Gabby's conscience made another effort to set things right, and she said, "Since Mr. Ashburn was under the mistaken assumption that this basket was his fiancée's, maybe an exception could be made."

"I'm sorry," the reverend said as he looked at Vernon Gatewood, "but Mrs. Tusk is correct. Besides, the baskets' owners are supposed to be a secret and if, after buying one and learning who the owner is, the man turns it down, he would be insulting the woman." He glanced at Gabby, and his expression soured. "No matter who the woman is."

Gabby turned her attention to Ty, who'd remained silent throughout the entire exchange. She could tell he was trying to decide whether to insult her or not.

Finally, he smiled tightly. "A case of mistaken identity isn't reason enough to insult a lady. Since this is Miss Gabby's basket, I'll be spending the afternoon with her."

Eleanor's cheeks bloomed with red splotches, and her father looked like he was trying to decide who to strangle first, Ty or Gabby.

"I'll call on you later, Eleanor," Ty said.

With her heart thumping against her ribs, Gabby walked over to Ty and placed her hand through the crook of his arm. His muscles felt like corded wood, which did nothing to ease Gabby's anxiety.

"Shall we?" she asked with a calmness that belied her turbulent nerves.

Ty's smile appeared brittle, and he spoke to the crowd. "It looks like the two mayoral candidates will be discussing the issues over lunch. If anyone has any concerns, don't hesitate to interrupt our meal. Isn't that right, Miss Gabby?"

Gabby knew her own smile was as fake as Ty's. "That's right, Mr. Ashburn. We're always happy to talk to our constituents."

She forced herself to walk slowly and ignore the gazes that followed them out the church door. She'd given Ty a way out of the supposed basket mix-up, but he'd behaved like a gentleman.

She didn't know whether to be thankful or upset. He should have taken his fiancée. Gabby had no right getting between them for her own selfish reasons, and hurting them in the process. It wasn't like her to be self-serving, but the thought of losing her home had frightened her more than she cared to admit, even to herself.

And in spite of her clamoring conscience, Gabby couldn't deny the rush of excitement at the prospect of spending time alone with Ty.

Chapter 13

Ty concentrated on each step rather than the shocked and disbelieving congregation, especially Eleanor and Vernon Gatewood, who watched him escort Miss Gabby Wade from the church.

Gabby tugged on his arm and he stopped, suddenly aware they were outside, standing in the middle of the street. "I know a pretty little place where we can have our picnic," she said, then added, "unless you want to change your mind. I won't be insulted if you'd rather escort Miss Gatewood. In fact, I think you should take her. After all, she is your intended."

If Gabby had switched the baskets on purpose, then why would she suddenly insist he take Eleanor?

He gazed down into her guileless eyes and saw only sincerity. It would be easy to take her suggestion, but he'd already made his decision. The picnic would give him time to observe his adversary, and the chance to spend an afternoon with the contradictory Gabby Wade was too tempting to resist.

"I bought *your* basket and I intend to honor my

side of the agreement. Unless you're trying to get out of it?" Ty asked.

Gabby shook her head, her ridiculous stuffed sparrows nearly flying off her dilapidated hat. "No, that's all right. I just thought . . ."

"Where is this picnic spot?" he asked.

She smiled and led him down a hard-packed dirt path. Her skirts brushed his leg and her rosewater scent washed across him, teasing him with the illusion of innocence.

He was going to be alone with Gabby for an afternoon picnic.

He reined in his momentary panic—he'd survived all these years without a woman clouding his judgment; he could overcome this temporary insanity.

"Here it is," she announced a few moments later.

Ty shook his thoughts aside and glanced around. They'd stopped on a small flat rise above a narrow brook that babbled quietly under the sun's warming rays. An ancient evergreen towered above them, its branches heavy with pinecones.

"Pretty, isn't it?" she asked in an awe-filled voice.

"How'd you find this place?" Ty asked roughly to hide his own appreciation of its quiet beauty.

She met his gaze with a hint of tolerant humor. "I haven't spent all my life in places like the Emporium. When I was a child I found places like this where I could lie down and daydream and wonder what I'd be when I grew up." She paused a moment, her eyes twinkling. "This might shock you, Mr. Ashburn, but I never imagined myself as a gambling hall owner."

Ty pictured her as a young girl with blond pigtails and sun-darkened freckles lying on the ground and staring up at the sky. The image was amazingly easy to conjure. "Most girls dream about getting married and having a home and children of their own."

"Not me. I wanted to be a pirate and sail the high seas," she confessed. "My uncle used to tell me stories about faraway places, and I figured if I was a pirate, I could sail to all those wonderful islands and see all the strange sights."

Ty should have been surprised, but he wasn't. He'd long since come to the conclusion that Gabby was unlike any other woman he'd ever met.

She glanced around sheepishly. "I forgot to bring a blanket. I hope you don't mind sitting on the ground."

"That's fine." He removed his suit coat, then spread it on the ground. "You can sit on this," he said gallantly.

"Thank you."

She lowered herself to his jacket, her legs tucked beneath her, and Ty could see a hint of her delicate ankles. He looked away and sat on the brown grass a few feet away from temptation.

"I promise I won't bite," she said, as if reading his thoughts.

"We're *not* a courting couple enjoying a fall picnic," Ty stated, although he wasn't certain if it was to remind himself or Gabby. "We're not even friends—we're political opponents."

"I thought we could forget that for a few hours and just be normal people."

She raised her arms to remove her hat. Ty's unruly gaze settled on her breasts, which strained against her jacket, threatening to pop the buttons.

The blood pooled in his groin, and his arousal pressed against his already snug trousers.

As his third official act as mayor, he'd make it a misdemeanor for Gabby to raise her arms in public. With a sidelong glance at her body's profile, he decided a felony would be more appropriate.

Reluctantly, he turned his attention to a gray jay that landed on a branch above them.

"A camp robber," Gabby said.

He glanced at her and saw her also looking at the bird. "Camp robber?"

She nodded and a gentle smile curved her lips upward. "My uncle called them that because they would steal anything they could carry. He swore that one actually stole a man's pocketwatch he'd left lying on a stump."

"I think your uncle liked to stretch the truth."

"I won't argue that, but he was the smartest man I've ever known." She opened the picnic basket. "Could you open the wine while I get the food out? You do drink wine, don't you?"

"I never said I was a teetotaler. I just don't drink in public."

She handed him the wine bottle, her fingers grazing his, and the fleeting touch jolted him.

"I won't tell the Temperance League," Gabby began with a conspiratorial grin, "if you promise to keep the ladies and your politicking away from the Emporium."

"It's a deal," Ty agreed, then added wryly, "it wasn't my idea to stand with them in front of your place. To be perfectly honest, I felt like a hypocrite."

"Then why did you do it?"

He shrugged as he poured a glass of wine for

each of them. "Vernon thought it would help my campaign."

Gabby handed him a plate heaped with chicken, biscuits, a couple of hard-boiled eggs, and a few pickles. "Here you are."

He took it from her, careful not to touch her fingertips again. "Thanks."

Ty took a bite out of a chicken leg and realized how hungry he was. He hadn't eaten anything since five o'clock that morning, when he'd had a bowl of oatmeal and a couple cups of coffee.

As he devoured his meal, he kept his gaze on Gabby. She ate heartily, without pretension, not taking dainty bites like Eleanor did. She seemed to savor food like she did life—with eager enthusiasm and little regard for convention.

Ty set his empty plate on the ground and wiped his hands on a napkin.

"I guess I should've made more," Gabby said with an apologetic look. "It's been a long time since I've cooked for a man. My uncle died about a year and a half ago."

"What about your parents?" he asked.

"They were killed in a wagon accident when I was seven years old," Gabby replied matter-of-factly. "After that, my uncle looked out for me."

So she was an orphan, like the children at the home. No wonder she felt obliged to help them. Ty gazed at the shallow brook, uncertain how to respond.

"Are your parents still alive?" Gabby asked.

He kept his eyes on the slowly moving stream. "No."

Ty could sense Gabby's frustration with his short

answer, but he wasn't about to expose his vulnerable past.

"Do you have any brothers or sisters?" Gabby pressed.

"A brother," he responded without thinking, then cursed inwardly for revealing that much.

"Where is he?"

"I don't know and I don't care."

Gabby studied him silently, but didn't ask any more prying questions.

"Would you like some dessert now?" she asked.

He nodded. "Sure."

Gabby lifted a round cake and a pie from the basket and sliced each one into generous pieces, unlike the slivers the Gatewoods usually served. Her slender hands drew Ty's reluctantly admiring gaze as they moved with fluid grace. He wondered if dealing cards had given her such smooth, sensual motions.

She handed him his dish with a huge piece of cake and a fourth of the pie on it. He forked some of the cake into his mouth and the sweet chocolate melted across his tongue.

"It's good," he said with more than a little surprise.

"Rose made it. I didn't even know she knew how to bake until a few weeks ago. Her parents owned a bakery back East."

"How'd she end up here doing what she's doing?"

Gabby smiled ruefully. "What she does is serve drinks."

"How long have she and Joe been seeing each other?" Ty asked curiously, yet at the same time hesitant to hear the answer.

Gabby frowned and took a sip of her wine. "They've been friends for a long time. I think he started courting her a couple months ago."

Disbelief filled Ty. "He can't be serious—a sporting gal never gives the life up completely."

Gabby's lips thinned in irritation. "That's not true with Rose. You don't know what happened to her."

"I have a pretty good idea."

"No, you don't!" Her cheeks bloomed with angry color. "You can't imagine how Rose was when I found her in that back alley." Gabby shivered and took a deep breath. "One of her 'customers' liked to hurt women. She almost died that night, and all because of a man's lust!"

Ty had heard of men who got their pleasure from hurting women, and even though Rose was a prostitute, she hadn't deserved that kind of punishment.

No woman deserved that kind of treatment.

He wasn't proud of it, but on a few occasions he'd used a prostitute to slake his needs. He'd never been abusive, but he'd never considered her feelings, either.

The fact was, he hadn't wanted to learn about them. Gabby had the irritating ability, however, to make him open his eyes.

"Not all men are like that," he said lamely.

"Maybe not, but all of them have the ability to hurt a woman if they want, and the woman has no say in the matter. If Rose had wanted to press charges against the man who beat her, her case would've been laughed out of court. She was a whore, so whatever a man did to her was okay as long as he paid up." Gabby's voice vibrated with fury. "I won't have any of my girls sell themselves. I could be making more money if I had rooms set up upstairs like most of the other places, but I won't do it."

Her heartfelt words unsettled Ty, and he suddenly realized he never had heard about any prostitutes working the upstairs rooms at the Emporium. If that was true, then perhaps he was wrong about other things concerning Gabby.

He watched her uncurl her legs from beneath her and draw her knees to her chest. She swept her skirts about her legs modestly, then wrapped her arms about her drawn-up knees and rested her chin on her forearms. She appeared so innocent that for a moment, he almost forgot she owned a gambling hall.

"How about you?" he asked in a low voice. "Have you ever had to sell yourself?"

She met his gaze squarely. "No."

Alone in the peaceful solitude of the woods, Ty wanted to believe her. When she'd first come to Sawtooth and opened her Emporium, he'd assumed she had bought the establishment with money she'd made on her back. He hadn't questioned that assumption until now.

"You don't know whether to believe me or not, do you?" Gabby asked.

He hid his uneasiness behind a nonchalant shrug. "It doesn't matter what I believe. It's you who has to live with yourself."

"The same holds true for you, Mr. Ashburn."

She scrutinized him with a steady, clear gaze, and Ty had the impression she saw straight to his soul. He looked away, troubled by the perception.

"Are you and Joe on speaking terms yet?" Gabby asked a few moments later.

"Only at work when we have to talk," Ty admitted, relieved to have the subject changed. He rubbed his cheek wryly. "He has a helluva right hook."

"He was right, you know. You had no call sticking your nose in their affairs," she said softly. "I know, because I tried it with Rose."

"Did she punch you, too?"

Gabby laughed, a sweet, unpretentious sound that slipped past Ty's defenses. "No, but she did tell me that she cares a lot for Joe. In fact, I would be willing to bet she loves him."

Ty swallowed the rest of his wine, along with the words of denial that sprang to his lips. "You think I should apologize to Joe?"

"And Rose."

He remained silent. Apologizing to Joe was one thing; apologizing to Rose was another.

"How long has he worked for you?" Gabby asked.

"When I started up the A-B, I asked him to come work for me. We started out as teamsters together years ago."

"If you don't make things right with him, he's going to leave," Gabby said quietly. She leaned forward and refilled his wine glass.

Her own glass appeared to be nearly full. For a woman whose business was liquor, she didn't seem to imbibe much herself.

"It's actually getting hot out here," Gabby announced. She unbuttoned her jacket and removed it, revealing a white blouse with lace frills adorning the front. He could see her filmy camisole beneath it, and the sight brought unwanted images to mind.

"Are you all right?" Gabby asked in concern.

"What?"

"You look kind of strange," she said. "You aren't coming down with something, are you?"

"Could be," Ty lied.

"Well, it wouldn't surprise me, the way you're always working and never getting enough sleep."

"Who told you that?"

Gabby shrugged. "Rose has seen your office lit up after midnight. You shouldn't work so hard."

"I happen to enjoy owning my own company," he said stiffly.

"That's fine and dandy, but all work and no play makes Jack a dull boy—and believe me, you were boring enough before. Lord help us if you get any duller."

Her twinkling eyes softened her comment, and Ty would have laughed at her audacity if he hadn't felt so offended. He was proud of his steadfastness—he'd worked hard to distance himself from his father's unreliable nature.

"When was the last time you chased frogs?" she suddenly asked.

A long-forgotten memory of himself and his brother catching frogs in the pond near his home emerged from some hidden corner of his mind. He'd been eight; Stephen had been six. They'd fallen into the pond and had gotten a licking from their ma for ruining their Sunday clothes.

"When I was a kid," Ty answered.

Gabby shook her head in sympathy. "Then it's been too long." She untied her shoelaces.

"What're you doing?" Ty demanded.

"Taking off my shoes so I can chase frogs in the creek."

"You can't do that."

She paused and looked up at him quizzically. "Why not?"

Ty searched for a plausible excuse. "It's fall."

"Maybe, but it feels more like summer." Gabby removed her shoes and stood.

"There aren't any frogs this time of year." Ty tried again to keep some semblance of propriety.

"Could you turn around while I take off my stockings?" she asked, ignoring his remark.

Ty growled and rose, then turned to face the brook. He could imagine her sleek calves and naked thighs, and an aching heaviness crept into his loins. If he had any brains, he'd go back to town. But his mind had been usurped by another part of his anatomy, one that had fewer scruples.

"You should take off your boots and socks, too, or they'll get wet," Gabby said.

"I'm not going to play, Miss Gabby," he said with a strained voice.

She moved around to stand in front of him and he spied her bare toes peeking out from under her skirts. He quickly raised his gaze to her sun-flushed face.

"I'm just trying to help you have some fun," she said. "Everyone needs to relax once in a while, and in the year I've lived in Sawtooth, I don't think I've ever seen you allow yourself to have a good time."

She turned away and walked gingerly to the brook. He could see her looking around, searching for the elusive frogs. She squatted down beside the water and animation lit her fair features.

"Ty, come look at this!" she called excitedly.

Startled, he realized she'd called him by his Christian name. He should have been offended, but he liked the way she said it, with a hint of huskiness. He liked it too much.

"What is it?" he hollered back.

"Come look!"

With an exasperated sigh, he joined her and hunkered down. "What?"

"Look at all the minnows," she said with childlike wonder. "I didn't think there'd be this many so late in the year. What kind do you think they are? Trout? Pike? Maybe bass?"

He shook his head, bewildered by her undisguised excitement over something as commonplace as minnows. "Not bass. They live in lakes."

She turned to gaze at him, her eyes wide. "I didn't know that. Have you ever fished for bass?"

Her enthusiasm seemed contagious and Ty found himself smiling at his memories. "A few times with my brother when we were kids."

"Do you miss him?" Her gently inquiring voice held him captive.

"Sometimes."

The breeze whisked a strand of blond hair across her brow, and without thinking, he reached forward to sweep it behind her ear. His fingers lingered on the cornsilk texture.

"I used to wish I had a brother or sister so I wouldn't be all alone," Gabby said in a voice with more breath than sound. "Where's your brother?"

He shrugged, rolling the blond strand between his callused fingertips. "I don't know. I haven't heard from him in nearly fifteen years."

"Have you looked for him?"

He shook his head. "We had an argument right before he left home."

"About what?"

Ty felt himself floundering in her topaz eyes, in the empathy he glimpsed. He released her silky hair, breaking the invisible bond. Rising to his full height so he towered over her, he took control of his chaotic thoughts. "That's none of your concern."

Stephen had betrayed him by choosing the life of a gambler. Wouldn't she just love to know his own brother had taken up the very profession that Ty opposed so adamantly?

Gabby ached to help him purge the bitterness eating at him. She'd never known a man so stubborn, so determined to keep himself apart from everyone else. Helplessness seethed inside her, and she wanted to force him to tell her about his brother. She wanted to know why they hadn't spoken to each other in so many years.

A man's past is his own, honey. You'd be no better than a thief if you took it without his consent.

Uncle Soapy's words came back to her as if he whispered them in her ear. She'd asked her uncle about his past, and with sadness in his expression, he'd given her that answer. It wasn't what she'd wanted to hear, but she'd accepted his advice and lived by it.

Maybe, in time, Ty would willingly give up his past. Until then she could do nothing but respect his wishes.

She glanced up and noticed fluffy clouds floating above them. "Have you ever taken the time to watch the clouds drift by?"

He seemed taken aback by her question. "Not lately."

"Then maybe it's time you did."

Gabby could see indecision in his well-honed features, and she was surprised he was considering it.

"Lie back on the grass," she insisted, pressing ahead. Lowering herself to the ground, she leaned back against the gentle upward slope of the creek bank. "Come on, it'll be fun."

She grasped his wrist and tugged him down beside her.

With a loud sigh, Ty lay down, crossing his ankles and stacking his hands beneath his head. "What am I supposed to be looking for?" he asked.

Gabby noted an impatient edge in his voice. "Relax, Mr. Ashburn. This isn't a contest." She pointed out a small cloud that seemed to have appendages. "See that one up there—doesn't it remind you of an elephant?"

He was silent for a long moment. She wondered if he would allow himself to play the game, or deem it purposeless in his world of numbers and neat columns.

Finally, he shifted his attention to the cloud she referred to. "More like a giraffe than an elephant."

Gabby let out the breath she'd been holding, and a bubble of relief filled her. She'd been so certain he would refuse to do anything this frivolous. "What do you mean, a giraffe? There's the trunk and the tail. And look, you can even see its ears."

"That trunk is its neck," Ty retorted.

She turned her head and noticed a slight smile on his lips. Giving her attention back to the sky, she tilted her head. "All right, maybe it could be a giraffe," she admitted.

"How about the dragon?" Ty said, surprising Gabby.

She followed his tapered finger to the cloud he singled out. Sure enough, she could imagine the billowing white cloud as the mythological creature. "It's a fire-breathing one," she said. "And look, there's the damsel in distress."

"What about the knight who has to save her?"

"His cloud hasn't come in yet," Gabby quipped with a grin.

Ty groaned, then rolled onto his side and propped his head on his hand to gaze down at her. "I don't know what to think of you, Gabby."

Gabby shifted to sit cross-legged on the ground, tugged at a grass stem, then stuck one end between her lips. "I'm not so hard to figure out. I just enjoy every new day and live it as if I may die tomorrow." She paused, and asked quietly, "Can you say the same?"

"A month ago I would've said yes," Ty said thoughtfully. "Now I'm not so sure."

His gaze turned skyward once more, and Gabby listened to Ty's deep, velvet-smooth voice as he described another drifting image. She hadn't known what to expect when he'd bought her basket, but it hadn't been this fragile camaraderie.

"I didn't figure you'd be so good at finding animals in the clouds," Gabby commented, turning to look at him.

He smiled, his straight white teeth brilliant against his wind-weathered face and his eyes lit with a teasing twinkle. It made him look devastatingly handsome and at ease—nothing like the man she opposed in the mayoral race. This Ty Ashburn was more dangerous, threatening something even more significant than her home.

"It's been a long time, but I guess it's not something a person forgets," he said. His grin faltered. "Even after twenty-five years."

"Do you miss being a child?" Gabby asked curiously.

"Sometimes," he admitted. "Things were a lot simpler back then."

"Only because you take life too seriously now."

His expression became shuttered and he studied her silently. "I can't be like you, Gabby. I don't see life as a game of chance. To me, making a good living and having the respect of other people is important."

For a moment the curtains lifted and Gabby glimpsed his haunted soul. She shivered with empathy, wondering what had conjured the dark ghosts and wishing she could chase them away.

"It's time we start heading back," he stated abruptly.

Ty helped her up, then released her. As he walked ahead of her up the hill, Gabby felt a sense of loss. For a brief time, she'd gotten Ty to share a little of the man hidden behind his sober mask; the same man she'd seen with the children. Why did he feel he had to keep that person locked away?

A frog suddenly hopped in her path, and she jumped, startled.

Ty spun around. "What is it?"

Gabby grinned sheepishly. "Just a frog." Mischief filled her. "Come on, let's get it."

She spied the green spotted frog a few feet away and hurried toward it. Before she could reach it, it jumped through the grass toward the brook.

"It's headed for the creek. We have to stop it before it makes it into the water," Gabby shouted.

"I'm not going to—"

"Hurry, or it'll get away!"

She saw his lips move in a muttered curse and hid her smile. Ty ran toward the brook, angling between Gabby and the water.

"Where is it?" he hollered.

It hopped past Gabby. "It's coming your way!"

She followed in the frog's wake and saw it stop in the grass. Gabby paused and tiptoed toward it. A few feet away, she lunged downward, intent on trapping it beneath her cupped palms. On her knees, Gabby raised her hands carefully, certain the frog would be under them. Nothing.

"Did you get it?" Ty called.

"No!" She searched the grass around her and caught sight of the creature as it jumped away from her. Scrambling to her feet, she shouted, "There it goes!"

Chapter 14

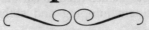

Ty had no idea why he was dashing pell-mell for the creek in an effort to catch a silly frog. He owned a freight company, was a respected member of the Sawtooth community, and here he was behaving like a kid. All because Gabby asked him to do so.

He watched her zigzag toward the water. Her blond hair had fallen out of its chignon and billowed behind her like a rich golden mane. He caught glimpses of her dainty feet and snow-white petticoat as she dashed after the frog. Ty had never known a woman so unconcerned about convention, so childlike in her joy in life's simple pleasures.

In his carefully constructed world there was no such thing as frivolity, yet here he was helping Gabby catch a frog. Just like he and Stephen used to do when they were children.

For a moment he could picture his brother, damp, dark hair plastered against his forehead and dirt smudges on his face. Stephen used to love to chase anything that moved. One hot summer day, he and Stephen had put a few inches of water in their ma's washtub and filled it with frogs and toads. They'd caught a couple garden snakes and added them to the menagerie, which had gone crazy when the snakes tried to eat the frogs. There had been critters jumping and slithering everywhere.

In Stephen's excitement, he tipped over the tub and slipped in the muddy mess. Ty had tried to help him up, but had only succeeded in getting himself as grimy as his little brother. It had been one of their best adventures, until their ma had discovered their shenanigans.

He'd buried the memories of those happy days beneath a blanket of disillusionment and disappointment. How had Gabby gotten under that cover he'd so diligently guarded, making him recall the laughter and innocence before his father had killed himself?

"Here it comes, Ty!"

Gabby's shout startled him out of his musings and he glanced up to see her charging directly toward him. Her attention was focused on the ground, on the frog that kept a foot ahead of her as it hopped toward the stream.

"Gabby, stop!" Ty called frantically.

He raised his hands to catch her before she dashed into the water. Her petite body collided with his, knocking him off balance. He flung out his arms to steady himself, but Gabby's momentum tumbled him backward into the stream.

Ty landed with a loud splash, and Gabby fell on top of him. Her full breasts were crushed against his chest, and despite the cold shock of the water, heat shot through him like a lightning bolt.

Lying in the four-inch-deep creek bed, Ty gazed up at Gabby, whose face was only an angel's sigh away. Her dark pupils nearly filled her golden-brown eyes, and her mouth gaped.

"I did it again, didn't I?" she murmured, making no attempt to liberate herself or him.

Ty's mind blanked, and the impatience he expected didn't materialize. Instead, he saw the humor in Gabby's penchant for disasters. He snorted and Gabby stared down at him as if he'd lost his senses.

"Are you getting a case of the vapors?" she asked in concern. "Should I go get the doctor?"

"Not unless you need him," Ty replied with a grin. "One thing about you, Miss Gabby: life is never boring in your company."

Confusion lit her features for a moment, then was replaced by a rueful smile. "Only when I'm around you."

Her musical laughter met his ears, and her breasts bounced against his chest, creating a sweet agony that worked its way downward. Her thighs framed his rapidly growing erection, and the heavenly friction threatened to undo the last thread of his self-control. He could hardly feel the chilly water with her soft curves scorching his body.

Her parted lips beckoned him to damn his resolution and kiss her. Soaked and bedraggled, she looked more desirable than the most beautiful, respectable woman he could imagine.

"I'm sorry, Ty," she said in between breaths. "I just wanted to catch the frog."

"Looks like he got us instead." Laughter, full and deep, spilled forth like a newfound spring. "I think the frog got the better deal. We'd better get out of here before we come down with pneumonia."

Ty placed his hands around her tiny waist and lifted her off of him. Then he rose out of the water, helping Gabby up beside him. Her soaked dress clung to her enticing curves like a second skin, and he could see her pebbled nipples as clearly as if she wore nothing at all.

Gabby raised wonder-filled eyes. "I've never heard you truly laugh before."

Framing her face in his palms, Ty brushed his thumbs across her flushed cheeks. "That's because I only laugh when I chase frogs and fall in the water with beautiful women."

"And how many times has that happened?" she asked in a thready voice.

"Only once," he whispered.

The distance between them sizzled like the air before a thunderstorm. He stared down into her unblinking, apprehensive eyes.

"What now, Miss Gabby?" he asked, his voice low and intimate. "Is this what you had planned for the afternoon?"

She shook her head.

"I thought you were a risk-taker, a gambler," Ty pressed. "How far will you go to stack the odds in your favor?"

Gabby blinked and her mouth opened, but no words came forth.

"This far?" Ty kissed her forehead. "Or maybe this far?" He pressed his lips to the side of her satiny neck, and she moaned, a primal sound from deep within her.

Ty's breath came out in short quick bursts, and her lyrical sighs sounded like heaven's choir. He was losing his self-control, losing himself in Gabby's irresistible spell. She was like a favorite candy where one taste of sweetness wouldn't suffice. He raised his head and slanted his lips toward hers, intent on recapturing the treasure she offered.

Then he caught a movement out of the corner of his eye and drew back before he completed his possession. At the top of the hill stood Floyd Sanders and his wife, staring down at them. Mrs. Sanders said something to her husband as she pointed down at him and Gabby.

Ty's passion dissolved, and he released Gabby. Stepping back a few feet, he noticed her look of surprised disappointment. He clenched his fingers into fists and pressed them to his sides.

"This isn't what you think," Ty hollered to the middle-aged couple.

"How can it be anything else?" Mrs. Sanders shouted back. "You should be ashamed of yourself, Mr. Ashburn, being an engaged man and all."

The incensed woman grabbed her husband's arm and propelled him out of sight.

Ty glanced at Gabby. She hugged herself against the chilly air, and her expression reminded him of a puppy that had been kicked.

"I'm sorry," he said, frustrated desire and anger with himself making his voice curt.

Without a word, Gabby turned away and hurried up the hill.

Cursing his lack of control, Ty followed her slowly. His wet clothing made the air colder, and he began to shiver.

He found Gabby tugging on her stockings, a strangely erotic sight that renewed his lust. Staring down at her bare foot, he was acutely aware of her tiny, pearllike toenails against the cold-reddened skin.

"At least my shoes and stockings are dry," she commented lamely. "Everything you're wearing is soaked."

He leaned over and picked up his jacket. "Not everything."

Gabby tied her shoes and stood. She glanced down at her limp skirt and dirty, bedraggled blouse, then shook her head. "My uncle always said I was too impulsive." She leaned over to pick up her hat and toyed with the frayed brim.

"I'm sorry," she suddenly blurted out. "I did it to try and hurt your reputation."

He froze. "What?"

"I switched baskets so folks might think less of you for spending an unchaperoned afternoon with a gambling hall owner."

She spoke so fast, it was a moment before Ty digested what she'd said. "You mean you expected someone to come by and see us in a compromising position so my reputation would be damaged?"

"No! I just figured the two of us being alone together would be enough."

Cursing his gullibility, he smiled coldly. "Congratulations, Miss Gabby. You're a much better actress than I suspected. You were especially convincing with the 'accidental' tumble into the stream."

"That *was* an accident!"

"To think I almost believed your little act at church about how I should take Eleanor even though I bought your basket by 'accident,'" he said sharply. He wasn't certain if he was angrier at her for lying to him, or at himself for letting her steal past his barriers with her seemingly innocent games. "You're going to win this election no matter

who you hurt in the process. I should've figured,
after you weren't able to buy the women's votes,
that you'd come up with some other damned
scheme."

Gabby took a step toward him, her hands outstretched. "No, Ty, it wasn't like that, I swear.
When I first came up with the plan to switch the
baskets, all I wanted to do was try to get a few
more votes. I never meant to hurt you, and I never
expected to have such a good time, either."

"You damn well better hope this worked," Ty
said. "Because if it didn't and I'm elected mayor,
I'm going to make sure you're out of my town by
sunset."

"It worked. Isn't that what you wanted?" Rose
asked in exasperation.

Gabby pushed back her desk chair and stood,
then moved around to the fireplace to warm her
chilled body. Ever since the picnic five days ago,
she'd been fighting a case of the sniffles. As well
as a guilty conscience.

"Yes. No." Gabby threw her hands in the air. "I
don't know. I didn't expect him to be the way he
was."

Rose narrowed her dark eyes. "You never did
tell me much about what happened, except that
you accidentally pushed him in the creek and then
the Sanders saw you."

"And the rest is history, thanks to the busybod-
ies in the quilting circle and the hypocrites in the
saloons of Sawtooth," Gabby said bitterly. "It
seems the gossip mill works even better than I
imagined."

"For pete's sake, Gabby, that's what you hoped

would happen. What changed your mind about old stiff-necked Ashburn?"

Gabby sent her friend a piercing gaze. "He's not so stiff-necked, and he's definitely not old."

Recalling the erotic sensation of his lips on hers, she shivered with sensual yearning. Ty had turned her body into a stranger and stirred her emotions into an unappeased tempest.

"He kissed you, didn't he?" Rose asked, her eyes narrowed.

Gabby glanced up, startled. "Why do you ask that?"

Rose laughed. "He did." She lowered her voice. "So where did he kiss you? Your hand? Your cheek? Your bosom?"

Shocked, Gabby stared openmouthed at her friend. "Rose! Why would he kiss my—my—there?"

Rose shrugged in her matter-of-fact way. "Because it's nice."

"Isn't there anything that embarrasses you?" Gabby muttered peevishly.

A grin lit her friend's face. "Not much. And quit changing the subject. Where'd he kiss you?"

Knowing Rose wouldn't leave her alone until she confessed something, Gabby turned to gaze into the fire. "He kissed my face and neck."

Gabby's cheeks burned, but not from the flames in the hearth.

"That's all?" Rose sounded disappointed.

Gabby twirled around, tugging her skirt hem away from the fire's orange tongues. "*Nothing* was supposed to happen! I figured folks seeing us go off on a picnic alone would be enough. I didn't plan to get kissed."

Rose crossed her arms. "Why not? You have a hankering for him, and by the sound of it, he's got it bad for you, too."

"That's ridiculous. He's engaged to Eleanor Gatewood. Besides, I swore I'd never let any man use me," Gabby denied.

Rose brushed her hand across the shiny sequins on her knee-length dress. "Sometimes being used is kind of fun, so long as you're using him, too. You should try it."

Gabby let her glower speak for her.

"Oh, all right, I'll mind my own business."

"That'll be the day," Gabby muttered.

"In that case, I won't tell you what Joe told me."

Her curiosity piqued, Gabby sighed. "I give up. What did Joe say?"

"He said that Ashburn hasn't been over to the Gatewoods' since the picnic. I figure Miss Priss got her nose bent out of shape. Maybe Ashburn'll get some sense and call the wedding off."

Gabby shook her head. "Ty cares what people think of him, and he's going to be even more determined to wed Eleanor and put the gossip to rest."

"I don't know," Rose said. "What if she won't take him back?"

Gabby hadn't considered that turn of events. Instead of feeling elated, more remorse crushed down on her. She didn't like Eleanor Gatewood, but Ty had chosen her to be his wife and Gabby cared about what he wanted.

"Then she's crazy," Gabby responded. She strode back to her place behind the massive desk and plopped down in her chair. "If you need help out there, give me a holler. I've got some paper-work to do."

Gabby picked up the closest paper on her desk and studied it unseeingly, waiting for Rose to leave. A few moments later the door slammed behind Rose, and Gabby winced. She dropped the document to her desktop, knowing Rose wouldn't stay angry with her very long, even though Gabby probably deserved it.

She propped her elbows on the desk's polished surface and clasped her hands together. The second debate was a little more than a week away, and the election a week after that. Why should she care if the paperwork gathered on her desk? Ty Ashburn was going to throw her out of Sawtooth soon enough. In spite of her too-successful strategy with the picnic basket switch, Gabby doubted she had enough votes to become the town's first mayor. All she'd done was cast some doubt on Ty's character; she certainly hadn't aided her own campaign by making people think better of her.

How could she explain the confusion and strange longings Ty had fanned to life with his delicious kisses? How could she make Rose understand her bewilderment when Gabby couldn't even fathom what had happened to her twice in Ty's strong, capable arms?

Although she enjoyed working and joking with the men who visited the Emporium, she always kept them at arm's length.

Until Ty Ashburn.

Ty *had* enjoyed their cloud-watching and the race to catch the frog. She smiled, remembering how he had actually run to the creek to head off the hopping creature.

Her smile faded. If only she hadn't been so impulsive. Then they wouldn't have fallen in the water and the Sanderses wouldn't have seen anything. Or maybe Gabby had just hastened the inevitable. Much as she hated to admit it, Rose was right. When she was around Ty the air seemed to crackle with tension, and not all of it had to do with being on opposite sides in a political race.

Now she'd be fortunate if Ashburn ever spoke to her again in a civil manner. If she'd been in his position, she wouldn't have believed her innocence, either. He'd been understandably upset.

Of course, *he'd* been the one to initiate the intimate touches both times. *He'd* been the one to kiss her.

And she was the one wallowing in a pool of guilt and self-pity.

Gabby's threaded fingers tightened, and her knuckles whitened. The only thing she'd done was have the picnic baskets switched. Then she'd even tried to make things right by insisting Ty take Eleanor, but his damned sense of honor had intervened.

She had nothing to be ashamed of, and if Ty Ashburn thought this whole affair was her fault, she'd be darned if she'd sit back and accept the blame.

No more hiding out in her office. She had an election to win.

With deliberate force, she pushed back her chair and stood. She tugged her shirtwaist down and smoothed her hair back from her temple.

Miss Gabby would be dealing at her regular table tonight, and tomorrow she would be out stumping for her bid to become mayor.

Miss Gabby Wade was *not* a quitter.

* * *

Ty didn't bother to check his dim reflection in the window of the Gatewoods' front door. He knocked and waited impatiently for Bentley to answer the summons. Although Ty had managed to change into a tie and jacket before coming over for dinner, he was also thirty minutes late. He suspected Vernon and Eleanor would prefer him being "fashionably late" rather than dressed in his work clothes.

Besides his irritation at having to change his attire, Ty didn't relish the thought of breaking the engagement to Eleanor. He wanted to call off the marriage; he *didn't* want to go through the unpleasant scene with Eleanor he knew would ensue. She'd been angry and hurt by the gossip of Sunday's fiasco with Gabby, but she'd forgiven him after she'd scolded him. He ground his teeth, remembering how he'd felt like a child under Eleanor's rebukes—another reason to be glad he was canceling the wedding.

Bentley swept open the door and greeted him in his usual polite monotone, "Good evening, Mr. Ashburn. Please step inside and I shall announce your arrival."

Ty stepped across the threshold and forced himself not to fidget.

A few minutes later, Bentley returned. "Please follow me."

Ty nearly choked on his retort—he'd been to the house numerous times and could well manage to find his own way to the parlor. Surprisingly, Bentley led him directly to the dining room, where Vernon and Eleanor were already seated at the table.

Bentley bowed at the waist and exited.

"Hello, Tyler," Vernon greeted formally.

Ty sent the older man a nod. "Vernon." He glanced at Eleanor, dressed in a dark blue dress and matching jacket. Her auburn hair, pulled back in a snug chignon, reflected the candle's flickering flames. There was no doubt she was an attractive woman. Why didn't *she* make his blood burn and his self-control disappear?

"Good evening, Eleanor. I'm sorry I'm late," he said without contrition.

Eleanor's gaze narrowed as she gave Ty a thin smile. "That's quite all right, Tyler. I'm pleased to see you dressed for dinner *this* time."

Ty nodded, but made no comment. If he hadn't been completely convinced before that he was doing the right thing calling off the wedding, he was now.

"Have a seat," Vernon said. "The first course is about to be served."

Following the characteristic ritual, Vernon tasted his soup and pronounced it acceptable. After Vernon's approval, Ty and Eleanor picked up their own spoons and began to eat. Ty decided to leave the conversation topic open, preferring that Eleanor or Vernon lead the discussion. He would say his piece later, after they'd all eaten and had retired to the parlor.

"I spoke with Floyd Sanders today," Vernon began as he cut into his prime rib.

Startled, Ty drew his napkin across his lips, buying time to regain his composure. "Oh? And what did he have to add to the already blistering gossip?" he asked.

"He said he could've been mistaken as to what he saw," Vernon said.

"What brought about this change of heart?" Ty asked suspiciously.

"There is more than one way to get a man to change his story."

The smooth, oily way Vernon said it told Ty what he'd done. "You bribed him?" he demanded in disbelief.

"I merely invested in his conscience," Vernon replied mildly. His eyes hardened. "As I have invested in you, Tyler."

"You haven't done anything besides get me into this election."

"I have given you a future," Gatewood said forcefully. He took a deep breath and spoke in a softer tone. "I still feel you'll win the election, but only because most people still trust you more than they trust Miss Wade. However, if you become embroiled in another such incident as the one last Sunday, I'm afraid your chance of becoming mayor could be in serious jeopardy."

"I can't help what people say or think. I know that nothing happened between Miss Wade and me." *Liar*, his conscience mocked him. "If they want to believe that we did something wrong, then they're going to believe it. I can't change their minds."

"No, but you can attack your opponent a bit more forcefully. Accuse her of using her bountiful charms to sway you. One look at her and no man would blame you for your slight indiscretion."

As much as Ty hated to admit it, Vernon's suggestion had merit. Hadn't Ty himself accused Gabby of trying to seduce him? Still, his lack of judgment earned a large share of the blame. And, try as he might, he couldn't forget her childish joy and radiant smile.

He glanced at Eleanor, wondering what she thought. She kept her eyes focused on her plate, although she seemed to be pushing her food around more than eating it. He suspected Vernon had already discussed this new strategy with her, preparing her for what may happen.

Ty shifted his attention back to Vernon, who watched him with a snake's unblinking gaze. "What if it wasn't all Miss Gabby's fault?"

Eleanor gasped and snapped her head up. She stared at Ty, her mouth agape. "Tyler! I can't believe you'd actually be attracted to that—that harlot."

Ty ground his teeth together and faced the woman. "Eleanor, we have to speak after dinner. There's something I need to tell you."

Her shocked disgust evaporated into wary uncertainty. "What?"

"It would be better if we discussed it after you've eaten."

She tossed her napkin on the table beside her plate. "Fine," she said petulantly. "I'm finished. What is it?"

Ty glanced at Vernon, who frowned his displeasure, then looked back at Eleanor.

"This is between us, Eleanor. Let's go into the parlor," Ty said.

"No," she exclaimed. "What you have to say can be said in front of my father."

Ty's stomach churned with anxiety and resentment. He hadn't wanted an audience, especially not Vernon, and he didn't like being put on the spot by Eleanor. But if she wanted "Daddy" there, that was her problem. He lifted his own napkin off his lap and set it on the table, then faced Eleanor and ignored her father.

"I'm calling off the wedding," he stated without preamble.

Eleanor's face drained of color and Ty thought she might faint.

"Are you all right?" Ty asked.

She laughed a shaky, near-hysterical laugh. "You want to call off our wedding less than two weeks before, and you ask me if I'm all right? Tyler, what in the world has come over you?"

Maybe something that should've come over him before he'd gotten engaged, he thought. "A lot has happened this past month, with the election and trying to meet all my contractual responsibilities," Ty said, feeling like a coward for skirting the real issue. "I don't feel I can give you what you deserve at this point."

Eleanor's eyes filmed with moisture. "I only want to be your wife."

Ty shook his head. "You want to be the wife of a mayor and have a home the size of this one. I may not win the election, and it'll be quite a few years before I can afford to build you a house this fancy."

"But we're going to live with Father—"

"That was *your* plan, Eleanor, not mine," Ty said bluntly. "If my cabin isn't good enough for you, maybe I'm not, either."

Eleanor stared at him, her tears drying and her expression hardening. "It's that Gabby Wade, isn't it? You want her, not me."

Ty swore silently; he hadn't wanted Gabby's name injected into this discussion. "She owns a saloon, and you know how I feel about gambling. That hasn't changed."

"You didn't answer her question, Tyler."

Vernon's low but commanding voice startled Ty. He'd forgotten about their audience. He settled a steady gaze on the older man and said flatly, "Yes, I did. The decision was mine and mine alone."

Eleanor stood quickly, and her chair crashed to the floor. "Fine! If that's what you want, then that's what you'll get." She tugged the diamond ring off her finger and flung it at him. The ring bounced off Ty's plate and landed in his lap. "I didn't want to marry you anyhow! It was my father's idea! He said you were destined for great things and I was foolish enough to believe him."

She spun around and stalked out of the dining room.

Silence hung in the high-ceilinged room.

Ty stared at Vernon, wondering if he had misjudged him. If Eleanor was only marrying him to please her father . . . Ty's injured pride demanded the truth. "You mean you forced her to accept my proposal?"

Vernon chuckled, startling Ty. "Don't pay her much mind—she's got her mother's temper," he said. "I'll give her a little time, then have a talk with her. After the election and things are back to normal, you two can reschedule the wedding."

"I'm not marrying your daughter, Vernon, especially now that I know the truth," Ty said forcefully. "I won't marry a woman who can't think for herself."

Vernon's nostrils flared slightly and he deliberately placed his elbows on the chair's armrests and steepled his fingers. "You've been so busy that you aren't thinking straight, Tyler. I know you don't love Eleanor, but that'll come later. You want what she can give you: respectability and a son to carry on your name."

Ty sprang to his feet angrily and leaned close to Gatewood. "Listen to me, Vernon. I'm not your puppet, and I'm not going to marry Eleanor." He took a deep breath to calm his temper. "I won't marry a woman I don't love."

"That's an odd statement from a man who once told me all he wanted was a successful business and people looking up to him," Vernon said mockingly, then narrowed his eyes. "A union with Eleanor will help you achieve those two goals. You know it and I know it."

Ty clenched his teeth, and his jaw muscle flexed. A month ago Vernon would have been right. But something had happened to him when he'd spent Sunday afternoon with Gabby. He still wanted a successful business and respect; it was his means to those ends he'd begun to question.

"I want to expand my business and you used that leverage to force me into running for mayor." Ty began to pace. "Without your financial backing, you knew I'd have to wait a couple more years. Maybe it'd be better if I just stayed patient a little longer."

Gatewood stood and stepped into Ty's path, stopping him. "Patience is for fools, and you're no fool, Tyler. What I did was offer you a chance to grab your dream. Don't be stupid and throw it all away for a whore!"

Ty bristled at Vernon's contemptuous slur. "This has nothing to do with her! It has to do with *me* and what *I* want. I've worked hard all my life to get where I am, and I've done it alone. If I win the election and you loan me the money, then I'm in your debt."

"It's a business arrangement, Tyler. If a bank loans you the money, you'd be in *their* debt."

Ty raked his fingers through his hair impatiently. "But they won't have a daughter they want me to marry."

Vernon's mouth thinned to a grim slash as he studied Ty. Finally, his expression relaxed and he nodded. "All right. If I stop badgering you about marrying Eleanor, would you be willing to stay in the election and accept my loan later?"

"Why?" Ty asked suspiciously.

The older man sighed and his shoulders slumped. "I own a bit of land around town. If you're elected, the bridge will be built and the road will bring people to Sawtooth. I'll be able to see some returns on my investment."

He sounded sincere, but a sense of unease swept through Ty. Vernon wouldn't give in that readily unless he had something else planned. Ty had admired the successful businessman since he'd moved to Sawtooth, and he'd sought Vernon Gatewood's advice on many occasions. The decision to marry Eleanor had seemed natural in the scheme of Ty's life and he hadn't questioned his reasons until now. Had he lost sight of his ethics in the race to leave his past behind?

"As long as marrying Eleanor isn't part of the deal," Ty acquiesced.

"If that's what you want," Vernon said with a voice as smooth as Kentucky bourbon.

"And I want it in writing."

Vernon's eyes widened momentarily, then he

nodded. "Of course. You can come by my office tomorrow and I'll have a paper ready to sign."

Vernon stuck out his hand, and Ty stared at it a moment, then slowly extended his. They shook firmly.

"I hope you can forgive an old man for wanting to see his only child married well," Vernon said with a sheepish smile.

Ty's antagonism faded, and he even managed a smile of his own. "Who knows, if I ever have a daughter, I might feel the same as you." He turned away. "I can see myself out."

Chapter 15

Once Ty had left, Vernon's affable expression disappeared. He glanced at the remaining food on his plate, but his appetite had fled.

Ashburn was becoming too damn maudlin with his ridiculous talk about marrying for love. What was love but another commodity to be bought and sold? Doubts began to plague Vernon, and he didn't like it a damn bit. Being Tyler's father-in-law would have enabled him to influence Ashburn's decisions, but Ashburn had taken away that venue by canceling the wedding. If, after he got elected mayor, Ashburn got too self-righteous on him, Vernon would have to find some other means to get him back under his thumb. And if that didn't work, there were more permanent ways to take care of him. But Vernon hoped it wouldn't come to that. He'd actually grown somewhat fond of Tyler.

"Is he gone?"

Eleanor's voice startled Vernon and he turned to see his daughter standing at the other end of the table.

"Yes," he replied. "I hope you aren't too upset about Tyler's cold feet."

"Maybe a little, but it wasn't as if I loved him," Eleanor said with a regal air. "In a way, I'm glad he called it off. I wasn't looking forward to the wedding night." She shuddered.

Vernon walked over to his daughter and swept the back of his hand gently across her cheek. "I know you weren't, darling, and I'm glad you won't be subject to such baseness. However, he may yet change his mind later on. Would you still be willing to marry him?"

"If that's what you want me to do, you know I'll do it, Father. I'm just worried about what people will say." She added crossly, "I'll probably have to stay prisoner in the house until the gossip goes away."

"No need to be so dramatic, my dear," Vernon said. "After this election is over, how about if we take a trip to Denver? You can shop to your heart's content, and I won't even scold you for spending too much. How would you like that?"

Her face brightened and her eyes sparkled as she clapped with childish glee. "Can we go before the election?"

"I'm afraid not. I have to make sure Tyler wins."

"But I thought that woman didn't have a chance."

"Due to your ex-fiancé's sudden attack of conscience, I'm afraid it's not as assured as it was," Vernon said, his anger rising once more.

She laid a hand on his forearm. "Is there anything I can do, Father?"

He could always count on Eleanor. He patted the back of her hand. "That's all right, my dear. I think I'll go for a walk and see if I can clear my mind."

"Would you like me to come with you?"

"No. You run along upstairs."

Acting like a child instead of a grown woman, Eleanor did as Vernon ordered.

A few minutes later, Vernon stepped outside carrying a walking cane with a carved snake-head handle. It had been a gift from one of his employees before Vernon had caught him embezzling. Ironically, the cane had served him well in ensuring the thief never robbed anyone again.

He strolled toward his town as voices and piano music floated to him on the cool breeze. Yipping from the foothills announced that the coyotes were beginning their night of hunting and scavenging. Glittering stars formed a cap over the valley that Sawtooth lay nestled in.

Six years ago, when Vernon had arrived in the area, there'd been nothing but a general store, a blacksmith, a livery, and five saloons. He'd brought Sawtooth to life and created his own little kingdom to lord over. When Tyler Ashburn had opened his business a few years later, Vernon had seen himself reflected in the young man's ambitious character and had been grooming Tyler to step into his shoes when he retired. And it had gone admirably well, until this election and Gabby Wade's infernal meddling.

He'd seen potential in her, too, when she'd arrived, but Miss Wade hadn't wanted anything to do with him. *Him*, Vernon Gatewood, the most wealthy and influential man in Sawtooth. His hold tightened on the cane's snake head, and he imagined his fingers around her slender neck while he took his pleasure in her pain.

Vernon breathed deeply of the autumn air. He couldn't afford to have voluptuous Gabby Wade sidetrack him and his plans. He paused and pulled his watch out of his pocket. Snapping open the etched silver cover, he held the face up to the light offered by a flickering gaslight. Nine o'clock. Time to pay a visit to a man he hoped would be his newest associate.

Vernon walked another block, then turned down a side street where a handful of sagging houses sat in a ragged row. Without hesitation, Vernon knocked on the warped door of one and, after a few seconds, was let inside.

"It's nice to meet you, Mr. Lowe," Vernon said, and extended his hand to the young, bespectacled man.

"Call me William." The bartender's palm was moist, but his grip fairly firm.

Vernon glanced around the sparse accommodations and the crumb- and dirt-littered puncheon floor. Articles of clothing were strewn across the few pieces of cheap furniture. He kept his revulsion disguised behind a friendly smile.

"Tom Bailey said you might be interested in achieving a higher economic state," Vernon began.

William clasped his hands in front of him. "That's right, Mr. Gatewood. I'm sick and tired of living in this decrepit hovel, but there's little room for financial growth in bartending."

"Where are you from?"

"Chicago, originally," Lowe responded.

Gatewood eyed the young man closely. His black wool trousers had seen better days and his boiled shirt had been washed so often it was limp and lifeless. Lowe's eyes, however, were shrewd and cunning behind the glass lenses. Vernon had an idea he'd been on the wrong side of the law before settling in Sawtooth, and that gave Vernon a decided advantage.

"What can you do for me?" Vernon demanded.

"Whatever you want me to," William replied without hesitation.

"Have you ever managed a place of business?"

"I've done a bit of managing here and there."

Vernon found himself liking Lowe, but he had learned not to make decisions based on instincts alone. "You've worked for Gabby Wade for nearly six months. Why would you be willing to work against her now?"

Lowe shrugged. "I don't look at it so much as working against her, as much as working for myself."

"If you become my associate, there is one thing I demand—loyalty." Vernon paused to let that fact sink in. "If you have any doubts regarding Miss Wade, speak up now, because it may come down to her against us. Do you understand?"

"I understand that I'm tired of being a bartender. I want my own place and I want to run it the way I see fit," William stated. "If that means ruffling Miss Gabby's feathers, or worse, so be it. When it comes right down to it, a person only has himself to look out for him."

Pleased, Vernon nodded. "I like you, William, and I think we have a fine future together." He clapped the younger man on the back. "As my first test of your loyalty, I want you to keep an eye out for some cowboys, men who'll do anything for a price. Do you know what I mean?"

"I understand." William appeared puzzled, but he was smart enough not to voice his questions, which raised Vernon's estimation of him a notch higher.

"Then when I may have need of the ruffians, you can act as my representative." Vernon paused. "I have great plans for this town, William. I'm hoping to someday share them with you."

"I'm looking forward to working with you, Mr. Gatewood."

The two men shook hands again, and Vernon left. As he walked back to his mansion, Vernon made a mental note to send a telegram to his agent in Cheyenne to check out one William Lowe from Chicago. If Lowe had been involved in any illegal activity, Vernon wanted to know. It would help him to decide how useful Lowe could actually be.

Gabby lifted her thick blond hair off her neck and allowed the air to cool her perspiration-soaked skin. The four orphans gathered around Gabby, with the two boys plopping down onto the Emporium's floor to catch their breath.

"I think that's enough sliding down banisters for today," Gabby announced.

"Come on, Miss Gabby, one more time. Pleeease?" six-year-old April begged.

Gabby looked down into the girl's huge violet eyes and weakened. Who could refuse such a plea?

She dropped her hair back into place and held up her forefinger. "*One* more time, and that's it."

April squealed in delight and dashed toward the staircase, followed closely by Harold and Tommy, who had miraculously regained their energy. Sara held back and walked with a bit more decorum beside Gabby, who noticed shadowed circles beneath Sara's eyes.

"Have the nightmares come back?" Gabby asked the girl.

After a moment, Sara nodded. "I had it a couple times this week. It's always the same." She shivered and Gabby put her arm around the child's thin shoulders. "This man dressed in black aims his gun at Ma and Pa, and shoots them. And I'm standing there like I'm frozen. I want to help, but I can't move."

"What would you do if you could move?" Gabby asked gently.

"Stop him," she said fiercely.

"How?"

"Put myself between him and my folks."

"Then you'd be killed."

"Sometimes I think it'd been better if I'd died with them."

Aghast, Gabby stared at Sara. "You don't really believe that, do you?"

Sara shrugged. "I don't know. Maybe sometimes."

Gabby stopped at the bottom of the stairs and laid her hands on Sara's narrow shoulders. "The pain doesn't go away overnight, or even in a week or a year. You have to let time work its magic, because you know what?" Sara shook her head. "You have your whole life ahead of you, honey. There are hundreds of new and wonderful things to be seen and done out there."

"Will the bad dreams ever go away?" Sara asked plaintively.

"Someday, Sara, someday."

"Come on!" Tommy shouted from the top of the staircase. "We can't start until you're both up here."

"What do you think? Should we join them?" Gabby asked gently.

Sara smiled slightly, easing the grief in her eyes, and nodded. "Let's go."

Gabby followed her up the flight of stairs. At the top, they decided to have the oldest go first, and Gabby obediently climbed onto the banister and slid down backward. Then Sara, Tommy, Harold, and finally April all arrived safe and sound at the bottom.

"How would you all like a treat?" Gabby asked the children.

"Yeah!" came the resounding enthusiastic reply.

"I heard that Mr. Tuttle at the restaurant got a new Shepard's Ice Cream Freezer and he made some chocolate ice cream. Doesn't that sound good?" Gabby asked.

"What's ice cream?" April asked, her cherub face twisted in puzzled curiosity.

"Can anyone tell April what it is?" Blank expressions met Gabby's question and she smiled. "I guess that means you're all in for a surprise. Get your jackets on and we'll go get some."

The children quickly shrugged into their coats, and Tommy and Sara helped Harold and April bundle up. Gabby retrieved her cape from the office and joined them.

"Are you sure it's all right for us to go there? Mrs. Edwards always tells us to stay out of the way and not go into any of the stores," Sara said tentatively.

"It'll be fine. We're not going there to get into mischief—at least, not too much," Gabby reassured her. "We're going as paying customers."

They all tramped out of the Emporium and

down the boardwalk. It was after one o'clock, so
the lunch patrons had already come and gone,
leaving most of the tables open. The few customers
that were inside cast curious glances at Gabby and
her young entourage.

Gabby led the children to a round table covered
with a red checkered oilcloth.

"I've never been in a place like this before,"
Tommy commented, his round blue eyes darting
about, trying to see everything at once.

"I was, with my folks, right before—" Sara broke
off and a tear trickled down her pale cheek. "Before
they died."

Gabby laid a comforting hand on the girl's arm.

"I don't remember my ma or pa," April piped
up. "Mrs. Edwards said they're in heaven."

"No, they ain't," Harold retorted. "She just said
that 'cause they didn't want you."

"How do you know, Harold?" Gabby demanded.

The eight-year-old boy squirmed in his seat. "I
just know."

"You're lying," April said, her lower lip trembling. "They're in heaven."

"Of course they are, sweetheart," Gabby assured.
"He didn't mean it, did you, Harold?" She cast the
boy a warning look.

He looked down at his short legs as he swung
them back and forth, and finally said, "Nah, I was
only joshin'."

April stuck out her tongue at him and went back
to looking around the café. Gabby breathed a quiet
sigh of relief. Now if she could get Sara's tears to
dry up so quickly.

The waitress came to their table and smiled

warmly. "Hello, Miss Gabby. Who are your friends?"

"Good afternoon, Sally." Gabby introduced each child, who shyly greeted the woman. "They all live with Mrs. Edwards at the home."

"I'm glad to meet you all," Sally said, her eyes twinkling kindly. "So what can I get you?"

"Ice cream," they replied in unison.

Gabby smiled at the zealous reply. "We'd each like a scoop of chocolate ice cream."

"Coming right up." Sally hurried back to the kitchen with her skirts swishing in her wake.

"You know *everybody* in town," April said in wide-eyed wonder.

Gabby laughed softly. "Not everybody. Sally used to work at my place, then she married Mr. Tuttle and now she helps him here."

She didn't add that when Sally had come to the Emporium, she'd been half starved and too proud to accept handouts. Gabby had given her a job and helped her regain her fractured self-respect.

The children settled back in their chairs, giving Gabby a moment to collect her thoughts. She'd never advertised her relationship with the orphaned children, thinking she'd spare them from the town gossip. But in the past few days she'd come to realize she had nothing to be ashamed of. She cared about the children and they enjoyed being with her.

Besides, she might have only a couple weeks left in Sawtooth. Her heart tightened at the thought of never seeing the children again. She gazed at each one of them, trying to memorize their features, from Harold's unruly cowlick to Sara's thin face.

A few minutes later Sally returned with a tray

bearing five bowls of ice cream. She set one down in front of each of the children and Gabby, and passed out spoons.

"Hope you like it. My arm darn near fell off when I was turning the handle," Sally said with a wink.

"I'm glad your arm didn't fall off, Mrs. Tuttle," April said solemnly.

Sally ruffled the young girl's hair. "Me, too, sweetie. Now you all enjoy your ice cream."

Tommy picked up his spoon and shoveled some into his mouth. He blinked rapidly and his mouth dropped open. "It's cold," he mumbled.

"Of course it is," Gabby teased. "That's why it's called *ice* cream."

The other children gingerly tasted the frozen concoction, and after a few spoonfuls all but Sara eagerly cleaned out their bowls.

"I never tasted anything that cold before," Harold commented, a chocolate mustache above his lip.

"Me neither," April remarked. "But I liked it lots. I think ice cream is my favorite food."

"I thought you liked licorice sticks," Gabby said.

"Can I have two favorites?" April asked earnestly.

"I don't see why not." Gabby glanced at Sara, who had only eaten a small portion of her ice cream. "Don't you like it, Sara?"

The girl glanced up, startled. "Oh, yes. I was just thinking about the last time I ate in a restaurant. I had chocolate cake for dessert."

Gabby wished she could ease Sara's suffering.

"Look, it's Mr. Ashburn," Tommy spoke up.

Gabby drew her concerned gaze from Sara to

glance up at Ty, who had entered the restaurant and now walked toward their table. He removed his hat and a dark curl spilled across his forehead. His eyes appeared tired, telling Gabby he was still working late into the night. Her throat tightened in empathy, and she curled her fingers into her palms.

"Hello, ladies, Tommy, Harold," Ty greeted them. He winked at April and Sara, sending the younger girl into a fit of giggles.

"Me and Sara aren't ladies, we're girls!" April corrected.

Ty smiled, giving creases to the corners of his eyes and throwing Gabby's thoughts into chaos. Her pulse skittered through her veins.

"Hi, Mr. Ashburn. Sorry we haven't been over, but we been helping Miss Gabby. We cleaned your place real good today, didn't we, Miss Gabby?" Tommy asked.

"That's right," Gabby managed to say. She forced herself to look at the children instead of Ty. "You all did a fine job."

"I'll bet the banister is all shiny, too," Ty said, a rare twinkle in his devastating blue eyes.

"Yep," April said. "We slided down it a hundred times."

"It wasn't a hundred," Harold said scornfully. "It was only about twenty or thirty times."

"Did Miss Gabby play with you?" he asked.

Nodding heads answered his question.

"She's best at sliding down," April said proudly.

"I'll bet she is," Ty said. "Looks like you all had chocolate ice cream."

Gabby glanced around at the children and chuckled at the chocolate ringing their mouths. "I think you all need to use those napkins and wipe your faces. It seems half the ice cream ended up on you instead of inside your bellies."

"You have to, too, Miss Gabby," Harold interjected. "You got a mustache."

Gabby's face heated in embarrassment and she quickly brushed the napkin across her lips. "Thank you, Harold."

"I hope you left some ice cream for me. I planned on having some for dessert," Ty said, keeping his gaze on the kids.

"Don't you worry, Mr. Ashburn, we have more than enough," Sally said as she sailed past. "I'll be right with you."

"Thanks," Ty said. "I'd best go sit down. Good day." He strode over to a table near the window facing the street.

Gabby leaned forward and asked in a low voice, "Do you see Mr. Ashburn very often?"

"He comes over to the home once in a while," Tommy replied. "And me and Harold and Alonzo went over to his place, where we helped clean the barn. He paid us a whole silver dollar each."

Gabby's mouth gaped, and she abruptly closed it.

"But we liked the ice cream just as good," Tommy said lamely, obviously misunderstanding her expression.

"I'm glad, Tommy," Gabby said absently. "Did Mr. Ashburn ask you to come over?"

Tommy shrugged. "Mrs. Edwards told us to go over there one day, so we did. He musta told her he could use our help."

"He must've," Gabby reiterated faintly. She shook herself free of her astonishment. "Is everyone ready to go?"

The children nodded.

Gabby dug some coins out of her cape pocket and set them on the table. "All right, let's go."

Chair legs scraped on the floor and the children hopped down from their seats. Gabby ushered them out, consciously ignoring Ty.

"Bye, Mr. Ashburn," Tommy and Harold called out.

"Good-bye," he returned.

Despite her resolve, Gabby glanced at him and found his unreadable gaze upon her. Her mouth suddenly felt parched. Did he still blame her for the picnic affair? Or had he decided to let bygones be bygones?

She paused on the boardwalk and opened the locket watch pinned to her bodice. Two o'clock. The Emporium wouldn't open for another couple of hours, so she had time to find out more about what had inspired Ty Ashburn's change of heart.

Flanked by the children, Gabby headed to the other side of town. A few minutes later, they arrived at the home and hustled inside to escape the burgeoning north wind.

Mrs. Edwards met them in the foyer and welcomed Gabby with a warm smile. "Miss Gabby, I wasn't expecting you to stop by today."

"I wanted to talk to you," Gabby said, glancing at the children meaningfully.

"Tommy, Harold, you have a woodbox to fill. And Sara, honey, you can go ahead and dust the parlor. Take April with you and have her help," Mrs. Edwards instructed.

The children obeyed with little hesitation, scurrying off to carry out their assigned tasks.

"Why don't you come into the kitchen where it's

nice and warm?" the kindly woman suggested.

"Thanks," Gabby said, and followed her down the hall.

Mrs. Edwards sat down, pulled a carrot out of a steel pan on the table, and began to scrub it vigorously. "Now, what's on your mind?"

"Tommy was telling me that Mr. Ashburn is letting them do some chores to earn money."

"That's right. He came by after he saw the children at your place and we had a little chat. Since then, he's been having a few of the boys over every few days to help clean up his barns and such."

"His business must be doing pretty well," Gabby said dryly.

Mrs. Edwards gave Gabby a disapproving look. "I shouldn't be telling you this, but the fact is, he's been a major benefactor since the home opened. He doesn't like folks to know that, though, just like you don't want people to find out about your contributions."

Gabby shook her head, still skeptical. "Why?"

Mrs. Edwards's stubby but nimble fingers paused in their task. "I've been raising youngsters for nigh on to thirty years now, and I've learned to read a lot just by looking in their eyes." She continued cleaning the carrot in her hand. "Mr. Ashburn has a few ghosts chasing him."

Gabby recalled the shadows she'd seen in his eyes when she'd asked him about his family. "What kind of memories could frighten a man like Tyler Ashburn?"

Mrs. Edwards shrugged. "Some of the most powerful men got to be that way because of the fears that followed them all their lives."

Gabby contemplated her words. She'd suspected

the same thing: Ty Ashburn was a man with something so horrible in his past that he refused to speak about it. Something that had scarred him, made him an aloof man with steely eyes who vehemently opposed gambling.

"Maybe you should go talk to him," Mrs. Edwards suggested.

"He'd rather have the plague visit," Gabby said dryly. "Especially after Sunday."

The older woman chuckled. "Seems to me it takes two to be doing what the Sanderses saw."

Gabby's face grew hot. "We didn't *do* anything."

"No need to get so riled, Miss Gabby. I'm not one to be judging other people. But I do have a word of advice, if you want it."

"What?"

"Sit down and talk to Mr. Ashburn—see if you two can work out your differences. He's not a bad sort; he might even surprise you."

Gabby had already learned he wasn't nearly as cold as he appeared. "He won't change his mind about the saloons," she said. "He's determined to close them, then he's going to make sure I'm driven out of town."

Mrs. Edwards sighed and heaved her weight out of the chair. "Pride's a person's own worst enemy."

Gabby nodded somberly. "Especially in Ty Ashburn's case."

"If you don't mind me saying, that's like calling the kettle black."

Gabby bristled defensively. "What do you mean? I'm willing to talk."

"Only if things go your way. You have a generous heart, Miss Gabby. Try sharing it with Tyler Ashburn."

A denial sprang to Gabby's lips, but she held it back. "All right. I'll go talk to him, but I'm telling you, it's not going to do any good."

"You can only try."

A howl from the backyard startled Gabby, and she and Mrs. Edwards hurried to the back door. They spotted Harold and Tommy running around the woodpile chasing a stray dog.

Mrs. Edwards opened the door and hollered out, "Leave that poor animal be, boys, and get back to your chores."

"Yes, ma'am," Tommy and Harold called, with far less enthusiasm than they'd shown trying to catch the animal.

The dog disappeared around the house corner, and the youngsters filled their arms with wood.

Mrs. Edwards moved back into the kitchen. "Just like all boys, those two want a dog. I told them we can't afford to feed one, but they keep trying."

Gabby's heart went out to the orphans, knowing what it was like to want something other children had. As a young girl traveling with her footloose uncle, she had watched other boys and girls playing games together and wished she could join in the fun. She'd tried once and had been rebuffed because she was different.

"What if I get them one and give you the money to feed it?" Gabby suggested.

"Who'll pay for it if you have to leave?" Mrs. Edwards asked softly. "I'm sorry, Miss Gabby, but my first concern is for the children's well-being."

The reality struck Gabby with despair. This was the first time she actually believed she would be forced to leave Sawtooth.

"I understand," she said around the lump in her throat. "I'd better go."

After bidding farewell to the children, Gabby left. She glanced up and saw the mountain peaks hidden by gathering gray clouds. Although it was only late October, it appeared winter would make an early entrance.

She wondered if Ty had gotten his extra shipments scheduled and hoped for his and the town's sake that he had. Pulling her cape's hood over her head, she decided to pay him a visit. Maybe Mrs. Edwards was right; maybe Gabby had to bend a little for the good of Sawtooth. She wouldn't give up her home, but perhaps she could change her stand regarding the road. That compromise might gain her enough votes to swing the election her way, as well as soften Ty's opposition to her.

Since she was closer to Ty's cabin than his office, Gabby walked there. She'd learned from Rose that he usually went home after lunch to check on his stock and equipment. If she was lucky, she'd find him there.

The brisk wind chafed her cheeks and her breath wisped in the cool air. A couple of men on horseback rode past her, tipping their hats respectfully and greeting her by name. Gabby recognized them as occasional customers at the Emporium. What would they do when her place was closed down? Where would they go to relax and engage in a friendly game of poker?

Ty Ashburn didn't have the right to decide what was best for anyone but himself. Picking up her pace, she arrived at Ashburn's place a few minutes later.

"Howdy, Miss Gabby." Joe welcomed her from

the nearest corral, where he was checking the horses.

She smiled at Rose's beau and waved. "Hello, Joe. Is your boss around?"

Ty stepped out of his cabin, and Gabby's gaze latched on to his familiar broad-shouldered figure. In his denim jeans tucked into black mule-ear boots, and blue shirt with the sleeves rolled up to reveal his undershirt, he didn't resemble a successful businessman or candidate for mayor.

She walked across the yard and stopped a few feet from him.

"What do you want?" he demanded, his expression hidden beneath the brim of his hat.

"I'd like to apologize for what happened on Sunday," she blurted.

Ty glanced over at Joe and found he'd turned away, then he looked back at Gabby. "Why don't we go into the cabin where it's warmer?"

The frosty tone of his voice didn't match the cordial invitation.

Ty opened the door, and she stepped inside and looked around, curious to see what his home was like. Although it wasn't very large, Gabby approved of the comfortable furniture and the fireplace made of fieldstone that covered half of one wall. She stepped over to the hearth and rubbed a finger along one of the smooth rocks, noticing veins of glistening white and pink quartz crisscrossing through it.

"It's beautiful," she said.

"I picked the stones myself." He paused. "You're the first one to notice the coloring."

She turned, startled to find Ty standing beside her, and she took an involuntary step back. "That's hard to believe. Surely your fiancée must've noticed."

Ty laughed, a harsh bitter sound. "If it were made of pure gold, she wouldn't notice."

Confused, Gabby shook her head. "I don't understand."

Ty crossed his arms, and her gaze was drawn to the muscles that flexed beneath his shirtsleeves. "Eleanor wouldn't lower herself to set foot in here, let alone live here. She's used to the finer things in life."

His underlying sarcasm surprised Gabby and piqued her curiosity. "I thought that was one of the reasons you're marrying her."

He glanced down at his boot toe, then back at Gabby. "Eleanor and I have reached an understanding—we're no longer engaged."

Chapter 16

66 I 'm sorry," Gabby said sincerely. "I hope it wasn't on account of what happened Sunday. If you want, I'll talk to her. I'll explain everything and apologize for switching the baskets." She sighed miserably. "I'm truly sorry, Ty. I know how much marrying her meant to you."

Confused, Ty stared at her. "What do you mean?"

"You want people to respect you and look up to you and Miss Gatewood is the leading citizen's daughter. Your standing in the community would've been assured if you had married her. Besides that, she's a beautiful woman and could have given you lovely children."

Gabby's succinct explanation made his decision to make Eleanor his wife seem equivalent to buying a brood mare. Still, she seemed to understand what he wanted more than he'd given her credit for. But was he so desperate to gain prominence that he would pick a wife based on such superficial qualities?

"What happened Sunday didn't have anything to do with my decision. I'd decided to cancel the wedding before that," he explained, his conscience not allowing Gabby to take the blame. "I figured I couldn't give her what she wanted." *And she couldn't give me what I needed.*

Gabby had forced him to open his eyes. She'd made him see the orphans as living, breathing children, not just another responsibility to bear, and she made him look at clouds as mythical beasts. Whether he liked it or not, she'd opened a door to a past when he'd believed in love, and he wasn't certain he could lock it again.

"Is a big home that important to her?" Gabby asked curiously.

"I figured it was, since she wanted us to live with her father after we were married." Suddenly feeling like he'd said too much, he asked dryly, "Was there anything else?"

She began to shake her head, then stopped in midmotion. "Actually, yes—I just had a little chat with Mrs. Edwards. She told me you were a major supporter of the home. Why didn't you tell me?"

He'd have to have a little talk with Mrs. Edwards about confidentiality. "I'm just doing my civic duty, and what I do with my money is my own business."

"And being the responsible citizen you are, you give the boys a chance to earn their own money, too." An understanding smile curved Gabby's lips upward. "Of course, you don't care for the children themselves. That's why you made it a point to stop by and say hello to them at the restaurant today. And why you took time out of your busy schedule to push the kids on the swings one morning."

Ty unfolded his arms and braced a shoulder against the mantel. Although he towered over Gabby by a foot, she didn't seem intimidated, and he was both annoyed and impressed by her mettle. "I was only trying to be neighborly. Don't read more into it than that, Miss Gabby."

Her eyes twinkled in that knowing way that discomfited him and made him wonder what she saw when she looked at him. He gave her his sternest expression.

Gabby twirled away from him and moved to the center of the room. "I would never do that, Mr. Ashburn," she exclaimed, her tone suggesting the opposite.

Her presence seemed to fill the empty corners of his cabin. He wondered what it would be like to have her there all the time: her laughter, like water dancing over the rocks, filling the corners of his too-silent home, and her dazzling smile that could stop his breath in his lungs. And sleeping with her soft curves pressed close to his body every night.

He shook himself free of the ludicrous thoughts. She represented everything he abhorred.

"Anything else?" Ty asked, keeping his voice cool.

She grinned like a young child with a secret. "No, I think that's it."

Disturbed by her cat-with-a-bowl-of-cream smugness, he opened the door and followed her outside. The afternoon had grown dark and gloomy, with angry clouds filling the sky and hiding the mountain peaks. The horses pranced nervously in the corrals as the weather affected their peace of mind, too.

"Do the animals always act this way before a storm?" Gabby asked curiously.

He nodded. "It depends on how bad the storm will be."

"By the looks of it, it'll be a bad one," Gabby replied anxiously.

"You'd better get back to your place before it starts," Ty said.

"Good idea." She turned to face him, and looked up at him with a clear, frank gaze. "Thank you again for helping the children."

Uncomfortable, he looked over her shoulder to Joe, who was unharnessing the latest team of horses to come in from Rawlins. "It's nothing."

"It's not nothing for the orphans."

He wished she'd leave him alone and stop thanking him. He glanced down at her, but the squeal of a horse sent his startled gaze back to Joe. The horse still hitched to the wagon reared up, catching Joe by surprise as he stood behind the animal, trying to release it. The chain, jerked taut by the horse's motion, caught Joe between it and the wagon tongue. Joe hollered in pain and fell, his leg trapped between metal and wood. The animal, startled further by Joe's cry, began to bolt.

Ty's heart jumped into his throat, and he shouted, "Joe!"

As Gabby gasped in horror, Ty ran toward the frightened horse to stop it before it could drag Joe. But the animal pulled the wagon and Joe nearly twenty feet before Ty caught its lead.

"Whoa. Easy, boy," Ty soothed. Holding on to the horse, he saw Gabby already kneeling on the ground beside Joe's still body.

"Is he . . . ?" Ty couldn't speak the word aloud.

Gabby shook her head, and Ty briefly closed his eyes in relief.

"He's got a bump on his forehead and his leg

looks broken," she said somberly. "I'll see if I can get his leg untangled from the chain."

Ty watched as she carefully maneuvered Joe's leg out from between the chain and wagon tongue. His trousers had been torn by the metal, and blood welled from the wound. Ty's stomach clenched at the sight of the injury, and he prayed Joe wouldn't lose his leg; for Joe that would be a fate worse than death.

"Okay, he's clear," Gabby said in a husky voice. She joined Ty. "I'll hold the horse so you can move Joe away from the wagon."

He nodded, and Gabby took hold of the horse's bridle with bloodstained hands and spoke in a gentle, easy tone to quiet the animal. Ty admired her calm. If it had been Eleanor, he suspected his ex-fiancée would have collapsed in hysterics, or fainted dead away.

Ty slowly tugged Joe's limp body out of the wagon's path, then Gabby led the hitched horse back to the corral and tied his lead to the top pole.

The injured man groaned, and his eyelids fluttered open.

Ty dropped down beside him and laid a hand on his shoulder. "It's all right, Joe. Don't try to move."

"What happened?" he mumbled, his freckles prominent against his milky pallor.

"The horse spooked." Ty felt his friend's leg to see how badly it was injured.

Joe let out a hair-curdling epitaph. "You trying to kill me?"

Ty's hands trembled, but he kept the worry from his voice. "If I was, I'd find an easier way."

Gabby dropped to her knees on the other side of

Joe. "How is he?" she asked Ty softly.

He shook his head tersely. "We have to get him over to the doc's."

"I can bring the doctor here," Gabby suggested. "That way his leg won't be moved any more than necessary."

"I like Gabby's idea better," Joe slurred. His eyes closed and white lines of pain showed at the corners of his mouth.

"I'll go," Ty decided. "Gabby, run into the house and get some blankets to keep him warm."

Gabby nodded and scurried into the house, her cape billowing behind her. A few moments later she returned, her arms laden with blankets. Working together, she and Ty covered Joe and made him as comfortable as possible.

As Ty stood to go, Gabby said, "Tell Rose, too. She'll want to be with him."

Ty tensed, but he bit back his argument. Gabby was right. What he thought of Rose didn't matter; Joe would want her with him. He nodded curtly, mounted Joe's saddled horse, and urged the animal into a gallop. A few minutes later he stopped in front of the doctor's office and charged inside. After telling the doctor about the accident and ensuring he was on his way to take care of Joe, Ty continued down the street to the Emporium to find Rose.

Ty pounded on the locked doors and waited impatiently for someone to answer. Silence resounded from within, and he tried again.

"Hold on to your drawers, I'm coming," Rose shouted from someplace inside.

Finally, she swung open the door. She wore a knee-length blue dress with thin straps over her shoulders, and black stockings adorned her legs. A friendly smile replaced her scowl. "Mr. Ashburn. What a pleasant surprise."

"Joe's been hurt," he stated without taking a moment to soften the pronouncement.

Rose's welcoming expression disappeared, replaced by fear. She grabbed Ty's arm. "What happened? How bad is he?"

Her genuine dread elevated Ty's opinion of her, and he spoke gently. "It was an accident. His leg was broken while he was unhitching one of the wagons. Gabby's with him, and the doctor is headed there now."

"I have to see him," Rose said, blindly moving past Ty.

He clasped her bare arm. "You can't go like that. You'll freeze. Where's your coat?"

Rose blinked like a sleepwalker awakening. "In my room."

"Run up and get it, then I'll take you to him."

Ty stepped inside as he waited for Rose. He hadn't expected her to be so frightened; women like her weren't supposed to care. What if she truly loved Joe? What if Ty had been judging her unfairly all this time? Maybe she *had* given up the profession, just as Gabby had said.

"I'm ready. Let's go," Rose said urgently.

Ty escorted her out of the Emporium and to the hitching post. "Do you know how to ride?"

"Some," she replied.

"Good," he said. "We'll ride double." He mounted up, then kicked his foot free of the stirrup and extended his hand to Rose to help her up to sit behind him. She wrapped her arms around his middle and they quickly set off down the main street.

Rose was uncharacteristically silent, and Ty could feel how tensely she held herself. If he'd been wrong about her, he owed her and Joe one hell of an apology, as well as Gabby.

When they arrived at his place, the doctor was already there. Rose scrambled off the horse's back before Ty could help her and ran over to Joe. Gabby moved aside so Rose could kneel beside him. She took one of his hands between hers, and a tear slipped down her cheek.

Ty couldn't deny his own eyes; Rose wasn't anything like he'd expected. If he were a gambling man, he would have bet she loved Joe. He joined them and hunkered down beside Gabby, who was cleaning the blood and dirt from Joe's leg. "What can I do?" he asked.

"Hold on to his shoulders while I set the leg," the doctor instructed.

Ty nodded and went to do as the doctor said. Joe's pasty-white face matched Rose's pale complexion, and Joe kept his gaze on her as if gaining strength from the mere sight of her. The truth of their love seared Ty, and his stomach knotted a little tighter.

As the doctor skillfully set the bone, Joe's body tensed and his neck muscles bulged. Suddenly he went limp.

"Joe!" Rose shouted frantically.

"He just lost consciousness," the doctor reassured. "Most folks let out a heckuva war whoop. Joe's a strong man."

Rose managed a slight smile through a sheen of tears. "Yes, he is."

"Miss Gabby, could you give me a hand with the splint?" the doctor asked.

Gabby nodded gamely and wrapped strips of cloth around the two splints to hold the leg in place to help it heal properly.

"Will he be all right?" Ty asked.

"Might be a slight limp with a bad break like that, but it shouldn't affect him too much. Of course, we gotta watch for gangrene," the doctor warned. "Let's get him over to his place while he's unconscious—it'll spare him a lot of pain."

Ty readied a buckboard, and he and the doctor lifted Joe into the back end. Rose climbed up to sit beside him. As Ty took the reins, the doctor joined him on the spring seat.

Ty glanced at Gabby, who seemed oddly forlorn standing in the yard, and he had the insane impulse to wrap his arms around her and hold her. "Are you all right?" he asked gruffly.

She rubbed her palms together and nodded. "I'm fine. Get Joe home and settled in before he wakes up."

Ty tightened his hold on the reins. "Don't stand out here, or you'll catch pneumonia."

Gabby only lifted her hand in farewell.

Ty flicked the leather over the horses' backs, but kept their pace slow so Joe wouldn't be jostled to much.

An hour later Ty returned home. Flakes of snow filtered down from the gunmetal-gray clouds and he quickly took care of the horses. He glanced over at the wagon that Joe had been tending to when he'd been injured. The panicked horse had been unhitched and let into one of the corrals. Ty frowned, wondering who had done it.

He hurried inside, expecting to find his fire out and the cabin cold. Instead, flames leaped in the hearth and warmth permeated the interior. The smell of fresh coffee tickled his nose. Puzzled, Ty went to the kitchen and spotted Gabby cutting a loaf of bread.

"What are you doing?" he demanded.

She jumped and spun around, one hand to her chest and the other holding the knife menacingly. "Are you trying to scare me to death?"

Ty stepped toward her, took the knife from her unresisting grasp, and laid it on the table. Given his record of accidents around Gabby Wade, he wasn't about to take any chances. "What're you doing?" he reiterated.

"What does it look like I'm doing? I thought you'd like something to eat when you got back, and a fresh pot of coffee to go with it." She piled thick slices of bread onto a plate. "Sit down and I'll get you some."

Not knowing what else to do, Ty pulled out a chair, turned it around, and straddled it. Gabby set a cup of coffee on the table in front of him, then sat down across from him with her own steaming mug.

"Did you get Joe settled at his place?" she asked.

Ty sipped his coffee, pleasantly surprised she'd made it strong, the way he liked it. He nodded. "Rose seemed to know where everything was, so I left her and the doctor to make him comfortable. Rose said to tell you she wouldn't be in to work tonight."

"I should hope not. Her place is with Joe," Gabby said. She gazed at him, her eyes disquietingly direct. "Thank you for getting Rose even though you don't approve of her."

He choked back the block of pride that willed him to keep silent. "I was wrong."

She tilted her head to one side in question.

"Rose really loves him," Ty said.

Gabby's expression turned thoughtful. "Why is that so hard to believe?"

She wasn't going to make this easy for him. "I've always thought women like her could never settle down with one man after having sold their body to so many."

Gabby leaned forward, her hands wrapped around her coffee cup. "Women like her are just like Miss Gatewood. The only difference is that Miss Gatewood has always had enough money to get whatever she wanted. Rose didn't even have money to buy food, and desperation drove her to do what she did."

He studied her earnest expression, her eyes that captured the light and spun it into gold threads. Again she was making him question his beliefs, what he'd always taken for granted. She had a knack for throwing him off-kilter and weakening the foundation of his control. It had been that self-command he prized so highly—his ability to be better than people like Miss Gabby and Rose.

And his father, whose weakness had destroyed his family.

"Understanding why she did it doesn't make it right," Ty stated through thinned lips.

"Maybe not, but it does let us forgive," Gabby said gently.

He hadn't forgiven his father for what he'd done,

and he never would. "Some things can never be forgiven."

"Are you saying you can't forgive Rose for what she did just to survive?"

Startled out of his own personal misery, Ty shook his head. "No. I'm saying it might take some time. I want to be certain she won't hurt Joe."

"You can still say that after seeing them together?" Gabby asked in disbelief. "I think you're the one hurting Joe, not Rose."

"What do you want from me, Gabby?" he demanded in frustration.

"Joe asked Rose to marry him at the picnic on Sunday. She said she wouldn't. She thinks she's not good enough for him."

He scowled. "That's not my problem."

"I want you to talk to Rose, to tell her that you approve of her marrying Joe. I think she'll change her mind. Your opinion matters to her because you're Joe's best friend."

Ty shifted uncomfortably. He had no doubt she loved Joe, and he already knew Joe's feelings toward her. If he had the ability to smooth their rocky road, he was obligated as a friend to do so.

He nodded slowly. "I'll talk to her tomorrow, but I can't guarantee anything."

Gabby's smile lit up her pretty face and chased away the darkness in Ty's soul for a few moments. "Thank you."

She stood and glanced out into the gathering dusk, where snow swirled and eddied. "I'd better get back to town before I can't see my way."

Ty rose. "I'll walk you."

"You don't have to. Besides, if folks saw us together, it would just add fuel to the gossip mill. I don't want you to get hurt any more than you already have."

"You didn't seem very worried about my reputation when you switched the baskets."

"That was a mistake," she said firmly. She wrapped her slender fingers about the chair's back, and her knuckles whitened. "And I didn't plan the fall into the creek, or what happened after that."

"You wanted me to kiss you again," Ty dared. Some perverse need within him had to hear her say that she wanted him as much as he'd wanted her.

"Maybe," she replied honestly. "You're a stubborn, self-righteous, inflexible man who is making my life miserable." Unexpectedly, she laughed. "But I like you a whole lot more than I ought to."

Gabby was the only person who made him feel like he stood at the edge of a cliff. He stepped closer until only the chair she gripped separated them. He feathered his forefinger across her flushed cheek. "You're a beautiful, generous woman who stands for everything I'm against. And I want to kiss you again even though I know I shouldn't."

Gabby's tongue swept across her lips, inciting Ty's desire. With a groan, he slanted his hungry mouth across hers, relishing her velvety softness and eager response. She wrapped her arms around his neck, drawing him closer and burying her fingers in his hair. A moan shuddered from deep within her, and Ty's blood burned for the taste of her. He coaxed her lips open, and his tongue swept across hers.

Ty's heart thundered in his chest. The sweet smell and taste of Gabby devoured his control. He wanted her with a need bordering on obsession. He wanted her compassion, her zest for life, and her spirit that soared with the clouds. He wanted her vibrant colors to chase away the ghostly shadows that haunted his soul.

He pressed closer to her and his knee rammed against the chair between them. Drawing away, he muttered a curse.

"It's a good thing the chair was there," Gabby said, her eyes filled with regret. "A kiss doesn't change anything—we're both still the same people we were."

Ty stepped back, reluctantly acknowledging her words. His hands clenched into fists at his sides.

"Unless you're willing to give a little," she added softly.

"I can't even if I wanted to," he said, his voice husky with lingering passion. "I'll walk you home."

Gabby stared at him a moment, then shrugged into her cape and pulled the hood over her head. The walk to Gabby's Emporium was a silent one, and Ty was strangely disappointed by her somber mood. She should have tried to catch snowflakes on her tongue or danced across the white blanket covering the ground.

For the first time, Ty admitted to himself that Sawtooth was going to be a boring place without Gabby's free spirit.

Chapter 17

~~~~~ Ꝺꝺꝺ ~~~~~

Gabby had little time to ponder Ty's unusual behavior at his cabin. With Rose taking care of Joe around the clock, Gabby filled in for her, serving drinks to her customers every night.

The last debate, only a few days off, also weighed heavily on her mind. After deciding Mrs. Edwards had a point about her own pride getting in the way, Gabby decided to support the new bridge. She had to win the election to ensure the survival of the Emporium.

Three nights before the last debate, Gabby's gambling hall was uncharacteristically busy. Because many of the cowhands had been unable to get into town on Saturday on account of the early snowfall, they'd taken advantage of the warm chinook wind that had blown in and melted the snow in the middle of the week.

"Here's those four refills," William called out to Gabby from behind the bar.

She managed a tired smile. "Thanks."

Piling the mugs on her tray, Gabby carried them over to a table where some hired hands from a local ranch sat. She set a glass down in front of each of them and picked up their empty ones.

"That'll be twenty cents, boys," she announced with forced cheer.

With a little good-natured grumbling, they tossed the coins on the scarred tabletop and Gabby scooped up the money. The youngest of the group looped an arm around Gabby's waist and pulled her against him, his forehead burrowed between her breasts.

"Hey, now, cowboy, you know the rules around here," Gabby reminded him, keeping her voice light. "The girls here serve drinks and that's all."

She tried to twist out of his arms, but he only tightened his hold.

"Come on, Miss Gabby. I bet you're a wildcat in bed, huh?" the teenage cowhand said, his words slurred.

His antics only exasperated her. "That's something you're not going to find out. Now, you let me go or I'm going to have to take your beer away."

She reached for his mug, and the others at the table chuckled.

"You watch it, Orville," one of them said. "She means what she says and she don't take guff from no one."

"She will from me," Orville argued, his immature masculine pride stung.

Gabby shook her head ruefully and poured the beer over the troublemaker's head. He sprang to his feet, releasing her. As he sputtered unintelligibly, Gabby slipped out of his reach.

"I think you gentlemen might want to take your friend home. He's had more than enough to drink," she suggested.

Orville glared at Gabby, but the oldest man

stood and took hold of his arm. "The lady's got a point. Besides, we got to work at sunrise tomorrow."

The other two finished their beer quickly and got to their feet.

"Now apologize for your bad manners," the older man said to Orville. "That ain't no way to be treating Miss Gabby, and you know it."

The young cowhand's face reddened slightly. "Sorry, Miss Gabby. I didn't mean nothin' by it. I was just havin' some fun."

Gabby smiled at the boy, who wasn't more than sixteen or seventeen and already doing a man's job. She knew what it was like to just want to have a good time once in a while.

"No harm done," she said. "Why don't you go on home and sleep it off? I have a feeling you're going to regret it in the morning if you don't."

The men tipped their hats to Gabby and shuffled out of the Emporium. Gabby sighed and picked up the mugs on the table. She carried them back to the bar and leaned against it for a moment.

"Trouble?" William asked.

"Nothing I couldn't handle." She laid a hand on his arm. "But thanks for asking."

"How's Joe doing?" he asked as he filled a mug from the keg's tap.

"Better, but he's still taking some laudanum for the pain. Rose doesn't want to leave him until she's sure he can take care of himself."

"She's got it bad for him, doesn't she?"

Gabby smiled. "No, she just loves him."

William set the filled glass on Gabby's tray and pointed to a table. "That's for that fella sitting by himself."

She groaned. "I've forgotten what it's like to be on my feet all night. Remind me to give Rose and the other girls a raise."

"Don't forget about me," William said.

"When you start wearing heels, I'll give you a raise, too," Gabby retorted.

"If that's the only way I can get one, I might just do that."

Although William's tone was light, his eyes seemed serious. Gabby wondered if he was as tired as she was, and decided he probably did deserve a raise. If she won the election, she'd have a talk with him, find out if he was interested in becoming the manager of the Emporium. She'd be busy with her mayoral duties and would need someone she trusted to look after the Emporium for her.

Heaving a weary sigh, she picked up the tray and continued working.

A couple hours later, the Emporium's crowd had dwindled to a handful of customers. The poker games had ended and William began to wash the dirty mugs gathered behind the bar.

"Could you fill the pail for me? I'll start wiping down the tables," Gabby said to William.

While he did as she asked, Gabby rested her chin in her palm. She enjoyed talking and joking with her customers and considered the regulars friends, but her worries over the election outcome exhausted her.

And with thoughts of the mayoral race came the intrusion of Ty Ashburn on her peace of mind. She tried to convince herself it was only because he was her opponent, but at the most inopportune times she remembered his kisses, and she'd press her fingertips to her tingling lips. Her body had become a stranger, wanting something Gabby didn't understand to appease the yearning ache. All she knew was she could no longer think of Ty as merely a businessman and her foe in the political race. But she refused to analyze her feelings toward him; she wasn't even certain she could.

She shifted her weight and groaned at her protesting feet. "Now I remember why I bought my own place."

"So you can order the rest of us around," William said with a smile that didn't reach his eyes.

Again puzzled by his ill humor, Gabby wondered if something was bothering him. Before she could ask, gunshots from outside distracted her.

"Probably a cowboy letting off some steam," William remarked.

"You'd think it was a Saturday night," Gabby added, and frowned. "Maybe Ty Ashburn's stand on not allowing firearms in town isn't such a bad one."

More shots sounded, punctuated by a scream.

Gabby's blood curdled, and she dashed out the door and onto the street bathed in shadows from the gas lamps. She spotted a weaving cowboy in the middle of the street, a revolver hanging loosely in his hand.

"He shot a little girl," a bystander hollered.

Gabby's gaze leaped to the slight figure lying on the ground not far from the drunken man. Raising her skirt hems, she raced to the body and knelt down. Carefully, she turned her over onto her back and Gabby's heart tumbled in her chest.

"Sara," she whispered hoarsely. Gabby pressed her ear to the young girl's chest, but there was no reassuring heartbeat. She held her trembling hand in front of Sara's face—no warm breath touched her palm.

A scream climbed into Gabby's throat, and tears burned her eyes. She pulled the girl's limp body into her arms and rocked her gently. Dear God, no, Sara couldn't be dead! Not quiet, gentle Sara who worried too much about propriety and who had never harmed a living thing in her short life. She would never slide down another banister or giggle when she landed safely in Gabby's arms at the bottom of the stairs. She, with her sad eyes and too-thin frame, would never grow into a woman or see the ocean or love a man. It wasn't fair!

Outraged voices circled Gabby.

"She's dead!"

"He killed a little girl!"

"Let's get 'im!"

The men moved away from her, toward the single figure who stood in the center of the street. Through misty eyes, Gabby watched the crowd overpower the drunken cowboy and wrest away his gun.

"String 'im up!"

"He deserves to hang."

The angry declarations gathered in strength and volume.

"Is she dead?" a man asked.

Gabby glanced at the doctor, who had silently joined her. She nodded mutely, unable to speak as tears flowed down her face.

The angry crowd shoved the shooter ahead of them, and they paused by Gabby. She glanced up at the drunken cowboy and recognized him as Orville. His dazed expression told her he hadn't known what he'd done. Until now.

"Is she alive?" he asked in a small voice that reminded Gabby of a scared boy.

She swallowed and shook her head. "You killed her."

His face crumpled, making him seem infinitely younger and more vulnerable. "I didn't mean to. I swear I didn't even see her."

"Someone get a rope. We'll show him what we do to men who murder innocent children," Bill Danvers, the sawmill owner, shouted.

"A man who kills kids is worse'n a rabid wolf," Floyd Sanders added.

The emotion-charged mob, fueled by rage and spurred on by Danvers and Sanders, shouted their approval and raised their fists. Orville was dragged away, his pleas and cries falling on deaf ears.

"Serves the son-of-a-bitch right," the doctor muttered.

Gabby closed her eyes, trying to shut out the angry mob and the frightened pleas of the boy. Her mind seemed numb, but her heart felt as if a knife had been driven through it. Her conscience screamed that it was her fault Sara had died. If she'd taken Orville's gun, he wouldn't have had the opportunity to shoot the girl.

As much as she hated him for taking Sara's life, though, she couldn't allow the young cowboy to be lynched. He was only a boy himself, with so much of his own life ahead of him. It had been a horrible accident, but an accident nevertheless, and Gabby had been just as instrumental in the tragedy.

"Take care of her, Doctor," Gabby said with a catch in her voice.

She gently lay Sara's body on the ground and hurried away, oblivious to the crimson blood that had soaked through her blouse and skirt.

The frenzied crowd had grown to include women with coats pulled over their nightrails and men with shirttails hanging around their hips. The "respectable" side of town had deemed the situation serious enough to interrupt their night's sleep, and their indignation added to the mad hysteria gripping everyone in its clutches. A few men carried torches that cast weird flickering shadows across the mob, making the scene more ominous and nightmarish.

Gabby caught up with them at the edge of town, near a huge oak tree with a limb that looked tailor-made for a hangman's noose. She shoved through the crowd, finally reaching the front, and shouted vainly to get their attention.

At first Ty had ignored the gunshots, but a sixth sense told him something was amiss. He arose from behind his desk and walked to his office window. Seeing the people gathered down the street, Ty's gut told him something was definitely wrong. The area where the commotion came from was near Gabby's Emporium, and his heart kicked against his ribs.

He nearly ran down the street, and when he arrived, he found the crowd had moved to the edge of town and only the doctor remained kneeling by a small body. Seeing it wasn't Gabby, an involuntary sigh of relief escaped him.

"What happened?" Ty demanded.

"Some cowboy killed this little girl," the doctor replied in disgust.

Ty studied the girl's face closer and his stomach twisted in recognition. She was one of the orphans he'd seen sliding down the banister with Gabby, and she'd also been with her at the restaurant the other day.

"Why?" Ty asked in a strained voice.

"He was drunk, shooting off his gun. She happened to get in the way of one of his bullets."

Sickness settled in Ty's gut. Did Gabby know what had happened? She would be heartbroken by the girl's death. "Where are they taking him?" he asked.

"He's going to get what he's got coming. They're going to hang him."

The mob's angry voices drifted to Ty in the crisp night air. He took off down the street, not certain what he should do, but knowing he had to do something. As he approached the unruly crowd, he heard Gabby's voice rising above the clamor.

"Stop it! Please, you have to stop this!"

Ty halted at the edge of the group and stared in shock at Gabby, who stood on a tree stump. Her hair was in wild disarray, framing her tear-streaked face. Her petite figure was ramrod straight, and a dark stain colored the front of her clothes. Ty's breath caught in his throat. Had she, too, been shot? She didn't move stiffly, though, and Ty realized it had to be the little girl's blood.

"We can't murder him," Gabby hollered above the shouts that demanded blood for blood. "He deserves a trial."

"Just like that little girl deserved what she got?" a bellicose voice hurtled back.

Pain flickered across Gabby's features and Ty's heart twisted again. She'd cared for the child; cared more than all these people gathered around who screamed for revenge. Yet it was she who was trying to stop another killing, in spite of the grief he knew was tearing her up inside.

"It was an accident," Gabby stated, her steady voice contrasting with the agony in her face. "He didn't shoot her deliberately."

"How do we know that?" another person demanded.

"I swear I didn't even see her," Orville said, his face gray and drawn in the torches' weird, flickering light.

Vernon Gatewood stepped up beside Gabby, his suit immaculate and each silver hair perfectly in place. "We can't let things like this go unpunished in our town. We have to make an example of this ruffian and hang him. We need to show others like him that we won't put up with drunk and disorderly behavior on our streets."

"Let the court decide what to do with him," Gabby argued. "If we allow him to be hung, we're no better than those so-called ruffians. We'll be killing someone outside the law, too."

Gatewood turned to Gabby, his face inches from hers. "You only care about your business, and men like this murderer keep you in business. You don't even care that a child was killed."

Gabby slapped him, and the sharp report hung over the suddenly silent crowd. Her cheeks blanched white and Ty stepped forward, afraid she was about to faint.

"How dare you!" she began in a voice that shook with rage. "How dare you say that, when you didn't lift a finger to help Sara when she was alive. You didn't even know her name was Sara, did you?"

Gatewood's face hardened like granite, and Ty

was shocked by the venom in the older man's expression. "If you knew her, it was only because you saw her as a future employee. Young, innocent girls are worth a lot in your business."

Unable to take any more of Gatewood's obscene accusations, Ty joined Gabby. Placing a hand on her arm, he felt her trembling. He turned his fury on Gatewood.

"That's enough!" Ty ordered. "Miss Gabby doesn't run that kind of business. She gives money to the home so the orphans are fed and clothed." His gaze swept across the crowd. "And I've seen her play with the children, giving them the care and affection nobody else in this town would."

Gatewood narrowed his eyes. "Even if you're right, which I don't believe, it doesn't change the fact that a little girl is dead and the man responsible has to be punished."

"If people want Sawtooth to become a civilized town, we have to take the first step tonight," Gabby spoke up. "We can't take the law into our own hands. If this man is guilty, he'll be punished, but that's not our decision to make."

A few grumbles met her impassioned speech.

"She's right," Ty stated forcefully. "If we can't do what's right tonight, we don't deserve to call ourselves civilized. We have a court system to determine a man's innocence or guilt, and to punish the criminal accordingly." He stared the crowd down. "Everyone, go on home. A girl is dead—we don't want any more blood spilled tonight. That's no way to honor her memory."

After a moment, a couple of people turned around and walked back toward town. A few more joined them, and soon the mob dispersed, leaving

Gatewood, Ty, Gabby, and Orville, who still knelt on the ground with a crude, hastily made noose around his neck.

"You shouldn't have interfered," Gatewood said coldly. "Especially taking *her* side."

"I took the *right* side," Ty corrected sharply. "We can't obey laws indiscriminately. This cowboy will get his day in court. Personally, I hope he hangs, but that's not for me to decide."

"I hope you realize what you've done, Tyler. You may well have lost the election this evening," Gatewood said flatly. His eyes glittered like obsidian. "Which means you've also lost your backing."

The older man spun on his heel and marched away.

Ty turned to Gabby, whose face was a pale oval in the inky darkness, her blond hair gilded by the moon's glow.

"Are you all right?" he asked softly.

She hugged her waist and nodded. "Thank you. I wouldn't have been able to stop them by myself."

"I'm surprised you tried."

Gabby glanced at the young cowboy on the ground. His shoulders were shaking and his face was turned away from them. "He's only a boy."

"He's a grown man, Gabby," Ty refuted. "He was old enough to drink, which makes him responsible for his actions. Besides, I would've thought you'd hate him for what he did."

She shook her head. "I hate what he did, but I can't hate him."

"I don't understand."

"He isn't a bad person, but he did a horrible thing which he's going to have to live with the rest of his life." She glanced down at the blood on her blouse and shuddered. Raising her grief-stricken gaze to Ty, she said, "That's the price of free will— but a cost we have to pay for all the rewards that go with freedom."

A tear rolled down her cheek, and Ty moved toward her to offer her comfort.

She cringed and took a step back. "Could you take him to the jail?"

Disappointed, he nodded. "He should be all right overnight. Once a mob like that is broken up, they lose their lust for blood. I'll send a wire to the circuit judge tomorrow morning."

"Thank you," she said, barely audibly. "Is there anything I can do?"

"Go home and get some sleep. You're exhausted," Ty said, tenderness creeping into his voice. "Good night, Gabby."

"Good night," she echoed softly.

His gaze followed her slow progress until the night swallowed her slumped figure. Appearances had fooled him. Gabby's unconventional lifestyle had hidden a generous and principled nature, and Vernon Gatewood's respectable facade had hidden a self-serving ego.

Who else had he misjudged in his quest to escape his past?

Chapter 18

The day of Sara's funeral reflected Gabby's bleak mood: grayish black clouds blanketed the mountains and cast a leaden pall over the autumn-colored valley.

Gabby stood at the edge of the black yawning hole, April clutching her hand on one side, Harold pressed close to her other, with Tommy trying to be brave beside him. Mrs. Edwards and Alma Tusk were nearby with the other children from the home, along with a handful of people from town who hadn't known the young girl except in her death. Absent were the men who had deemed it their duty to see Orville lynched, despite the fact that they'd ignored the shy, self-conscious girl while she was alive.

" 'Ashes to ashes, dust to dust,' " Reverend Tusk droned.

Gabby blocked out his monotone and concentrated on the small pine coffin that held Sara's mortal remains. She tried to imagine Sara's thin face shining brightly as she ran to her family, greeting them after being separated for so long. But all she could see was the limp, blood-covered figure she'd held in her arms on the dark street.

274

Gabby swallowed a sob.

"Amen," the reverend said, and the scant mourners echoed him.

Using ropes, two men lowered the spartan casket into the earth. After the coffin was settled in its final resting place, they picked up shovels and tossed dirt into the hole. The soil thumped on the wood, and Gabby flinched at the desolate, hollow sound.

The small crowd began to move away. Alma Tusk dared to give Gabby a quick hug before she followed her husband. Gabby remained motionless, except for a slight jerk each time a shovel of dirt was heaped onto the casket. Tommy and Harold shifted restlessly.

"Why don't you two go on back to the home with the other children?" Mrs. Edwards suggested, her tone gently maternal.

Reluctantly, the boys left Gabby's side and walked out of the cemetery with the other orphans. April remained beside Gabby. "Is Sara in heaven with my ma and pa?" she asked curiously.

"I suppose she is, sweetheart," Gabby said softly.

"Then why is everybody so sad?"

Gabby's eyes filled with moisture, and she squatted down beside the child. "Even though she's in heaven, we're going to miss her."

April thought for a moment and pushed back the pale blond strands that had blown across her face. "I'm going to miss her, too. She used to buy me a licorice stick when we went to the store." She looked up at the ominous clouds. "Do you think she can see us?"

Unable to speak, Gabby nodded.

The small girl lifted her hand and waved to the sky. "Bye, Sara. Don't forget me."

Gabby pressed her fist to her mouth to hold her tears back. If only she had a tiny piece of April's innocence and faith.

Mrs. Edwards stepped forward and took April's hand. "I think we better get back to the home and make sure the others are behaving themselves."

"Okay. Bye, Miss Gabby, and don't be so sad. Sara wouldn't want you to be sad."

Feeling as ancient as the massive oak in the corner of the cemetery, Gabby pushed herself upright. "I'll try," she promised in a husky voice.

"You take care, Miss Gabby," Mrs. Edwards said. "Sara was a good girl, but sometimes she liked to sneak out of the home late at night and go for a walk. It probably had something to do with those nightmares she'd have. So don't you go blaming yourself."

Gabby wished she could heed her advice, but she knew the truth. Gabby had known the cowboy was drunk and she hadn't taken away his gun, as she'd instructed her employees to do after a man drank too much. Instead, she'd only sent him on his merry way, on to another establishment, where he'd finished the job of getting completely sotted.

"I'll stop by the home in a couple days," Gabby said somberly.

Mrs. Edwards frowned and laid a hand on Gabby's shoulder. "I'll be watching for you."

The men finished covering the grave, then slung their shovels over their shoulders and left Gabby alone.

She raised her head and gazed silently at the slate-gray clouds that hung over the land like a funeral shroud. The wind sifted through the tree branches, rustling the last of the dying leaves—a lonesome sound.

She took a deep, shuddering breath. She had insisted that Ty Ashburn's worries were groundless, that she could control the drunken behavior before it got out of hand and nobody would get hurt.

She'd thought Ty had too much pride, but she'd been guilty of the same.

She stared down at the new mound of dirt, silently begging for a forgiveness that would never be given. Sinking to her knees beside the grave, Gabby laid her hand on the soil. The dampness crept through her glove and chilled her hand, but she kept it there as if to punish herself.

Tears rolled down her cheeks and dripped onto the grave. "I'm so sorry, Sara. I hope you can forgive me."

Her whisper sounded harsh in the hushed quiet.

The rustle of footsteps startled her, and she turned to find Ty standing behind her. Dressed in a dark suit and holding his hat in his hands, he appeared to be paying his final respects.

She stared up at him for a long moment, searching his face for a sign of condemnation, but found none. He remained mute, and she gave her attention back to the newly formed grave. Ty hunkered down beside her and rested a hand on her shoulder.

"You did more for her than anybody else in this town ever did," Ty said softly.

Gabby's throat tightened, and she waited a moment before she could speak. "I got her killed."

Ty shook his head. "No—that cowboy killed her."

"If only I'd taken away his gun," she said, ignoring his words, "Sara would still be alive."

"You don't know that for certain, Gabby," Ty said gently. "I heard you refused to serve him another drink after you thought he'd had enough."

Gabby smiled without humor and with a large dose of self-reproach. "A lot of good it did. He just went someplace else to drink."

"That wasn't your fault. You couldn't have stopped him," Ty reiterated firmly.

"If I'd supported your stand to forbid firearms in the town limits, this wouldn't have happened."

"Or if the bartender in the last saloon he went into took his gun away—or if his friends did. Life's got a lot of 'ifs,' " Ty said.

Guilt gnawed at Gabby's soul. She didn't deserve his understanding; she deserved his contempt. She got to her feet, and he rose also.

"Tell me it was my fault!" Gabby demanded, glaring up at him. "Tell me Sara would still be alive if I hadn't settled in Sawtooth and opened the Emporium." She fisted her hands and struck his chest, self-hatred and bitterness welling within her.

Ty grabbed her wrists and pulled her against him. "Nobody can see the future, Gabby."

The feel of his hard body brought some sanity back to Gabby and she tilted her head back to stare up into crystal-blue eyes that reflected her own misery.

"Sara's gone, Ty," Gabby whispered hoarsely. "And it's my fault."

He brushed back a strand of her hair and gently cupped the back of her head in his palm. "Listen to me, Gabby Wade. It wasn't your fault. You cared for Sara, probably more than anybody else did.

Don't punish yourself for something you had no
control over."

Gabby studied his drawn features and finally believed him. She buried her face in his shirt and
cried out the agonized grief that twisted her heart
into a strangled knot.

Her body shuddered with sobs, and Ty wrapped
his arms around her, drawing her into a comforting
embrace. Moisture blurred his vision, although he
didn't know if it was for the young girl who lay in
the earth or the woman whose pain was like a
physical entity between them.

By all rights, he could blame Gabby, but the
thought of using Sara's death as a political tool
sickened him. He suspected she saw herself in Sara
and to publicly blame Gabby for the accident
would be worse than unfair; it would be cruel and
inhuman.

"Shhh, it's all right," he crooned tenderly, rubbing her back with gentle circular motions. To see
her so heartsick and pale pierced him with helplessness.

Finally, Gabby's sobs turned to hiccups and she
wiped her streaked face with her gloved hands.

"I'm sorry," she said with a grief-husky voice.
She brushed at his chest. "I got your shirt all wet."

"It'll dry," Ty said. "Are you feeling better?"

"A little." She gazed up at him with regret-
shadowed eyes. "Why are you here?"

Ty glanced away, unwilling to let her see the uncertainty in his own eyes. "I came to say good-bye
to Sara."

"You hardly knew her."

The north wind swept through Ty, chilling him
straight to the bone. He fixed his gaze on her. "You

taught me to care for all of them, including Sara."

He studied her, noting the exhaustion creasing her brow. Gabby's concern for the orphans was heartfelt, not a facade she took off and put on like a coat. He remembered the people in the town where he'd grown up, and how they had pretended to care after his father had lost everything. Later, when Ty, his brother, and mother needed their help, all they'd gotten were a few reluctant scraps of food anybody would have given a stray dog.

Gabby wouldn't have abandoned two young boys and a sickly woman.

"It hurts to care," she finally admitted with a heavy sigh. "Even though we'd miss out on so much in our lives if we didn't."

Ty remembered his father's bloodied corpse, and he closed his eyes a moment to banish the grisly picture. "Sometimes not caring is the only way a person can survive," he said softly.

"An animal survives, but a person has to live," Gabby replied, equally quiet.

"Something else your uncle taught you?"

She shook her head. "I learned that myself, and that's what I have to believe." Gabby glanced down at Sara's newly formed grave, and a tear rolled down her cheek. "It's what I tried to teach Sara and the other children."

Ty thumbed her tear away gently, the warm moisture searing his skin.

He'd never known anyone like Gabby. Because she possessed the courage to defy convention, and the inner strength to do what her heart told her, Ty had misjudged her. He had passed judgment on her based on society's rules. It was his way to escape the past's recriminations, and if he hadn't gotten to know Gabby Wade, he undoubtedly would have lived the rest of his life holding rigidly to others' expectations.

"And sometimes we don't decide to care or not care. It just happens," he said softly, gazing into her eyes.

A sad smile tilted her lips upward. "I guess it does." She lifted her hand and rested her palm against his cheek. "I guess it does," she repeated gently.

Raising herself up on her tiptoes, she pressed her warm, soft lips to his. He trembled as a wave of emotion passed through him, but he didn't try to deepen the kiss. Instead, he held her as if she were a fragile flower, afraid he might crush her in his embrace.

All too soon, Gabby stepped out of his arms. Her hat lay askew and she tipped it back in place.

"You should get a new hat," Ty suggested.

"This is the only hat I've ever worn—it was my mother's. I remember her wearing it when we went to Sunday service, and it's the only thing I have left of hers."

Startled by her revelation, he remembered how he and Eleanor had made fun of it. Now that he knew what it meant to her, he felt ashamed by his callous remarks. Gabby prized the memories of her parents, and a pang of jealousy struck him. Ty had wanted nothing to remind him of his father, and when his mother died, he'd buried his past with her. But Gabby had kept her mother's hat all these years and had worn it with pride despite its frayed appearance. To Gabby, it was beautiful because it had been her mother's.

"I'll walk you back to your place," Ty said with a husky voice.

After one last look at Sara's grave, Gabby moved ahead of him toward the gate. Ty placed his hat back on his head once they were out of the cemetery.

"How's Joe?" Gabby asked as they followed the narrow path back to town.

"He's off the laudanum, and just as ornery as ever," Ty replied. "He said Rose went back to work last night."

"I think she felt guilty after what happened to Sara and all." Gabby shook her head. "I told her she could stay with Joe longer, but you know how Rose is when she gets something in her head."

"I'm finding out," Ty said dryly.

They walked in silence for a few minutes.

"I apologized to both of them last night," he said. "I said I'd be honored to be Joe's best man if he'd have me."

Gabby paused and turned to look up at him with expectant eyes. "And?"

"Rose still won't give him an answer. She said she couldn't until we find out who wins the election."

"Why?"

"She didn't say."

Gabby spun away from him and marched toward Sawtooth, her arms swinging stiffly at her sides.

Ty caught up to her in a few long strides and grabbed her, bringing her to an abrupt stop. "Where are you going in such a huff?"

She narrowed her flashing eyes. "Rose has a real chance at happiness, and I'm not going to let her get all noble on me. She loves Joe and he loves her. From what little I understand about marriage, that's a good beginning."

Reeling from her offensive barrage, Ty shook his head and grinned. "Just when I think I have you figured out, you go and say something that makes me wonder if I'll ever understand you."

Gabby tilted her head, an unaffected gesture Ty was fast becoming fond of. "If I can make you smile by doing something you don't expect, I'll have to come up with some more surprises."

"Try not to spring them on me all at once. I don't think I could handle it," Ty teased.

"Don't worry. After I'm elected, I'll have lots of time to surprise you."

She turned and continued into town.

Ty chuckled. Losing the election could have some definite advantages.

He hurried after her and gently took hold of her elbow.

She glanced at him, startled.

"I said I'd escort you to the Emporium, and I never go back on my word."

They garnered a few curious looks, but Ty ignored them. With the election less than a week away, he had done everything he could to let people know where he stood on the issues. If they didn't like his platform, they didn't have to vote for him. If they disapproved of the company he kept, he didn't want their vote.

In front of the Emporium, Gabby paused to draw a key out of her reticule. Ty took it from her and unlocked the door, pushing it open. He handed the key back to her.

"Thank you," Gabby said, her cheeks rosy from the cool, wintry air.

"You're welcome," Ty replied. "I'll see you tomorrow night at the debate."

She nodded, a twinkle in her eyes. "I'm looking forward to it."

"I am, too," he said, surprised to realize he meant it.

Her expression sobered. "Thank you for paying your respects to Sara."

"You don't have to thank me. I did it because I wanted to."

She smiled gently and clasped his hand. "I know."

Ty's heart skipped into his throat, and he leaned forward to kiss her forehead tenderly. "Good-bye, Gabby."

"Good-bye."

Reluctantly, Gabby released his hand and watched him leave. Out of all the people in Sawtooth, he was the last one she'd expected to offer her comfort.

Beneath his reserved, aloof exterior lay another side to Tyler Ashburn, a side that he'd buried, and Gabby was finding too much to admire about that other man. She lifted her fingertips to her forehead where he'd kissed her. There was definitely more to Ty than she'd suspected.

She entered the Emporium and closed the door behind her.

"Hello, Gabby," Vernon Gatewood greeted her, his tone disrespectful.

Gabby's heart missed a beat, and she stumbled in her shock to find him sitting at one of the poker tables. She crossed her arms and glared at him. "I don't remember inviting you," she stated.

He smoothed his white shirtfront and adjusted his silver vest. "I invited myself."

The silence of the Emporium, usually soothing, seemed ominous, settling on Gabby's shoulders like a heavy mantle. She walked past him to the bar and removed her hat. "Then uninvite yourself. I have things to do."

Gatewood turned slightly in his chair and settled his black, fathomless gaze on her. "How was the brat's funeral?"

Gabby trembled with rage at his mocking tone and retorted sharply. "You weren't there. I think that says it all."

He smiled, the gesture a mere formality. "I'm glad to see you still have your claws."

"What do you want?" Gabby asked bluntly.

"I always liked that about you, Gabby. You cut straight to the chase." He paused dramatically. "I have a business proposition for you."

"Like the 'proposal' you made Ty?"

His brow lifted. "So you two are on a first-name basis. That may change things."

Gabby chastised herself for allowing her guard to slip. "What do you want?" she repeated impatiently.

He stood and approached her. With every nearing step, Gabby's heart beat more frantically. She schooled her expression into a cool mask, afraid to reveal her revulsion and fear.

Gatewood leaned against the bar with only a couple feet separating them. "I can ensure you'll win the election."

"And what's the price of this generous offer?" Gabby made sure Gatewood heard her sarcasm.

"Would you believe it's offered freely?"

She shook her head. "Nothing is free with you, Mr. Gatewood. I'm sure Mrs. Gatewood learned that too late."

Rage twisted the older man's face. "Shut up!" He shook his finger at her. "Don't you ever speak of my wife again!"

Gabby stood her ground. "Why—because women like me are only good enough to take to bed?" she taunted. "But I turned you down, and you've never forgiven me. That's the only reason you're backing Ty's stand to get rid of the saloons."

Gatewood's jaw muscle clenched and unclenched furiously. After a few moments he seemed to regain control of his emotions. "And he will, too, unless you're willing to make a deal."

"A deal with the devil? No, thank you, Mr. Gatewood. I'd rather take my chances."

"You're making a mistake, Miss Gabby. A *fatal* mistake."

"You're the one who made the mistake—both with Ty and myself. Ty decided he didn't need you or your daughter, and I have all I need right here." She lifted her arms expansively, gesturing around the Emporium. "You'd better face it, Mr. Gatewood: whether Ty or I win, your days in Sawtooth are numbered."

Gatewood narrowed his eyes. "Are you threatening me?"

"No, I'm only telling you how it is."

Gatewood's chuckle rasped across her nerves, bringing goose bumps to her arms. "No one tells me anything, Miss Gabby. *I* tell *them*."

He strolled out of the Emporium, his insolence leaving a stench in his wake.

Gabby leaned heavily on the bar. She hated Vernon Gatewood and all the two-faced men she'd known like him. To the community they were pillars of respectability; in the upstairs room of a saloon, they were hypocrites who proclaimed to love their wives while they lay with a prostitute. Marriage vows were only words to such a man, while women were expected to remain faithful to their husbands under the threat of divorce or worse. Although she'd never known Eleanor Gatewood's mother, Gabby suspected she'd had worse.

Straightening, Gabby picked up her hat and walked toward the staircase. At the bottom of the steps, she halted.

The Emporium had been locked—how had Vernon Gatewood gotten in?

Chapter 19

Ty buried his chin deeper into his fur-lined coat and tightened his hold on the leather reins. With Joe laid up, Ty had taken his scheduled run to Rawlins the day before the final debate. He had started back to Sawtooth the next morning but had had a run of bad luck starting with one of his horses throwing a shoe. Then a wagon wheel had loosened, so Ty had to tighten and regrease it. It was a good thing he'd gotten an especially early start.

With only about ten miles to go until he arrived home, Ty relaxed and allowed his thoughts to wander, only to return to the same question that had plagued him the last few days. Of all the issues he'd taken a stand on, the issue of closing the saloons bothered him the most. The more he learned about Gabby, the more he wondered if he'd made the right decision. What gave him the right to decide if a person should visit a saloon or not? As both Gabby and Mrs. Williams, the dressmaker, had told him, most men played a friendly game of poker without losing more than a dollar or two. Those like Ty's father were the exception.

Still, Ty wasn't sure if he could change his stand.

He'd be going against everything he believed in.

Ty spotted a fallen tree blocking the road up ahead and he drew back on the reins, bringing the horses to a halt about twenty feet from the obstruction. Frowning, he tied the leather to the brake handle and jumped down. He walked over to the massive pine, and his gaze latched on to the easily distinguishable marks at the base. Somebody had purposely chopped down the tree. He glanced around nervously, the hair prickling at the back of his neck. What if the person who'd downed it was still nearby?

Moving cautiously back to the wagon, Ty pulled the Winchester from the floor beneath the seat. Feeling better with the weapon in his hands, he searched the area but couldn't see anyone. With rocks and uneven ground on either side of the road, he couldn't chance driving the heavily loaded wagon around the tree. He could unhitch one of the horses and ride into town to get some help, but if the wagon's goods were stolen, Ty would lose more money than he could afford.

With a sigh of exasperation, he lifted an axe from the back of the wagon and set to work.

Two hours later, sweat-drenched in the early evening air, Ty moved the last of the fallen tree from the road. He shrugged back into his coat and climbed up on to the seat. Urging the rested horses into a fast gait, Ty tried to determine who would gain the most by his absence at the debate. The obvious answer was Gabby, and considering her past record of campaign strategies, it shouldn't have been too difficult to believe she'd done this, too.

Except Ty didn't believe it.

That left only one other person.

Gabby crossed the upstairs hallway of the Emporium and knocked on Rose's door.

"C'mon in," Rose called out.

Gabby entered her friend's room and shook her head at the typical disarray that greeted her eyes. Clothes were thrown across the bed, chest, and open armoire; shoes littered the floor, resting where Rose had tossed them.

Rose stepped over a pile of underclothing and walked around Gabby to eye her spring-green skirt and jacket. "You look very nice."

"I'm surprised you can find me in here," Gabby teased.

"I don't complain about your room, do I?"

"That's because there's nothing to complain about. I wasn't sure you'd be going to the debate or staying with Joe."

Rose's expression grew serious. "I want to be there for you, like you've always been there for me. Joe knows that."

"Have you told Joe about everything?" Gabby paused and added, "Including how that man nearly beat you to death?"

Rose nodded and leaned over to retrieve a pair of shoes. She sat on the edge of her unmade bed to put them on. "He wanted to go find him and kill him." She grinned wryly. "How's that for true love?"

Gabby pushed aside a hill of blankets and sat down beside her friend. "Surely you know he loves you, Rose."

"That's what he keeps telling me."

"Do you love him?"

Rose finished lacing her heeled boots, then turned dark, troubled eyes to Gabby. "The first time, after I sold myself for two dollars, I knew no decent man would ever want me. Right then and there, I swore I wouldn't go and do something stupid like fall in love. For six years I kept that vow."

Gabby ached for her friend and wished she could have helped Rose escape the shame she'd endured. "Joe *wants* you for his wife."

"I don't know if I can do it."

"What do you mean?"

"I don't know if I can suddenly start believing in love after all this time. You know what it's like, Gabby. Most of my customers were 'happily' married men."

"Joe isn't like those men," Gabby argued, praying she'd judged him correctly. "He'll be faithful to you, Rose. And he can give you a lot more security than I can."

"What'll you do if Ashburn wins?" Rose asked with a troubled look.

"I don't know yet. The only thing I know for certain is that if you love Joe, you should marry him. He'll take care of you, keep you safe, and maybe you two will even have a houseful of children."

Rose snorted. "Can you see me with a dozen kids hanging on to my apron strings?"

Gabby smiled slightly, bittersweetness in her breast. "Yes, I can. I think you'd make a wonderful mother."

Rose blinked, and Gabby saw moisture lurking in her eyes. "I love him more than I thought I could ever love someone, but people will talk and make

Joe's life miserable for marrying someone like me."

"You have nothing to be ashamed of! Joe is the only person who matters, and he doesn't care what you've done in the past. It's the future that matters. You accept his proposal and show everybody you're proud to be Mrs. Joe Hedley."

Rose wiped her eyes, a new resolve on her tear-stained features. "I'll give Joe my answer tonight."

"Good!" Gabby stood and walked to the door, stepping over the items scattered across the floor. "I'll be ready in about five minutes."

"All right," Rose said. "And Gabby?"

She paused, her hand on the doorknob. "Yes?"

"For what it's worth, you'd be a better mother than me."

Gabby thought of Tommy, Harold, and April. If she could, she'd adopt them and raise them as her own—but the courts would never agree to give her custody. The law didn't care that she could love them as if they were her own; they only saw a single woman who ran a gambling hall.

She shook her head and smiled too brightly. "Not me. I like being able to give them back when I'm done playing with them."

Gabby slipped into the hallway and ducked into her room. She couldn't allow her mind to linger on the orphans, or on the possibility of having to leave them behind. If she did, she wouldn't be able to get through the next few hours.

Five minutes later, she hurried down the stairs and was surprised to see Rose was already waiting for her.

"Are you ready?" Rose asked.

Although Gabby's heart raced in anticipation of seeing Ty again, she was nervous about what to expect. So much had changed since the first debate, including her feelings toward him. "As ready as I'll ever be. How about you—you *are* going to accept Joe's proposal, aren't you?"

"Yes. And after the debate is over, I'll go see him." Rose clutched Gabby's hand. "You're a good person, Gabby, and don't let anyone tell you otherwise."

"Anyone like Vernon Gatewood?"

Rose grimaced. "Especially him."

Gabby and Rose left the Emporium and walked down the street toward the stage. After tonight, the platform would be taken apart and the lumber re-used. If Gabby had her way, the boards would be used to build an addition to the Home for Orphaned Children. She knew Ty would support her idea; he'd turned into a powerful ally in helping the orphans.

Once Ty recognized his responsibilities, he took them seriously, and his scrupulous honor dictated his actions. In spite of their differences, she trusted Ty Ashburn more than any other man she'd known. She'd loved her uncle because he was family, but Gabby could never be certain if he was telling her the truth or trying to con her.

She caught sight of Ty's tall, broad-shouldered figure as she and Rose approached the growing crowd. Her heart did a funny little jig, and she couldn't seem to pry her gaze from him.

"You're wearing your heart on your sleeve," Rose whispered.

"What?" Gabby asked, confused.

"It's as clear as those ugly birds on your hat that you've got feelings for Ty Ashburn."

"They aren't ugly," Gabby retorted.

"Yes, they are, but you missed my point."

"I didn't miss anything. I merely ignored it."

Even if she was attracted to Ty, nothing could ever come of it. She couldn't allow a man, even one who made her senses spin and awakened her desires, to sidetrack her. There was no choice to be made: in order to keep her home and her independence, she had to defeat him in the mayoral race.

"Good evening, Miss Gabby, Miss Rose," Ty greeted them.

"Hello, Mr. Ashburn," Rose said, flashing him a saucy grin.

Gabby noticed his haggard expression, and concern filled her. "Are you all right?"

He nodded grimly. "I just got in from Rawlins about twenty minutes ago. Somebody felled a tree across the road."

"Why?"

"To keep me from getting back here in time for the debate."

Gabby's eyes widened. "I didn't do it."

"I know," he said with a certainty that warmed her. "You aren't that ruthless, but I know someone who is."

Gabby could guess who he referred to, and one look into his somber eyes confirmed her suspicions.

Ty turned to Rose. "Have you seen Joe lately?"

She nodded. "I was over there this afternoon. He wanted to get up, but the doctor said he has to stay in bed awhile longer to make sure the bone is knitting right. I'm not sure who's getting worse-tempered, him or me."

"Joe was never one to be lying around," Ty said. "You may end up having to tie him down."

"I got my lasso all ready."

Ty smiled. "I don't doubt that you'd use it, too."

"Tell Mr. Ashburn your decision," Gabby prompted.

Rose flushed. "I've decided to marry Joe, only he doesn't know it yet."

"Congratulations," Ty said, genuinely glad. He leaned down and kissed Rose's cheek, startling her and shocking Gabby.

Rose overcame her surprise and winked at Gabby. "If I'd known I'd get a kiss from Tyler Ashburn, I would've told Joe yes a long time ago."

Gabby laughed at Ty's puzzled embarrassment. "Don't worry, she was only joking—I think."

She looked up at the debating stage and saw Tom Bailey motioning for her and Ty to join him.

"I think it's time," Gabby said.

Ty nodded and escorted her up the steps, his solid presence calming Gabby, yet at the same time tying her stomach into knots.

Bailey quieted the crowd and reintroduced Gabby and Ty. The debate followed the same agenda, with the constituents asking questions which the two candidates answered.

"Because the weather has grown considerably colder, and the candidates have already stated their views, we will take only one more question," Bailey said thirty minutes later. He pointed to Vernon Gatewood. "Go ahead, Mr. Gatewood."

Gatewood stood, gripped his lapels, and asked in a clear voice that rang through the frigid air, "What are your stands on the construction of the bridge?"

Gabby glanced at Ty, who gave her a small nod.

She rose from her chair and stood in the center of the stage.

"Most of you recall how it was my opinion that we didn't need the bridge, or the addition of more people to our town." She paused. "That *was* my opinion. Tonight, however, I wish to change my stand on that issue. I would be willing to support the maintenance of a new road to link us with the proposed bridge."

Gatewood appeared surprised, and people began to mutter among themselves.

"Why the change, Miss Wade?" Gatewood asked.

"Because it will bring families into our town and help it grow in a direction we all wish it to go."

"You're telling me that a saloon owner wants God-fearing families to populate Sawtooth?" Gatewood demanded.

"Why is that so hard to believe, Mr. Gatewood? I want what's best for our town, and I think establishments like mine can coexist with other legitimate businesses."

Gabby felt Ty's curious gaze upon her, but she didn't dare look at him.

"Thank you, Miss Wade," Bailey said. "Mr. Ashburn, your stand on this issue?"

He took Gabby's place at the center of the platform. "My position hasn't changed. I will support the construction of the bridge and maintenance of a new road."

"What about the saloons? You still plannin' on closin' them down?" a man shouted from the audience.

Gabby held her breath.

"My position on public drinking and gambling

hasn't changed. If I am elected, I'll do everything in my power to shut down those establishments which cater to those vices," Ty replied.

Gabby's heart thudded to her toes. With all the other changes she'd seen in him, she'd hoped he would change his mind about closing the saloons, too. But that conviction just ran too deeply.

Bailey concluded the debate and reminded everyone to vote in three days, then invited people over to the schoolhouse for the Harvest Dance. In the chilly evening air, folks hurried away to the promise of warmth, food, and music.

"I'm sorry, Gabby."

Ty's contrite voice startled her out of her disappointed reverie.

"I considered taking the saloon closings off my agenda, but I couldn't." His eyes held genuine apology. "I hope you realize it's nothing personal; I just can't abide a place where a man can gamble his life savings away."

"Nobody has ever lost his life savings at my tables," Gabby said quietly. "I would never let that happen."

"I know that, but there are other owners who aren't so conscientious," Ty said. "Isn't there something else you could do in Sawtooth—like maybe open a dress shop?"

Gabby laughed sardonically. "Me, own a dress shop?" She shook her head. "I can't even sew a button on straight. Besides, I like having a place people can come to and forget about their troubles for a little while. Life wasn't meant to be taken so seriously, Ty, and people forget that. If I can ease someone's burden for just fifteen minutes, it's worth it."

Her amber eyes pleaded for his understanding, and Ty wished he could give it to her. The fact was, he did understand, only too well. Gabby Wade delighted in making people happy; hadn't he been on the receiving end of more than one of her schemes? Her sunshine-filled laughter itself tempted his smile and, more dangerously, his heart. He'd lived in the darkness so long, he'd forgotten that billowy clouds and blue skies existed. Gabby had reminded him, and he only wished he could give her something in return.

"What about the home? Mrs. Edwards is getting on in years; maybe you could take over there," Ty suggested.

"If I didn't know any better, I'd say you wanted me to stay in Sawtooth," Gabby teased. A sad smile touched her lips. "Because of who I am, they would never approve of me working with children."

"If I'm the mayor, I can put in a good word for you and press them to accept you."

Gabby toyed with her reticule's drawstring, then met his gaze with troubled eyes. "I wouldn't accept the position even if, by some miracle, it was offered to me. It would hurt too much."

Ty had seen her suffering with Sara's death, but surely that wouldn't happen again, especially with the saloons gone. If he could only get her to see how much better it would be than owning a gambling hall.

"But you have the gift to bring joy into their lives, just like you do with your customers," he argued.

"That's different. Children comes to the home because they've lost their families. That's a deeper hurt than any of my customers have, and I'm not sure I could deal with those tragedies without losing my own ability to see past the pain."

He couldn't imagine Gabby losing her gift to instill joy and pleasure into others' lives. She fairly glowed with a light that burned brightly from within and illuminated every life she touched, including his own.

Ty straightened Gabby's hat brim and allowed his hand to linger on her beloved keepsake. He didn't want her to leave town, but he couldn't change his long-held opinion on gambling halls. He'd lived with the humiliation for too long, and nothing could purge the memory of his father's cowardly suicide and the reason behind it.

"So what'll you do after the election?" he asked, hoping his voice held only curiosity.

Her buoyant optimism resurfaced, and her eyes twinkled. "I'll set up my mayor's office in the back room of the Emporium and hire a sheriff who'll work on commission."

Ty chuckled and shook his head. "I should've known." He glanced around to find they were the only two people left. "Would you like to go to the dance?"

She cocked her head coquettishly. "Is that an invitation, Mr. Ashburn?"

"It is."

"Then I accept."

Her sparkling smile dazzled him, and for a moment he forgot the election, her gambling hall, and his reasons for keeping her at arm's length. Instead he imagined waking to her bright smile and enticing curves every morning. Her hopeful optimism and ability to see good in everything might someday give him the strength to let go of his festering bitterness.

Fairy tales were for children, and happily-ever-afters were for fools, and he was neither. Yet he couldn't help wishing he still believed in both. If he did, maybe he and Gabby would have a chance together.

He extended a crooked arm to her and she put her small but capable hand through it. He escorted her toward the schoolhouse, which was lit up like a beacon. Fiddle music danced amid the buildings and through the treetops. Ty heard Gabby humming softly to the Stephen Foster tune, and her dulcet tone wrapped around him, lulling him and bringing forth years-old memories.

"My mother used to sing to my brother and me when she'd tuck us in at night," he said in a low voice.

Gabby sighed. "I've always been jealous of people who have brothers or sisters."

"Don't be. More often than not, they'll let you down when you need them the most."

"Is that what happened with you and your brother?"

He choked back a wave of bitterness. "He did something I can never forgive."

"Never is a long time, Ty, and he's your only family. You should let it go," Gabby suggested gently.

"I can't, Gabby. Some things just go so deep that you can't ever get rid of it."

"So you let it poison you. Is it worth it?"

"Yes." Ty didn't need to think about his answer. Stephen's betrayal had been almost as brutal as his father's.

"When you're seventy years old and you haven't seen him since you were children, will it still be worth it?" Gabby pressed.

"You don't know anything about it."

"Then tell me, so I can understand."

They arrived at the schoolhouse, and a few people called out greetings to them. Ty was glad for the interruption. He allowed Gabby to enter ahead of him and blinked in the bright light. After taking Gabby's cape and his jacket to the cloakroom he rejoined Gabby, who appeared strangely pale and stiff. She'd removed her hat and held it in her trembling hands.

"Is something wrong?" he asked close to her ear.

A brief shake of her head gave her answer. Ty frowned. Something had upset her. He glanced around the room and spotted Eleanor and a couple of her equally snooty friends. Eleanor was staring at Gabby and speaking to the two girls beside her. A word or two drifted to him, and he saw Eleanor point toward Gabby's bonnet. He had an idea of what she was saying.

"Did Eleanor say something to you?" Ty demanded.

Gabby didn't answer, but stared down at her hat as if seeing it for the first time. Ty put two and two together and strode across the room to Eleanor.

Although the music continued, Ty was aware of the cessation of voices as the townsfolk strained to eavesdrop on his conversation with his ex-fiancée. He kept his voice low to spare Gabby's feelings.

"What did you say to her?" he demanded, staring into Eleanor's wide eyes.

Her lips thinned and she smoothed her pale pink

taffeta gown with a gloved hand. "Nothing that would interest you."

Ty stepped closer, forcing her friends to move back. "Pull in your claws, Eleanor. Gabby never did anything to hurt you."

Hatred glimmered in the dark depths, stunning Ty. He'd never seen this side of Eleanor before. "She humiliated me when you broke our engagement to be with her."

"I broke the engagement because I decided we weren't meant for each other. Gabby had nothing to do with it."

Eleanor's flat smile was a caricature of her father's. "Who are you trying to convince: me, yourself, or everybody else? You've been making a fool of yourself over that—that woman ever since the election began."

"You're the one making a fool of yourself," Ty said grimly. "Gabby has more compassion in her little finger than you'll ever have, even if you live to be a hundred."

"If it's compassion you wanted, you should've told me. I might have been able to come up with enough to satisfy you." Eleanor's tone was acidic, burning through Ty's limited patience.

Ty studied Eleanor like a bug under a magnifying glass. Respectability, like her fashionable appearance, was merely skin deep. And this was what he'd wanted to marry, what he wanted to become?

"I never thought I'd say this, but I actually feel sorry for you," Ty said.

"You'd better save some of that pity for yourself," she retorted with narrowed eyes. "I have a feeling you're going to need it." She flounced away, with her entourage close behind.

Ty rubbed his brow. His ex-fiancée's contemptuousness made him wary. He thought the break had been clean, but obviously Eleanor had other ideas. He wondered where Vernon stood: if he disapproved of his daughter's vindictiveness or if he would use it to his advantage. If Vernon could use his own daughter for his greedy purposes, Ty suspected he was capable of using anything to his advantage.

Gabby had been right about not knowing those closest to him.

A commotion at the door drew his attention and he saw Gatewood enter, followed by a young man with dark hair who stood a couple inches shorter than Ty. The newcomer's clothing, beneath his unbuttoned greatcoat, appeared expensive and tailor-made to his lean body.

"Tyler," Vernon called out. "I've got a surprise for you."

Ty frowned and crossed the floor. As he approached Vernon and the stranger, Ty's heart missed a beat and he stumbled slightly.

"This young man was looking for you so I thought I'd bring him over," Vernon said, his expression too smug.

"Hello, Ty. It's been a long time." Stephen Ashburn extended his hand to his brother.

Chapter 20

Gabby gaped at the younger image of Tyler Ashburn. There was no doubt the two men were related. But where Ty's rugged face had been creased by the burden of responsibility, Stephen's face appeared smooth, with laugh lines at the corners of his sky-blue eyes.

Ty made no attempt to shake his brother's extended hand, and Stephen brought his arm back to his side. The air between the two men sparked with tension, threatening to explode at any moment. Gabby stepped between them and faced Stephen.

"Welcome to Sawtooth, Mr. Ashburn," she greeted him, putting on her friendliest hostess smile. "You chose a perfect evening to visit, with the Harvest Dance going on. At least, I was under the assumption this was a dance." She deliberately swung her gaze to the three-man band. "Can we have some music, please?"

The gray-bearded fiddler nodded and struck up a lively tune. Conversations picked up where they'd left off, and Gabby was caught between Ty's fury and Stephen's guarded wariness.

"You never mentioned you had a brother, Tyler," Gatewood commented, drawing Gabby's star-

304

tled attention. She'd forgotten he was there.

"I didn't think it was any of your business," Ty growled.

Stephen smiled crookedly. "Same old Ty. It's nice to know some things never change, big brother."

"What the hell are you doing here?" Ty demanded.

Gabby noticed Gatewood's avid interest in the hostile exchange between the Ashburn men, and unease curled in her stomach. She wouldn't put it past him to use Ty's animosity to hatch some scheme that would benefit himself.

She took hold of Ty's taut arm. "Why don't we go someplace more private? Like the Emporium. You two can talk there without an audience."

Stephen's blue eyes, a mirror of Ty's but friendlier and more open, settled on her. "And who is this beautiful angel?"

Gabby laughed at his obvious flattery. "Miss Gabby Wade."

"The same Miss Gabby Wade who's running for mayor against my big brother?"

"That's right," she said, instinctively liking him. She glanced at Ty's thunderous expression, and her smile faltered. "Come on, Ty, let's go."

His jaw muscles clenched and unclenched, revealing his anger and indecision. Finally he nodded curtly. "All right. I'll get our coats."

He spun away to the cloakroom.

"I thought maybe he'd changed in fourteen years," Stephen commented, and raked a nervous hand through his raven hair. "I guess I forgot how muleheaded Ty can be."

"Why did you come here?" Gabby asked

bluntly, knowing Ty would be back at any moment.

He shrugged. "I was in Rawlins when I read that he was running for mayor, so I thought I'd swing up this way and see how he was doing."

Gatewood leaned closer and Gabby's skin crawled. She took a step back to put more distance between herself and the older man.

"And what business are you in?" Gatewood asked.

"Here's your coat," Ty broke in, elbowing Gatewood aside. He helped Gabby into her cape, then donned his own wool-lined jacket. He glanced at Gabby. "Don't forget your mother's hat."

Startled, she nodded and retrieved the headpiece from a nearby desktop. Instead of putting it on, though, she merely held it at her side. Eleanor's cutting remark about how Ty had laughed at the hat had hurt Gabby. She didn't want to believe Eleanor, but she'd been shaken by her venomous barbs.

"Aren't you going to put it on?" Ty asked, glancing at the bonnet.

She shook her head curtly. "I'll just carry it."

He frowned and took it from her hand. With a tenderness that nearly brought tears to Gabby's eyes, Ty set the hat on her head, gently tugged one side to straighten it, then tied a bow beneath her chin. His fingers brushed her neck, and his warm breath caressed her cheek.

"There, that's better," he said softly. "Your mother would be proud of you."

Gabby raised her head, straightened her shoulders, and sent Eleanor Gatewood a cool stare. The pampered woman merely glared back at her, then lifted her nose in disdain and whirled away.

Ty leaned close to Gabby and whispered in her ear, "That's my girl."

His affectionate and intimate words brought a secure, cozy feeling to Gabby, but his nearness brought goose bumps to her arms.

Then Ty turned to his brother and his expression once again grew stormy. As Ty ushered her and Stephen out of the crowded schoolhouse, Gabby noticed Gatewood's eyes narrow when they passed him, and she shivered from the arctic chill in his black stare.

Walking between the two brothers, Gabby could feel the tense silence stretching, threatening the fabric of the night. What had Stephen done to make Ty so bitter toward him?

A few snowflakes gently spiraled down to land on Gabby's cape and in her hair. She usually enjoyed these crisp evenings with a gentle snowfall, but tonight her mind was on the puzzle of Ty and Stephen Ashburn.

She scurried into the Emporium, followed by the two men. Only a few customers occupied the tables, and William appeared bored behind the bar.

"Is the dance over already?" William asked.

Gabby shook her head. "Mr. Ashburn's brother arrived unexpectedly in town, and I volunteered my place as neutral territory to talk."

Ty glared at Gabby, while Stephen sent William a helpless shrug.

"Could you bring a pot of coffee and three cups to the office?" Gabby asked her bartender.

He pushed his spectacles up on his nose and frowned, but replied curtly, "I'll have it for you in a couple minutes."

She sent him a nod of gratitude and motioned for Ty and Stephen to follow her. Noting that Ty did so grudgingly, Gabby wanted to box his ears. Couldn't he see he had an opportunity to forgive and forget whatever had come between him and his brother? Stephen had made the first step; it was up to Ty to meet him halfway.

Once in the office, Ty turned to the fireplace, giving his ramrod back to her and Stephen. His stiff shoulders and clenched fists reminded Gabby of the man he'd been at the onset of the mayoral campaign.

"Have you eaten supper?" Gabby asked Stephen, deciding to ignore Ty for a moment.

Stephen nodded, and an easy smile slipped across his handsome face. "I had something at the restaurant."

Gabby couldn't help staring at the younger man, wondering why he and Ty had turned out so differently.

"When did you get into town?" she asked, trying to dispel the uncomfortable silence.

"Yesterday."

"So why didn't you look up Ty right away?"

At her question, Ty turned slowly to fix a hard stare on his brother. "Because he was scared."

Stephen's face reddened, although Gabby wasn't sure if anger or embarrassment caused it.

"Why would he be scared?" she asked Ty.

He dipped his chin at Stephen. "Ask him, not me."

Puzzled, Gabby looked to the younger brother. "Were you scared?"

Stephen slipped off his overcoat and draped it over the back of a wing chair. He wandered around the office, examining each picture on the wall as if it were a rare portrait. Finally, he faced Gabby and hooked his thumbs in his brocaded vest pockets. "I suppose I was. Fourteen years ago, we didn't part on the best of terms."

"What happened?"

Gabby noticed a flicker of apprehension in Ty's gaze, and a silent message seemed to pass between the men.

"Doesn't she know?" Stephen asked Ty.

"Nobody does, and that's the way I want it." The underlying threat in Ty's voice startled Gabby.

What had happened between them that was so terrible he wouldn't talk about it?

A knock on the door sounded, and William entered the room bearing a tray with the requested coffee. He set it on Gabby's desk.

"Thanks, William," she said.

He nodded and exited without a word.

Her mind aswirl, Gabby poured them each a cup. Stephen picked his up, and Gabby handed Ty a mug.

He took it with a slight easing of his angular features. "Thanks."

"You're welcome," she said softly.

Stephen took a sip from his cup, then spoke to Ty. "You were always too concerned about what other people thought."

"And you didn't give a damn about anything," Ty fired back.

Stephen lowered his eyes, and Gabby saw in the younger man's expression the same haunting sadness she had glimpsed in Ty.

"You're wrong, big brother," Stephen stated, bringing his gaze back to his brother. "I cared about you and Ma and Pa before he . . . before he passed on. I worried about how hard you worked and I thought I could help."

"By gambling?" Ty demanded in disbelief. "You knew how I felt about it, and still you'd sneak out of the house and go to a saloon to find a poker game."

Comprehension dawned on Gabby. She should have seen it right away: the expensive clothes, the smooth white hands that had never done manual labor, and the easy smile that hid his thoughts.

"And I helped pay some of the bills, too," Stephen retorted defensively. "But you were too damned full of self-righteousness to accept the money. But Ma, she didn't care where it came from. She just wanted to take some of the burden off you, too."

"I made enough to take care of both of you. I didn't need blood money." Ty shot a nervous glance at Gabby.

"You're a professional gambler?" Gabby asked the younger man.

Stephen nodded slowly, and kept his gaze fixed on Ty. "Much to my eternal damnation."

Ty closed his eyes, humiliation in the slump of his shoulders. Gabby knew how deeply Stephen's seeming betrayal must have wounded his pride, and she ached with empathy. With Ty's strict code of ethics, he could never abide Stephen's choice or admit to anyone he'd failed with his own brother. And now, three days before the election, Stephen's arrival in Sawtooth could undermine Ty's campaign.

"Did you really come here to patch things up

with Ty, or was there another reason?" Gabby demanded.

"What other reason would there be?" Stephen asked. He appeared confused by her question.

"Maybe you thought you'd get some revenge by hurting Ty's chance to be elected mayor."

Stephen faced Gabby. "Wouldn't you like that? From what I understand, if Ty wins, you and the other saloon owners will be forced out of Sawtooth."

"At least I'll know he remained true to his beliefs," Gabby said. "From what I've seen of professional gamblers, you rarely even understand what the word 'ethical' means."

Stephen's intent gaze settled on Gabby, then moved to Ty. Suddenly he laughed, startling her. "That's a strange comment from a gambling madam. Are you sure you and Ty aren't on the same side?"

Gabby's mouth dropped open. "We don't agree on anything," she said after finding her voice.

Stephen only chuckled. "The lady gambler and the righteous entrepreneur: that just proves that even Cupid likes a good practical joke now and again."

"You're crazy," Ty said forcefully. "Gabby's right. We're on opposite sides of each issue."

"Whatever you say, Ty," Stephen said with a straight face. His eyes, however, twinkled mischievously.

Ty strode to the door, his footsteps heavy on the carpeted floor. He paused, his hand on the doorknob. "I want you out of Sawtooth. The sooner the better."

He jerked open the door, then slammed it behind him on his way out.

Gabby sank into her desk chair and rubbed her temple with her fingertips. "There's no doubt you two are brothers: you both know how to make quite an impression."

"Thank you," Stephen replied smoothly.

"I didn't say a 'good' impression," Gabby corrected.

Stephen plopped down in the chair on the other side of the desk. "But I was right, wasn't I?"

Gabby refused to dwell on his absurd claim that she and Ty . . . Even Cupid wasn't that blind. "*Ty* was right: you're crazy."

"I only have one question. How can you two run against each other when you're on the same side?"

Gabby glared at the man who resembled Ty Ashburn a little too much. "He's going to close down the sal—drinking and gambling establishments. I run a gambling hall. How, pray tell, are we on the same side?"

"Gabby, in the grand scheme of life, there are only two sides; those who love and those who don't. You and my brother are obviously on the same side."

Although Stephen resembled Ty on the outside, they had little in common on the inside. Ty was practical, down-to-earth, while his brother was more like her.

Shocked by her abrupt revelation, Gabby suddenly realized one of the reasons Ty hadn't liked her: she reminded him too much of his brother. Of course, she hadn't liked Ty in the beginning, either, because he was too much like those pseudo-pillars of society who cheated on their wives Saturday night and attended church service Sunday morning.

"I'm glad for Ty," Stephen said softly.

"What?"

"I was afraid he'd end up with one of those so-called respectable women who would never make him smile."

Unable to stop herself, Gabby laughed. "He almost did. Last week, he called the wedding off. In fact, his ex-fiancée is the daughter of Vernon Gatewood, the man who escorted you over to the schoolhouse." Her eyes narrowed. "Why would he be so friendly, since he knew you were the brother of the man who jilted his daughter?"

Stephen shrugged. "I have no idea. I ran into him in the hotel and asked him where I could find Ty."

Gabby studied him, speculating on her suspicions. Had Vernon Gatewood brought Stephen to Sawtooth to sway Ty to his way of thinking? Or had Gatewood and Stephen been in cahoots from the beginning? She didn't know or trust Stephen well enough to dispel her wariness. If he had come to town to hurt Ty, he would answer to her.

"It's hard to say what motivates Vernon Gatewood," she said, keeping her voice casual. She stood. "It was nice to meet you, Stephen. How long are you planning on staying?"

Dismay clouded his eyes. "I'm going to give Ty a couple more chances to put the past behind us. He wasn't always so serious, Gabby—we had a lot of fun times when we were kids. I was always getting him in trouble, but even back then, he took all the blame." Stephen sighed. "Now we've only got each other, and I was hoping he'd let bygones be bygones."

"What happened to your father?"

His gaze skipped about the room. "It's not my place to tell you. If Ty wants you to know, he should be the one to answer that question." He got to his feet and threw his coat over his arm. "If you don't mind, I think I'll check out your poker tables."

"You're more than welcome to. House rules are simple: no cheating and no bets over ten dollars without my approval."

Stephen grinned. "A woman of beauty, intelligence, and a fair sense of play. If Ty hadn't found you first—"

Gabby cut him off before he could continue. "I've worked too hard to get where I am, and no man, not even one as 'charming' as your brother, can force me to give it up."

"Then perhaps you'd consider a partnership with me?"

Despite herself, Gabby smiled and gave him a friendly shove. "Go on, and don't take too much from my regulars."

"Your wish is my command, beautiful lady," Stephen said gallantly.

After he'd gone, Gabby settled in the wing chair in front of the fireplace. She'd known many men who called themselves professional gamesters, who only cheated better than everybody else. If Stephen was one of them, she would have him removed from her Emporium. And if he were such a man, would he consider selling out his brother no worse than stealing at the poker table? She'd have to keep a close eye on him.

It was almost impossible to believe Stephen and Ty were brothers. Ty with his too-somber countenance was the dark half, while Stephen with his too-easy smile was the light. What had happened with their father that had made them that way?

Gabby recalled the torment in Ty's hunched posture as he'd stood by the hearth, and her throat tightened at his anguish. If only he would share it with her—surely nothing could be as bad as he believed this family secret was.

Ty Ashburn was the most prideful, infuriating man she'd ever known. He was also the most honorable and principled, not to mention the only man who'd stolen her resolve with a single kiss.

Her wayward thoughts returned to Stephen and his absurd comment about her and Ty. Hadn't Rose made the same ludicrous observation?

Gabby admitted she'd enjoyed Ty's kisses more than she should have. But that was merely a physical attraction that had nothing to do with love.

Yet if it was merely lust, why had he comforted her at Sara's grave? And why had it felt so right in the circle of his secure arms?

Ty wanted to smash something—anything. His fingers curled and uncurled into futile fists as he strode down the boardwalk. He avoided the schoolhouse, where the dance continued undisturbed by the chaos his brother had brought into Ty's predictable life.

Stephen had a lot of nerve showing up a few days before the election. Now Ty would be lucky if he offered Gabby any opposition in the election. He'd more than likely lose Gatewood's shaky support, too, which might not be such a bad thing.

Especially since he believed Gatewood had tried to keep him from the debate, though Ty wasn't sure why. Unless he merely hoped Ty would blame Gabby.

Ty paused in front of his office, and his breath misted in the wintry air. He didn't want to work tonight. Yet the thought of returning to his solitary cabin didn't appeal to him, either.

He'd go see Joe. He'd understand Ty's frustration with his brother.

His boot heels clicked sharply on the wood made more brittle by the cold, and he buried his hands in his coat pockets. A few minutes later, he arrived at his friend's place and pounded on the door, then entered without waiting for a reply.

Rose hurried out of Joe's bedroom, her face flushed and her black hair spilling out of its knot. "Mr. Ashburn. We weren't expecting you."

"Obviously," Ty said dryly, embarrassed heat spreading upward from his neck. "I'm sorry. I'll talk to Joe tomorrow." He turned to leave.

"Ty, is that you?" Joe called out.

"Yeah, sorry I bothered you. I'll stop by tomorrow," Ty replied.

"Get back here and tell me what's bothering you," Joe growled.

"How do you know anything is?"

"Rose, would you haul him in here for me?" Joe shouted.

She arched a pencil-thin eyebrow and grinned. "What do you think, Mr. Ashburn—do I haul you in there or will you go peaceable-like?"

The thought of the much smaller woman dragging him across the floor brought the first genuine smile he'd had since his brother had shown up.

"When you put it that way, I don't have much choice," Ty teased.

He walked into Joe's bedroom and found his glowering friend sitting up in the carved oak bed. His splinted leg rested on top of a pillow, and he wore lightweight woolens with the sleeves pushed up to his elbows. "You're looking as ornery as ever," Ty greeted him.

Joe flashed him a scowl. "You'd look ornery, too, if you were held prisoner in your own bed."

Ty laughed. "I hear congratulations are in order."

The red-haired man's face flushed, and he smiled proudly. "Word sure gets around fast."

"I had an inside source."

"Her name wouldn't happen to be Gabby, would it?"

Ty pulled a ladderback chair over beside the bed and straddled it, resting his forearms across the top. "She and Rose happened to mention it before the debate. I'm happy for you and Rose, Joe. Really."

Joe narrowed his suspicious gaze. "As I recall, you and I had some words over Rose a couple weeks back. What changed your mind about her?"

"A lot of things," Ty responded vaguely.

Joe brushed a hand across his brow. "She's had a hard life, Ty. When you and me were learning how to freight, she was surviving the only way she could."

"Gabby told me pretty much the same thing."

Joe studied Ty for a long moment, his eyes unreadable. "You didn't come over here just to congratulate me and Rose. What happened?"

Ty rubbed his eyes with his thumb and forefinger. "My brother showed up tonight."

"Here in Sawtooth?"

Ty nodded wearily. "He said he came to patch things up between us, but he hasn't changed."

"You never told me much about him. What's he do?"

"He went against everything I tried to teach him." Ty paused, inundated by the painful memories of their last argument. "He's a professional gambler."

"Does he cheat people?"

Ty glanced up sharply at Joe's curious expression illuminated in the yellow glow of the lantern. "I don't think so. I never heard he did."

"Then I don't see a problem, Ty. Look, I know you're against gambling, but if a person plays square, I don't see anything wrong with it."

Joe didn't know the full story, and Ty didn't have the courage to tell him. Nervous agitation brought Ty to his feet and he paced Joe's small bedroom. "What're folks going to think when they see my own brother is a gambler? I'm going to lose their support and more than likely lose the election."

"You're not your brother's keeper, Ty. He's a grown man and you can't control what he does."

"Why'd he have to show up now?"

Rose entered the small bedroom carrying two cups of coffee, which she gave to Ty and Joe. She lowered herself to the feather mattress to sit by her intended.

"Why'd who have to show up?" she asked curiously.

"Ty's brother's in town," Joe answered.

Rose smiled. "That was mighty nice of him to come visit you."

"They don't get along," Joe added.

Rose's cheerful expression faltered, and she looked up at Ty. "It's a shame when a family can't patch up their differences. A lot of times I wish I could do that with my folks, but there's too many bad feelings under the bridge."

"Maybe we can go visit them after we're married," Joe suggested.

"Naw, they don't want to see me."

"But they're your parents," Ty argued. "They should be able to understand why you did it and forgive you."

"Look who's talking about understanding and forgiving," Rose lifted one brow. "A man who can't even give those things to his own brother."

Ty's pacing came to an abrupt halt and he stared at Rose. She was right. He had no right dispensing advice he couldn't follow, but it seemed to Ty it would be easier to forgive a daughter gone astray than a brother who'd gone against everything he believed in. Or a father who'd abandoned his family.

"I'll stop by tomorrow, Joe." He sent Rose a respectful nod. "Good night, Rose."

After he left Joe's place, he walked back to his cabin. Rose's parting words plagued him the entire way, compelling Ty to relive that day twenty-two years ago when he'd found his father lying face-down in a pool of his own blood. He'd never forget how he'd gotten sick and vomited from the horrific sight. Even now his stomach cramped with the memory.

Stephen had only been nine years old at the time

and he'd been spared the last image Ty had of their father. The tragedy wasn't Stephen's fault; so why did Ty blame him? Because he'd become a gambler himself?

Ty pictured his younger brother that morning their father had killed himself. Stephen had been told there'd been an accident, that John Ashburn had been cleaning his revolver when it discharged. Neither the sheriff nor Ty told Stephen or their mother how the bullet had left blood and gray brain matter spattered on the wall behind him.

Nausea assaulted Ty, and he pressed his lips together. He had to dismiss the past from his thoughts. He had to look ahead, to a future that no longer looked as promising even if he won the election. For if he won, Gabby would leave.

It would be for the best. Despite Stephen's outlandish claim, Ty and Gabby had no future together. Maybe someday Ty would find a respectable woman who also had Gabby's zest for life and her generous compassion.

But I don't want any other woman.

He couldn't even consider courting her. She was a gambler, a woman who lived on the fringes of society and represented everything he'd struggled to overcome for so many years. Still, the thought of her having to leave after the election weighed on his conscience.

But if he changed his stand on saloons now, he would lose all the respect he'd attained in Sawtooth—and he couldn't risk that. Not even for Gabby's smile.

Chapter 21

Stephen Ashburn's untimely arrival was an unforeseen complication in Vernon Gatewood's scheme to gain control of Sawtooth and all its commerce. Gabby Wade's refusal to consider his proposal was yet another stumbling block to all the plans he'd made.

Vernon leaned back in his smooth leather chair that sat behind the massive mahogany desk. Everything about his home gave the illusion of breeding and wealth. The fact that he'd been raised in a sequence of upstairs saloon bedrooms where his mother had worked had never been discovered, and he'd climbed the ladder of respectability by stepping on anyone who stood in his way.

The two mayoral candidates were merely ladder rungs he would climb over if it became necessary.

Gabby Wade thought she was too good for the likes of Vernon Gatewood, but she would get her comeuppance. He had believed Tyler to be much like himself: single-minded in his quest for success and esteem. But Ashburn had unexpectedly turned soft, and it was up to Gatewood to ensure Ashburn's victory. If that meant eliminating the opposition, or using a bit of extortion, he would do so. And he had the means to do just that.

A knock sounded on the door.

"Come in," Vernon called out.

Bentley opened the door. "Mr. Lowe to see you, sir."

"Send him in."

"As you wish."

Bentley stepped out of the doorway to allow William Lowe past him. Once the visitor was in the study, Bentley retreated and closed the door behind him.

"Have a seat."

Lowe did as Vernon said, then pressed his spectacles up on his nose.

"I was surprised to see Tyler Ashburn at the debate," Vernon stated.

Lowe shifted uncomfortably. "I told the men to do like you said, but Ashburn started out earlier than we figured. Why didn't you just have them ambush him?"

"Because I don't want him killed. I have other plans for him." The tree had merely been a test to see where William's loyalties lay. "I have another job for your hired men tonight, if you think they can be more successful than they were with the last task."

"I'll make sure they don't you let you down again."

"Good." Vernon waited a moment, savoring the power behind his next order. "I want them to destroy the Emporium, and Gabby Wade along with it."

William's eyes widened. "Is that necessary?"

"Are you having second thoughts about our collaboration?" Vernon asked in a deceptively mild voice.

The younger man moved in his chair nervously. "I just don't think you have to kill her."

"I'm not going to kill her. She'll be a victim of an unfortunate accident, much like that pathetic waif she was so fond of."

William appeared shaken. "I wasn't counting on being party to murder."

Vernon opened his desk drawer and withdrew a telegram message. "Perhaps you'd like to go back to Chicago instead?"

Lowe wrapped his fingers about the armrests and his knuckles turned white.

"There seems to be a warrant for your arrest there for the rape of a young girl," Vernon continued calmly.

Lowe looked like a rat caught in a trap. "What time do you want them to go to Miss Gabby's?"

Vernon studied the Emporium's deceptively innocent-looking bartender. "Between eight and nine, when it's the most crowded."

William nodded reluctantly. "That way it'll be more difficult to pick out the five men who actually do the shooting." He removed his glasses and wiped them with his shirtfront, his hands shaking. "Have you considered my proposal?"

Vernon smiled smugly—William wouldn't give him any more trouble. "I have, and I think it's a good idea," he said. "After Ashburn is elected, you can take a trip and gather some working girls. By the time you return, I should have the Sawtooth Social Hall started."

"And I'll have fifty percent ownership?"

"That's right." For now, Vernon would appease

his hunger for control because he needed him. Later, after Vernon gained control of the appointed city positions, he would renegotiate the terms of the agreement.

William replaced his round spectacles. "How can you be so certain Ashburn will allow the Social Hall to commence business? Won't he try to stop it?"

Vernon shrugged. "He might try, but I shouldn't have a problem gaining his cooperation, either."

"The same way you gained mine?"

Vernon laughed. "I like the way think, William. If our partnership proceeds well, I may even allow you to court my daughter."

The bartender's eyes gleamed behind his lenses.

"We have to make sure Ashburn becomes the mayor, and that means the plan has to go without a hitch tonight. You make sure those men leave Sawtooth as soon as they've done their job. I don't want them hanging around for somebody to possibly recognize."

Lowe seemed to accept his fate. "You can count on me, Mr. Gatewood."

"I know I can, William. You've already proven your loyalty."

Vernon stood and offered the young man his hand. William got to his feet and shook it firmly. "Don't worry, Mr. Gatewood, everything will work out."

"I'm certain of it. Good-bye."

He watched the traitorous bartender leave and sank back into his comfortable chair. After tonight, the whore would get her due for denying him not once, but twice. Gaining revenge against Gabby Wade was almost more satisfying than the thought of pulling Tyler Ashburn's strings once he was mayor.

Despite the cool morning, Ty had to mop the sweat from his brow after helping one of his men hold steady an injured horse. The animal had somehow gashed its fetlock overnight and the wound had to be sewn up.

Ty replaced his Stetson and stuffed his handkerchief in his breastpocket. The drivers had shown up an hour ago and taken their wagons to Rawlins for supply runs. With only a few horses left in the corral and all but one wagon gone, the yard was nearly deserted.

He gazed up at the snowcapped mountain peaks against the azure sky and listened to the silence broken only by a sorrowful keening high above him. It had been a long time since he'd appreciated the stillness of a clear day or the single lonely cry of a hawk riding high on the wind currents.

He had Gabby to thank for forcing him to see beyond his business, to open his eyes to the simple pleasures he'd left behind with his childhood. Maybe enjoying a moment of tranquillity didn't increase his profits, but it did feed a need inside that had been hungering for something beyond material gains.

His thoughts turned to the woman who had invaded his peace of mind, trespassed on his dreams, and thrown his well-structured world into disarray. He wondered if she made love with as much passion as she approached life. Remembering her eager response to his kisses, he grew hard. He'd fought his craving for her, telling himself any redblooded man would lust after someone like Gabby.

But it was more than her hourglass figure and silken blond hair that drew him; her sunny outlook and fearlessness captivated him even more than the physical attraction. That allure was also more dangerous, appealing to Ty's heart.

He headed toward his cabin to change his clothes before going to the freight office, and noticed a man on horseback approaching. Squinting against the morning sun, he recognized Stephen and swore under his breath.

"Morning, big brother," Stephen greeted him, flashing a smile too reminiscent of their childhood days.

Ty glared at him. "I hope you're only stopping to say good-bye on your way out of town."

Stephen's friendly expression faltered, and he dismounted. "Actually, I thought we could talk some more."

"We've got nothing to talk about." Ty spun away from him and strode toward his cabin door.

A hand clasped his arm, jerking him around.

"Can't you give your only brother a few minutes of your valuable time?" Stephen's tone oozed sarcasm.

"Nope." He stared pointedly at his brother's hand. "Let go."

Stephen shook his head. "Not until you agree to talk."

"About what?"

"Our father."

Ty's heart pounded in his chest. "There's nothing to talk about."

Stephen swore. "Still stubborn as a mule and twice as dense." He gripped Ty's arm tighter. "I knew it wasn't an accident."

Ty stiffened. "What're you talking about?"

"You know damn good and well what I'm talking about. Our pa didn't have an 'accident' when he was cleaning his gun. He killed himself!"

Ty's heart jumped into his throat, and his gut coiled into a knot. "Whoever told you that is a liar!"

"Nobody had to tell me." A weary smile fell on Stephen's face. "It wasn't that hard to figure. He'd just lost everything he owned. He probably thought he didn't have a choice."

Ty wrenched out of Stephen's grasp. "He had a choice," he said savagely, "and he took the coward's way out."

"Not everybody can be as strong as you," Stephen said with large dollop of cynicism.

"You're making excuses for him!"

His younger brother shrugged. "Maybe—and maybe it's time to let it go. He didn't kill himself to hurt you or me or Ma; he probably thought he'd spare us his shame."

"He would've spared us his shame if he hadn't gambled in the first place!" Red-hot anger hazed Ty's vision, and he stabbed Stephen's chest with his forefinger. "And then you shamed Ma and me by becoming a gambler."

Stephen silently studied Ty, his hooded gaze giving nothing away. "Ma knew, too."

Ty froze. "What?"

"Ma knew," Stephen repeated. "When I realized Pa had killed himself, I asked Ma about it."

"You told her, you son-of-a-bitch?"

"I didn't have to. She knew the night he did it that it wasn't an accident."

"You're lying! Before she or anyone else could

see him, I got the sheriff and he had some men take Pa's body to the undertaker's. The sheriff and I were the only ones who knew."

Stephen shook his head sadly. "Ma knew Pa wasn't strong enough to face what he'd done. The whole town knew, Ty."

Ty didn't want to believe him. "Then why didn't she tell me? Why didn't *you* tell me?"

"She wanted to protect you," Stephen said dryly. "Isn't that something? Ma didn't want to hurt you, since you tried so hard to keep us from learning what really happened. She didn't want you thinking you'd failed."

Dazed, Ty swung away from Stephen. All along, everybody had known Pa had killed himself. He'd spent most of his life hiding the truth: from them, from the townspeople, and even from himself.

A hand settled gently on his shoulder. "I'm sorry, Ty, but Ma thought it was best. She knew how hard you worked to make ends meet, and she didn't want to burden you with anything more."

Ty jerked away. He'd struggled alone to hide the shame of his father's cowardice, and all along everybody had known. He'd thought all the pitying looks were on account of his father's losing everything at the poker table. Instead, they'd been talking behind his back the whole time he'd been eking out enough money to buy food and clothing for Stephen and his mother.

His insides churned and aching hollowness filled him.

"Everyone admired you, Ty, including me," Stephen said, coming up behind him. "You never asked for handouts and worked hard for everything you got. You were always the strong one."

"Is that why you became a gambler—because you 'admired' me so much?" Ty demanded furiously. "Or were you laughing at me, too?" His whole life had been based on a lie!

"Nobody was laughing at you, Ty," Stephen said gently.

Ty turned away as rage pounded through him.

Stephen touched his arm and Ty spun around, swinging his fist with the anger that had accumulated for twenty-two years. The force of the blow sent numbing shock up Ty's arm and knocked Stephen to the ground.

"Does everybody in Sawtooth know my dirty little secret, too?" Ty demanded.

Stephen sat up and gingerly touched his jaw. He shook his head. "I haven't told anyone."

"And I'm supposed to believe you, you bastard!"

Stephen struggled to his feet, then swayed a moment as he regained his balance. "I swear I'd never do anything to hurt you, Ty. Geezus, I'm your brother."

Feeling as sick as he had when he found his father's body, Ty felt as if he had no idea what was real and what wasn't anymore.

"I don't know what to believe," he said hoarsely.

Stephen took a step toward him. "Ty—"

"Stay away from me," Ty cried. "Just leave me alone."

He staggered away and mounted his brother's horse. Wheeling the animal around and keeping his mind blank, Ty headed toward Sawtooth.

A few minutes later, Ty pounded on the Emporium's locked door and waited impatiently until Gabby unlocked the door and swung it open.

He stared at her, at her bright green dress and

the golden hair that spilled over her shoulders in shimmering waves. His whole world had tumbled in around him, yet Gabby remained the same amid the chaos.

"What're you doing here?" she asked warily.

"I came to get a drink," he replied, and pushed past her.

Ty went behind the bar and pulled a bottle of whiskey off the shelf. He grabbed a shot glass and tugged the cork out of the bottle with his teeth. Glancing at Gabby, who watched him with her arms crossed, he asked, "Want a drink?"

She shook her head. "What's wrong, Ty?"

He laughed bitterly. "What could possibly be wrong, except that my whole life has been a damn lie?"

"Is it Stephen? Did he do something?"

Ty downed the whiskey, then slammed the glass down on the bar. "You mean other than making a fool of me all these years?"

"Nobody in town knew he was a gambler until he showed up last night," Gabby said, apparently confused.

Ty refilled his glass and held it up to the light to stare at the amber liquid. The color reminded him of Gabby's eyes—golden brown hues that sparkled with sunshine. "All this time, I thought I was the only one who knew the truth," he said.

"What truth?" Exasperated, Gabby grabbed hold of his hand that held the glass and suddenly noticed his bloody knuckles. "What in the world is going on? Did you and Stephen fight?"

"I wouldn't call it a fight exactly," Ty said. "More like a past-due payment." He gazed at her, at this woman who now seemed to be the only person in his life who was who she appeared to be. "You're the only person who's been honest with me, and I've treated you the worst. Why is that, Gabby? Why aren't people who they're supposed to be?"

She glanced down at his skinned knuckles and touched them gently. "Because everyone feels that who they are just isn't good enough. They haven't learned that they'd find happiness if they'd only accept who they are."

Ty cupped Gabby's cheek and stroked her satiny skin with his thumb. "Like you." His anger spent, Ty only felt hollow desolation. "I've been running all my life, Gabby, and I just found out nothing was chasing me."

He dropped his hand from her face. "When I was eleven years old, my father lost everything we owned in a poker game."

Gabby gasped. "I'm sorry, Ty."

He damned the moisture that filled his eyes. "He killed himself that same night—put a gun to his head and pulled the trigger. I found his body."

"Dear God!" she said hoarsely, covering her mouth with her hand.

"Do you know what it's like to find your father like that?" Ty rubbed his eyes so Gabby wouldn't see his weakness. "I tried to keep it a secret. Only the sheriff and I knew what happened—at least, that's what I thought. All those years, I thought Ma and Stephen didn't know. I thought I'd spared them the shame."

"But they knew all along?" Gabby guessed, her voice a bare whisper.

Ty nodded. "Everybody did. It seems I was the only one I was fooling."

Gabby moved around the bar and placed her palm against his whisker-roughened jaw. Her soft, womanly scent wrapped itself about him.

"Maybe everyone thought you didn't know and they were trying to protect you?" she said.

"My father was a coward, Gabby," he stated. "And everyone knew it!"

"He was probably ashamed. He couldn't face the fact that he'd let you and Stephen and your mother down."

"That's *no* excuse for what he did to us." Betrayal and childish fear swept through him, and for a moment he was that eleven-year-old boy again.

"What was your father like before?" she asked gently.

Ty closed his eyes a moment, thinking back, remembering the time before. . . .

"He was a good father when he didn't gamble," he began. "He used to take Stephen and me fishing. We'd get up before the sun rose and catch night crawlers to use as bait, then head for the pond and fish all day. Ma would bring a picnic basket down around lunchtime, and we'd all eat together and tell her about the ones that got away." He gazed down at Gabby, who looked up at him with understanding and no hint of condemnation. "Ma used to be a lot like you—always smiling and playing games with us. Until Pa killed himself." Despair crushed Ty. "After that, she hardly ever smiled."

"It wasn't your fault, Ty." She framed his face in her palms and searched his eyes. "You were only a boy. You couldn't have known what he was going to do."

"I could've followed him out to the barn and I could've stopped him."

"Maybe that time—but what about the next time he tried to kill himself? You can't take responsibility for everyone's actions, Ty. You couldn't control what your father did, and you can't make Stephen be somebody he's not. Everybody makes their own decisions, right or wrong." She glanced away. "And we all have to live with the wrong ones."

Ty knew she was thinking of Sara, and he also knew her guilt—it was the same guilt he carried. "What about my decisions, Gabby? Has my whole life been based on one bad decision after another?"

"Nobody can answer that but you, Ty. We each make our own path in this world, and we choose what's right and what's wrong based on our own conscience and beliefs." She smiled tenderly. "The good news is that every day gives us a brand-new start on our lives and another chance to make the right decisions."

"I don't understand—you lost both your parents when you were a child, but you aren't bitter about your life."

"I wish you could've met my uncle. He'd been educated back East, but he preferred to travel around the frontier, taking hold of each day like it was his last. He used to tell me that nobody has the right to tell us how to live our lives. And nobody can tell us that how we choose to live it is wrong."

Ty smiled faintly. "It seems I've been telling you that how you live is wrong ever since the election began."

"And I've been ignoring it," Gabby tossed back with a mischievous smile.

He stared at her, his heart constricting.

"Is something wrong?" she asked.

"Did I ever tell you your smile is the prettiest thing I've ever seen?" he asked, his voice husky.

Gabby shook her head. "No," she whispered.

"It chases the shadows away." He held her beautiful face between his hands. "Smile for me, Gabby," he said softly.

She looked at him with wonder and bewilderment. Then, as she gazed into his eyes, her lips curved upward once more.

He soaked up her radiance, allowing it to flood the darkest recesses of his soul. And finally the past began to fade, replaced by the brilliant light of the woman he held in his arms.

Throwing caution to the wind, he slanted his lips down on her sweet mouth and his tongue met hers. He plunged his fingers into her thick, riotous tresses, the satiny strands caressing his hands like a skillful lover. Need obliterated the last trace of his resistance.

He wanted all of generous, courageous, beautiful Gabby Wade.

Chapter 22

Gabby was caught in a whirlpool of emotions and feelings she'd never experienced before. Eyes wide, she drew away from Ty, breathing deeply to cool the heat that poured through her veins. She'd never known anything as powerfully alluring as Ty's touches and now understood only too well why a woman would give herself freely to a man.

"What is it?" Ty asked, taking a step toward her.

"Please don't come any closer," she whispered hoarsely, her breathing harsh and labored.

Confusion filled Ty's eyes. "Why?"

She swallowed and closed her eyes as her hands trembled uncontrollably. "I'm afraid."

He stared at her, at first uncomprehending, then with shocked amazement. "You mean, you've never—"

She shook her head vehemently. "But that's not the reason. I vowed I would never let a man use me."

"But this is different."

"How?" Gabby demanded.

"Because it is," Ty said helplessly.

Gabby wrapped her arms around her waist. "Be-

335

ing independent is the most important thing to me, Ty. If I let you . . . if we . . ."

"I'd never try to change who you are."

She gazed at Ty, instinctively knowing he spoke the truth. But to throw everything she'd believed out the door because he made her heart beat faster was difficult to do.

He took a step toward her and Gabby had a crazy impulse to move back into the circle of his arms, but uncertainty kept her rooted in place.

"It's because of who you are that I care for you so much," he said in a low voice.

Would he care for her so much if he knew the truth—that she and her uncle had conned dozens of people out of their hard-earned money? That Soapy had taught her how to deal from the bottom of the deck? That they'd been run out of town more times than Gabby could remember?

And would she be able to bear Ty's disappointment if he found out?

Slowly, gently, Ty drew her into his embrace. Gabby chastised herself for her unreasonable fear. The only way he'd learn about her past was if she told him, and she wouldn't—couldn't—do that.

She laid her palms against his shirt, the material warmed by his body, and she could feel his heart's steady rhythm. As she raised her head, her eyes collided with his tender gaze. She felt as if she were wrapped in a favorite quilt—toasty and secure— but another strange and frightening and wonderful feeling also encompassed her. Is this what Rose felt when she looked at Joe?

"I can show you how good it can be between a man and a woman, Gabby," Ty said. "No strings attached."

"You'll want nothing in return?"

Ty shook his head, and his blue eyes twinkled devilishly. "Only what you want to give me."

His titillating smile blazed a path straight to the middle of her newfound desire, and Gabby knew that no matter the cost, she had to satisfy this restlessness Ty had created within her.

"I feel so strange, Ty—like I don't know who I am anymore."

"I feel the same way. Everything I believed was a lie, including you."

Gabby stiffened. "I never lied to you."

"It was *my* lie, Gabby. I thought you were someone you weren't, even though the truth was always right in front of me." Ty grinned wryly. "I guess my brother was right when he said I was stubborn as a mule and twice as dense."

She shook her head, tenderness welling within her. "You were trying to be someone you weren't. And to be honest, I didn't like that man nearly as well as I like the real Ty Ashburn."

How could she not trust Ty after all he'd shared? He'd freely given his past to her, and she wanted to give him something equally as precious. Gabby raised herself on her tiptoes and kissed him as naturally as she breathed life-giving air.

Ty felt her acquiescence the moment her sweet lips touched his. He deepened the kiss, and his heart pounded with urgency. Initially shocked by her confession that she was a virgin, Ty wanted to show her how good their lovemaking could be, and share her discovery.

He swept her into his arms, and Gabby locked her hands together behind his neck. As he carried her toward the staircase, she drew away from him.

Ty stopped at the bottom of the stairs. "If you don't want this, say so now, Gabby, because once we're upstairs, I don't know if I'll be able to stop."

For a moment indecision clouded her face; then it was gone and she nodded firmly. "I've never wanted anything more."

Relief flowed through Ty, along with a powerful need to make her his. As he carried her upstairs, he could feel her heart beating rapidly against his chest. At the top, she pointed to her room and Ty entered it. A big four-poster bed, draped with a sky-blue crocheted coverlet, stood in one corner, and he crossed over to it. He sat down on the edge of the mattress with Gabby in his lap.

After a second's hesitation, her hands moved to his shirt. Awkwardly, she began to unbutton it. The dark crinkly hairs on his chest tickled her fingers and made her clumsy as her breathing grew more labored. His masculine scent was like an aphrodisiac, invading her senses and banishing her remaining doubts.

Once she'd finished with the buttons, he removed the garment. His shoulder and chest muscles flexed with the movement, and Gabby placed her hand lightly against his firm biceps. "I'm glad you don't spend all your time behind a desk," she teased.

Ty's chuckle rumbled in his chest and brought a smile of delight to Gabby. "I like it when you laugh," she said. "There ought to be a law that says everyone has to laugh at least three times a day."

If it made Gabby happy, he would gladly make that his fourth—or was it fifth?—official act as mayor.

She lightly brushed her palms over his torso,

skimming down to his waist, and Ty's breath caught in his throat at the unexpected sensuousness of her feathery touch.

His need for her increased tenfold and he took her hands in his, kissing her palms lightly. She inhaled sharply, and her breasts pressed against her dress, drawing his greedy gaze.

"I want to see you, Gabby," he said huskily.

She licked her lips and nodded in a short, jerky motion. He undid the pearl buttons at the back of her dress slowly, drawing out the moment while Gabby's breath shallowed. Once all the buttons had been released, he paused, giving Gabby the choice.

"Go ahead," she said in a barely audible voice.

He drew her dress down off her shoulders, and Gabby pulled her arms free of the sleeves, leaving her bosom covered only by a white eyelet chemise. Her coral tips peeked through the undergarment, teasing Ty with a hint of their glory.

"You're so beautiful, Gabby," he said as his fingers traced the slope of her pale breasts that rose above the chemise.

Ty kissed the valley between her breasts. Gabby tipped her head back and clutched his arms as she groaned. Dear God, she'd never expected it to be like this—like water sizzling on a hot skillet. Ty kissed the hollow of her throat lightly, then dragged his tongue slowly down her slender neck. The air cooled the blazing path he made and added to the eroticism that danced through Gabby's veins.

Ty undid the bow at the top of the undergarment and bared her full breasts. For a moment he stared hungrily, and Gabby forced herself to remain still in spite of the instinct to cover herself. She shivered when he cupped her breast in his palm. He rolled the nipple between his fingers, and her whole body throbbed. All of Gabby's awareness settled someplace below her stomach, to her moist center that ached for appeasement.

Then Ty's mouth replaced his fingers and he laved a pebbled crest, wresting a cry of startled wonder from her.

"I didn't know anything could feel this good," Gabby said, her voice husky with longing.

"There's more—much more," Ty whispered.

He pulled the camisole off over her head, then Gabby stood between his knees and allowed her dress to puddle on the floor at her feet.

Clad only in her shoes, stockings, and drawers, Gabby felt wickedly wanton. She kicked off her shoes, then removed her drawers. Keeping her back to Ty, she rolled down her stockings, intensely aware of his smoldering gaze following her every movement.

She pivoted slowly to face him, both excited and fearful. Ty's eyes widened as his gaze traveled down her body, and Gabby wondered if he could see her heart thumping in her chest. He stood and removed his jeans, revealing muscled thighs with a light coating of hair. Her gaze settled on his arousal outlined beneath his underwear and another wave of heat pulsed through her. When he slipped his fingers into the waistband of his drawers, Gabby quickly averted her gaze.

A moment later, Ty took her hand in his and gently tugged her down to lay on the bed beside his lean body. She came eagerly into his arms, and when he began to explore her body with his hands and mouth, she whimpered in ecstasy. She ran her hand across the curve of his backside and up his firm back and shoulders. With more confidence, she pressed her soft lips to his nipples, and Ty immediately stilled, closing his eyes.

"Did I do something wrong?" she asked in concern.

He opened his eyes and shook his head. "It's just that a woman's never done that to me before."

She frowned. "But you've been with other women?"

His smiled faded, and he framed her face between his callused palms. "None that ever made me feel like you do, Gabby."

Her heart fluttered. "It's not the same every time?"

He chuckled at her sweet innocence, so different than what he'd believed about her. "No. With you, I feel like I'm capturing a ray of sunshine." He lifted a hand and drew it through her hair, the satiny tendrils slipping through his fingers like pure silk. "With you, I feel like I'm alive, like I've never lived before today."

Gabby traced his lips with her fingertip. "I feel the same way, but I thought it was because this is my first time." She bestowed a kiss on his mouth, then his chin and each cheek, enjoying the feel of his whisker stubble. "I like to kiss you and touch you, Ty. I like how your skin feels against mine. I like that look in your eyes that makes me feel like a bowl of chocolate ice cream."

"But you taste a whole lot better," Ty said with a devilish glint.

Gabby felt herself blush, and Ty's smile grew. He moved his mouth over hers, and Gabby's thoughts spun out of control. Faintly aware of his hand upon her leg, she jerked in surprise when his fingers moved to the curls at the juncture of her thighs. He became bolder and traced her womanly flesh, then moved his thumb within her. Gabby's hips lifted off the mattress, instinctively urging him deeper.

Now she understood why women gave themselves wholly to a man. If Ty asked her at this moment to withdraw from the mayoral race, Gabby wasn't so certain she could deny him. Not if it meant he would stop the wonderful things he was doing.

"You're so wet," he whispered hoarsely, fragmenting her coherent thoughts.

Wrapping his hands around her tiny waist, Ty lifted her over him so she straddled his torso. The scent of her increased his passion. Gabby shifted her thighs so that she pressed on his erection, bringing a groan to his lips.

Grasping her hips, he raised her slightly, placing his masculinity at her damp entrance. He gazed into her passion-clouded amber eyes. "I want you now, Gabby."

Her breath quickened and she lowered herself upon his hardness. Her slick heat enveloped him, drawing him farther inside her tight channel. He met the proof of her innocence and Gabby uttered a slight moan.

"This will hurt only for a moment, I promise," Ty said hoarsely.

For a split second indecision filled her, then she gazed into his breath-stopping eyes. Only Ty could quench her sweet agony, and she murmured, "I trust you."

With a deft motion, he rolled her over so he lay on top of her. He kissed her deeply, and as she moaned, he thrust into her, breaking through her virginity. Gabby stiffened a moment at the sharp pain, and Ty kissed her more tenderly.

He held himself motionless inside her and smoothed her hair from her temples. "I'm sorry, honey."

"Don't be." She had known there would be some discomfort the first time, but the fast-fading ache was a small price to pay for the wondrous intimacy they shared. He filled her completely, but she wanted more. She moved her hips slightly. "I didn't know a man could feel so good inside a woman."

He smiled. "It gets even better."

Ty skimmed his hands up her sides and cupped her breasts. He thumbed the nipples and felt her tight sheath convulse around his hard length.

He began to move within her and his world suddenly became her—her sunlight, her laughter, her joy. Without her there would be no life, only darkness and the hollow cold.

His breathing became labored, and hers came in gasps as she met his long, even strokes. Pleasure like he'd never known hurtled through him. All too soon, he lost himself within her throbbing heat, and her climax merged with his in a moment of perfect completion.

Gabby pressed her lips to Ty's neck, tasting the saltiness of his sweat. He lay over her, resting most of his weight on his arms so Gabby could savor his nearness a few moments more. How could she ever have thought Tyler a frozen, unfeeling man?

With a boldness she didn't know she possessed, she laid her hands on his muscled buttocks, the intimacy feeling inherently right. Ty had made her whole in a way she didn't understand: he'd filled a need within her she hadn't even known existed until this moment. But it was more than that—they'd shared a communion of body and soul that Gabby knew she would never share with anyone else.

He raised his head and gazed down at her with a gentleness that made her heart dip and soar. He dropped a tender kiss on the tip of her nose, then rolled to her side, keeping his arm across her waist.

"It was nothing like I thought it would be," Gabby said.

A teasing smile tilted his sensuous lips upward. "Is that good or bad?"

"Most definitely good," she replied without hesitation. "Now I know what Rose meant."

"What?" Ty asked, puzzled.

Gabby grinned mischievously. "Let's just say that she had you pegged right."

Ty opened his mouth as if to ask another question, but thought better of it and shook his head. "I don't think I want to know."

Gabby turned on her side and pressed close to him. "Good, because this time I want to be on top."

Ty laughed—a full, deep-timbered sound—and Gabby thought it was the most beautiful thing she'd ever heard. Even if Ty beat her in the mayoral race, she had a feeling he had won something even more valuable: the secret of happiness.

Then all thoughts were set aside as she and Ty explored each other's bodies until passion exploded between them once more.

Gabby rested her head in the hollow of Ty's shoulder as she trailed a lazy hand across his chest.

Her flesh still tingled where Ty's lips and hands had branded her. If she never left Ty's arms, Gabby would be more than satisfied. Was this what love was all about? Her breath caught in her lungs—no, it couldn't be. She wouldn't allow herself to even consider the possibility. This had been an enlightening and delightful experience—one Gabby would treasure forever—but she had no intention of tying herself to a man, even one as magnificent as Ty Ashburn.

"Gabby?" Ty said, his voice low and husky.

"Yes?"

"Will you marry me?"

Gabby's pulse roared in her ears, and Ty's handsome face swam in and out of focus. She pushed herself upright. "What?"

He shifted so that his eyes were even with hers. "I want you to be my wife."

Gabby licked her suddenly dry lips. "We can't get married," she blurted out.

"Why not?" he demanded.

"I'm not the marrying kind."

"Why not?" Ty pressed.

Because I've swindled and cheated people—things you could never forgive.

"You want a woman who's respectable and doesn't play marbles or slide down banisters. And who certainly doesn't own a gambling hall."

"I want Gabby Wade," Ty stated. "I want her laughter and her generosity, and I want her in my bed every night."

She should have known his code of honor would demand it. He'd taken her virginity, so that meant he had to marry her, even if he didn't love her. She had never planned to marry, and she certainly wouldn't wed a man who didn't love her.

Damn him for ruining everything! She'd enjoyed what they'd done together and had been tempted to suggest meeting in secret, but Ty spoiled it all by getting noble on her. If she gave in to the temptation of marriage, he would no doubt start telling her how she could and couldn't live her life. And sooner or later, her past would come between them.

It didn't matter that she might be a little bit in love with him.

She scrambled off the bed and began to dress. "You don't owe me anything, Ty," Gabby said. "I knew what I was doing, and like Rose always says, it takes two to have a good time."

Ty sat up, and Gabby blushed at the sight of his nude body. She concentrated on tugging on her drawers over her stockings.

"I love you, Gabby," he said plainly.

Startled, she looked at him, and the honest sincerity in his face nearly undid her precarious will. Tears threatened, and she turned away to hide her weakness. She couldn't let him know how much she cared for him, or how much she'd give to be respectable, a woman he'd be proud to call his wife. No, she had to stay strong for both their sakes.

"You love what we did, but that's not real love. A man and a woman need more than this"—she motioned to the mussed bed—"between them to get married. We argue about everything—from gambling to taxes to what a lady should be."

Ty stood and approached Gabby. His towering figure had never frightened her before, but his blatant masculinity was something else entirely. Deliberately, she kept her eyes focused on his face and held her ground.

"That's not important. What matters is how we feel about each other," Ty said.

He started to put his arms around her, and she backed away. If she allowed him to get too close, she might give in to his foolish whim and say yes; then they'd both have to live with regrets.

"We'd come to hate each other," she said. "When you look at me, you'll see the gambler who destroyed your family. I can't change who I am, Ty. Not for you, not for anybody."

"I'm not asking you to change—I don't want you to change," he said, exasperation evident in his voice.

"You say that now, but if I agree to marry you, you'll have second thoughts. Pretty soon you'll be telling me how to dress, how to act, who I can have as friends." Despair crushed down on her, and a dull, empty ache gnawed at her heart. She picked up her dress from the floor and held it in front of her. Facing him, she hoped he couldn't see the agony she desperately tried to keep hidden. "I have to open the Emporium in less than an hour. You should leave now; you have your reputation to think about."

Ty cursed, then jerked his pants and shirt on. "Dammit, Gabby, I don't care what people think. I'm not going to let you go—not after I've looked for you for so long." He shoved his shirttails in his waistband, then tugged on his boots.

The thought of marrying Ty and having his— their—children tempted her far more than she could have imagined. "You don't know anything about me," she cried. "If you did, you could never love me."

He paused, and stared at her. "What do you mean?"

Gabby wanted to turn away, to hide and pretend nothing had happened between them. But, as her uncle had said so often, *Time is infinitely precious; you can never go back and change the past.* In order to make Ty understand, she had to be brutally honest, and that meant she'd lose his respect and the love he claimed to have for her.

She fought back her cowardice and tried to ignore the awful churning in her stomach. "My Uncle Soapy raised me after my parents were killed."

Ty nodded impatiently. "I know that."

Gabby took a deep, ragged breath. "Did I ever tell you how he got his nickname?" She didn't wait for his reply. "He was a con man, Ty. One of his games was to sell bars of soap for fifty cents with the chance that the bar they bought would have a twenty-dollar bill wrapped inside of it. I used to be his shill—his helper—but nobody was supposed to know that. I'd go up and 'buy' some soap from him and unwrap it in front of everyone, showing them the money inside of it."

A muscle twitched in Ty's jaw. "You cheated people?"

Gabby nodded. "It was what my uncle did—what he did to make enough money to take care of me. There was one town where the people came after us, ready to tar and feather my uncle and me. We barely escaped, but I had forgotten my mother's hat, so I sneaked back into town that night. I got caught, and Uncle Soapy came to get me. Before we were set free, those 'righteous' folks used the tar and feathers on us." She trembled from the horrible memory. "My uncle had to cut all my hair off that night. I swore I'd never cut it again."

"How old were you?" Ty asked.

"Twelve," she replied.

"You were only a girl."

She met his eyes defiantly. "I was old enough. After that, I never cheated anyone again." Sadness suddenly overwhelmed her. "But my uncle, he kept right on until the day he was killed."

Ty took a step toward her, the lantern light shimmering in his sympathetic eyes. "How did he die?" he asked softly.

"He was shot during a poker game because he was dealing from the bottom of the deck," Gabby replied as sorrow clutched her chest. "We got away, but he died on the trail. Rose was with us then. She helped me bury Soapy, then I took the money he'd won in that crooked game and bought the Emporium."

Ty didn't know whether he should be furious or offer her comfort. Her uncle had been like the gambler who had taken everything his family had owned, and Gabby had learned the tricks of the trade from him. Still, he couldn't believe she had followed in her uncle's footsteps. "I'm sorry, Gabby."

She knew he might feel sorry for her now, but that would pass, and then he wouldn't be able to look at her without feeling disgust at what she'd done. And Gabby couldn't live with his loathing. She forced herself to remain harsh. "Don't be. It was a good life on the whole, and better than most." She raised her chin challengingly. "My uncle was the one who taught me to enjoy each day, to live it as if it were my last, and that's something I'll always be grateful for."

Now he *had* to realized the absurdity of them getting married. It was a fool's paradise to believe they could be happy together.

"I have to go talk to Vernon Gatewood," Ty suddenly said.

"Why?" Gabby asked, startled.

"I'm going to tell him I'm withdrawing from the election. You'd make a better mayor than me, and I'm going to make sure Gatewood knows it, too."

Shocked, Gabby argued, "After everything I just told you, how can you say that?"

Ty smiled and the gesture touched his eyes with bittersweetness. "You were the one who convinced me that we have to let go of our pasts. How we live now is what's important."

"But—"

"Before I do go see him, I'm going to buy you a ring. And later I'm going to ask you again if you'll marry me. If you say no, I'll ask you every day until you say yes or until I die, whichever comes first."

He grabbed her and kissed her with savage possessiveness, then stormed out of her bedroom. Gabby's knees wobbled like tapioca pudding, and she dropped into a nearby chair. Although his parting kiss had been anything but gentle, it had shaken Gabby as deeply as their lovemaking.

Living her life as she wanted had always seemed the most important thing to her, but now she wasn't so certain. Ty had turned her whole world upside down.

She couldn't weaken. Ty may think he loved her,

but he didn't. Gabby wouldn't let him throw away everything that he'd worked for just because of his misplaced code of honor.

What was best for him would be for her to leave Sawtooth, no matter the outcome of the election. And she loved him enough to do just that.

Chapter 23

Later that evening, Gabby sat dealing poker at her usual table. Although she couldn't concentrate on the game, the cards seemed to be stacked in her favor.

Lucky at cards, unlucky at love, she thought dourly as she laid her cards face up on the table. "Full house, jacks over eights."

Stephen Ashburn and the three other poker players playing with her groaned.

"I got a feeling you're Lady Luck herself," one of the men complained good-naturedly.

Gabby flashed him a halfhearted smile. "Only in some things, gentlemen." She shuffled the deck. "Another game?"

All but Stephen shook their heads and stood. Bantering good-naturedly, the men thanked her for lightening their pockets by a few dollars and departed.

She glanced around to make sure all her customers were having a good time. Rose was delivering a tray of drinks to a table of men, and Gabby could see her laughing and joking with the playful cowhands as she expertly evaded their playful advances. With a smile, Gabby continued to survey the Emporium and found nothing amiss.

She shifted her attention back to Ty's younger brother. Although his clothes—a scarlet brocaded vest, a white shirt with frills at the cuffs and down the front, and fancy garters encircling his upper arms—made him appear a dandy, the look in his cool eyes dispelled that presumption. Gabby suspected Stephen could be cold and ruthless if the situation warranted it.

She'd kept a close eye on him, having learned that how a man gambled revealed his true character, and she'd found Stephen to be cautious—more cautious than most professional gamblers. Gabby also noticed he'd lost more than he'd won that night, unusual for a man in his profession.

"Are you normally this bad a poker player, or do you have other things on your mind?" she asked curiously.

Stephen glanced at her and Gabby's gaze was drawn to his swollen jaw, as it had been all evening. He hadn't explained it, and remembering Ty's scraped knuckles, she had an idea where he'd gotten the black and blue mark.

He sent her a crooked grin too reminiscent of Ty's smile. She struck the image from her mind, not wanting to be reminded of Ty or what they'd shared that afternoon. She'd only grow more confused by the strange feelings he'd awakened within her.

"Is it that obvious?" Stephen asked.

Gabby nodded.

Stephen picked up the deck of cards she had set down and with his long, slender fingers began to shuffle them with amazing dexterity. Gabby wondered anew if he and Gatewood had formed some type of partnership. It still struck her as odd that the cunning businessman had gone out of his way to escort Stephen to the schoolhouse—it didn't fit with his self-serving manner.

"Have you seen Ty lately?" Gabby asked cautiously.

"I tried to talk to him this morning—he wasn't much for conversation," Stephen said.

"I figured so by the bruise on your face," Gabby said dryly. "You might want to try again."

"So he can get the other side of my face?" Stephen asked with a sardonic lift of his brow.

Gabby laughed, then placed her elbows on the table and leaned forward. "I think he wants to finally put the past to rest."

"Did he tell you about—"

"About your father and how he lost everything in a poker game? Yes, and he also told me he thought he was protecting everyone by hiding his suicide." Gabby took a deep breath. "Your brother is the most stubborn man I've ever met, but he's the most decent and honorable man, too."

Stephen's blue eyes twinkled. "What were you and Ty up to this afternoon?" Gabby's face heated with embarrassment, and he chuckled. "I guess my notion wasn't as crazy as you thought it was."

Gabby tried to come up with a clever retort, but a disturbance at the entrance caught her eye. A rough-looking character wearing a battered hat and a low-slung gunbelt was arguing with one of the men Gabby had hired to confiscate customers' weapons. Although her decision wasn't very popular, most of her regulars relinquished their weapons out of respect for her. Those who refused to surrender their guns were denied entry. The few antagonistic customers she'd lost by prohibiting firearms was a small price to pay if she could save just one life.

"Excuse me a moment," she said.

Stephen followed her gaze and frowned. "Do you need some help?"

She sent him a smile of gratitude, but shook her head. "That's all right. I've had a little experience at taking care of this sort of thing."

Stephen didn't appear convinced. "I don't like the looks of him, Gabby. He could get ugly."

She smiled wryly. "He's already ugly, but I'm sure he can't help that. This is my place and I have to deal with the troublemakers. It comes with the territory."

Gabby touched Stephen's shoulder lightly as she walked by, hoping she hadn't hurt his pride by refusing his assistance.

Gabby strode across the room, readying herself for a battle of wits. By the looks of the ruffian, it would be a short altercation.

She stopped beside her employee. "Is something wrong here, Vince?"

"He don't wanna give me his gun," Vince, a short but muscular man, replied.

"Can I help you?" she asked, turning toward the burly cowboy.

A scar tracked across the bridge of the man's nose and down his right cheek. His deep-set eyes bored into her, and Gabby shivered at the brutality lurking in them. "You the Miss Gabby that owns this place?"

She forced herself to hold her position and not let his appearance or foul breath intimidate her. "That's right. What can I do for you?"

He smiled, revealing rotting and tobacco-stained teeth. "Nothin', but I can do something for you." He drew his Colt and fired at the ceiling. Four more men, as mangy as their leader, charged into the Emporium, their own guns drawn and cruelty in their dirty, unshaven faces.

Then all hell broke loose.

By the time Ty traded Eleanor's engagement ring for one that suited Gabby, and had waited for the Gatewoods to finish dining, it was after eight.

"Have a seat, Tyler," Gatewood said as Bentley closed the door to the study. He waited, his elbows on the armrests and his fingers steepled, until Ty sat down. "To what do I owe this unexpected visit?"

Ty studied Gatewood as if he were a stranger, finally seeing him clearly and not liking what he saw. What he once thought was shrewd business sense now appeared as cruel cunning, and gentility a transparent mask.

"Why did you try to keep me away from the debate?" Ty asked flatly.

"I don't know what you're talking about, Tyler."

"If you were trying to drive a wedge between Gabby and me, it didn't work. I know her well enough to know she couldn't have done something like that."

Gatewood's eyes narrowed, but he remained silent.

"I'm dropping out of the mayoral race," Ty announced.

"You're what?"

"You heard me. Gabby would be a better mayor than I could ever hope to be."

Gatewood jumped out of his chair and came around the desk, his eyes dark with fury. "You can't do that! The election is just a few days away. What will people think?"

Ty shrugged calmly. "They can think what they want. It was my decision, not theirs."

"Have you thought this through carefully? Do you realize you're throwing away your chance to expand your freight business?"

Ty smiled, enjoying his victory over Gatewood's extortion attempt. "No, I'm not. I'm only postponing it—and this way I'll do it on my terms, not yours."

"You didn't think you could wait six weeks ago when I made the proposition. What's changed?"

"I have," Ty said. "I'm not interested in doing business with you anymore, Gatewood. Whatever respect I had for you is gone."

"Gabby Wade did this, didn't she?" Gatewood demanded. "She'd say anything to turn you and me against each other so she'll win the election."

Ty shook his head. "Gabby doesn't like politics— which makes her the best candidate for mayor. She won't let anyone sway her from what's right."

"Look what she's done to you, Ashburn—she's turned you into as big of fool as she is," Gatewood taunted. His dark eyes narrowed slyly. "When this election began, I had my man in Cheyenne look into her past. Do you want to know what I found?"

Ty clenched his hands to keep from strangling Gatewood. "I think I can guess," he said tightly.

"I don't think so." Gatewood rounded his desk and pulled a sheet of paper out of the top drawer. He tossed it across to Ty. "Your Miss Gabby, along with her uncle, Horace Wade, were a couple of two-bit con artists.''

Ty kept his murderous gaze on Gatewood. "I know.''

If Ty hadn't been so angry, he would have laughed at the other man's stunned look.

"Then how can you think she'll be a good mayor?'' he demanded.

"Because I know her—and I know she's generous to a fault, as honest as you are crooked, and she wants the best for Sawtooth,'' Ty stated flatly.

Gatewood stared at Ty a moment, then shook his head in pity. "You're such a fool, Tyler. You're never going to get ahead in this world if you allow people like her to influence you.''

"*You* were the one who tried to manipulate me, Gatewood. You had your own agenda all along and you were just using me.''

Gatewood stared at Ty coldly. "I always get what I want, Tyler. And don't be so sure your Miss Gabby will be our first mayor.''

"If you try to use Gabby's past to discredit her, I'll stand against you and support her. She was just a girl at the time.'' He rose to his feet. "Make no mistake, Gatewood, I *will* protect Gabby,'' he swore.

"And who'll protect you?''

"Are you threatening me?'' Ty demanded.

"Think about your reputation, Tyler. What would people say if they knew how your father gambled away everything your family had, then killed himself? Do you think they'd be so eager to trust you with their goods?''

"Did my brother—''

"He's as closemouthed as you about your past.

But I had other avenues at my disposal." Gatewood's eyes narrowed. "So you have two choices, Tyler: stay in the mayoral election, or be ostracized by the fine citizens of Sawtooth. Which is it to be?"

Ty's mind raced. If he caved in to the blackmail, he would continue to live a lie. Gabby knew the truth, and she hadn't condemned him. Stephen also shared his secrets, but he'd kept his silence out of respect for his brother.

Ty's throat tightened. Gabby and Stephen were the two most important people in his life, and he was amazed to realize he didn't care what others thought. It was time to set things right in his life.

He smiled coldly. "Go to hell, Gatewood." He turned to leave, a heady sense of victory and freedom filling him.

The older man's face reddened, and a vein pulsed angrily in his forehead. "It's interesting how accidents can happen at any time," he said coolly. "Fires are especially common hazards in a town like Sawtooth, don't you think?"

Cold dread snaked through Ty, and he whirled around. "You hurt Gabby and I'll kill you."

"All I said was that accidents happen." His eyes became as black as death. "And the funny thing is, there's nothing you can do to prevent them."

Vernon Gatewood's evil went deeper than Ty had imagined. How had he been so naive as to think Gatewood had gotten as far as he had by playing by the rules?

His fingers itched to close around Gatewood's throat. "You son-of-a—"

The sound of faint gunshots drifted in, and Ty froze. He looked at Gatewood, who smiled thinly.

"What's going on?" Ty demanded.

The older man shrugged. "I have no idea—except that maybe you'd better consider staying on the ballot."

Ty jerked open the door and ran out of the hollow mansion. He caught a faint whiff of smoke and spotted an orange glow coming from Gabby's side of town. He burst into a dead run.

The five gunmen forced their way inside and pistol-whipped Vince, who dropped to the floor in an unconscious heap. They began to kick over tables and chairs, bottles and glasses breaking as they tumbled to the floor. Customers and employees alike raced for the door to escape the carnage as the outlaws began to shoot wildly.

Gabby dashed toward the bar, keeping her head low. "William, get the shotgun!"

He shook his head, a hostile smile creating a thin slash across his face. "Get it yourself. I quit."

Shocked, Gabby watched him remove his apron and run out of the Emporium, like a rat abandoning a sinking ship. A bottle crashed above her head and she ducked, her heart thundering in her chest.

Running crouched over, Stephen hurried to her and grabbed her hand. "Come on, Gabby, we have to get out of here."

One of the shooters threw a kerosene lamp down, and fire raced up the tasseled velvet curtains she'd ordered all the way from Chicago.

"No!" she cried, and jerked away from Stephen. "I have to stop them!"

Gunpowder mixed with the acrid smell of burning cloth, and Gabby coughed as she ran around to the end of the bar. Her eyes teared from the smoke and moisture rolled down her cheeks. Bullets struck the wall-sized mirror behind the counter, and glass exploded all around her. She covered her head with her hands to protect herself from the sharp fragments, and leaned over to get the shotgun. Her fingers closed around the metal barrel. A bullet skimmed past her ear, fracturing a whiskey bottle behind her.

"Get down, Gabby!" Stephen shouted, hurtling himself over the bar toward her.

He yanked her down behind the cover of the heavy wood, and the shotgun slipped from her sweat-coated palms. Stephen grabbed it, stood and shot at the nearest gunman, then ducked down beside Gabby.

"One down," he said grimly. "We have to get out of here. This place is going up like a tinderbox."

"This is my home!" Gabby pleaded. "Please, I can't leave. I've got no other place to go."

"It's going to be your coffin if you don't get out now!"

Keeping low, Stephen dragged her to the end of the bar. Dense smoke hazed the room except where hungry orange-red flames devoured the Emporium. Despair cramped Gabby's stomach and her lungs constricted, making it even harder to breathe. Smoke burned her eyes, just as the fire burned her heart and soul.

"There's still four men left and they're shooting at anything that moves. We have to make a run for it. There's no other way," Stephen said close to her ear as they hunched down. "I've got one shell left in this thing. I'll use it to cover us. Are you ready?"

She nodded, her mind reeling. This couldn't be happening! The Emporium was coming down around her and there was nothing she could do. She'd never felt so helpless in her life.

"Okay, get ready," Stephen began. "Go!"

He surged to his feet, and Gabby rose with him. A man loomed ahead of them in the gray haze, a revolver raised. Stephen fired his last shell and the outlaw staggered back, his chest riddled with shotgun pellets.

Gabby pressed her fist to her mouth and turned her gaze away, her eyes watering from the intense smoke as she dashed through the inferno. She staggered out of the Emporium and fell to her knees on the boardwalk, coughing desperately for air.

"Gabby, are you all right?"

Through streaming eyes, she saw the naked anguish in Ty's face. "I'm okay," she managed to say hoarsely, her throat raw and painful.

He lifted her into his arms and carried her to safety across the street. His heart pounded so hard Gabby could feel it against her arm, and she gazed up into his face to find a tenderness so intense it punched the air out of her lungs. She lifted her hand and laid her palm lightly against his cheek, feeling the rasp of whiskers against her skin.

He looked down at her. "My God, Gabby, I could have lost you! If you had died in there—"

"I didn't, thanks to your brother, " she said huskily.

Gabby's confused gaze turned back to the smoke arising from the Emporium and the fire threatening the neighboring buildings. Stephen—where was he? She frantically searched the frightened and curious faces, but he was nowhere in sight. He'd been right behind her, hadn't he? Ty's only brother had saved her life, maybe at the expense of his own.

She grabbed Ty's shirtfront. "Stephen—he's in there!"

Ty's eyes widened with alarm.

"Gabby, you're all right," Rose exclaimed, running over to them, her face streaked with sooty tears.

"Take care of her, Rose," Ty ordered.

He set Gabby down on the boardwalk gently, then rushed toward the fire that raged out of control.

Terror gripped Gabby, and she could hardly breathe past the panic that squeezed her chest. "Ty!"

She tried to stand up, to go after him, but Rose wrapped an arm around her shoulders and held her back.

"Where's he going?" Rose asked.

"Stephen," Gabby replied brokenly. "He's still in there. He saved my life."

She heard the muffled roar of falling timbers, and sparks ascended from the roof, rising high above the town like sputtering fireworks. But now it wasn't the Emporium's death that wrapped her in agony. If Ty died in the fiery flames, Gabby would never forgive herself. "Oh, God, please, not Ty!"

Rose hugged her tightly, rocking her, murmuring comforting words that Gabby couldn't hear past her fear. Instead, Gabby listened to her mind's echo of the words Ty had said to her that afternoon. *If you say no, I'll ask you every day until you say yes or until I die, whichever comes first.*

Gabby whispered an agonized plea. "Please don't let him die."

Seconds became a lifetime as Gabby prayed for

Ty's and Stephen's safety, her eyes locked on the door of the Emporium. When she finally saw Ty stumble out of the burning Emporium, Stephen slung over his shoulder, she nearly collapsed in relief.

Two bystanders rushed over to carry Stephen, and Gabby could only stare when Ty's gaze met hers as he crossed the street. Her heart seemed ready to explode as she climbed to her feet.

Ty's soot-covered face and scorched clothing told her how close she'd come to losing him forever. He stopped a few feet in front of her.

"Stephen?" Gabby asked huskily.

"He was shot, but he'll be all right," Ty replied.

Relief nearly overwhelmed her. For an eternity, Gabby couldn't seem to move. Her gaze flickered to the collapsed and smoldering Emporium that had been her only security. Then she looked at Ty. He slowly opened his arms, offering her something far more valuable than a building.

"Take a chance, Gabby," he said in an achingly tender voice.

Take a chance. The same words she'd spoken to him so long ago when she didn't know the real Ty Ashburn—the man who'd stolen her heart not with flowers and fancy words, but with the gift of himself. With a sob, she ran into the circle of his arms and he enfolded her in his loving embrace. She was truly home at last.

"I can feed myself," Stephen said impatiently.

Gabby glared at his frowning countenance as he lay in his bed at the boardinghouse, recovering from his brush with death. A sling held his left arm close to his side, and the minor burns on his face and hands had been covered with salve. "There's no doubt you and Ty are brothers!" she exclaimed.

"I'd take that as a compliment if I were you," Ty said as he entered the room.

"Don't bet on it," Gabby retorted.

Ty removed his hat and walked over to Gabby. His crooked grin nearly stopped her heart, and when he leaned over to kiss her, Gabby gave up her pretense of irritation. She threaded her fingers through his thick ebony hair and opened her mouth to his.

Stephen coughed deliberately, and Ty drew away.

"Thought I'd better stop you two before you started the honeymoon early," Stephen commented, his blue eyes twinkling mischievously.

Ty grinned boyishly, and Gabby glowed at his newfound ability to smile and laugh more easily.

"Did you vote?" Gabby asked.

He pulled a chair close to the bed and took Gabby's hand in his. He swept his thumb across her knuckles and the engagement ring she proudly wore. "Yep. I wish I'd gotten my name off the ballot in time. Folks are saying it's going to be a close one." Ty took a deep breath. "Your bartender Lowe made a confession to the circuit judge."

Gabby shook her head sadly. "I completely misjudged him. I thought he was my friend."

"For his loyalty, Gatewood offered him a stake in the new Sawtooth Social Hall he was going to start once all the other saloons and gambling establishments were shut down. It seems Gatewood had his own plans for Sawtooth after he had me elected. He thought he could control me through

Eleanor." He gazed at Gabby with a love so powerful, she couldn't breathe for a moment. "If you hadn't helped me see the truth, I would've married Eleanor and he would've succeeded."

"You couldn't have known, Ty." Then she asked curiously, "Was Eleanor involved in her father's scheme?"

He shrugged. "I doubt it. She knew he sometimes bent the rules, but I don't think she knew the whole story. Besides, the man was her father and she loved him in spite of everything he did. She's leaving on the stage tomorrow and I doubt we'll ever see her in Sawtooth again."

Gabby looked at Stephen. "I misjudged you, Stephen, and I'm sorry. I thought you might be involved with Gatewood."

Stephen smiled warmly. "You were only protecting Ty." He glanced at his brother. "You'd better hold on to her, big brother, or I might take her myself."

Ty wrapped his arm around her waist. "Don't worry. I don't plan on letting her go. Not after all the trouble I had convincing her to marry me."

He shifted his gaze to Stephen, and Gabby could sense his nervousness. She knew where this conversation was leading, and she squeezed his hand reassuringly.

"There's something we need to talk about," Ty began.

It had taken almost losing Stephen in the fire for Ty to realize how much family meant to him. If he'd died, Ty would have lost his only chance to reconcile with his brother. He wasn't about to throw his opportunity away.

"How did you forgive him?" Ty asked his brother softly.

Stephen didn't need to ask who he meant. "He was a good father, Ty."

"How can you say that after what he did to us?"

"He didn't do it to hurt us—he did it because he was ashamed of what he'd done," Stephen explained. "We had a lot of good times before he took to gambling. Do you remember how he'd always bring us something from the general store? And how he taught us to fish and hunt? And there were the times when he and Ma thought we were sleeping, and we'd look over the edge of the loft and see them hugging and kissing. Remember what we used to say?"

Ty smiled at the memory. "We swore we'd never kiss a girl." He glanced at Gabby, who was smiling, though her amber eyes glistened. "That's one promise I'm glad I never kept."

Stephen chuckled, then sobered. "We've got a lot of happy memories, Ty. Don't let Pa's killing himself overshadow everything else he left us with."

"I don't know if I can, Stephen. You don't know what it was like to find him that way."

"Thanks to you, I'll never have to know," Stephen said gently. "You can be proud of that, Ty—you saved Ma and me from having to remember him that way."

Ty swallowed the block of sorrow in his throat. He gazed at Stephen, and instead of seeing the man, he saw the small boy he remembered so well. He missed those days when he and his brother had been so close, sharing all their secrets. By working so hard to deny his father's cowardice and the subsequent shame, Ty had buried all of the good memories, too.

"In your own way, by trying to hide the fact that Pa killed himself, you were trying to protect him as well," Stephen said. He swallowed and tilted his head against the headboard to stare at the ceiling. "He doesn't need your protection anymore, Ty. You can't let his shadow be at your back forever." Stephen returned his gaze to his older brother. "Pa wouldn't have wanted that."

Tears burned in Tyler's eyes. Stephen was right: Pa had given them so much more than he'd taken from them, and he wouldn't have wanted that final night of his life to be Ty's lasting memory of him.

"Can you put the past behind us?" Stephen asked, cautiously extending his hand to Ty.

Ty gripped his younger brother's hand firmly, and the look that passed between them began the healing process.

Ty continued to hold his brother's hand as he wrapped his other arm around Gabby's shoulders. It was time to forgive and start his life anew, with his father's ghost laid to rest and Gabby at his side.

Epilogue

Gabby shaded her eyes against the snow that glittered under the January sun and gazed up at her brother-in-law. "You don't have to leave so soon. We'd love to have you stay, wouldn't we, Ty?"

"The offer for one-third ownership of A-B Freight still stands—with Gabby's backing, we'll be expanding a lot sooner than I'd figured," Ty said.

Stephen grinned wryly and tugged at the frilly cuffs hanging below his green frock coat sleeves. "Three months is longer than I've stayed anywhere since I left home." He stared into the distance, beyond Sawtooth's main street and civilization. "There's a lot of poker tables out there I haven't played yet. Maybe after I've seen them all, I'll come back." His gaze returned to Ty. "Maybe I'll take you up on that offer then."

Ty nodded at his brother, and Gabby was relieved to see his expression remained relaxed. She was proud of her husband—he'd come far in healing the emotional wounds he'd carried for so long. Stephen's presence had helped, and the two of them had spent many hours together talking and learning to trust one another again.

"Don't stay away too long. In another month or so, April, Harold, and Tommy will officially be ours, and I want them to grow up knowing their uncle," Gabby said. Then she glanced wickedly at Ty. "And you may have a baby niece or nephew before long, too."

Stephen smiled and his eyes crinkled at the corners. "I'll be like a bad penny—I'll keep showing up when you least expect me." He leaned over and embraced her. "You take good care of my big brother, all right?"

Gabby nodded, unable to speak past the lump in her throat.

Stephen released her and she stepped back. For a moment, Stephen and Ty only stared at one another, then Ty extended his hand. His brother gripped it and Ty pulled him into a hug.

"Take care of yourself," Ty said, his voice husky.

"I always do," Stephen replied.

The two men separated and Ty wrapped his arm around Gabby's waist, holding her snugly by his side. Stephen climbed into the stagecoach and Ty closed the door behind him.

The stage handler slapped the horses' rumps with the reins and yelled, "Hiyah!"

As the Concord coach rolled away, Stephen waved from the window, and Ty and Gabby waved back until he was out of sight.

"Are you all right?" Gabby asked Ty gently.

He smiled sadly. "I'm going to miss him."

She squeezed his hand. "I am, too. It's nice to finally have a brother, but it hurts to see him leave." Gabby gazed up at her tall, handsome, honorable husband, and love filled her near to bursting. "I love you, Ty."

"I love you, too," he said tenderly. He took a deep ragged breath. "I don't know what I'd do without you, Gabby."

Mischief danced through her. "You're going to find out for the next couple hours. I have a town council meeting to preside over."

Ty groaned, but his blue eyes twinkled. "April, Tommy, and Harold will be over for supper—will you be home in time or should I make them the Ashburn special?"

"Beans and beef?" She wrinkled her nose. "I'll make sure I'm home in time to cook. Mrs. Edwards wasn't too happy about all the beans you fed them while I was at the quilting bee the other night. I think Rose and Joe are coming over after the meeting, too, and I have a feeling Rose will be bringing some goodies with her."

Ty rolled his eyes. "She always does when the children are over."

"She's just practicing for their own—after all, July isn't that far away."

He grinned. "So what's on the agenda today?"

"I'm going to push for approval of a sheriff who works on commission, and enforcement of the firearms prohibition in the town limits. Most of the saloons are already taking weapons at their doors, but it doesn't stop the gunplay when they leave. It's too late for Sara, but not for the rest of the children."

"Forgiveness starts from inside yourself, honey," Ty said firmly, and he pulled her into his embrace. "You were the one who taught me that."

Gabby brushed a tear away and looked up into his devoted gaze. "And maybe someday I'll be able to follow my own advice. Right now, all I can do is make sure it never happens again." She gathered her composure and straightened her spine. "You know, Gatewood actually did us a favor when he bribed the officials to start the bridge before it had been approved. It's too bad he and Tom Bailey weren't patient enough to do things legally."

"They're going to be forced to learn patience after spending ten years in prison," Ty said with a chuckle.

"At least this way the bridge will be done come spring and Sawtooth can start growing."

Ty eyed her teasingly. "I thought you liked the town the way it was."

"Oh, I don't know; sometimes change is a good thing—especially when it comes from the heart."

Ty's humor faded, and his expression grew troubled. "I was wrong about so many things, Gabby. Why did you put up with me?"

"Because I wanted to see you laugh," she replied simply. "Wasn't that enough?"

"Only for you," he said. Then he laughed, a full, rich sound that filled Gabby's eyes with tears of joy and happiness.

Later that evening, after Ty and Gabby had walked the children back to the home, Ty stopped in the middle of the street. Darkness enveloped them and the notes from a tinny piano drifted out from one of the saloons.

"I believe I have a debt to pay, Mrs. Ashburn," he said, his eyes twinkling. "Would you care to dance?"

Gabby smiled and moved into his arms.

Beneath a canopy of stars, Ty danced a jig in the middle of town with the woman who'd gambled everything on love.

And won.

Dear Reader,

If you're looking to put more romance in your life, then don't miss next month's romantic selections from Avon Books, starting with the return of those irresistible Cynster men in Stephanie Laurens' *Scandal's Bride*. Richard Cynster, known to his family as Scandal, has decided he'll avoid the fate of most Cynster men—he'll never marry. But then he meets beautiful Catriona Hennessy. Will Scandal soon be headed to the altar?

Next, it's the moment many of you have been waiting for—the next contemporary romance from Susan Andersen, *Be My Baby*. I know that Susan's *Baby, I'm Yours* is a favorite of her many, many readers, and if you haven't yet experienced the pure pleasure of reading one of Susan's fast-paced, sexy contemporary love stories...well, now is the time to start! It's contemporary romance at its finest.

Eve Byron has charmed countless readers with her delightful heroines and strong heroes, and in *My Lord Stranger* she gives both. It's a Regency-set love story you're not likely to forget.

Margaret Moore is a new author to Avon Romance, and *A Scoundrel's Kiss* is sure to please anyone who loves a rakish hero tamed by the love of a woman. Here, our hero makes a bet with his friends that he can seduce any woman in England...even the prim-and-proper heroine.

Enjoy!

Lucia Macro
Lucia Macro
Senior Editor

AEL 0299

Avon Romances—
the best in exceptional authors and unforgettable novels!

ENCHANTED BY YOU   by Kathleen Harrington
79894-8/ $5.99 US/ $7.99 Can

PROMISED TO A STRANGER   by Linda O'Brien
80206-6/ $5.99 US/ $7.99 Can

THE BELOVED ONE   by Danelle Harmon
79263-X/ $5.99 US/ $7.99 Can

THE MEN OF PRIDE COUTNY: by Rosalyn West
THE REBEL   80301-1/ $5.99 US/ $7.99 Can

THE MACKENZIES: PETER   by Ana Leigh
79338-5/ $5.99 US/ $7.99 Can

KISSING A STRANGER   by Margaret Evans Porter
79559-0/ $5.99 US/ $7.99 Can

THE DARKEST KNIGHT   by Gayle Callen
80493-X/ $5.99 US/ $7.99 Can

ONCE A MISTRESS   by Debra Mullins
80444-1/ $5.99 US/ $7.99 Can

THE FORBIDDEN LORD   by Sabrina Jeffries
79748-8/ $5.99 US/ $7.99 Can

UNTAMED HEART   by Maureen McKade
80284-8/ $5.99 US/ $7.99 Can

Buy these books at your local bookstore or use this coupon for ordering:
....
Mail to: Avon Books, Dept BP, Box 767, Rte 2, Dresden, TN 38225   G
Please send me the book(s) I have checked above.
❑ My check or money order—no cash or CODs please—for $_____is enclosed (please
add $1.50 per order to cover postage and handling—Canadian residents add 7% GST). U.S.
residents make checks payable to Avon Books; Canada residents make checks payable to
Hearst Book Group of Canada.
❑ Charge my VISA/MC Acct#_____Exp Date_____
Minimum credit card order is two books or $7.50 (please add postage and handling
charge of $1.50 per order—Canadian residents add 7% GST). For faster service, call
1-800-762-0779. Prices and numbers are subject to change without notice. Please allow six to
eight weeks for delivery.
Name_____
Address_____
City_____State/Zip_____
Telephone No._____   ROM 1098

Avon Romantic Treasures

Unforgettable, enthralling love stories,
sparkling with passion and adventure
from Romance's bestselling authors

❋❋❋❋❋❋❋❋❋❋❋❋❋❋❋❋❋❋❋❋❋❋❋❋❋❋❋❋❋❋❋

TO CATCH AN HEIRESS *by Julia Quinn*
78935-3/$5.99 US/$7.99 Can

WHEN DREAMS COME TRUE *by Cathy Maxwell*
79709-7/$5.99 US/$7.99 Can

TO TAME A RENEGADE *by Connie Mason*
79341-5/$5.99 US/$7.99 Can

A RAKE'S VOW *by Stephanie Laurens*
79457-8/$5.99 US/$7.99 Can

SO WILD A KISS *by Nancy Richards-Akers*
78947-7/$5.99 US/$7.99 Can

UPON A WICKED TIME *by Karen Ranney*
79583-3/$5.99 US/$7.99 Can

ON BENDED KNEE *by Tanya Anne Crosby*
78573-0/$5.99 US/$7.99 Can

BECAUSE OF YOU *by Cathy Maxwell*
79710-0/$5.99 US/$7.99 Can

Buy these books at your local bookstore or use this coupon for ordering:

Mail to: Avon Books, Dept BP, Box 767, Rte 2, Dresden, TN 38225   G
Please send me the book(s) I have checked above.
❑ My check or money order—no cash or CODs please—for $_____ is enclosed (please
add $1.50 per order to cover postage and handling—Canadian residents add 7% GST). U.S.
residents make checks payable to Avon Books; Canadian residents make checks payable to
Hearst Book Group of Canada.
❑ Charge my VISA/MC Acct#_____ Exp Date_____
Minimum credit card order is two books or $7.50 (please add postage and handling
charge of $1.50 per order—Canadian residents add 7% GST). For faster service, call
1-800-762-0779. Prices and numbers are subject to change without notice. Please allow six to
eight weeks for delivery.
Name_____
Address_____
City_____State/Zip_____
Telephone No._____   RT 1098

W'eve got love on our minds at

http://www.AvonBooks.com

𝒱ote for your favorite hero in
"HE'S THE ONE."

𝒯ake a romance trivia quiz, or just
"GET A LITTLE LOVE."

ℒook up today's date in
romantic history in "DATEBOOK."

𝒮ubscribe to our monthly e-mail
newsletter for all the buzz on
upcoming romances.

ℬrowse through our list of new
and upcoming titles and read
chapter excerpts.

RWS 0898

America Loves Lindsey!
The Timeless Romances
of #1 Bestselling Author

KEEPER OF THE HEART	77493-3/$6.99 US/$8.99 Can
THE MAGIC OF YOU	75629-3/$6.99 US/$8.99 Can
ANGEL	75628-5/$6.99 US/$8.99 Can
PRISONER OF MY DESIRE	75627-7/$6.99 US/$8.99 Can
ONCE A PRINCESS	75625-0/$6.99 US/$8.99 Can
WARRIOR'S WOMAN	75301-4/$6.99 US/$8.99 Can
MAN OF MY DREAMS	75626-9/$6.99 US/$8.99 Can
SURRENDER MY LOVE	76256-0/$6.50 US/$7.50 Can
YOU BELONG TO ME	76258-7/$6.99 US/$8.99 Can
UNTIL FOREVER	76259-5/$6.50 US/$8.50 Can
LOVE ME FOREVER	72570-3/$6.99 US/$8.99 Can
SAY YOU LOVE ME	72571-1/$6.99 US/$8.99 Can
ALL I NEED IS YOU	76260-9/$6.99 US/$8.99 Can

And Now in Hardcover
THE PRESENT: A MALORY HOLIDAY NOVEL
97725-7/$16.00 US/21.00 CAN

Buy these books at your local bookstore or use this coupon for ordering:

Mail to: Avon Books, Dept BP, Box 767, Rte 2, Dresden, TN 38225   G
Please send me the book(s) I have checked above.
❏ My check or money order—no cash or CODs please—for $_____ is enclosed (please add $1.50 per order to cover postage and handling—Canadian residents add 7% GST). U.S. residents make checks payable to Avon Books; Canada residents make checks payable to Hearst Book Group of Canada.
❏ Charge my VISA/MC Acct#_____Exp Date_____
Minimum credit card order is two books or $7.50 (please add postage and handling charge of $1.50 per order—Canadian residents add 7% GST). For faster service, call 1-800-762-0779. Prices and numbers are subject to change without notice. Please allow six to eight weeks for delivery.
Name_____
Address_____
City_____State/Zip_____
Telephone No._____   JLA 0898

Timeless Tales of Love from
Award-winning Author

KATHLEEN EAGLE

REASON TO BELIEVE
77633-2/$5.50 US/$6.50 Can
"Kathleen Eagle crafts very special stories."
Jayne Anne Krentz

THIS TIME FOREVER
76688-4/$4.99 US/$5.99 Can
"Ms. Eagle's writing is a delight!"
Rendezvous

FIRE AND RAIN
77168-3/$4.99 US/$5.99 Can
"A hauntingly beautiful love story that will touch the
heart and mark the soul."
Debbie Macomber, author of *Hasty Wedding*

SUNRISE SONG
77634-0/$5.99 US/$7.99 Can

THE NIGHT REMEMBERS
78491-2/$5.99 US/$7.99 Can

Buy these books at your local bookstore or use this coupon for ordering:

Mail to: Avon Books, Dept BP, Box 767, Rte 2, Dresden, TN 38225   G
Please send me the book(s) I have checked above.
❑ My check or money order—no cash or CODs please—for $_____is enclosed (please
add $1.50 per order to cover postage and handling—Canadian residents add 7% GST). U.S.
residents make checks payable to Avon Books; Canada residents make checks payable to
Hearst Book Group of Canada.
❑ Charge my VISA/MC Acct#_____Exp Date_____
Minimum credit card order is two books or $7.50 (please add postage and handling
charge of $1.50 per order—Canadian residents add 7% GST). For faster service, call
1-800-762-0779. Prices and numbers are subject to change without notice. Please allow six to
eight weeks for delivery.
Name_____
Address_____
City_____State/Zip_____
Telephone No._____   KE 0898